Little Disasters

Little Disasters

Randall Klein

Viking

VIKING
An imprint of Penguin Random House LLC
375 Hudson Street
New York, New York 10014
penguin.com

ISBN 9780735221680 (hardcover)
ISBN 9780735221703 (ebook)

Printed in the United States of America
10 9 8 7 6 5 4 3 2 1

Set in Fairfield LT Std

For my family
And for Midge

Little Disasters

Michael Gould

Present Day: July 19, 2010

7:45 AM

Jennifer Sayles and I are a terrible idea. The two of us together is like touching a stove to see if it's hot, or cutting through the park at night, or eating strange, ripe berries straight off the bush.

We're that moment right before the world becomes catastrophic, when we are more alive than we have ever been or ever will be again, and we embrace our commitment to the bad idea, because that's the idea that makes perfect sense.

I've learned this lesson, step by heavy uphill step, trees sagging wearily around me, looming over the paved path, as if in judgment. I've learned this, on a quest up to the entrance of the Cloisters, a fortress of an art museum located at the northern tip of Manhattan, about as far across the city from my sliver of Brooklyn as one can get.

I slipped out this morning when the sun was just starting to come up and the temperature was still merciful. I waited on the platform with men in uniforms—security guards, orderlies, janitors. These are the men who ride the subway before rush hour, who sit and catch a few minutes of sleep, narcolepsy by necessity, their heads hitting their chests the instant the doors close, some global positioning alarm clock springing them awake when the train rolls into their stations. I hunkered down, sipped milky bodega coffee, people-watched, voyaged north and north and farther north, people coming on, people getting off, the hourglass swell of riders crowding the train, then dwindling more and more as we zipped our way

1

up until there was no one getting on, only people departing. And then we arrived at 207th. Blocks go that high in Manhattan. I started searching for the park, walking through a neighborhood that woke and stretched as I passed.

We chose the Cloisters because neither of us had ever been. We have ignored this guidebook staple, full of medieval art and tapestries. It's an intimidating stone building in the middle of a park, the type of place that might have been besieged by dragons in another time. When I get to an entrance to the park and look up at the distant edifice of the Cloisters, I realize immediately that Jenny is not going to meet me up there. She's not going to want to walk through the park and up this hill in the humidity and rising heat. I check my phone; it's already eighty-eight degrees and the sun has been out for maybe an hour. But we agreed. If I'm not waiting at one of those entrances in fifteen minutes, and there is the skin-of-her-teeth chance that she is, I'm pretty much fucked. And so, uphill.

8:00 AM

My phone tells me it's ninety degrees. The air saps moisture from every pore, leaves me drenched in sweat. When Jenny gets here we'll stroll for a bit and laugh about this, work a shower into wherever the rest of our day takes us. Now that we'll have been to the Cloisters I can't see us ever coming back. It's beautiful—there's a view of the Hudson through trees, winding paths for hand holding—but this will be, at best, a place we take our kids *once*. It's too far from everything. One day we'll pack a picnic, rent a car by the hour, and take li'l Wassily or wee Austen up to see where Mom and Dad committed to one another once and for all. My breath stinks sour of coffee, and I plan to kiss her when she arrives, so I smoke a cigarette to balance out the taste.

Jenny is supposed to be here by now, but she hasn't been on time to a single thing in her entire life. I'll need to work on that with her, subtly and without eliciting resentment. Or I'll have to learn to live with it. Today isn't about punctuality, though. Today isn't about the people we'll become. That sounds pedantic in my own head; I'll need to revise that in case it's something I say out loud to her when she finally does arrive.

8:30 AM

I check my watch, wondering what route she took to get here. Leaving the apartment this morning—opening the front door and stepping into the stairwell and closing the door behind me, testing the knob to make sure it's locked, hearing the neighborhood around me still but for the drone of cicadas and the distant belly rumble of truck noise—I thought it would all be more difficult. I thought I would leave some part of myself behind. But it wasn't and I didn't. I have a grasp of what I have done and cannot undo. That's on my mind, still sitting here waiting for Jenny. But it doesn't feel like loss. It doesn't feel like the pains of a phantom limb callously discarded in Red Hook.

At some point in the future I'll stare forward blankly and let my mind wander into every hidden room of the past to the black, rotted core of exactly what I've done. How I became the villain. But if I feel anything now, still waiting for Jenny, it's resolute. I made my choices, and now come the ramifications. I can deal with those.

Before that fall, though, come so many gorgeous moments—shared secrets, shared joys, shared sins. It's entirely possible that Jenny is at some other entrance, waiting patiently for me as I do for her, anticipating the same lateness, though my slavish devotion to punctuality would suggest otherwise. Give me six months to live, and rather than bargain with God I'd throw myself into traffic to meet the deadline early. Jenny knows this about me. I take out my phone and find her in my contacts. There she is, one of many, but her name may as well be encircled in neon.

> Hey Love, I'm staring at a castle and
> waiting to kiss the sweat on your
> shoulders. You close?

And ten minutes later, that happy chirp.

> I couldn't. Michael, I'm sorry. Please don't
> hate me.

Just like that, I'm running through the park, downhill, away from the Cloisters, where I had never been before, and where meeting Jennifer Sayles was a lovely idea that made no sense whatsoever.

Michael Gould

One Year Ago: July 18, 2009

I'm smiling, grinning really, deeply in love with my life and all that the day holds. And the smell of freshly baked cookies—always the smell of freshly baked cookies—enveloping me like a straitjacket.

The egg timer beeps. Rebecca waddles into the kitchen. The timer is one of those magnetic models that leeches onto the fridge and, when it hits zero, starts counting upward, so irresponsible bakers can see how many seconds they've let something overcook. Rebecca is not an irresponsible baker. That electronic whistle, like a homing device, draws her to the oven from anywhere in the apartment. Why she takes the extra step of turning off the timer before reaching into the oven I don't know; she could just as easily flip the process. That's not exactly true, or it's more kind than accurate. Rebecca turns it off first to emphasize that she didn't fuck up, that another perfect batch cooked not a second longer than her handwritten recipe instructed.

I can't say the same for our son, who is late by two weeks. Rebecca had designs on July Fourth. "A fireworks baby," she said, as if that's a thing. It's now July 18, her own egg timer beeping shrill as the seconds mount up, and her doctor wants to get this little bun out of the oven.

"Our son will share a birthday with Nelson Mandela," I say, impressed. "Also Harriet Nelson, Hunter S. Thompson, Screamin' Jay Hawkins . . ." I scroll through a few more names, debate whether to add Hume Cronyn to the list. "Ooooh, also *Mein Kampf* was published in 1925. That's ominous."

I close my laptop and join Rebecca in the kitchen. She takes another batch of cookies out of the oven, each one perfect—perfectly round, perfectly plump, perfectly browned—and sets the timer to let them cool for five minutes. I intercept her as she's hitting start and kiss her flush on the mouth, kiss my wife the way I always promised I would, like I intend to still once our son is born. She responds with a hum of pleasure, her body relaxing under my hands, cradling her tummy. When we break she says, very quickly, "I love you."

"Dammit," I curse under my breath and she laughs. It's a competition we have, who can say it first after a long kiss. She wins four of every five. I lose myself somewhere in her lips, but a part of Rebecca always stays alert, always thinks of the next thing on her to-do list. "I love you too," I grumble.

"My bag is packed and so is yours." I follow her into our bedroom. She has packed an overnight bag for herself; I helped with that one. She's laid my backpack next to it, packed without my knowing. There are books, of course, and my iPod. Three bottles of water, and enough energy bars to keep me fed through hiking the Pacific Coast Trail.

"You know there's a bodega across the street. You're not delivering in the Gobi."

"In case you can't leave the hospital."

"There's a cafeteria too."

"Say thank you, Michael, and keep looking. There's more."

She's also packed candy cigars. "To share with the other dads. They're bubble gum." Oooh, and a flask. My flask, a gift from my dad when I turned twenty-one. I unscrew the cap and smell Blanton's, my special-occasion bourbon.

"I say thank you, Rebecca." I kiss her again. "Thank you for being amazing, and thank you in advance for the unspeakable gore you are about to endure."

The timer beeps, and she's past me and out of the room faster than a blink.

Thirty minutes later I pull the truck up to the front of the apartment and we walk down the stairs together. I'm holding the bags in the lead, and she has her hands on my shoulders, slowly and carefully making our way outside. It's nine in the morning and already blisteringly hot. A storm passed through a few nights earlier, the humidity finally coalescing into actual raindrops, but now we're back to hatefully heavy air. Rebecca has Rorschach blots under each breast seeping through her gray T-shirt. I left the engine running and the air-conditioning on, and she glances back at me gratefully for this small mercy as I help her into the passenger seat.

"Did you turn everything off?" she asks. She means in the house. God forbid we let Con Ed gouge us more than they already do.

"I did."

"Did you lock the door?"

"I did. Did you remember the baby?"

She pats her stomach.

"Okay," I say. "Let's go become parents."

It's already been decided that my role today is to wait, patiently, in the waiting room. I am allowed to check up on her, and if the doctor gives me any news, I am allowed to go back into her room and discuss it with her, specifically if decisions need to be made.

But I am, under no circumstances, to sit in her room and add to her stress. This isn't some spiritual choice that Rebecca made so that our son would not be born into a world of negative chi; she simply doesn't want me irritating her. I can respect that. Rebecca likes to have her accomplishments to herself. This child will be *ours*; the labor, however, is *hers* and *hers* alone. The doctor and the nurses won't even factor into the games she plays with pronouns.

We drive under the Gowanus Expressway and pull onto Ninth Street. The warehouses give way to brownstones. Rebecca stares out the window silently. She does this when she's tense, goes spooky and mute. I reach across and grasp her hand and she clutches mine right back.

I stroke her bare fingers, one knuckle to the next, with my thumb. She took her wedding ring off a few months ago when her fingers grew too swollen. Something clicked in me that day, seeing my wife visibly pregnant, wearing her jeans with the spandex waistband hidden underneath a long-sleeved T-shirt. Without that ring, some quality that defined her in my mind changed from a minor to a major chord, and I saw her anew as a stranger—a stranger I profoundly wanted to fuck.

"What brought that out?" she asked afterward.

I couldn't tell her the truth. I looked at Rebecca, her body supine, her belly distended, her swollen breasts rolling like uncooked dough into her armpits, her hair limp and lifeless, her skin spotted like a teenage boy's. "You just turn me on like lights," I said instead. "You flip the switch and *pop*."

That was the last good lay. Rebecca and I discussed this, in tones serious and somber. We discussed that I'm finding it difficult to view her vagina as an orifice designed for pleasure when it is now preparing itself to be an orifice for procreation. Those are her words, incidentally, cribbed from a baby book, recited with solemn understanding. I tried to protest ("No . . . !"), but if that were a reason she'd accept as justifiable, I'd cop to it. Since then, Rebecca will initiate sex and I'll respond, softly poking at her. She moans and grunts and says words of encouragement, and I can tell she's faking enthusiasm; sex for her now is like having an itch that I pat gently instead of scratching. That will change. I promise myself to take whatever journey I need to take in order to return us to the days when she'd wax for me.

I hang a left on Eighth Avenue. We're in the posh part of Park Slope now, a neighborhood whose pretensions we mock from the comfort of our kitchen. But we're also a block away from Prospect Park, its lush green scent wafting in through the vents, triggering fantasies in Rebecca of our son ambling down the hills by the baseball diamonds, shrieking with laughter at dogs swimming in the filthy pond that's always pudding-skinned with algae.

We turn onto Seventh Street. The hospital stands on both sides of the block. Rebecca sucks in breath as if through a straw. Her mouth goes tight and her eyes clamp up. I quickly veer the truck over to the side, stick it in front of a fire hydrant.

"Hey." I make her turn to me. "This is happening."

"I know," she says, and the waterworks start.

"He's coming out, it's time."

"I know."

"And he's coming out in a good hospital, with a doctor you trust."

"I know."

"You've done everything right. All the vitamins and the bed rest and the exercises. Reading to him, playing him music. Of course he doesn't want to come out yet. You're too good a hostess."

She giggles a bit through tears. "I know."

"But this is happening, no way around it."

She wipes her eyes. "I know. I know. Thank you. I don't know what this is. I'm not sad or scared, it's just . . ."

"It's a stressful fucking day," I offer.

She nods. "It's a stressful fucking day."

"You're going to push a baby into the world today."

"Our baby."

"Yes, ma'am."

She rubs my hand. "Thank you. I'm ready. Let's do this."

I pull into the circular driveway and help her out of the truck. An orderly comes out with a wheelchair and Rebecca considers it, shrugs, and sits down. I bend over and give her a deep, lingering kiss. "I love you," she says into my mouth.

It takes me another five minutes to find a space, something that isn't in front of a hydrant or someone's driveway or too tight because three hybrids are parked far enough apart to fit a sectional couch in between their bumpers. I luck out when an SUV pulls out of a space down the block. I grab it and start walking back toward the hospital.

I want to stroll into the waiting room and have a kindly, plump nurse straight from central casting tell me, "Mr. Gould, your wife went into labor and delivered a healthy baby boy. Mother and son are doing great. Let's get you scrubbed up so you can come see them." I want it to be over and done with by the time I cross the street and go through the revolving doors. I want to take all the stress out of today, all the doctor periodically sticking her head out into the waiting room to tell me how many centimeters my wife's cervix is now dilated, leaving me to nod, as if I know whether that's eye-of-a-needle width or canyonesque and to hide how I have little medical or practical knowledge of how a woman's anatomy functions. I want that nurse to grab me in the lobby and lead me upstairs, telling me as I go that my son is in all the highest percentiles and nowhere near the autism spectrum and will do fine on all standardized tests and not be the smelly kid in class or the stupid kid, will never get called a faggot on the playground or call some other kid a faggot, will date a few good-looking girls who won't crush his self-esteem or make him feel like his body needs to be gym-hardened in early adolescence and won't make him self-conscious about the size of his cock, whether it's too small or too big or just bent at some odd angle, and that he will have a choice between some good state schools or a few decent liberal arts colleges, and that his wife will be a good partner who has roughly similar goals in life and his kids will look up to him with the same adulatory eyes that he uses to look at me.

I want that. All of it. I want it so badly that if the hospital had a karmic trading post I'd hand over one of any organ I have two of in exchange for any one of those things to be positively true.

At the corner of Seventh and Seventh, still across the street from the hospital, I walk into a froufrou market. It's essentially a bodega, but they added a few prepackaged vegan entrées in plastic clamshells and slapped FARM on the awning outside to give the aura of freshness. I don't need to go through the aisles to find what I'm looking for. I go straight to the counter and grab a pack of peppermint gum, then point behind the cashier.

"Camel Lights," I say.

His hands run across the Camel suite before settling. "Yeah, those. And a book of matches." I tuck the gum into my pants and the smokes and matches into my backpack, in a different compartment from everything else. There's no way I'm getting through today without smoking, and while Rebecca would forgive me for it, I'd rather not ask her to.

Paul Fenniger

Present Day: July 19, 2010

8:26 AM

It was difficult to leave this morning. Jenny said to go, and she said it in a reassuring voice loaded with the insinuation that she would still be there when I got back and that we would talk more. I'll cook and she'll sit on the counter, tell me about her day. I love that Jenny tells me about her day in such detail, even when it doesn't involve leaving the house. She tells me about everything she's read, all of the tin-eared sentences in the papers she edits, funny stories about typos, then all of her thoughts big and small. I'm not going to have a fun day at all; the office doesn't provide those. I don't need to relive my day by talking about it. Hearing the calming canter of her voice is better than a massage. I'll chop vegetables and savor her words, and once we've had a few drinks we'll continue our conversation from last night.

And it'll be okay.

The conductor has cranked up the air-conditioning on the L train this morning. It keeps everyone a little more sane at rush hour. We're packed in, my crotch at the head level of a man lucky enough to be sitting, reading *The New Yorker* and patently ignoring the people around him, lest he look up and notice we're all pregnant women and he's the jerk who won't give up his precious seat. It's okay, though. The heat makes everyone cranky, a little more aggressive to push their way into or out of the train car, a little less likely to listen to the conductor's aggravated pleas that there is another train right behind this one. No one ever believes that there is another train behind this one. There is only this train, this one solitary train to take us to the island of Manhattan.

When the train pulls into Bedford, the last stop in Brooklyn before crossing underneath the river, the doors open and a few tattooed bodies nudge their way out before a sea of people floods in. I glance in both directions to see if I can shift my body, shrink myself to make room for others. The doors open and shut repeatedly into people who can't fight back, who push against the rubber strips that slam them from both sides to no avail. At the last second one more lucky person slips into the train car, everyone else left on the platform. This last person is like me, a guy in a suit that already shows the wrinkles of being sweat through. He looks around the car in solidarity but gets glares in response. It's his fault this ride will take an additional ten seconds. But we'll forget—aggression

11

dissipates like steam in the subway, white-hot one moment and gone the next.

The train slows, then stops, somewhere under the East River. Some mornings I zip through the tunnel without raising my eyes from a script. Not today, though. I turn my eyes up, let the pause gift me a moment.

There's an audible exhalation all around me, a collective shrug. *Ladies and gentlemen, we are delayed because of train traffic ahead of us. We apologize for any inconvenience. Thank you for your patience.* That's the automated voice. Strong, male, authoritative. The intercom clicks on and the conductor gives a sharp intake of breath, then it clicks off again.

Ladies and gentlemen, we are delayed because of train traffic ahead of us. We apologize for any inconvenience. Thank you for your patience. I wonder if it's a button that the conductor pushes from a console of prerecorded statements or if it's all computerized, a synapse between the signals we pass and the speed of the train. After another minute or two, a few arms drop around me. Then a few more. A minute later I let my own fall to my side, nursing the circulation back in. BlackBerrys emerge. People remove earbuds, loop them around their neck, and wait for the next announcement. We wait for the train to churn itself back to life and pull into First Avenue, where virtually no one will get off but dozens more will try to filter on, the remnants who couldn't get onto the train in front of ours, who have to rely on faith that there is, in fact, another train right behind. I wait to get to the office, put in my eight hours, and then rush home to Jenny.

Ladies and gentlemen, we are delayed because of train traffic ahead of us. We apologize for any inconvenience. Thank you for your patience. New Yorkers roll their eyes. What choice do we have, we think. We get on the subway and we are at its mercy, a show of faith we perform every day.

We wait.

Paul Fenniger

One Year Ago: July 18, 2009

I make egg whites for Jenny. Scrambled egg whites and turkey bacon, extra crispy. She fantasizes out loud about breakfasts of Bloody Marys and pots of coffee, real coffee, caffeinated coffee. She talks about eating undercooked meat and raw, egg-based sauces. She stares in the windows of liquor stores, mixing drinks in her head. I bought her a breast pump in preparation, a gift she nearly cried over because of the freedom she claims it will provide. I love her for her reckless enthusiasm. This is the last morning, she decrees, that she will ever drink herbal tea.

She comes into the kitchen, already dressed, rubbing the sleep from her dormouse eyes and crinkling her nose at breakfast. "I'm not hungry," she says.

"Come on, just a bit."

She holds two fingers up, no space in between them. "Just a bit."

"Last day you're eating for two," I remark.

When I sit down at the table she comes around behind me, lays her head on top of mine. I tilt my head back and she kisses my forehead. "Tell me you love me," she says.

Easiest thing to say. "I love you." That gets her to sit down, and she soon finishes her eggs and bacon and half of mine.

We stand outside in the rising heat and Jenny's hands twitch and click. She still hasn't gotten used to standing in one place and not smoking, all these many months later. I gave her rubber bands to fidget with but that's cold comfort. Her bag sits at my feet. "Did you pack anything for yourself?"

"I'll keep myself occupied," I promise.

"Fenn," she whines my nickname. "It will take hours."

"It's okay," I insist. She pulls a face at me. "It's okay. I'm very patient. I'll sit in the waiting room and come up with names."

"I don't like the names you pick."

"Seymour . . . Max . . . Rupert . . ."

"Those are awful names."

"Harrumph." I kiss her neck.

"Those are all dog names."

"Not all of them. What about Fido? Or Sir Barks-a-Lot? Sir Barks-a-Lot is a great name for a boy. Strong." She giggles and nuzzles me on the cheek. Comedy isn't my strong suit, so when I make her laugh I feel godlike. I look down, and her hands have stopped twitching.

We get in the black sedan, and when I tell the driver the name of the hospital he turns in his seat and looks at Jenny. "You sure you don't want an ambulance?" he says nervously.

"She's not in labor," I reply, before Jenny can get cranky with him. He shrugs and starts off toward Park Slope.

The most difficult part of being a father will be having to share my wife. That seems so petty a thought that I don't say it out loud, especially not to Jenny. For the longest time it's been the two of us, getting to live selfishly. I'm going to be a good father, though. For the first year it's all processes anyway: changing diapers, scheduled feedings, scheduled naps. It's repetition and mechanics—that I can handle easily. I think that's the part Jenny is most worried about, those years before our son is ready to have a conversation. So we make a good couple. I'll handle the diapers, and once he's potty trained and starting to speak in sentences, she'll take over.

When we arrive at the waiting room, Jenny sits down next to me. Her hands are back at it, her mouth puckering every few seconds. I rub out the tension from the back of her neck. She purrs in appreciation. I love her sighs of contentment, how she vocalizes happiness. Then the nurse comes to take her back to see Dr. Mulitz, and she gives me a look as she stands, to remind me that I should wait right there. "I don't need you all aflutter *doing*, Fenn," she instructed me when we got the appointment. "There will be people doing in the delivery room. Let me have my people." I had hopes, or thoughts, that the first person our son would see would be me. I know that he'll be virtually blind, that I would at best be daddy shapes, but it would have been something to tell him later, that mine was the first face. Instead it will be the doctor, and that's okay. The doctor, then Jenny, then nurses, in some order. Down the line, daddy shapes. Jenny turns and gives me a smile as she's being wheeled away. When she's gone, I get to have my own jitters. Now it starts.

Before a show, we have exercises to keep ourselves loose, to keep nerves to a minimum. I sit on the floor of the waiting room and breathe, visualizing the air looping underneath my diaphragm, filling me, and rushing out, taking all of my stress with it like the tide. Some nurses look over, probably to check if I'm about to pass out, but I'm in my own happy world, meditating my way into a placid state, completely unself-conscious.

I'd know what to do if I were back in the delivery room with her. Scrub in, mask over my face, then keep out of the way. If I could, I'd hold her hand and let her seethe at me, whisper back words of encouragement, a background noise underscoring the doctor's instructions. No one trained me to do that, I just think that it's innate human knowledge. When another pregnant woman rolls by, I give her a small smile and she returns it. Her child will have the same birthday as my child. So many children will be born today, and mine will be one of them. For a split second, my child will be the youngest child in the world, just like his mother and his father were.

A man, about my age, comes and sits down near me in the waiting room. He pulls a granola bar out of his backpack and wolfs it down. I'm tempted to start a conversation with him but then he pulls out a book, thick as an almanac, and starts reading. He doesn't acknowledge me at all.

So I wait. I wait for my son to be born. And it's okay.

Michael Gould

Present Day: July 19, 2010

9:03 AM

Oh this clusterfuck of streets. Spoil me with a grid system and I can find my way in the dark. I try to double back, to retrace my steps back to the subway that took me here, but I'm lost in New York. On the island of Manhattan, where it's virtually impossible to get lost. Fort Tryon Park isn't some byzantine labyrinth—the streets seem to lead somewhere—but in a near sprint downhill, beads of sweat hanging from my eyelashes, I can't see through the trees to where I exit. The run-down amphitheater area that I passed on my way up the mountain is nowhere to be found, and instead I jog over a bridge I know for a fact I've never been over before. Those few other people—the stroller walkers, the tourists, the park weirdos—have all vanished. I am the only man in Fort Tryon. Even the expanse of the Cloisters is once again hidden behind foliage.

I finally come upon a man walking a beagle. "How do I get out?" I huff. My wind sucks, I can't run more than a quarter mile on a good day; today it's like wading through soup. He points behind himself, doesn't want to address me more than he needs to. I thank him and I'm off again, feet slapping the ground.

When I emerge, it's in an entirely new place, a cul-de-sac where, again, I have never been. But I no longer need a map or a guide, there's the blessed green plinth of a subway marker. Once I'm underground, I can get anywhere.

I'm confronted by a bank of elevators, signs instructing me to take the elevators down to the platforms, and for a moment I have forgotten how to operate them. When one opens up, seemingly on its own, I get on and wait, but the doors don't close. Finally, an older woman steps on as well, eyeing me with mild discomfort, clutching her wire mesh rolling cart close, ultimately deciding I'm not a threat, heaving and sweating profusely in the corner. She presses a button clearly marked PLATFORM and the doors close.

The platform itself is near empty, which always frustrates me, because it usually means a train has just left. I wait among the scattered few, people spaced out from one end of the tunnel to the other, all of us craning our necks and peering down the tracks to seek out the lights of an oncoming train, reassure ourselves. I check my phone for more texts from Jenny but there aren't any, and I neglected to charge last night, so I'm running on a battery one-third full. I did remember to charge my iPod last night, but that's still plugged into the charger, attached to a wall. I'm completely without external stimulation—no podcast to distract me, no music to measure time by, not even a book to stare at numbly. Only my thoughts, all of them anxious, waiting for this fucking train.

Speakers crackle to life. A tinny voice, transistor radio hiss and scratch, swells in the station, bouncing off the tunnels. *After an earlier incident, all train service is suspended in both directions. Please seek alternative transportation.* I haven't heard that announcement before. I've never heard the subway people tell us that we are shit out of luck and should see if we can't hail a cab instead. The half dozen of us waiting on the platform look at each other for answers, for reasons. Then everyone assembles back at the elevators, silent and sepulchral, to make our way back to the street.

Draining my battery a bit more, and cursing myself for not thinking to do this when I was lost in the park, I call up my map on my phone, pinpointing myself and zooming in and out to find another subway. If the A train isn't running, hopefully the 1 train over at Dyckman is. Which train doesn't matter, I'm going to transfer anyway once I get to a line that will send me back to Brooklyn. Keeping my phone out so as to follow myself (actual Michael doing the running, blue-dot-Michael rolling at a steady clip toward his

17

destination), I race to the Dyckman station, this one luckily above-ground. No elevators at Dyckman, which, in my manic state, I take as a good sign. As I'm running up to the platform I nearly collide with a woman coming down the stairs. She has a baby strapped to her chest, and she recoils from me, taking two quick steps back up. The child's legs dance a spastic jig in its sling. "I'm so sorry," I say to her. She walks by me without acknowledging my apology. "I'm sorry," I call out again.

Some terrible bubble just burst in me. A pinprick found its way through a membrane and now my sense of unease overwhelms me. It cuts my strings. I sit down on a step for a minute, catch my breath. I need to get back to Brooklyn.

I need to get back to Brooklyn now.

Standing back up, I take my place in the crowd. The platform has the same smattering of confused commuters, but it's above-ground. They're all on their phones.

After an earlier incident, all train service is suspended in both directions. Please exit the station. The voice sounds urgent, clipping its consonants. A few people immediately obey, rushing past me with their phones at the ready. The rest of us wait, either out of obstinacy or some misguided faith in the New York subway system. We each have at the ready some anecdote from a night long ago when we were drunk and it was late and we were just trying to get home and they said this train wasn't running but, like, thirty sec-onds later it rolled into the station and everyone who left was fucked but I got home, no problem. That's what we're holding out hope for, the phantom train that will appear and open its doors to us, welcome us into its air-conditioned intestine and shoot us through the pipes wherever we want to go. The announcement comes again, this time even louder, as if the station agent is shout-ing into the microphone, hoping to herd us out with her voice, but we're not budging. I'm not budging. I have to get back to Brooklyn.

Five minutes later I hear the same announcement shouted at me from down the platform. A woman in a maroon vest and parachute pants, sweating as badly as we are, yells at all of us, with only her annoyance as amplification.

"Trains are not running," she says, enunciating each word, like we're simple. "I need you to leave the station."

"Is the A running?" a man yells back. He came from down the platform and seemingly waited until he was right behind me before shouting.

"No trains are running. Not here, not anywhere. I need you to leave the station immediately. Come on." A few more people start to trudge toward her. She beckons the rest of us, me included, with her hip cocked. "There's not going to be a train and I need this station evacuated right now. If you don't leave I'll have you arrested." No mincing those words, and we last few stragglers make our way to the exit. On the way past, I slow down, meet her vexed eyes with a look of incredulousness in my own.

"How do I get back to Brooklyn?" I ask. That earns an eye roll. "What's going on?" I prod, as if a reason will make the situation any better.

"I don't have any further information at this time," she says officiously, actually pushing me in the back to keep me moving along.

We mill about outside the station. We loiter under awnings, taking what little refuge we can from the cruel heat now that the sun has fully risen. If this were an airport, we'd start discussing our destinations, seeing if anyone wants to go in on a car rental, travel quicker alone but farther together. Some of the faces seem genuinely troubled, more than inconvenienced, as if the trains will never work again and we are stuck here on Dyckman Street in unbearable heat, commanded to ford the Hudson if we are to get anywhere ever again. I wonder, briefly, if my face mirrors theirs, if my look is also one of unenlightened fear.

Separating from the crowd, I retrace my steps in the hopes that, if I make my way back to the subway I emerged from, I might somehow go back in time and not come up here in the first place. But I need to get back to Brooklyn—there's no way around it. If the trains aren't working, I will seek out the slow, monotonous, but ultimately reliable trudge of a bus. Back to Brooklyn. Back to . . . I check that last text again . . . back to Jenny Sayles.

Michael Gould

One Year Ago: July 18, 2009

−4:00 hours: I've read as much of my book as I'm going to. It was a struggle four chapters ago. When Rebecca picks up a book, she finishes it, turning pages at a steady rate. I timed her once, without her knowing. A page turned every thirty-three to forty-six seconds, probably determined by how much dialogue is offset, or those end-of-chapter pages. I, meanwhile, hit a wall; it becomes physically arduous to move my eyes from line to line. There's another guy in the waiting room, wearing a thin white linen shirt and a tank top underneath. He hasn't done a thing but sit still since I got here. As far as I know, this is just his hangout, or one of the nurses is his girlfriend. He keeps glancing at me, I can see in my periphery, like he's aching to strike up a conversation.

I put the book down and pick up some pamphlets on child care off the end table. They're divided into the categories of shit you should do for your baby and shit you should do for your baby *for the love of God*. The first set comprises step-by-step instructions on how to install a car seat, at what age vaccinations are needed, numbers you can call for postpartum depression. The second category is made up of pamphlets on the dangers of secondhand smoke to an infant, as if any asshole is going to see that in tri-fold format in the waiting room and put two and two together. Here's the kicker, so amazing to me that I almost want to finally turn and acknowledge this other guy just to get his take on it. The people in the instructional pamphlets, they run the ethnic spectrum. But the people in the warning pamphlets—uniformly dark. The cartoons all have brown or black skin. Jesus Christ.

−3:00 hours: A nurse comes into the waiting room. "Michael Gould?" she calls out. I raise my hand and she beckons me over to the nurses' station. There she runs through the details of inducing labor, like a flight attendant reciting safety features. I catch every third word, and the words aren't particularly complex or jargony; blood has broken the levy and flooded my brain and the next thing I know I'll be able to do cogently is hold my son and probably sob. So I nod, and make polite hums of understanding whenever her voice goes up at the end of sentences. She smiles and I actually shake her hand, like we've concluded a transaction. Then I sit back down. She shuffles my chart to the back and lays another one over it. "Paul Sayles?" she calls out. The other guy leaps to his feet. "It's Fenniger," he corrects politely. She checks the chart and then looks at him again. "I'm Paul Fenniger," he continues. "Jennifer Sayles is my partner." Aha, she nods, then guides him to the desk for what looks like the same speech.

−2:00 hours: I'm out of granola bars and two of my three bottles of water are gone. I've thrown them out, which was idiotic, because now I can't refill them from the water fountain. I try picking my book back up, get through the same paragraph four times, and tuck it back into my backpack. I close my eyes, lean my head against the chair, and divide up my son into small parts. I hope he inherits Rebecca's eyes but my mouth. Rebecca has thin lips that are going to get thinner as she ages. Mine are fuller. I want him to have my mouth. Rebecca's ears. Rebecca's nose. My jawline. My hairline. My height. Rebecca's skin. Rebecca's generosity. Rebecca's optimism. Rebecca's entrepreneurial spirit. Rebecca's fortitude. Rebecca's obstinacy. Rebecca's perfectionism. Rebecca's monomaniacal, myopic ability to latch onto a goal, clamp down her jaws, and twist until she feels its bones give way. My sense of humor. My elegant piano fingers. Rebecca's kneecaps.

−1:00 hours: Sitting. Sitting. Waiting. When a nurse, any nurse, emerges from those sliding doors, her eyes don't go anywhere near the waiting room. They all keep laser-guided focus on the desk. Sometimes they go there and joke with the other nurses, trilling laughs of the islands and the barrios blending together. Sometimes they disappear to another part of the hospital, return ten minutes later. Dr. Mulitz comes out twice, stands at the entrance to the waiting room the first time. Both the other guy and I look directly at her and she holds our gazes for a few seconds too long, a tiny smirk playing at her mouth. "Nothing yet to report for either of you, I'm afraid. It's going to be a long night. But your wives are both doing great." The second time she just smiles at us both on her way to the desk. On her way back she says in a saunter-by-shouting, "Hold tight. I'll be out as soon as I have something to report."

−0:03 hours: I walk up to the nurses' station. The woman behind the desk doesn't look up, though she clearly senses my presence, if not my stench. Rebecca says that I'm a shower-twice kind of guy when the temperature gets past eighty. "Excuse me," I say, so gently, as if to not wake her up. She looks up more haughty than weary, preparing to test for how few words she can let me get out before she tells me that there's no news and when there is news Dr. Mulitz will be the one to deliver said news. So I jab her first. "Can I smoke?"

"Not on hospital grounds."

"I know. I mean, do I have time, do you think?"

Her face relaxes into something akin to pity. "You have a cell phone on you?" I write down the number on a pamphlet (*The Hazards of Shaken Baby Syndrome*, for fuck's sake) and she promises to call me in the next twenty minutes if anything is up. Then she adds, "You can't smoke within fifteen feet of hospital grounds."

I walk half a block and stand outside of a Baptist church, the sun starting its descent, the temperature still inhumane. I'm about to light up when the other guy comes jogging across the street. "Hey." He nods to me.

"Something up? They need me?"

"No. No, sorry. Look, I'm sorry to be that guy—" he starts, and I cut him off by handing him the pack. There's not a noble reason to bum a cigarette off of anyone, I don't know why people bother to ask with such an apologetic tone. I light his cigarette for him and he sucks in deeply. "Thank you."

"Of course."

We stand and face each other for a few puffs. He looks at the sky, as if searching for an explanation for this heat, steps out of the way of a few passersby. "They told me it can take more than a day from when they induce," he says.

"I know. Christ." I can see the outline of a tattoo on his shoulder through the thin fabric of his shirt. He's bigger than I am, rangier. He'd fight one weight class up from me. Handsome guy now that I'm looking at him. He's got the toast stubble and a sharp nose. "Mine is getting induced."

"Mine too." He bobs his head.

"Guess they bundle those together. Maybe they have an inducement team of nurses." This doesn't even warrant a response, but his face constricts, as if he's trying to determine whether to give me one anyway. "I admit, I have no fucking clue what any of this entails."

He belches a laugh of smoke. "Me neither. I keep thinking of movies and TV shows and all I know is that babies get delivered in elevators."

I toss him a smirk like a coin. You earned that, handsome fella. "I'm guessing this is your first."

"Yeah." He smiles sheepishly. "You?"

"That it is."

"I'm Paul." He switches the cigarette and extends his hand to me.

I shake it. "Michael. You live around here?"

"Oh no." He laughs. "Park Slope? Couldn't afford it even if I wanted to. You?"

"Me and my wife live in Red Hook."

"That's a nice neighborhood." He nods.

"Up and coming," I reply.

"Greenpoint," he offers.

"Oh, I want to get up there more. I hear good things. How nice it is."

"Up and coming." He smiles again. "Far from here, but Dr. Mulitz . . ."

"I know. She's their cult leader." We chuckle, stand awkwardly for a few beats. "So, Paul, what do you do?" That's the next question on the New York checklist. First is where you live. Then it's what you do. If I approve of both of those, we can continue the conversation.

"I'm an actor," he answers. Adds, almost but not quite an afterthought, "And a paralegal. You?"

"I'm an artist. A painter." I tack on an addendum of my own. "And I work in construction."

We share a conspiratorial grin. "Everyone gets to be a slash these days. Great economy, huh."

"One thing for rent, another for sanity."

"What kind of construction do you do?"

"It's not really construction," I clarify. "Sorry, that's my canned answer. I share a workspace in Red Hook with other guys like me, doing a little bit of everything for the home. I build custom furniture. I'm not a steel girder and hard hat kind of guy, but I make a nice coffee table."

Paul clicks his fingers a few times, like he's trying to place me. He takes another drag off his cigarette and says, "Can I get your number? Jenny up there is my wife—my partner," he corrects in a stammer with a noticeable hostage twitch, "and she's a novelist. She has thousands of books that are just sitting on the floor, so some built-ins in our living room might be perfect. I don't know what that sort of thing costs, but I've been wanting to do something to thank her for whatever is going on now."

"Absolutely." I fish a card out of my wallet. Rebecca had them made up for my last birthday. MICHAEL GOULD: HOME DESIGN AND IMPROVEMENT. I almost hesitate to hand one over, they're such gorgeous cards. As with everything, Rebecca picked out the perfect paper stock, the perfect design. But I offer and he slips it into his front pocket. "Shouldn't be too expensive, and I'm happy to offer you a discount, seeing as how our kids are going to be born on the same day."

"They are." He chuckles. "Jesus. My son. You know yet what you're having?"

"A boy as well. You have a name picked out?"

"No!" he shouts, manic and joyous. "Jenny and I can't agree on one. She wants something literary and I don't have a problem with that, but she's going for deep cuts. Diggory, Rodolphe, Fitzwilliam." I don't know where any of those are from, but Paul dances in place, enamored with all of them. I'd hate to be the first guy to prick his balloon with a blank stare, so I nod knowingly instead. "You guys have a name picked out?" he asks.

"It's between Mark and Willem. After Rothko and De Kooning, the abstract expressionists." If he's not going to help me with his references, he can Google mine, though I add, "Those are the artists I like. I paint that style of art." Rebecca likes Willem, because of the two syllables. She thinks Willem Gould sounds better than Mark Gould.

"Fitzwilliam Sayles-Fenniger," he recites. "When this is all done our kids should meet."

"Absolutely," I reply. I'm down to the filter so I take a last drag and stamp it out underfoot. Though he still has a few drags left Paul does the same. I guess we're friends now. I reach into my bag and make a decision, take the flask out, and unscrew the cap.

"Paul, we're going to become fathers tonight. My wife packed this for me so I could celebrate. Will you drink with me?"

"I'd like that very much, Michael. Thank you." And I give him the first sip, which he takes, standing in front of a church in Park

25

Slope, tilting his head back and making the universal face for when a shot of bourbon hits your throat. All squints and smacked lips. "Blanton's?" he inquires, and I decide then and there that I like him.

"Nothing but the best for our sons," I reply, taking a slug of my own. Then we chew some peppermint gum, and laugh together because the combination of tastes is disgusting.

When we get back to the waiting room the nurse is standing in our way. We both slow our stride, time itself slowing down. She's got a grim set to her face, and bad news can't reach us unless we allow ourselves to be sucked toward it. But it's like an undertow, we keep getting closer, and she bridges the gap by striding up to both of us.

"Michael Gould?" she says, and my heart shatters. Paul audibly exhales next to me.

"That's me," I say hoarsely.

"We've been trying to call you," she says tartly. And I take out my phone, realizing that, per hospital policy, I turned it off when we came inside and never turned it back on again. And when I look up, her face isn't grave anymore. It's stern. She disapproves, that's all.

"Is everything all right?"

"Everything is more than all right, Mr. Gould. You have a son."

Michael Gould

One Year Ago: July 21, 2009

My son, his head a giant garbanzo bean in shape and color, turned toward Rebecca's swollen breast, one of her arms cradling him, the other stroking his tiny, booted foot. I watch them, idly stirring pasta in a pot of boiling water, steam fogging up the kitchen, masking the scent of freshly baked cookies. I smile at this portrait of domesticity and think about the lengths I would go to again and again to protect it.

If four strung out meth heads came barreling into our apartment right now I would draw upon untapped stores of brutality latent in my being and destroy them, one at a time. I would pummel and choke, splatter their brains across our eggshell-painted walls before they could make their first demand, before my family could even notice the intruders. When my wife looked up, she would see four bodies on the floor, their heads caved in, and me standing over them, bloody entrails dangling through my fingers, merciless and primal. "Oh," she'd say, "I thought I heard something," and then she'd go back to cooing a culling song to our boy.

If a tornado ravaged Brooklyn I would gather my family in my arms, swallow them whole into my belly like stones, protect them from all wind and weather, my feet planted in the floorboards like roots, waiting for the storm to pass. Then I would regurgitate them, slick but unharmed.

If a plane flew low into our front window I'd grab it by the nose, push it with locomotive force back onto the street, and serve Rebecca dinner while the sirens blared and the police cordoned off the area.

If the plague swept through the streets they could breathe with my indestructible lungs. I'd purify water, boiling it in the heat of my rage toward any bacteria brazen enough to try to shatter our tranquillity. And we would thrive. Our son would grow iron-boned, like an earth-bound god, able to withstand the most biblical of calamities, power and courage passed through the blood of his father.

I'd destroy the world to keep this scene intact.

We named him Jackson Thomas Gould. Jackson after Pollock. Thomas after Rebecca's father's father. Gould after me.

Paul Fenniger

Present Day: July 19, 2010

9:38 AM

The announcements stopped fifteen minutes ago. We continue to stand, elbow to elbow, marinating in our own sweat. Headphones have come off, books have been dog-eared and tucked into bags or onto laps. We're playing a favorite game, speculating about what's wrong.

"Signal failure," the *New Yorker* man speaks, in tones of information delivered from on high. "Some malfunction in red lights and green lights and we have to sit here until they figure it out."

"How come we have to wait here then? Take us to the next station and figure it out there," he's asked. Some voice in the crowd. He considers this, his seated position giving him the air of kingly condescension.

"There are trains ahead of us. They can't move if the signals don't work in front of them. It's a domino effect. Probably backed up all the way to Bushwick."

"Definitely a jumper," the suited man—the last man to squeeze in—counters. "I've seen this before. Some guy dives into an oncoming train and they have to clean it all up before the next train rolls in. Some asshole's last act was to make me late for work."

Cell phones can't get a signal down here, but that doesn't stop people from checking, from clicking through again and again, reaching to the ceiling in the hopes that an extra inch will help the signal penetrate through the East River, bore through the tunnel, and meet their device. I've taken my jacket off and folded it over my forearm. I'm taking all of this in, absorbing it to recount to Jenny. I have a lot of trouble starting conversations. Sometimes she jokes that she is my director; if she didn't cue me to speak, I'd amble through life like a background extra. When I get home today I don't want to dive into the serious talk. We should orbit it instead, wait for the right moment to approach. If she doesn't have much to share with me about her day, though, I'll tell her about the cast of characters who got stuck on the subway.

"How long are we going to be stopped here?" One voice speaks for many.

"If it's a jumper, could be a while. They have to get as many pieces as they can." He's trying to sound insouciant, but he clearly relishes this. This man will laugh later in a bar about a subway jumper.

I'm exhausted, but that's okay. I don't need to be particularly energetic to fetch and file for the law firm. Jenny didn't sleep well, which means I didn't sleep well.

I want Jenny back. I want Jenny back, and that occupies every idle thought.

"If a guy jumps from the end of the platform when a train is coming in at full speed, he can get everywhere."

"Why don't you shut up," a voice in the crowd responds.

Then the steady hiss of the air-conditioning goes out and the train car immediately feels thirty degrees hotter. There's a horrible mix of sounds—gasps of horror, groans of anger, the clicking of tongues, as if the air-conditioning is being inexcusably rude.

Shortly after the air-conditioning goes out, the lights follow.

Paul Fenniger

Eleven Months Ago: August 13, 2009

I come home to find Jenny in pajama pants. This is an improvement. Yesterday she woke up in a T-shirt and underwear, and I came home six hours later to find her still barelegged. She doesn't acknowledge me as I drop my briefcase (a ludicrous gift from her for my last birthday, solid and leather—it looks like it should be holding stacks of unmarked bills, not the paperback I brought on the train and the Tupperware with remnants of my half-eaten lunch), or even when I come up behind her, bundle her hair in my hands, and kiss the top of her head. The ashtray on her desk is empty. This tells me it was at saturation point before I arrived.

"Did you write today?" I ask.

"I did write today," she replies.

She's not going to apologize for smoking in the house, not that I think she needs to. It's okay, I guess, that she does. I'm just concerned. I don't want the slammed doors or the tears that sharing my concern would provoke, so instead I rest my face on the crown of her head. I'd like to know if she's been drinking. I'd like to know which Jenny I'm going to get tonight. I spin her chair and she doesn't resist, doesn't resist when I cup her chin in my hand and doesn't resist when I kiss her mouth. She doesn't touch me back, and her lips barely twitch in response, but this is also an improvement.

"In medieval times," Jenny says, "husbands would come home and kiss their wives less to show affection and more to detect notes of alcohol, see if the missus has been in the liquor cabinet."

"Have you been drinking my mead?"

"No."

"Well then." I kiss her again.

I kneel, because she's not going to stand up, and we have our daily stare-off. I look into her eyes, the crevices deepening by the day, and she looks back into mine, challenging, daring me to acknowledge her grief. Jenny didn't go outside today, or shower, or do more than throw on pants and come in here to type. Jenny may have taken a nap, if sleep came for her, or she may have blearily watched an hour of television, flipping absently through channels, settling on some show she'd seen before—the comfort of familiarity, of knowing the joke a second before it's delivered, of having the resolution of the drama determined in her mind while the conflict still raged. She's got a coffee mug on her desk, so the pot I left her this morning went to some use. I'll check the fridge downstairs to see if she's eaten. I'd look in the sink to see if she dirtied a dish, but Jenny has taken to washing and drying dishes immediately after using them, of making the bed the instant she leaves it, of erasing all signs of her presence outside of this desk, so if I weren't to stand in the stale smoke air of our bedroom, next to the wooden desk she's had since college and that has followed us, like a stray dog, from apartment to apartment, I wouldn't know she ever existed.

"What should I make for dinner?"

"I'm not hungry."

I lower my head, then curse myself. I shouldn't show frustration with her. "Please, babe, can we eat something together?"

"Can you not call me babe?"

"Sorry."

"Babe or baby or . . ."

"I won't. I'm sorry."

"It's cruel."

"I wasn't thinking."

"You're being cruel."

"I'm sorry."

She runs out of steam. Jenny scratches her arm absently, leaving a jet trail that immediately glows red. I ask again, "Can I make chicken and rice?" She sticks out her tongue, shakes her head. "How about hamburgers? I could grill them." Another violent shake. "Do you want to order a pizza?" Nope. "Umm . . . Chinese?" Ew. "Indian." A moment's hesitation, then another headshake. "Steak?"

She accepts this, bobs her head in tacit agreement. Steak. She gestures at me, waves her hand around like a sorceress. "With the . . ." She chokes up. Tears start.

"With the marinade?" I complete her thought. She knows that I know she loves it when I marinate skirt steak. But she's gone now, crying into her hands, knees drawn up into her chest. Quiet, almost silent sobs. "It's okay, Jenny," I reassure. "It's okay." I try to rest my hands on her legs, unpry them so I can hold her, but she's shut fast. She wants to be left alone. I know this mood; I've learned this language in a crash course. So I leave to get the ingredients for marinated skirt steak. On another night I may have tried something new with it, some citrus or adventurous spice. Not tonight. Not for a while.

On my way out I pass by the closed door. Jenny doesn't want it opened. I can't even open it when she's down the hall in our bedroom; she'll come and yell at me. She did the one time I tried, actually beat my chest with her hands. It was the closest she'd come to blaming me. I leave the door shut and walk out of the house. On our front stoop I withdraw a cigarette from one pocket and my cell from the other. I light up and scroll through my contacts, searching for the name of the man I met in the hospital, the one who knows how to improve a home.

Michael Gould

Eleven Months Ago: August 13, 2009

The Brooklyn I grew up in was splintered by race and ethnicity, then by class. Cooking a big meal would find you venturing from neighborhood to neighborhood, grabbing one thing from the Italians, another from the Chinese, a third thing from the Blacks. That's what my mother called them, collectively—The Blacks. Like a family. She'll deny to this day that the term is racist in the slightest.

The Brooklyn of my childhood kept its nice things across the river, in a cabinet of curios called Manhattan. We kept our money in their banks, our hopes in their skyscrapers. We bought our daily clothes down the street (from the Jews) but our funeral and bar mitzvah suits from the shops of Fifth Avenue. Their Fifth Avenue. We have one too, but we shopped on theirs.

And then came the new wave of gentrification, this mysterious houseguest who claimed squatters rights before both feet were across the threshold, a salesman Santa with all sorts of goodies in his sack. Lower crime rates, an influx of business, new development. The homeowners loved it because trust-fund kids flooding Brooklyn from Long Island, from New Jersey, from parts unknown with only their bank accounts on their backs raised property values every time they signed a lease. The renters, people who may have lived in a neighborhood for decades but could never quite get over that down-payment hump, weren't as fond of these nattily dressed kids flipping the demographics of their block like a game of Othello.

And then came the bar owners—mustachioed, pomade-slick vinyl hair, with nautically themed tattoos crisscrossing pipe cleaner forearms, lending heft to the underlying skinniness. They too came to our neighborhoods, joined by the artisanal shopkeepers and bookbinders, terrifically strange men and women who dressed as if dragging the Jazz Age and the Weimar Republic into this century, willfully ignoring that hell followed those pale horses.

And then we came. To Red Hook, where I marvel that the man who writes calliope music is afforded the same respect as the stock trader. I rented a work space in a warehouse to store canvases and build furniture. That's another great thing about gentrified Brooklyn—no matter how esoteric your living (or hobby), you can always find three other people who will go in on loft space with you.

The wood swallows my chisel. It's a hot knife into butter, and I pull up to avoid cutting too close. I don't hear my phone chirp when the text message comes in. I've tuned it out, listening to my iPod, metal scraping wood at high speeds underslung by whatever angst rock I have playing. Rebecca complains that if I can't hear my phone when I'm in the shop, I should put it where I can see it. But I'm steps from home. In an emergency, she can step outside our apartment and hurl a rock through the window of the shop floor. My phone stays in my pocket, where I won't lose it. I don't hear my phone because I'm focused on this cherrywood table leg, on shaping it in the style of a modified Latchee twist. I'm focused on the money this chiseling will bring in.

Rebecca wiped down our kitchen table the other night while I cradled Jackson, shushing him to sleep. Feeling a baby fall asleep in your arms provides immeasurable peace, better than watching fish. The rest of it has been pretty boring thus far. It's marvelous, he's astonishing to gaze upon, but every emotion, sustained too long, becomes rote. It's exhausting to be this appreciative all the fucking time.

"We should get a new table," Rebecca observed.

"What's wrong with that one?"

"Nothing is *wrong* with it. We should just think about a new one. We can afford it."

"But why would we need a new table?"

"Why not? You could build one, manly man."

"Why would we replace a table that still works fine? It's still a table, isn't it?"

She shrugged, hummed to herself while she finished cleaning up. Rebecca has planted her seeds; she wants a new table. And since then, every time I look at the table, I see its flaws, how it does look like the sort of thing two people significantly less far along in life should have. It's not that there's a problem with it—the problem lies within Rebecca and myself. We're not poor enough, not young enough (God help me . . . not hip enough?) to have a table that is one step removed from particleboard set on two sawhorses, aka the much-loved table I had through college. And I miss the person who was suited to my kitchen table. He traded something unawares to earn the right to be too good for a piece of functional furniture.

Marc welds over in his corner. Neither Tony nor Regina is here today, but if they were, Tony would be spinning a potter's wheel and Regina would be competing with me for table saw time. The three of them have been here longer—I started renting the space six months ago, after my predecessor (I've been told) stole "three or four cars." His incarceration is to my benefit—a workshop space a few blocks away from my house, use of a truck, shared supplies.

My shopmates are a cordial bunch, but they've been slow to warm. Tony molded a clay giraffe for Jackson, something to sit on a high shelf for the foreseeable future, and I appreciate the gesture. I offered to take them all out for a beer to celebrate Jackson's birth, but Regina and Marc demurred. Tony was initially up for it but followed their lead. I bring in Rebecca's cookies and they're devoured gratefully within a few minutes. Still, there's a thin plane of ice between shopmates and friends that needs a bit more thawing.

Would be nice to have a beer with someone—I didn't realize that would stop once my wife pushed out a baby. I didn't realize that having a child would lead to the immediate death of my social life. I'm not an adolescent and I don't exist in a sitcom; I knew sacrifices would be made. I knew I wasn't going to be stumbling home while Rebecca provided the 2:00 AM feeding, but I didn't anticipate the full stop at the end of the sentence. Plug up that release valve and it has to go somewhere, doesn't it? So I spend more time in this shop, or I volunteer for all sorts of errands so that Rebecca can stay at home with Jackson. She's not going stir-crazy, doesn't matter to her. I keep running back and forth to Fairway, so often the produce manager recognizes me now as the guy who always forgets one or two ingredients and has to keep coming back. "You sure you got everything you need?" He laughs. I smile and nod, because fuck him in the teeth. He doesn't know my needs.

My foot finally catches up to the rest of me and stops pressing the pedal. The lathe gradually slows, the table leg transforms from a blurred cylinder to the twisted, bulbous shape I've been hoping for. Wood like pulled taffy, ready to be sanded. Polish this one, then do it all three more times.

When I take out my phone it's to check the time, make sure I'm home for dinner. There's nothing elaborate waiting for me, just leftover chili, possibly reheated. Our new habit is to cook a giant one-pot meal to last us for three or four days, based primarily on what's on special.

Hi Michael. This is Paul Fenniger. We met at the hospital. Was hoping I could buy you a drink and we could talk projects.

This guy. The actor slash something else that doesn't pay. I've sat across from dozens like Paul, guys who read too much GQ and crave bespoke suits but don't want to pay the tailor. In my case, it's custom furniture, and depending on the wood and the hardware, it's expensive. Tell that to a guy like Paul and his mind starts downgrading from dining room table (like the one I just spent hours lathing a leg for, that I myself could never afford) to coffee table, still not considering my time and labor in the cost. Or, you know, my expertise, the fact that I make beautiful furniture and others don't, and there's value in that. My father used to have an expression: *Everybody wants to pay only for the burger, no one wants to pay for the grass.* He probably still says that, shakes his hands like he's reciting Talmudic wisdom instead of a quaint shtetl idiom.

Paul Fenniger didn't give off the musky cologne of trust fund, but I've been wrong on that count before, and if mine eyes don't deceive me, he's offering to buy me a drink. Sitting across from another guy, especially one going through the same shit I am, could be therapeutic.

> Hi P, I remember you. Sure lets drink.
> when and where

A minute later . . .

> Do you want to meet in the Slope? Or I
> can come to Carroll Gardens or Boerum
> Hill. You're in Red Hook, right? And how
> about tonight? Does that work for you?

> Your buying, Ill come to you. Gpoint?

> Thanks. That would be great. How about
> Black Rabbit, Greenpoint Avenue?

> I know it give me ninety to get there. See
> you 8sh.

> That's great. Thank you.

I wave to Marc on my way out, but he's hidden behind a veil of sparks and a steampunk nightmare mask. Back at home Rebecca has already started eating the chili without me. She sprinkles a few semicongealed strings of shredded cheese over each bite. "I was starving." She covers her greeting and apology. I tug back her pony-tail and kiss her swollen mouth. I kiss Jackson's garbanzo bean and stare for a moment, take in the sight of his hostile expression, limbs twitching, fighting off sleep in his vibrating papoose chair. He is literally the most spectacular fucking thing I will ever lay eyes upon, and other than this one moment of grace, I have not had a single thought since I stepped back into this house that was not undercut with notes of getting the hell out as fast as possible.

"I have to run to Greenpoint for a client meeting."

"Now? Which client?"

"Potential client," I correct, both myself and Rebecca. "Guy I met at the hospital."

"What does he want you to build?"

"Don't know yet. Going to go to Greenpoint and find out."

And her face says it all. It says that I shouldn't leave, that my priorities are out of alignment with hers, and that the good father I'm supposed to be, as all boys are supposed to be when they've grown into men and put obsolete playthings behind them like so many discarded bikes left in backyards to rust, is the man who sits down on the carpet and watches his son fall asleep, tidies up a bit, converses with his wife about the banalities of their day, makes an effort to get her to laugh, kisses her until she relents and breaks away, goes to wash the scent of cookies from her skin; or doesn't, instead continues to kiss, wants to be made love to (that hideous phrase makes me softer than Marshmallow Fluff), draws her gently into the bedroom, one ear alert for the waking, shrieking child, the rest of his attention on her mewing pleasure, the affectionate hold-ing that replaced the ferocious clutching somewhere along the way, as if fathers aren't supposed to have nail marks. That's what her face says. It says that with a harmonizing look reminding me that I am also supposed to provide for this family, and so she under-stands that I need to go to Greenpoint for business, and that she trusts both the business element of that sentence and the needing to go. It says that too.

But it's just her face that says that, not her words, and so I kiss her again, make some vague promise to be back before she's asleep, which I guarantee I will not be, and make my way to the bus stop. I get lucky and catch a passing B61. I'll be there early, with enough time to enjoy a drink on my own.

At twenty to eight, I'm sipping the house beer at the bar, passing time, paying close attention to a couple on a date without being too creepy. They are something new, it's laced throughout every furtive pause and every perfunctory interview question. But each answer warrants a small noise of surprise, delighted squeaks to discover that this new person has also been to London or has an older sibling as well.

I don't know if there's a single question I could ask Rebecca and be shocked by the answer. I'm guessing she'd say the same thing about me. She told me she doesn't like the taste of capers a few weeks ago. That resonated enough for me to remember it now, weeks later. We're the last four minutes of "Hey Jude," the coda everyone sings along with because they know the words and the tune. No surprises, only the comfort of shared experience. When that song comes on, I let McCartney get through one go-round, then click forward to "Revolution."

Eight on the dot and Paul Fenniger walks in. We do our man shake and settle into a booth, Paul covering both my last and my next (a Manhattan this time), as well as something honey-colored and neat for himself. When he sits across from me, even in the low light of this hipster bar, I can tell he's not how I remember him. His face projects spilt ice cream and skinned knees. We clink glasses.

"Here's to not having to breast-feed," I quip. He smiles politely in reply. "How's it going?"

He bobs his head, his rounded shoulders hunched so tightly it's making me tense. "It's going. How's your family?"

"Everyone is great." I beam. "Jackson keeps doing cute baby things. Mostly sleeping still. Rebecca is exhausted, so there's that. I'm sorry, I don't remember your wife's name."

"Jenny."

"That's right," I confirm. "How's fatherhood? You got a few too many two AM's under your eyes, Paul."

It's in this moment that I cross the threshold. I've just made a faux pas there's no way I could have known I was making. It's in the tightening of his mouth, the look askance at the bar, as if I can't see that he's got tears welling up if he's not facing me straight on. "We didn't . . ." he starts, bundles his hands into fists. "He never left the . . . he had . . . he had a hole," and he taps his chest twice. "Right here."

Everything sinks at once. The floor of the bar falls away and I stare openmouthed at Paul Fenniger, this bottomless well of sadness, and I thank every deity imaginable that I am not this man, that I don't know his pain. That I am better than he is. That I am better than he is. That I am better than he is. A broken record thought, repeated and repeated while he composes himself and I mask the bile and the . . . what is this . . . fucking schadenfreude? Am I actually comforted to know that his child leaped into the bad statistical pool in the false hope that Jackson, conversely, will now be safe? Am I glad? Paul looks directly at me, like he knows what I'm thinking, like he doesn't blame me for being reassured it's him and not me.

"Jesus, Paul," I sputter out. "That's the worst thing. I'm so sorry. How are you holding up?"

"I'm okay. Jenny's okay," he insists. "She's been having some bad days, kind of what I wanted to talk to you about."

"Okay . . ."

"We turned her office into a nursery, and now we don't need a nursery for a while. I want to turn it back into an office. I have money."

I wave him off, hate myself for doing so. "That comes later, Paul. Tell me how I can help."

"I was thinking shelves. Like built-in bookshelves. She has a lot of books."

"She's a writer. I remember you telling me that. Shelves are easy enough."

"Maybe some other stuff. I was hoping you could come over one night. Not tonight. I haven't spoken to Jenny about this yet. But you could come for dinner. See the room. Tell me what you think. You and your wife could both come. I mean—I'm sorry—she'd be busy, or you both would be busy."

"My parents can watch Jackson," I reassure. It feels dirty to say the name of my son in front of a grieving father.

"Thanks." He wicks a tear away from his cheek. When he looks back at me his eyes are dry. He's once again stoic and manly. "You want to go smoke?"

"Sure. You need one?"

"Nope." He taps a private code on the table. "I've got."

For the next hour, Paul Fenniger and I talk about where we grew up and what sort of work we do. We talk about our wives. I get the feeling that whereas my drinking buddies simply don't see me any-more, Paul never had any to begin with. He's a little too enthusias-tic to share trivial details about himself. Then there's a pause, and his voice stays steady when he tells me, "I'm just worried about Jenny." He repeats that twice, an incantation to the bottom of his glass, and he leaves it at that. He's worried about Jenny. Fair enough.

He pays the full bill and we separate at the train station. This time, when we man shake, he throws an arm around my back and I do the same. I start down the stairs but come back up a second later, watch him walk away, see his body transform once again into something heavier, rounded, walking in the fetal position, bracing himself for the next blow.

Then I break into a dead sprint down the stairs and through the station. I run as fast as I can for the train. It's not here yet, and it'll be another fifteen minutes before it arrives, but I couldn't take the chance of having just missed my way home.

Michael Gould

Present Day: July 19, 2010

9:49 AM

For our honeymoon, my parents sent me and Rebecca to Paris. I'm an artist, she's a baker, it made sense. When we got there, starving, we went to find something to tide us over until dinner. A man at a crepe cart asked us what we'd like, and I opened my mouth and said, "I'll have banana caramel, please."

Every word in an English accent. Upper crust. More Laurence Olivier than Michael Caine.

Rebecca looked at me askance but said nothing. We ate our crepes and strolled toward the Eiffel Tower. There, after getting *deux* tickets, I bumped into another set of tourists and apologized, "Sorry."

Soar-eee.

Rebecca made fun of me for it, thinking that I put on a stupid fake accent for strangers to amuse her. For the rest of our trip, she'd sometimes lapse into a hideous cockney, only when speaking to me, of course, and demanded Cornish pasties for every meal.

My fake accent wasn't entirely intentional. It never came out to the customs agent at the airport or the concierge at the hotel, and I couldn't understand why until I realized that they had my passport. They knew where I was from. But to a stranger, I was determined to be as much a stranger as possible. And I couldn't control it.

The accent came out again, unwelcome as spittle, when I paid for my bottle of water on West 181st. A dozen blocks north of there, four buses had passed without stopping, without passengers. The drivers hadn't even looked in our direction, we few standing at the ass end of Broadway, trying to go south. I checked my phone again for incoming texts, had none, saw the temperature had crested ninety-three, and my battery power was down to 20 percent. I also grew fairly certain I was dying, since my body had jettisoned every drop of water.

"Fuck it, I'll walk," I announced to the small crowd. And so I pointed my feet south and got started.

Three people stand at the counter at a bodega on 181st, two leaning over a candy display to watch a small rabbit-eared television with the clerk. They don't pay any attention as I grab the biggest bottle of water I can find from the fridge and chug a third of it walking back up to the front of the store. "What's going on?" I ask, hearing my voice overenunciate its consonants, my upper lip stiffening. Far enough away from home, speaking to strangers, I myself become strange.

"Something happened in midtown," the clerk grumbles. He notices the bottle in my hands and says in the same dejected monotone, "Four dollars."

"Four bucks? Is this a movie theater?"

He immediately escalates. "You opened it!" he shouts. The other two customers turn and glare at me, a united front.

I haul out the ten in my wallet and hand it over. "What happened in midtown?"

"They don't know."

"Trains aren't running," I offer. Provide a little information, hope to get a little in return.

"Nothing is running," he huffs. The other customers nod stoically. "Everything is completely shut down. TV says they are trying to evacuate the area."

"Jesus, is it . . ." I let my tea-and-crumpets voice trail off. I don't want to say *terrorism* out loud, not in front of the dark-skinned clerk and his other customers. The youngest customer, a guy who probably isn't older than twenty, starts fiddling with his phone.

"Reporter said possible train crash," the clerk provides.

"Train into another train," the older of the two customers clarifies.

"It's terrorism," the younger interjects. He holds up his phone, waves it around. "I have no bars. My cousin works for Verizon. He told me they can turn off the towers by flipping a switch if they want to shut down cell service to an area."

The other two men shake their heads. "No, really. There must have been a bomb underground. You can trigger that shit with any piece of shit phone. Even those." He points behind the counter at the small collection of burners hanging on a pegboard.

"Not those." The clerk chuckles uneasily. He's simultaneously shooting daggers at the kid and offering up a *what can you do* chuckle to me.

"Yes! Those exact phones! My cousin told me any phone. It's real Al-Qaeda shit. But they shut down the towers so there's no signal. No signal, no detonation. I'll bet a bomb went off and they don't want to report it because people would panic. Those assholes wait for the first responders to come in and then they set off a second bomb, so the phone companies shut down the tower. I'll bet anything that's what happened."

I check my phone, and sure enough, I don't have any service.

"Definitely terrorism," the kid insists. "And if they're not even reporting it, it must be massive."

Michael Gould

Twenty-one Months Ago: October 16, 2008

She calls it the Interior. Geographically, it's a misshapen triangle of land bordered on one end by the hip commerce of Van Brunt Street, on another by the slowly reclaimed industrial wasteland of Beard Street, and severed from the rest of Brooklyn by its third border, the Brooklyn-Queens Expressway. I point out to Rebecca that at the point it reaches our neighborhood, the BQE is actually more aptly termed the Gowanus Expressway, or even Hamilton Avenue, but to her it's fast cars zipping by on two levels, plunging headfirst into the gaping anus of the Brooklyn-Battery Tunnel.

The Interior is everything within. The Interior is the projects, though that's the term she learned in Connecticut, when projects were settings for movies. The projects were fictions to Rebecca, settings for drive-by shootings and ghetto poetry until she moved to Red Hook. She learned that term over there, and I had to be the one to break it to her that they've come up with a less-loaded term by now. No one calls them the projects anymore, and if she'd noticed the well-manicured courtyards and the families around picnic tables, the aesthetics have changed a bit since she rented a VHS of *New Jack City*.

We call it the Interior and we don't go there as much as travel through it. The bus makes its way slowly through Red Hook from the body of Brooklyn, like a blood cell voyaging to an oxygen-starved extremity, and it picks up and drops off people along the way until it reaches Van Brunt and we get out.

I call my wife a racist. I don't say it like I mean it but make a joke of it, to be kind, if vaguely barbed in that kindness. Michael Gould, born and raised in Brooklyn, has no qualms about walking through the Interior. But I hang back, stay on Van Brunt, patrolling like a dog on an invisible leash, because I know how uncomfortable it would make Rebecca for me to venture inward.

Instead I call her a racist. I used to say it only in response to her issues with the Interior, especially anytime she would invoke our term for it, but now I say it about anything, widening the scope of the humor. Whenever I sense discomfort in her, I contort my face and say, "You racist!" to her in as horrifically broad a stereotype as possible.

The first time I brought Rebecca to Red Hook, an act as mysterious and portentous as introducing horses to the Indians, we stepped off the subway one neighborhood over, at Smith and Ninth streets, descending from up on high, the novelty of the above-ground subway and the spectacular view of downtown Manhattan from the platform transfixing us both. This could be our view, whenever we wished. "See," I said, "you like it already." And she did. She positively glowed, making her careful calculations in her head, running fingers along a mental abacus, budgeting the cost of smiling at my comment.

She wanted to take a bus, but I insisted that we walk, to approach this new neighborhood on foot, see it appear before us from its fringes to its core. I wanted us to map out our future in the storefronts we passed, to find the future anniversary restaurant, the wine store that carries Gewürztraminer, the boutique where I could buy her birthday gifts.

The walk became a horrific miscalculation on my part, and lazy scouting to boot. I hadn't done the advance work to see how much the neighborhood had gentrified over the years from when I last saw it, when it was an uninhabitable shipping yard, subway-null and crime saturated. We crossed over the expressway, scurrying to make the light, and turned right, past gas stations and garages. Past cracked sidewalks, barely able to hear each other over the truck noise. Rebecca's look clouded over.

Rebecca hasn't breathed a stupid breath in her lifetime. She saw through the facade, this choreographed first trip, designed to dip her toes into the waters of Red Hook. She knew, sure as sugar, that I had already decided that we're getting the hell out of my parents' place and that this is where we'd settle, possibly even seen where we'd live, and that I was practically humoring her to believe she had more agency in the process. On that first trip I took her to the gigantic Fairway market, where we bought ingredients and assembled our lunches on the picnic benches outside. Our very own picnic. I pointed out the small shops up and down the waterfront, artisans hawking their wares in buildings like forts. That's where she'd buy her earrings. That's where she'd buy her ornamental scarves.

"What is this place like in winter?" she asked.

"It becomes Santa's workshop. Elves and reindeer everywhere."

"I'm serious." A long pause to show me how serious she was. She layered shaved turkey and slices of cheese, building a sandwich of unimpeachable structural integrity rather than look me in my face. She added, half to herself, "This isn't where I saw us moving."

"Where did you see us moving?" I asked the question I already knew the answer to.

"Park Slope. Or Carroll Gardens. Or Brooklyn Heights."

"We can't afford any of those places."

"We can if you ask your parents."

"Then we can't afford any of those places. I've asked as much as I'm going to ask." We've had this discussion so many times it reads as two actors testing each other to see if they have their lines memorized. "You won't be the only white lady in Red Hook," I promised.

She looked around quickly to see who'd heard. I'd aired a dirty secret and put my thumb in a very deep wound. "That isn't what I meant and that's not fair," she spat. "Red Hook has bad parts; I know what happens in bad parts; I've been to bad parts. Are you going to be okay with me calling the police the first time I see kids loitering on our block? Or sitting on our front steps?"

She had a point. It's not one I considered valid, but it's a point I couldn't argue with her. Nevertheless, give Rebecca enough time and she'll argue both sides in her own head. The pro–Red Hook side of the debate will win if I can wait out the other side's acquiescence.

I took her to the end of the pier and we looked out at the Statue of Liberty, never so close before, never seen from this angle. She was almost facing us. I kissed my wife there. "I love you," she blurted the second our lips parted.

And I walked her around those small streets that exist outside of the triangle, tributaries that jut off until they are stopped by the amorphous shape of the shoreline. I showed her a restaurant that specializes in key lime pie and is so popular and so renowned that it can exist in Red Hook selling mostly key lime pie.

We sat across from one another at Hope & Anchor, her sipping a white wine, me a beer. She glanced around the restaurant, and everyone looked like they too were from affluent Connecticut. Everyone digging into their artisanal sandwiches looked like they grew up in a town that puts tinsel on the train station railings starting in the middle of November. Children of university professors and bank vice presidents. Sons of gynecologists and daughters of orthodontists.

She sipped her wine furtively. I told her she resembled a sparrow drinking from a birdbath, but I knew how nervous all of this made her, so I reached across the table and grasped her hand.

"Red Hook is far from all of our friends," she posited. "No easy way for us to get to them or vice versa."

"You'll have to rely on me for entertainment," I replied. This doesn't placate, so I continued, "The friends who are friends will come and see us. I can't base our life decisions on how easy it is to get drinks with Alice and Peg and Carly."

"You just named three of my friends."

"Or Sam, or Aaron, or Tanya. I'll see them when I see them. I want us to have our own place."

She paused for another skim of a sip, asked me, "Where is it?"

"We passed it. It's an open-plan loft, second floor of a two-unit building. We can build up the kitchen for you, put in a few ovens, and put up partitions to make rooms. It's in our price range, with a little room left over."

"Room for three?" she asked me. The debate had been settled; now came the terms for surrender.

I smiled and repeated it back to her, assuredly. Meant it too. "Room for three."

The move into Red Hook was a process, a step-by-step march into our own space. The landlord gave us free rein to, as he put it, "put a few nails in the walls," meaning he had our security deposit and couldn't be bothered to care how we renovated an open–floor plan loft space. The first thing I did was divide the giant room into two halves, essentially creating an efficiency with a kitchen next door. A few beams, a few tubs of joint compound, and up pops a bedroom. Split that in two and there's room for three. Slap a couch and dining room table on the other side of the wall and line the whole thing with bookshelves and even Rebecca didn't mind spending the night with me on an air mattress, though the alternative was staying alone with my parents, so I take only some of the credit.

The lion's share of the work happened in the kitchen. My father called in a few favors and a team of Hebrew-speaking electricians showed up to argue with one another, knock some holes into the walls and ceiling, and curse in heavily accented English about the construction of our building. But they also gave us a second line for a second oven.

"She could keep both ovens going all day, run a mixer, and blow-dry her hair without tripping a circuit," Dov bragged to me, smoking his unfiltered Israeli army cigarettes in my apartment.

Why the second line? For that, go back twelve years, give or take. Rebecca's family studiously avoids one another, four drops of vinegar in a pool of oil. Her father lives at his office, penetrating the psyches and occasionally the labia of his patients. Her mother throws herself into community service, chairing town committees like a petty tyrant. Her sister, Jolie, drives through the gateway drugs and vanishes for weeks at a time. Rebecca, very much alone at home, takes up baking. Discovers she has a talent for it. Discovers she has a marketable talent for it and pays for her own car with the proceeds from running a perpetual bake sale out of the house. Becky's Bites was born, continued through college, and brought south to Brooklyn.

Rebecca started by baking the cookies herself, selling them in gift boxes. A few enterprising coffee shops put in orders and Becky filled them, providing five-dollar desserts to people already sipping four-dollar lattes. Then the restaurants came calling, but with caveats. It made no sense for Rebecca to bake two dozen cookies for them three times a week. Depending on when she filled the order, the cookies could be stale by the time they hit the plate, and customers kept sending them back to the kitchen in the hopes the chef could warm them up, like mom used to make them, which was because they were Toll House.

So Rebecca toyed with ingredients, with storage, and perfected the cookie log—an almost fanatically cylindrical mass of dough, notches run through with a serrated knife in precise eighteen-millimeter increments, wrapped first in wax paper, then plastic wrap, then tin foil. Baking instructions taped to the package. Now, she makes a delivery once a week to her restaurants, and they can cut and bake as needed.

A year after we moved to Red Hook, and Rebecca hasn't called the police once. She waits out further "improvements" to our neighborhood with a dogged determination. The day a Starbucks opens she will stand triumphant in its doorway and personally remind everyone that bathrooms are for customers only.

She finds me on the roof of my studio, prolonging a ten-minute smoke break from alternating between stretching canvas and restoring a set of antique chairs. I proffer the cigarette to her but she declines, a sour twist to her mouth. "Too nervous even to smoke?"

"I need you to drive me," she replies. For a moment, I consider mounting an argument—it's certainly not convenient, but that's my sharpest dull weapon. There's no one else in the shop today, and the sign-out board for the truck is empty for the next thirty-six hours. By the time I pull up in front of the apartment she's waiting for me on the curb, logs of cookie dough cradled in her arms.

"Which did you bring?" I ask.

"Maple walnut, lemon thyme, white chocolate blueberry, rum raisin," she replies, wide-eyed. "Should I have gone with something else? I don't have anything with chocolate."

"I thought you said white chocolate blueberry."

"That's white chocolate. It's not real chocolate."

I give her question due consideration. "Maple walnut is your best cookie."

"That's your opinion."

"Yes, but I eat a fuck-ton of cookies, so my opinion counts for something. Maple walnut is the best, lemon thyme is a good example of a more savory cookie, so she'll be able to envision it paired with different things. White chocolate blueberry is just yummy, and it's denser than your other cookies, so that's another weapon in your arsenal. Rum raisin tastes like fellating a homeless man, so that one was a mistake."

She laughs, "I'm serious, Michael."

"I am too. Rum raisin cookies wouldn't even make the menu at Dachau. But the other three she'll love."

She is the immaculately poised Dawn de la Puente, owner of four restaurants in Brooklyn. All farm-to-table, at the vanguard of the locavore movement. Half of her vegetables come from rooftops scattered throughout the boroughs, the sources for every ingredient listed on the menu. Rebecca and I ate at Riziki, her flagship in Bed-Stuy, and while I couldn't discern the difference between lettuce that came from California and lettuce that came from three floors up, Rebecca savored and swooned.

"How do you know she's not lying?" I asked. "How do you know this chicken isn't from some factory farm in Kentucky?"

"I can tell," Rebecca replied sagely.

"How's that?"

"When you eat factory farmed animals, you taste the sadness in the meat." She meant it too. Every word.

Dawn will quiz her on where she sources her ingredients, and Rebecca has the expensive fanaticism about getting her supplies locally. All of the basics—the flour, the eggs, the butter—all come from New York State, close enough in horseshoes, hand grenades, and the militant wings of the locavorian army. She has to go farther afield for the sugar—the cane fields of Westchester have gone by the wayside—but she did spend over a month finding the right independently owned and operated sugar plantation in Florida, so she gets her sweets from there. The rum she uses isn't from a local distiller, the raisins aren't from local grapes. I couldn't begin to tell you where half the nuts come from. This weighs on Rebecca's mind; I can tell from how she narrates the signs she sees on our drive to meet Dawn, her chatter an old standby from her stable of tells.

"'Bud Lime. The night starts here,'" she mutters.

"It's going to go fine," I reassure.

"I know that." Then, "'Have you been injured in an automobile accident?'"

I grab a beer and watch bowling on television at a bar down the street from Riziki. On a weekday, at two in the afternoon, I'm both the youngest by twenty years and the whitest by three shades. So I sip my beer and avoid conversation until my wife is done baking and taste-testing cookies with an enterprising restaurateur. Part of going to any other neighborhood now involves absorbing the reasons why our neighborhood is better and feeling smugly superior. Bed-Stuy is a little more worn around the edges, no Fairway as a supermarket, no river view, and it smells vaguely like wet metal. Growing up, my father told us around the dinner table that "Bedford-Stuyvesant has a slogan. It's Bed-Stuy: Do or Die. Can you imagine living in a place like that?"

And my mother, bless her heart, couldn't understand why the community would allow such a seemingly negative phrase as its welcome mat. "Why not Bed-Stuy: Have Some Pie?" she offered. I like Red Hook better, and scanning the bar, I can't see anyone who wouldn't gladly swap neighborhoods with me, if not lives.

Rebecca texts me an hour later and I meet her outside of Riziki in the truck. Dawn comes out and waves to me, though we haven't met. If she's not proceeding directly to a gala, I cannot fathom how anyone can look that put together on a weekday. Dawn hugs Rebecca. That's a good sign, that and how Rebecca's hands are now empty.

"She's in for eight dozen a week." She radiates light.

"Is she going to serve them in all of her places?"

"Starting just here."

"Is that . . . good?" I don't want to pop her balloon, but I'd think someone with four restaurants would want more than (quick math) ninety-six cookies a week. My parents have helped with start-up costs for both of our businesses, and mine has steadily grown to where I write them a check every month rather than the other way around. If Rebecca is going to do the same, and God help me I don't want to have the conversation wherein I ask Rebecca to start doing the same, she can't sell cookies to the restaurants of Brooklyn like running a bake sale out of our nonexistent front yard.

"It's eight dozen per flavor," she clarifies. "She wants eight dozen maple walnut, eight dozen lemon thyme, even eight dozen rum raisin."

"Fool."

"And she put in an order for the caramel pine nut and the Mexican chocolate sight unseen. Or flavor untasted."

"So eight times twelve times six."

"Five seventy-six."

"A week."

"Every week."

"Every week?"

"From here until Armageddon."

We celebrate by having sex in our new apartment, napping, and then getting dinner at Hope & Anchor. The staff there has started to know us by sight, not yet by name. Red Hook feels tonight like the edge of the globe whereupon we dance, gleeful to be in such proximity to oblivion. When Rebecca and I curl around each other in bed later that night, exhausted and joyous, mapping out our future like we're plotting a heist, she runs a finger through my paltry chest hair and whispers in my ear.

"Today went so well."

"That it did."

"It went so well, Michael."

"You make amazing cookies."

"Soooooooooo well." Then she starts crying. I turn my head toward her and the faucet has spun open, she's shaking against me, crying and heaving and laughing, cackling at the top of her lungs. Like a mad witch. Like someone triumphant over death. "I'm pregnant," she bellows, a huge admission made through wracked sobs and maniacal giggles. "I'm pregnant. I'm pregnant! I'm pregnant!"

My first instinct is to crack a joke, and thank God I force that down, because she's going to remember how I reacted to this moment for the rest of our lives. Rebecca possesses within her limitless patience, boundless kindness, unending generosity. She can also recite past fights verbatim. Every slight goes into a cabinet, reliably forgiven but never forgotten.

We're going to have a baby. It hits me the way it's supposed to, nothing to force or contort. My face lights up, I cry right along with her, I laugh as loudly as she does. We laugh and cry, so loud that our neighbors could reasonably call the police. Then I drag her, naked, into the empty guest room and we laugh and cry some more, pointing at where the crib can go and the changing table and the glider. A baby a baby a baby, we repeat, sleep-dumb and slack-jawed, wild and in love and unhinged.

Somewhere in this mirth I pause to consider that we don't use condoms because Rebecca is on the pill, and thus totally in control of her own, and by proxy our, fertility. And it occurs to me that, unlike condoms, the failure rate on the pill is so minuscule as to be totally disregarded. And I search the recesses of my mind for a memory of having ever had a conversation with Rebecca about her going off the pill.

And draw a complete blank.

Paul Fenniger

Present Day: July 19, 2010

10:10 AM

We stand so as to not ruin our suits. It's our last vestige of pride, this miserly held belief that a suit we've sweat through is still fixable, that the dry cleaners and their magic chemicals can polish it like new, but by sitting, by lowering ourselves to the filthy rubber floor and the stains of a million footprints, we will absorb a residual grime that will never come out.

Everyone else sits down, men crisscross, women in skirts with legs tucked demurely underneath themselves, crooked to the side. When the air-conditioning went out, more than a few people started shouting, but they hushed almost immediately. A ranting lunatic wants to be alone on his or her soapbox. That so many people were shouting the same thing, in tone if not exact phrase (*"Like caged animals!"*), took the oxygen out of the fire.

The ranters gave way to the sneering derision of the pack, a slower burning fire, more heat than light. The sarcastic comments, the veiled threats, the promises of retribution. These went on for a bit, while clothing got stripped off and bags were set down. Our eyes adjusted to the dark on the train; we could make out shapes by this point, follow a withering comment to the outline of a head.

Once the pack got it out of their system the lieutenants emerged. Not leaders, but not followers, these were the people who started getting others to sit down if they wanted, to clearing space where space could be cleared, to calming kids.

The rest of us, myself included, stay silent. We wait for some action to be requested before we take action on our own. Some of us are, understandably, ambivalent. It's not our place to . . . do

55

what, hijack the train and take us to the next station? We are, ultimately, powerless, and so the best thing to do is to not make matters worse, and to plug our ears to people who have made their point multiple times and were now at risk of being punched.

"You touch my ass again I'm going to break your fucking hand," a woman's voice rings out ten feet to my left.

"I'm not touching your ass," a male voice shoots back.

"That's the third fucking time, pervert."

"Listen, bitch, just because you have a huge ass—"

"Both of you!" a voice barks over to my right. It's all voices at this point, no one can tell how big her ass is, how close his hands are, or whose voice just rang out, but it resonated deep. A weight-lifting voice. A black voice. The voice of the possible pervert, on the other hand, is a cask-beer-appreciating voice. A white voice. "Miss," the black voice instructs, "see if you can't move to another part of the train. If that guy touches you again, I'll deal with him."

"Can fight my own fucking fights," she grumbles, but there follow the sounds of her heels and muffled *excuse me*'s on the way across the aisle.

The loudspeaker crackles, and there's a collective shushing, though no one speaks. A voice tries to sound strident, but it quivers as it descends from the ceiling. *Attention passengers, there is an emergency situation and we are unable to proceed. We have no further information at this time. We ask that you remain calm. In the next few minutes, the conductor is going to come through with an officer of the New York City Police Department. Please do your best to make way for them; they will be opening the emergency doors in between the cars while we await further instructions.* And quiet muttering behind the conductor, something unintelligible to us. *Okay. I've been instructed to tell you that no one is in any danger, and that we have no further information at this time, but to repeat, no one is in any danger. We'll come through now. Please clear a path.*

"They fucking did it again," a voice says. He means terrorists. We all know he means terrorists. He means that somewhere on the surface something has exploded or collapsed or there are particles floating through the air making people fatally ill. Maybe all three. And it could be the heat, or the fear, but no one disagrees, posits an alternate theory. No one even bothers to check a phone. The sitting rise and, in a practiced gesture of anticipating the first responders, they push themselves to the sides of the car, creating a path down the middle.

A flashlight sends a beam through our car, revealing grimy faces, hair like wet paintbrushes, shirts see-through with sweat. The ground is littered with empty water bottles, Tupperware containers, Clif Bar wrappers. I'm momentarily reassured to see this, to know that people were surreptitiously sneaking water so that they wouldn't be forced to share. That's survival instinct. It would be a glorious thing to witness if I weren't already panting.

The click of a key against metal, then the turn of a lock, and the door at the front of the car pops open. "Please remain calm! I am Officer Gutierrez of the NYPD. I do not have any information to share at this time beyond what I am about to tell you, so please do not badger me with questions like the other damn cars did." A low laugh responds. All right, Officer Gutierrez, good on you, banding us together against those idiots in the front cars. Screw those guys.

"We're going to have to evacuate this car. All of the cars. We're going to walk in an orderly fashion out the back and walk back to the Bedford Street stop along the tracks. I'll say this more than once, and it's important to keep this in mind—you are not in any danger. Whatever is keeping us from moving forward is not a threat to us down here; the electricity on the tracks has been turned off so there's no danger in the third rail. There are supposed to be emergency lights, but those aren't working. I don't have any information on that, other than it's dark. I'm not afraid of the dark, but my kids are, so I understand that some of you may be as well. If you are, hold hands with someone who isn't, and walk with them. Walk carefully and slowly, anywhere you want along the tracks. Again, the third rail is off and it's not going back on until every last person is out of the tunnel. I don't have any more information than that. You are not in any danger.

"We still have a few cars to go. You have all been incredibly patient and I know there is help waiting for you on the surface, medical help if you need it, and definitely water. Once I get all of the doors open, I'll start coming through again and letting you know when it's okay to go. Everyone standing will go first, as orderly as possible. There's no rush. I repeat, you are not in any danger. Then the people sitting will go. If you need additional assistance, I encourage you to arrange for it now while we get the doors open. Ask your fellow passengers, and we'll make sure everyone who needs it has a guide through the tunnel.

"Everyone got all that? I'm not taking questions now so don't ask me. I'm going to walk through and give this speech to the next car, then the one after that, and then I'm at the back of the train. One last time, you are not in any danger."

He sweeps through the carriage, the only person who can see in front of himself, thanks to the beam of light, carried by a conductor who leads the way like a henchman, beady eyed and eager, key at the ready. At the back end of the car, the keys jangle once more, the door swings open, and we hear more or less the same speech, with the same insulting quip about the too-inquisitive car (*Hey, make sure they know it's not us,* I think) and the same promise, said hoarse and rote, spoken sincerely but believed by not a single person on any of the cars, that we are not in any danger.

Paul Fenniger

Eleven Months Ago: August 14, 2009

Jenny missed her calling. She's a spectacular editor, I know this firsthand from how she used to fix my papers in college, but where she truly would have excelled is as an interrogator. Black ops. The military would swoop in, pick her up in a chopper, spirit her away to undisclosed locations, warehouses in the bowels of the third world where, in flannel pajamas, Jenny would sit across from the world's most battle-hardened terrorists and get them to spill their secrets. Sometimes she'll start asking me questions, weaving her way around to the topic she actually wants to get to, luring me into a trap of my own design until (*snap!*) she springs and I'm left totally exposed. In this respect, she is an emotional ninja. Other times, she'll lie in wait, still and silent, as she does now, reading a J.Crew catalog at the kitchen table as if she's barely conscious of my existence. I know better, though, not that there's anything I can do about it. When she's ready, which is when I'm most vulnerable, she'll ask the penetrating question that will make my head explode and splatter every iota of information she seeks. In this respect, Jenny Sayles is an emotional sniper. I glance over at her, beautiful and deadly, and she looks up, flashing a wan smile.

"Can we listen to something else?" she asks. I picked Erik Satie. He scores the moment, slow and achingly gorgeous in three-quarter time. It's my favorite. My fingers dance on the air, on the countertops, on top of the chicken, once on Jenny's bare back, playing those same notes over and over again, languid and melancholic. She doesn't usually mind. Tonight is different. She knows I'm hiding something and she wants to keep me uncomfortable, off balance. So she changes my comfortable music. She's brilliant. I slip a step ahead of Jenny, all the while aware that she's going to destroy me in the end. There's no winning for winning.

I ask, "What do you want to listen to?"

She gets up and is halfway to my computer when she says, "Anything else."

Jenny puts on the Replacements. She hops and bounces into the kitchen. Four weeks of torpor and now Jenny has springs in her heels. She's an awful dancer, but that's okay. I love her for her inability to stay on time, for her reckless abandon. She doesn't dance in public, only here, frequently in the kitchen, poking me, teasing me, rubbing up against me while I work with hot pans.

She still has the body she had when I met her, slender hips and skinny thighs. Her hands go to my ribs and I feel her sway behind me, her hair brushing my bare arms, her fingers migrating south.

It's been so long. I've been so patient waiting for her, waiting for her body to recover, for the fissures and fractures of her mind to once again fuse. And she knows how long it's been for me, her fingers teasing around my belt, pressing me, turning me toward her.

But when I reach for the knob to shut off the oven, to perform this last task before taking her into our bedroom, she grabs my hand and pulls it back. "What are you hiding from me, Fenn?" she asks.

My mouth is dry. It takes a second to form words. "What makes you think I'm hiding something?"

"Because you just stalled." She smiles, but she's not amused. "What have you done?"

"Nothing bad."

". . . and . . . ?"

"I invited some people over."

"Fenn!"

"You'll like them."

She lets my hand go, like it burned her, or disgusts her. "Fenn, I don't want guests. Not right now. I would hope you'd understand why."

"I do. But the guy works in construction."

She shakes her head, incredulous. "I don't understand any of that. Where did you meet this guy?"

"At the hospital," I say quietly.

"Oh." She matches my volume. I turn off the oven, now because I'm fairly certain I've ruined dinner. "And why was he in the hospital?"

"His wife was having a . . ." I can't say the word yet, can't make the leap.

"A b-b-b-b-baby?" she mocks me. "You invited them to do what, rub my nose in our dead child? Are they going to bring their kid with them, remind me that I killed ours?"

"Please stop saying that."

"Why did you do this? Why would you do this to me?" She balls up her hand into a fist and hits me once, pounds my chest with a gavel strike that hurts but only a little, more for the seismic change in the room. Jenny takes a step back after impact, half-worried that I'm going to clock her back, which I never would, and half-amazed at what she just got away with. Her expression goes from rage to numb shock.

"It was a surprise," I offer. "He's going to look at the nursery and talk about turning it into an office for you."

She cries, and I know I won't be redeemed for my good intentions. "I don't want anyone in that room, Fenn. That room isn't . . . no one goes in there."

I take a step toward her and she backs away, but I follow through, gathering her into my arms, letting her weep into the spot she just punched. "If you want to move, we can move. We can move anywhere you want."

This only makes her cry harder. She doesn't want to leave Greenpoint, or this home on Franklin Street. It took us so long to find it, longer to afford it. So instead she goes limp in my arms, lowering herself to the floor, taking me with her, until I have her cradled on the kitchen floor, both of us in tears, the oven growing cold.

Michael Gould

Present Day: July 19, 2010

10:02 AM

If hell has a chorus, the soprano section is made up of sirens. Hi-lo's and Klaxons, horns blaring to reinforce the message. The only time I pay attention to them is when I'm driving. And now, standing on the corner of 179th and Broadway, looking north, watching a convoy of emergency vehicles head south, speeding through inter-sections. Fire engines wail like banshees at the vanguard, clearing the path. Ambulances follow, one after another. Dozens of police cruisers in the back. The noise concusses everyone around me. We cover our ears, a shameful line for New Yorkers to cross. We dull our own senses for no one and no thing, but the cacophony is too great, the horror of this frantic armada too powerful.

When it passes, I notice for the first time the cars traveling in the opposite direction, without benefit of siren or flashing lights. No one is around to stop them from speeding, from running the red lights, from blocking the box and preventing the flow of cross-town traffic. These are the first rats to flee the ship.

I race downtown, block by block. My phone still gets no service, and thanks to the proliferation of cell phones, pay phones are harder and harder to find. The few I've passed have lines twelve deep, people elbowing, demanding that the front of the line finish his fucking call because they need to check on family too. People keep waving their cell phones in the air, trying to get attention from a satellite, eyeing one another contemptuously. *Must be that too many people are making calls at the same time, right? Must be you who is putting us over, right?*

I've heard nothing concrete about what has happened, only that police have closed off midtown, that it's gridlock from the park to the ferry. Latest speculation still has this as terrorism, but those are street corner wagers.

With what battery life I have left, I open up Google maps and try to chart a route home, but without service, I can't get the map to expand. I'm left with the last place I was, the subway station twenty blocks up from here. A few blocks south and the picture won't clarify, my city dissolves into terra incognita. Broadway will take me home, I think. To Central Park at least.

I contemplate waiting this out. There are diners with bottomless cups of coffee for me to sit at, wait at least until buses start running. Even if midtown is ricin confetti right now, some contingency plan will emerge. It has to.

But every second up here prolongs those other uncertainties: where Jenny is, what prompted her last text, who was standing over her shoulder as she sent it. And Rebecca and Jackson, glimpsing Manhattan from the front window. Rebecca won't stop shaking until she sees me again; a phone call, even if I could make one, wouldn't satisfy.

I will walk home from the tip of Manhattan back to Red Hook. It's insane, a marathon, but it's my duty; I signed up for it the moment Rebecca took my name and Jackson took my blood. I think that is where my feet will take me, but I have time to decide. I have literally hundreds of blocks to walk, a bridge to cross, and God knows what chaos to walk through in order to get home. That I've mapped it out in my head is enough commitment for now.

Standing just off from the foot traffic, I consult my amorphous blur of a map one last time. Scanning it, pinching my fingers along the screen to zoom in and out, I still see the route in my head, and there I also see the alternate route, to Greenpoint. Filing my way back into the stream of people heading south, I still have time to decide.

Michael Gould

Eleven Months Ago: August 21, 2009

Rebecca shoves a variety tray of cookies into the oven. She's timed it so that they'll come out as my parents arrive, if they are on time, which they will inevitably be. I watch her run the countdown in her head, as if she can see them driving over. They don't expect cookies, and were she to have asked, my mother would be horrified that Rebecca went to any trouble on her account. Of course, ask my mother if she would ever have someone over to her house and not put out something to eat, and she'd look at you like you were raised by Cossacks.

Really venture back, far back, to a Sunday afternoon. Pre-Jackson. Pre–Red Hook. Pre-marriage. Early, but not too early in our relationship. Bar in Connecticut. Rebecca has a book open on her lap and something blanc sweating in front of her. I'm on my second beer, watching my beloved Mets on the bar's television. Every few minutes I sigh, or grunt, or groan, vacillating between noises she connects to sex and noises she connects to leaf raking. Finally she looks up, sees that my team is losing, eight to three. I'm shaking my head, back and forth, a weary, sullen metronome.

"Rooting for the Mets," I say, "is like rooting for my relatives in Auschwitz. All I want is for them to retain a shred of dignity before they hit the showers."

And that's when it twigs my girlfriend that she's seriously dating her first Jew.

She presents her credentials, as if it's a job interview. She hadn't deliberately avoided dating Jews growing up. There were plenty of them in Connecticut, plenty at her school. She always remembered to wish people happy holidays. I still called her a closet anti-Semite.

Meant it as a joke, but that light poke left a bruise. She turned the conversation serious then, to an evergreen serious topic, to Jolie.

"I had other things to worry about," she argued. "I was eight and Jolie was getting in trouble at school. I was ten and Jolie was sneaking out of the house. I was thirteen and stealing drugs from my sister's room so I could flush them. Managing her and managing my parents took up a lot of time and kept me out of the bar mitzvah circuit, I guess."

She didn't meet my parents until we moved to New York. I hadn't met Jolie before then either. Until those fateful meetings, our families were inventions, stories we'd tell each other, almost like sharing celebrity encounters. None of her sister's exploits seemed plausible to me within the context of the Rebecca I knew. There's no way two such disparate people could have been raised in the same household. Rebecca apologized to inanimate objects when she bumped into them. Her sister fellated men for heroin. It took a while for me to be properly introduced to Jolie. We had to find her first.

My parents, on the other hand, were easy to find. Rebecca met them in the house where I grew up, in Midwood, one of those neighborhoods in Brooklyn that seem permanently sepia to the outside world. Racial strife existed solely among European immigrants. The deli two blocks away had the sourest pickles. The Dodgers never left.

Marty Gould worked on the subway for decades, though I couldn't offer Rebecca anything more specific than that. He wasn't an engineer, more of a designer, a man who devised timetables to keep the system running efficiently. "Me and Mussolini," my father remarked jovially. "We made the trains run on time." Thirty seconds into an explanation of his job and all eyes glazed over, so he quipped instead.

My parents settled in Midwood because of the strong Jewish community. It gradually grew more Orthodox around them, black hats and gabardine at every bus stop, shop windows advertising in

Hebrew, suspicious glances at Marty's bald, uncovered head. Miriam and Marty considered moving for the duration of one tense meal before concluding that they liked Midwood, that they wouldn't be ostracized from their perch as community pillars. Miriam set forth with new resolve to meet her new neighbors and make a good impression. As she put it, "one thing led to another," and my mother became a Shabbos goy for her entire block. On the Sabbath, when any number of households around the Goulds spent the day avoiding all work, keeping the lights off, observing laws that Marty and Miriam found, at best, arcane, Miriam went from house to house, helping however was needed. She'd turn on reading lamps and heat up suppers, doing the tasks those more spiritually observant could not. She confided to us that she suspected her neighbors liked having her as their designated goy, even though she wasn't a goy ("Not like you, dear," she said to Rebecca, dripping with intent), because she wasn't a *schvartze*, like the Shabbos goyim of adjoining blocks.

Of course, the *schvartzes* also did their tasks for money, whereas Miriam refused all cash payment on the premise of being a good neighbor. It's entirely possible that a bunch of Jews used Miriam because she was free, a point Rebecca never made aloud, partly because I made it for her. "What a terrible thing to say," Miriam chastised but didn't correct.

Instead of accepting cash, the neighbors made sure my parents were kept well fed in Old World cuisine: jars of chicken fat, herring in cream, gefilte fish suspended in gelatin, rugelach and sundry other pastries, and disc after disc after disc of potato pancake. Marty never called a plumber, or an electrician, or a mechanic. His neighbors all knew someone who owed a favor and who took care of virtually any nuisance right away, bowing gratefully to Marty after replacing a valve, as if it were he who had done them the favor. Miriam would venture out on Friday, an hour before sundown, and she'd return late at night, kiss my forehead whether or not I was asleep, and wake up early the next morning to work again until sundown, walking house to house while I played in the yard, the only child out that day, the only one with his head uncovered, un-shaved, with his forelocks uncurled, his clothes *treyf,* tossing a baseball to himself. My mom would return Saturday night and soak her feet in Epsom salts while my dad heated up a leftover *cholent,* and the Gould family wanted for nothing.

A conversation later recounted, my father doing his best Topol impersonation of our neighbor:

"Marty," his neighbor beckoned one day. "I cannot thank your wife enough for what she does for me."

"It's her pleasure. It's what good neighbors do," Marty replied.

"True." His neighbor nodded. "Still, I want to thank you. My son—he is a stockbroker. He works on Wall Street."

"That's so impressive. You must be very proud."

"I wish he spent a little more time in synagogue, but when they hit a certain age, what can you do?" His neighbor shrugged. That his son was so far from the flock was a major topic of gossip, an-other benefit my mother had picked up in her weekly rounds. But Marty kept his face a mask of deep understanding. "He passed along a tip to me, and I'd like to pass it along to you. You know kids with the cursing music?"

"Yech," Marty replied.

"Well there's this thing coming out, and it's called . . . hang on . . . I wrote it down . . ." His neighbor fumbled through layer after layer. Marty sweated just to look at this man. ". . . em pee three player."

My father listened. My father talked it over that night with my mother. My father made a call to his neighbor's son.

He retired a year later. He no longer needed to make the trains run on time. My mother, flush with cash, wanted to keep her hands busy, so she continued to perform her rounds and stock the fridge with cabbage soup.

My parents drive from Midwood, which they hate to do, to babysit for Jackson, a name they aren't fond of, at our place in Red Hook, a neighborhood that alarms them. Miriam rushes over to Jackson, happily vibrating in his papoose chair, and scoops him up, shrieking into his neck, rubbing her perfume all over his face, pressing kisses into his tiny nose. Marty breathes deeply the air of cookies, but squints disdainfully at our lighting. Last time it was the flooring.

"It's very dark in here," he comments.

"Who said that?" I reply.

"I'm serious. It can't be good for his eyes."

"It's fine, Dad."

"Let me buy you some lamps."

I take a deep breath. It's a move I've practiced, that Rebecca has rehearsed with me more than once, to look like I'm giving the matter some thought, to not come off as petulant, but in reality taking the beat to keep my cool. "If we want any additional lighting I'll come ask you, okay?"

"Just dark in here," my father says again, before diving in with my mom, tickling Jackson with twenty arthritic fingers.

I don't like taking money from my parents. Most of the time. I didn't mind asking them for the seed money for my business, or Rebecca's, or this apartment. They didn't mind giving it, and to their credit, they haven't lorded it over us in any way. Haven't even mentioned it. That largesse provides me with limitless stores of patience when my mother is smearing my son against her, making him smell like a department store, and when my father shit-talks my home.

Rebecca has narrowed her choice of earrings down to either gold hoops or gold studs, and she comes in leading with them. I point at the hoops. She gets a second opinion from my parents. "Go with the little ones," my father counters. My mother stands at attention, enough tact to pretend to listen as Rebecca goes through her instructions for when to feed Jackson, what schedule he's more or less keeping, and where emergency numbers are located. She inserts the studs into her ears as she runs through this.

"It's so sad," my mom says to Rebecca, apropos of nothing,

shushing Jackson back and forth. He's got his cheek pressed up against her breast, and he's confused. He knows Rebecca by her boobs, and these ain't them. "Losing a baby. Outliving your child. No greater tragedy," she elaborates.

We all nod, stare at Jackson and nod sincerely. Not my father. Pose a tragedy to my father and he spins to the nearest window, stares out as if looking for the answer on the horizon.

"Before Michael, I miscarried twice. Very early on. You're having a baby and then you're not."

"It is very sad," Rebecca agrees, hoping that will end the conversation.

But it doesn't. "We've become conditioned as a culture to assume that everything that is supposed to happen will happen. A generation ago we were lucky just to live a little better than our parents did, for our children to live a little better than we did. Now everything is a done deal before it even starts, and that leads to very sad moments." She cradles Jackson, who looks around vacantly through half-lidded eyes. Rebecca thought it would be more difficult for her to leave him for the first time, but it's not. With cheek kisses all around, I take her hand and we're off. Just like that.

"You know they're going to go through our apartment," Rebecca says to me.

"Just your things," I reply.

I lay my raggedy backpack over my lap on the train. I've brought my tools and a digital camera and a batch of Rebecca's cookies, caramel cashew, along with a bottle of red and a bottle of white. "I plan on drinking tonight," Rebecca says.

"Then drink you shall."

"God, I haven't had a glass of wine in I don't know how long. I want one more than my next breath." Whether she makes it through an entire glass is dubious. She's so exhausted she lays her head on my shoulder, dozes for the trip. I plug my headphones in and flip to a podcast. We sit in comfortable silence as the poor, much-maligned G train slithers its way through the less affluent areas of Brooklyn.

We alight in Greenpoint, heads on a swivel, staring at the stores. The signs in Polish, letters with tails and hats, us with our fingers intertwined, reading out loud, phonetically, under our breath. This strange hamlet of New York, of Brooklyn, no less. Here, I can't tell how we don't fit in, only that we don't. There are the requisite hipsters, but here they stick out, as if they wandered up from Williamsburg in search of something new to gawk at or co-opt or disdain. The locals pay them, and us, no mind. Old men smoke cigarettes on the steps of a majestic church, a restaurant has a full suit of armor, actual metal armor, on either side of its doors, the legs chained to the facade. The dress code appears to be track suits for men, ample cleavage for women. I stare at strained tops, at rounded bums in stretch pants, as subtly as I think polite, until I glance over at Rebecca and realize I've been ogling with the subtlety of a self-immolation.

Paul and Jennifer live one long block over, on Franklin, close enough to the water that we see it peeking through buildings, see the neighborhood cede its houses to industry, to fences and smokestacks and truck exhaust. I squeeze Rebecca's hand on the front steps. "Ready for this?"

And she says yes, because what else is there to say?

Dinner, in four courses

FIRST COURSE
Seasonal vegetables, served with homemade hummus

"I'm Paul." He says this to me while shaking hands with my wife. He's all facial tics and quick movements. He waves his arms in front of himself like dealing three-card monte when he apologizes, amping up the wattage on his head shot smile. "Jenny is still getting ready."

First word that comes to mind to describe the apartment is *cute,* though that rings dismissive. It's maybe a little larger than ours, when you add up the square footage, but its ceilings are lower, its kitchen is smaller, and the paint on the walls is the chalky whitewash that corner-cutting landlords the city over slap on in two coats, leaving ridged blotches that make a wall look like it has eczema. They've got posters and playbills up in plastic frames, but very few pictures of themselves. Paul instructs us to make ourselves at home, because that's something people say to one another, so I take a mini tour of the living room, walking in a loose box step, peering at their shelves, scrutinizing their tchotchkes, marking off the comparisons to our apartment as they come up. The entire room is ringed with stacks of books, shin-high, a ridge of literary baseboard. Rebecca shuffles behind me the whole time, like a kid on her first day of school. Paul slips away down a hallway and Rebecca and I share a look. I kiss her forehead and she squeezes my hand to say *Thanks, buddy.*

She finally breaks off and sniffs around, explores the same shelves, makes idle sounds of approval. I respond in kind. The first time I see Jennifer it's in a frame next to a wooden bowl filled to the brim with pennies. The two of them beam at the unseen photographer, the Washington Monument stretching phallic behind them. They look younger, though it's difficult to tell with Paul of the lineless face and the boyish energy. Jenny's face hides halfway behind his in the picture, seemingly kissing him on the back of the ear, too distant to reveal what she looks like. Paul sweeps back into the room, clapping his hands and grinning to the cheap seats. "Let me take drink orders," he declares.

He pours wine for Rebecca, puts a glass of red in her hand, and I can hear the tension crackling off my wife's shoulders as she raises it to her lips, polishing off half before Paul has time to rummage through his drawers and find a bottle opener for my beer. He keeps shooting cautious looks down the hall and then reassembling his too-wide smile for the both of us, and I get the sneaking suspicion that either Jennifer isn't quite up for tonight or this is a trap and Rebecca and I are about to be murdered.

"Greenpoint is beautiful." Rebecca throws this statement into the air, waits to see where it lands. Paul grabs a tray of vegetables from the fridge and puts them on the table along with hummus, coarse and khaki. Then he looks up with surprise, anxiety rippling the pond, his mind rewinding to the last thing said. I want to tell him to sit down, that Rebecca and I are low maintenance; we're not expecting to be entertained as if we own the factory. I want to tell him that we've spent the past few months eating while a child intermittently shrieks at us, or that Rebecca has to work the fork around his body on the way up to her mouth while he lampreys to her nipple. Seems a cruel gesture more than a comforting one, though, so I say nothing and sip my beer.

"Thank you. We really love it here. And it keeps changing, even this street. We have the bookstore, and clothing stores, and a tattoo parlor, and bars, and a bodega . . ." He runs out of steam. Then he leans forward to both of us and says, quiet, almost conspiratorial, "How is your son?"

Rebecca bobs her head, and for a moment it gives me pause, the question's phrasing and her response making me wonder if something is wrong with Jackson, if Paul's asking because the last he heard, Jackson wasn't doing so well but was still fighting. "He's good?" I whisper back. Rebecca confirms with a sharp nod.

Footsteps emerge from down the hall and Jennifer Sayles steps into our lives. Her arrival charges every ion in the room, displaces the air into the corners. She catches me tilting a bottle of beer between my lips, lingering there, staring. My first impression of her is so outright bitchy that I have to brace myself on their table to keep from doubling over in self-hatred. My eyes dart from face to face, checking to see if everyone notices the same thing I do. Paul may be used to it by now, but Rebecca must see what I see.

Paul's face has such symmetry, he's such a boilerplate beautiful man, and Jennifer looks so drained, so emptied out and haggard, with none of Paul's humor or vitality. My first thought is how vastly more attractive Paul is than Jennifer. I pull on my beer, draining half of it in one go, because I can't fathom what is inside of me for that to be the first thing that comes to mind.

"Sorry I'm late," she says, voice hoarse with false cheer. "Fenn, do we have wine?"

"Red or white?"

"Whatever's open."

"Red is open."

"Then a bottle of that." She laughs, brash and hacking. "Glass! I meant a glass. I'm sorry. I'm out of sorts."

Rebecca steps forward and approaches Jennifer. She says, "I remember you." My wife lays her glass on the table so that she can stretch out her arms, reach forward like a zombie narrowing its scope on the kill. Jennifer starts to recoil, but her body freezes, goes rigid. "We both were in T-shirts and yoga pants, and you had a wraparound sweater, and I remember thinking how smart that was in case it was cold, even in the summer, because of the air-conditioning. You told me how horrible you looked, but you didn't. You looked beautiful. We both were too self-conscious to look anything but perfect in front of Dr. Mulitz."

Then she wraps her arms around Jennifer and holds her tightly. Rebecca is an inch shorter, so her cheek cradles Jennifer's jaw. Jennifer, for her part, accepts the hug uncomfortably, like she's being sniffed by a strange dog. Then she settles into it, though she doesn't hug my wife back. Her arms remain at her sides, hands slack. Stiff but unbowed, Jennifer raises her head and stares at Paul, gaze fixed, looking every inch a painting of one of those martyred women flayed alive for their faith.

When the hug breaks, Jennifer pats Rebecca on both shoulders. "I remember you too," she assures, before lunging for a glass of wine.

SECOND COURSE
Gazpacho with Parmesan croutons

"Paul tells me you're a writer," I say. Jennifer, who has been raising spoonfuls of soup halfway to her mouth, then tilting them back into the bowl for the past five minutes, gives me a wry smirk, to make clear that I will regret engaging her on any level throughout this meal.

She opens her mouth and leaves it like that for a few beats before sound emerges. "Did he now?"

"What kind of writer are you?"

"The unaccomplished kind. Paul says I'm a writer because it's kinder."

"That's not what I do," Paul corrects gently. "You're an as-yet-unpublished author." He has stared at his soup since sitting down, intermittently glancing at Jennifer across the table (a much nicer table than ours, but ours has *character*). Rebecca and I sit across as well, foot pressed to foot, united in our effort to overcome this meal. It helps that my wife is alternating sips of soup with gulps of wine.

"How did you two meet?" Rebecca takes her turn at bat. She's on her third glass. Jennifer keeps pace. Paul and I eye each other over our second beers.

Jennifer clangs the spoon against the bowl and leans back in her chair. She glares across the table at Paul, who shrinks before her gaze. Then she looks at my wife with a sweet, vacant expression, and says, "We met at a party. I was already there, and Paul walked in. Our eyes met and . . . I know this sounds cheesy, but is music supposed to play when you see the person you'll end up loving? Because at the time it didn't. The room didn't even lower its volume to an ambient hum. But when I picture this scene in retrospect it's Paul's song in my ears. Do you know Erik Satie?"

Rebecca shakes her head. Jennifer doesn't even bother checking with me. "You should seek him out. *Gymnopédies*. The most beautiful thing you'll ever hear. That's the composer who scored the moment I met Paul. I hadn't heard it before Paul and now I can't hear it and not think solely of him, as if Paul himself wrote it. I first fell in love with Paul Fenniger through my ears."

"That's beautiful." Rebecca reaches across the table to squeeze Jennifer's hand, but Jennifer, with no small measure of irritation, tucks them both in her lap.

"But it's not entirely true. I'm not being honest, just artful. He's a beautiful man. That's actually the first thing I noticed. Loved him first with my eyes. Taken apart, piece by piece, I grew to appreciate the high forehead and the flat planes of his spotless face. I came to lust for the perfect knob of his Adam's apple, the notch below it sized as if designed for my jaw to rest in. His guileless eyes. The slight pursing of his lips. A nose sculpted with one of God's finer chisels. When I cut him up into small parts I can hold him up to the light and scrutinize each lovely piece, but in that first moment, I noticed, simple as breathing, that the man who just walked in was unspeakably beautiful."

A stillness sets over the table. Who the fuck is she speaking to? Who is this performance for? I can see Rebecca's gears spinning, striving to name the movie Jennifer is quoting. "Jenny . . . ," Paul says, low and pleading.

Jennifer throws her head back and laughs, the sound of a plucked guitar string, steady and tinny. "I can make it prettier than it is, Paul," she chides. "I'm a writer after all. Fine, you want to know how I met Paul Fenniger?"

Rebecca looks to me for support. I bury my eyes in my soup. There's no way I'm diving headfirst into this hornet's nest of crazy. My plan is to wait Jennifer out until she goes from giddy, chatty, sociopathically drunk to maudlin, exhausted, unconscious drunk. Once her head hits the table, I'll feel comfortable rejoining the conversation. With no one to overtly disapprove, she commences.

"I met Paul my senior year of college. I'd pretty much only had weekend boyfriends up to that point. My freshman year, I started hooking up during orientation with a sweet boy named Chris, who called his mother twice a week and thought buying me a single rose on my birthday was the height of romance. I liked him, but it ended before sophomore year, when I seriously dated a less sweet boy named Kyle, who didn't believe in romance but had an opinion on every other subject. That also went an entire year, though a flowerless one. But I did learn a lot about Thomas Pynchon. In my junior year I became a gal about town, arm in arm with athletes and poets, a junior professor, and a townie named Curtis, who didn't go to the University of Wisconsin and resented everyone who did except for me."

"They don't need to hear all this." Paul rubs his eyes.

"She asked, Paul. Our guest that you invited asked, and I want to be a good hostess. I'll skip a few chapters. It's mostly blow jobs anyway. One night my roommate Molly whined me into going to a party. It was close enough to walk in heels so I said fuck it. It ended up being a theater party and no one was more entertaining than the bottom of a plastic cup. But I did meet a guy there that I fell deeply in love with. His name was Danny Perlis and he designed sets and he had these pellucid blue eyes that made me learn the word *pellucid*. That night we got high and had sex on everyone's coats and two months later we were living together. And a year after that he asked me to marry him and I said yes and two weeks after that I met Paul, who was one year younger and a virgin from Cadott, Wisconsin, who had terrible grammar and who thought that rainbows flew out of my snatch and twelve years later we live in Greenpoint. Just the two of us."

She punctuates the story by finally spooning gazpacho between her lips. I give Jennifer an appreciative smirk. Shine on, you crazy diamond. You roped me back in. "What happened to Danny Perlis?" I ask.

"He gave me a lecture that he clearly thought was eviscerating and I thought was directed entirely to my tits. Probably a good thing that we didn't elope like he wanted. I loved him, but the thing

I loved most about him was how much he loved me. I mailed his ring back after graduation."

Jennifer pushes her virtually untouched bowl of soup forward. She drains another glass of wine and reaches halfway across the table for the bottle, but Paul's arm shoots out and grabs it first. He holds it just out of Jennifer's reach and the two of them glare at each other. Rebecca has on her no-lipped mortified face, but I cannot imagine a better standoff. Either they will go the full George-and-Martha and my wife and I will get to go home (or to a bar, so long as we have our babysitters . . .), or she'll wrestle the bottle from his hands and deliver another meandering monologue of her checkered sexual history. Either way, I'm getting dinner and a show. There's a vitality in the room, an electricity I discover that I've missed. Rebecca fusses with her lap, but I've engaged all five senses.

Paul stands up from the table and carries the bottle over to his wife. Then he turns to Rebecca and pours her a half measure, a bold act of defiance. But he knows exactly how much is left, because he next takes Jennifer's glass and fills it up just a shade more. "Shall I clear bowls?" he asks no one before taking mine to the sink.

"And that's how I met Paul Fenniger. How did you two meet?"

Under other circumstances Rebecca and I would laugh at this question. This subject is a longstanding inside joke between us. "Neither of us remember," I say. "We just sort of happened. There we were."

"That's sweet," Jennifer murmurs, sipping her fresh glass of wine. "I like your story better."

MAIN COURSE
Pork chops with homemade applesauce and minted peas

Whatever hostility Jennifer needed to expel has burned off. No sooner had Paul set the plate in front of her than she'd tucked her fingers into the pockets of his jeans and tugged back and forth, like a child demanding attention. Paul's face relaxed, and he leaned over and kissed the tip of her nose.

"You did have atrocious grammar when we met," Jennifer says sweetly.

He raises a glass to her. "And you fixed it. Now I'm ready to meet the queen."

The mood lightens, and it's once again okay to joke without malice or sneer the answer to simple questions. His mood elevated, Paul talks about how his father was the single, solitary bus driver in Cadott, Wisconsin, where his dad did one sweep for the school kids, and then doubled back to take the elderly and anyone else who fit on the twelve-seater around to run errands.

"This may be a silly question," Rebecca slurs. I stopped counting glasses by the time I started counting bottles. "But why did you decide to keep your name? I mean, I thought about keeping mine, but I ended up taking Michael's. I have this strange attachment to feminism, like I think of myself as a feminist, even though I make cookies all day, but that's neither here nor there. It's just something I notice, when women take their husband's name."

"Paul is my partner," Jennifer notes lightly. "And there was no way in hell I was taking his ridiculous name."

Rebecca scrunches her face. She turns to Paul. "What is your name again?"

"Paul Fenniger."

"Oh," Rebecca replies. She doesn't press further. Jennifer Fenniger. She of the self-satisfied smirk. I got it. Clever girl, avoiding that one. Say it out loud.

But no one explains it to Rebecca, and the rest of the main course passes by swapping safe New York stories, lamenting the trust-fundification of Brooklyn, as if we weren't the canaries in that coal mine. My father would want to slap me for even listening to a conversation so lacking in self-awareness.

Nevertheless, Paul clears the plates once only bones are left, curved like the body of a harp, picked clean and white. I notice this when I find myself staring at Jennifer's plate, relieved that she's finally eaten something. She catches my dumb gawk and raises an eyebrow—first one, then both, like asking a question and a follow-up in one go.

———

DESSERT COURSE
Becky's Bites

"I'm not much of a hostess tonight," Jennifer admits, half-apologetic, half-defiant.

Rebecca, glassy-eyed, takes her hand. She's reached for it all night and now finally Jennifer has left it languid on the table long enough for my wife to clutch. I've never seen her this drunk. "It's okay, it really is."

"No, it's not. I'm being rude, and you and your husband are doing us a huge favor just by being here. How is your son?"

"We don't need to talk about him," Rebecca says quickly.

"No." Jennifer punctuates with her free hand, delivering a hard slap on the table. "I live in a world where people have children. I have to get used to being around them. Parents and kids. Can't avoid walking past playgrounds, right?"

"That's strong of you. I don't know if I'd be that strong."

She takes Rebecca in, searching her foundation for structural weakness. "What an awful thing to think about yourself."

"Jackson is fine," I step in. "Thank you for asking."

"Good." She takes a bite of cookie. "That wasn't so hard."

"How have you been holding up?" I cringe at how stupid that question sounds. It's possible that, four or five beers in, I'm a bit drunk myself. But Jennifer absorbs it, considers it as she lights a cigarette at the table. Paul opens a window.

"Not great," she admits. "I keep thinking about all the little things I might have done that killed my kid."

"You can't think like that," Rebecca interrupts.

"You wouldn't know." Jennifer's voice sharpens. She blows a thin stream of smoke over the table. It sinks into the plate of cookies. "I don't mean like smoking or drinking. I'm not a fucking idiot. I didn't do any of that. I mean like yoga poses or sitting a certain way. Things like getting out of bed too fast. I was doing something or not doing something when my child's heart got ruined. There's no way to separate out my behavior from what happened. I know as a rational human being—I'm a rational human being—I know that I didn't kill my child. That's not how it works, or that's what our doctor told me."

"Dr. Mulitz?" Rebecca says, smiling sadly. "I'd kill for that woman. Anyone she asked me to. Even Michael. Especially Michael." She snorts a laugh. "If she says you couldn't hurt your baby, then you didn't."

Jennifer stares out the window. "Something I ate. Walking up too many steps."

"Are you and Paul going to try again?" Rebecca interjects. She does this whenever anyone displays what she deems negative emotions. Sadness or anger, especially. Rebecca goes into Saturday morning cartoon mode and won't stop until everyone joins hands and sings. "I hear you can try within a few months."

"Beck," I caution.

"Probably. Maybe not within the next few months, but eventually. I mean, this wasn't the most deliberately planned of pregnancies. I can't take hormonal shit because it makes me act like a fucking lunatic and I have a latex allergy, so Paul and I have pretty much always been like Christian teens, but this is the first time our methods failed. Or succeeded. Or succeeded and then failed. Not sure how to phrase it."

Rebecca parts her lips to sally forth with another platitude, but I cut her off and lie. "I'll bet someday you'll be a terrific mother."

She tilts her head toward me, smiles without teeth. "Thank you, Michael."

AFTER DINNER
Cordials and work

As soon as Paul clears the last of the plates, Jennifer stands up and exits the apartment, sweeping out at celebrity force. Paul watches the front door close but lets it go without comment. "Let's go take a look at the room?" He puts it out there as if that might be a fun idea. Rebecca teeters on unsteady legs. "Go," she says to me, rich with meaning. "I'll be outside."

Paul and I take a moment at the table to decompress. This is the point where one of us should say something, apologize for our respective significant other so that the other person can say it's no big deal. That muscle goes unflexed, Paul instead leading me back down the hall, opening the only closed door.

The room itself is small, big enough for the crib still sitting in the middle, and a nursing chair over by the window. I'm about to say that Rebecca has one of those as well, and comment on how comfortable a chair it is even for nonnursing mothers, but I catch myself in time to realize how that might come across, that while Rebecca has a nursing chair, Jennifer has an expensive rocking chair decked out in cow-jumping-over-the-moon upholstery.

Paul stands in the doorway, watching me evaluate the room. If he's expecting alchemy, that I'll wave my arms and gut renovate the nursery that wasn't, he's going to be sorely disappointed. The magic starts with my taking a tape measure from my belt loop and a pad and golf pencil from my back pocket.

"Is there anything I can do?" Paul asks.

"Give me ten minutes. I'll take some measurements."

Paul nods. "Okay," he says. "It's okay." And another nod. I prod him gently along; it doesn't benefit either of us to have him here. "Just ten minutes should do it. I'll come out when I'm done. You can shut the door if you like."

"Okay. Okay. I'll start cleaning up." He closes the door. I hear him pause in the hallway before his footsteps go off, leaving me to my tape measure. It takes eight minutes to get all the info I need.

When Rebecca and I leave, there aren't hugs or hollow promises to do this again. Jennifer slipped back into the apartment and into her bedroom while I was working, and Rebecca helped Paul clean up until I was finished. At the door, he leans forward to kiss Rebecca on the cheek but catches himself a foot from her face, as if he stumbled with his lips pursed. Instead he shakes both of our hands, thanks us for the cookies, and gives us one last perfunctory smile. No mention of when I'll be coming back. Jennifer's name goes unspoken in our farewells, as if she were a ghost we all hallucinated.

On our way home Rebecca asks me about the job I'm going to do for them, working at a severely cut rate. It's a kindness we can afford, more or less, so long as it doesn't prevent me from taking on better-paying work. Becky's Bites can cover our bills this month.

Most of the work will be building shelves, to turn the nursery into more of an office. There's only so much I can do in a room that size, but giving Jennifer space for books and a place to write seems the absolute least of it. Next time I'm over I'll dig deep for more inspiration, assuming my work goes beyond tonight. I can very easily see a long discussion between Paul and Jennifer tomorrow in which the whole idea is scrapped and I never see either of them again.

I hold Rebecca's hand, our fingers intertwined. I grip it in my own like she's going to get sucked from the moving train. "What did you think of them?" I ask.

"I liked them," she replies. "Did you like them?"

My answer comes out unfiltered. Poisonous. "I think they're damaged goods."

She considers this. Doesn't disagree. "Did you look across the street?"

"From their place?"

"It's a playground, Michael. They live across the street from a playground."

And I say, "Jesus"—because what else is there to say?—and we clutch our hands together all the tighter.

When we get home Rebecca plows past my parents and into the bathroom. My mom shuffles over, holding Jackson in her arms like a porcelain football, and sniffs my breath. I must pass whatever test she's administering because she hands off my sleeping son, and he barely stirs. When Rebecca comes back out, the overwhelming stench of mint doesn't mask the mist of wine wafting from her pores, but she has put herself together enough to seem dignified, hugging my parents, gracious in thanking them for our night out. I give Jackson over to her, to put him in his crib, and I walk my parents to their car while Rebecca lays our son's sleeping head down on his mat, with his blanket and stuffed animals and chirping mobile and everything else designed to placate not only his overstimulated mind, but ours as well.

Paul Fenniger

Present Day: July 19, 2010

10:32 AM

The full weight of the situation hits once we hear the car behind us start its shuffle out. As much as we all ride the subway—descending the stairs, swiping our cards, passing through the turnstiles, waiting on the platforms, and then getting on the train, sitting down or holding on to a pole, and emerging at our stops, having endured a noisy, hassled journey—we never go into the tunnels. We never see the path itself the way we do at street level, where the asphalt is something tangible, something we actively navigate. The tunnel exists to us as a blur seen through windows, the tracks only squeals below. But listening to the collective movement of hundreds of people shuffling out, the low moans and quiet sobs of fellow passengers, we realize that this is really happening, that we are entering a dark, ignored, terrifying place.

A voice says, "I can't do this." I look down at a woman. Her head comes up to my stomach. No, she's bent over, trying to tilt her head between her knees from a standing position, breathing in fits and starts. When she straightens up, still whistling in shallow huffs, I see tear streaks on her face through the sheen of sweat. "I can't do this," she repeats. She's talking to me.

I have maybe a minute before it's my turn. I'm one of the standing. I'm supposed to exit first. She dives her head back down, so I kneel down to her level. "It's okay. We're all going to go," I reassure.

"I can't," she cries. "I can't go on the tracks. I'll wait here until it's safe."

"It's safe now."

"You don't know that."

"The power's off. There's no current going through."

"I'm not worried about being electrocuted," she snaps. And then she whispers aloud the fears of many. "There are rats."

There are rats. There's no denying that there are rats. They scamper through every station, gawked at by tourists. Even hardened New Yorkers take a moment from their days to watch the show before the rumble of the train sends rats back into drainpipes, into the storm grates built into the track beds, into the lip under the platform where I can only assume there is enough space to fit a rat. Or a couple thousand rats. The small ones are no bigger than golf balls. The big ones are . . . noticeable.

"Too many people." I try to calm her, speaking loud enough in case others are listening. "We'll scare them off. Rats aren't going to bother us."

"I can't," she says again. I take another deep breath, the humidity forced into my lungs, and think of something else to say, some offer to make, that I'll hold her hand, that I'll carry her through the tunnel the entire way, until I can lay her gently on the platform, but before I do there's a shift in the car. I'm jostled and pushed forward, then to the side, and she joins the amorphous dark blob of people on the other side of the car. Officer Gutierrez has come back in with his flashlight and is waving us along.

"People standing first. No pushing, let's keep this as orderly as possible. The conductor is on the tracks to help you down."

No one moves at first, except a few enterprising souls who nudge their way past him, as quickly as possible. "Come on," he scolds. "We've got a lot of people to get out."

And like that, I'm swept up, shuffling along with the rest of the straphangers, those who weren't lucky enough to get a seat, now somehow luckier to get off the train first, not that any of us ever wanted to leave the train this way.

It's okay, I tell myself, again and again. When I reach the door to the car behind ours there's a logjam, and I let a few women drag their feet in front of me, searching for the woman from before. We're all taking geisha steps, and once we reach the next car it's easier—there's no one seated except for a few elderly riders who are waiting their turn, who can't make it out without more help than can currently be provided. All the brash chatter has ceased; it's a solemn, unholy ceremony. At the next door we constrict, and again, I let a few more women pass in front of me until I hear an audible and irritated huff from a man behind me. Then I feel a hand on my back, pushing me forward, not aggressive but assertive—definitely not an accident.

I spin to see who it is: he's small, my age, and he starts apologizing before our eyes meet. "Please, just keep moving," he says, his voice hushed, as if giving words to his worst secrets. "I can't stop or I won't start again. Please." He steps in place.

In the last car I see the flashlight at the exit, and we stand in line until, one at a time, we step to the end and drop three feet, like getting off a carnival ride. Some take longer than others. The passengers from the car behind have started to creep up on us, their voices growing louder, gaining strength from anger and fear. "Fucking move!" someone yells, and the man in front of me, in his suspenders, shudders.

My turn comes after what feels like an eternity. A single hand emerges from the darkness, the flashlight illuminating where I'm supposed to land. I wave him off and hop down. The conductor, portly and wheezing, continues to wave people along. "Just start walking. Help is waiting at Bedford," he repeats.

I step to the side. "Who's helping you?" I ask.

"Sir, please just walk down the tunnel," he bellows. Speak loudly and hope I'll fall in line. Otherwise he fears the same chaos everyone fears, the sense that any actual danger will be met with people screaming, then running, then falling.

My hand goes up to the next person, mirroring him. The small, pushy man grabs it, takes the conductor's hand with his other, and sits down on the back lip of the train, sliding off onto the ground. The next person is a woman who takes both of our hands and seems to float down. An older man puts his hand on my shoulder while the conductor illuminates his path with the beam. And on. And on.

After the tenth person there's a brief respite, only a second long, before the next body appears. It's then that the conductor pauses his instructions to say, under his breath, "Thank you."

Paul Fenniger

Eleven Months Ago: August 26, 2009

I open our door to Ryan and Stephanie Locke. They hold hands on the front step, beaming at me. It's honestly a little threatening. "We love this neighborhood," Ryan says by way of greeting, grabbing my palm and pumping it twice. His wife nods, keeping both her own hands around her midsection. "We'll come back here for dinner," she adds. Then amends, "Not here, sorry, but to Greenpoint." She and Ryan laugh awkwardly. I don't understand why they feel a need to impress me. It's no longer threatening, just unnerving. I invite them up.

Ryan helps Stephanie up the stairs, one hand on her back, guiding her along the railing. None of it is necessary. She has a small tummy, like she swallowed a honeydew. Ryan supports, physically and vocally. *Couple more steps. Easy does it.* I used to do the same for Jenny. She shrugged me off the first time I tried it. "I'm pregnant, not crippled," she bit at me. Seeing my hurt expression, she stroked my face and wounded ego and instead put her hand around my back and guided me up the steps. We laughed at that, how little help she wanted, even up to the end, when she couldn't see where she was stepping anymore and allowed me my small measure of gallantry.

I love her for her independence. I love her in spite of how fearful I am of that independence.

Stephanie and I stand back while Ryan inspects the crib, testing the guardrails, running a finger along every screw. "How old is your . . ." She trails off.

"Son," I finish. "He's turning three. It's time for a big boy bed."

"That's so sweet." She looks around the room, tries to not point out that there aren't pictures of our child anywhere, that there isn't a changing table, only this crib and a rocking chair. This doesn't look like the room of a child. I'm too conflicted to tell her the truth, fearing it would depress them into leaving.

"We only moved here a few months ago," I explain. "We found this amazing furniture maker in Red Hook who's building a bed and we're going to put it here." I point to where Jenny's desk will go. "Then a little play area over there. He loves music, so we're going to paint the walls to look like sheet music and put little notes all around."

"I love that idea!"

"What's his name?" Ryan slides the guardrail up and down, up and down, up and down, testing and retesting it, putting his weight on it while it's locked to ensure that his future child can't lean on it and go tumbling to his or her death.

"Diggory," my dry mouth answers. It elicits appreciative (or horrified) oohs and ahhs.

"I want to name this one Sophia if it's a girl or Aidan if it's a boy." Stephanie rubs her stomach methodically.

"Those are popular," I reply, hopefully without implying judgment.

Ryan comes up from his crouch, grinning. "So, two hundred?"

"Yes, please."

"Would you go one-fifty?"

I give it the obligatory moment of contemplation. "I'd go one-sixty."

"Done." And Stephanie claps. Then she starts welling up, runs her hands along the slats of the crib. This will be where her baby sleeps. "Where's Diggory now?" Ryan counts out twenties on the windowsill.

"His mother took him to the park across the street. Then they were going to run some errands. If you want to add the glider, I'd do the pair for three-fifty."

Stephanie sits down. "It's Dutailier," she says, appreciatively. She glides back and forth, positions her arms under her breasts, conjuring the baby who will nurse there. "This is so comfortable." She gives Ryan a subtle nod, but we're both staring at her so the hint is lost. Ryan reaches back into his wallet and counts out seventeen twenties and a ten.

"You've kept everything in great condition," he remarks as I help him carry it down to their rented van.

"Diggory's an easy child," I reply. "The only thing he really pounds on is his toy piano."

"That's so cute. Do you have a picture?" Stephanie stares into the park, perhaps looking for him. I do the same.

"I don't. Not on me. I know, I'm the worst dad."

"No," she reassures loudly. We make our last pleasantries and they drive off with the baby furniture. All in all, we took less of a loss on it than I thought we would, but Jenny would have been fine scrapping it. The three-fifty will help matters, though, assuming she doesn't declare it blood money and insist that I give it to charity. We can be our own charity on this one.

I lock the front door behind me and knock gently on our bedroom door. When there's no answer I open it to find an empty room. I sit on the bed for a moment, close my eyes, and take a few cleansing breaths. Center myself. It's okay. Then, with both hands trembling, I open the closet door and sit down next to Jenny, curled up into a ball and sobbing. Now that she's alone she's free to give her voice heft, to wail at the top of her lungs, to howl like a wounded animal. I gather her into me; it's the tightest she's let me hold her since.

I've come to hate that word. *Since.*

And we rock, back and forth, tears streaming down both of our faces, Jenny's wailing like a wind strong enough to knock down our house of bricks.

Paul Fenniger

Eleven Months Ago: August 27, 2009

I click open three tabs. The first one I set to Playbill, the off-Broadway listings. I scroll halfway down the page past a blur of shows I didn't get to audition for. I click over to the second tab and type in the address I've memorized. My hands know where on the page will lead me to a group. I sift past everyone else's questions to my own, posted yesterday.

> Howdy All,
> My wife returned to work this week, so it's just me and my buddy
> (6 mos.) and a fridge full of bottles. Not complaining—I'm not the
> one being asked to pump, but the little guy is a lot fussier about
> mealtimes than he used to be. Any advice on how to get him
> better at hitting the bottle?

And below, the answers. So many answers. I wonder whether, if it all had turned out differently, I would be one of those answering. Would I have made the time? I read through the first of three pages of responses.

> Let him futz with the bottle. If he's at six months, he's probably
> grabbing at everything. So proud he can grip!!!! Plus he loves
> putting things in his own mouth. Let him discover it on his own.
> And good for you. Breast is Best!!! J

> I went through the same thing with Rowan at five months. My
> doctor said to wait until he is just going down for a nap and then
> give it to him, because his "defenses are down" and he might be
> more ready to take a bottle. Good luck!

> Hell eat when hes hungry. Dont worry.

I hit the back button and search further down the page, to Friday's question.

> Dear Group,
> My son is ten months old and is a fairly good napper. The other day I went into his room to check on him and discovered he was tugging at his hair while he was asleep. Is this normal? Is he going to pull it out?

Each response brings with it a stone that presses down on my chest. When it gets too heavy I click over to the third tab and type in an address, also memorized. A few more clicks and I'm again in a group room, of sorts. It's a difficult shift, but it drives away the demon I need out before letting the devil in.

> Username: Volpone814
> Password: ********
>
> *Loading live show*
> *Connecting to Lexxy*
>
> LEXXY: Hi
> VOLPONE814: Hi.
> LEXXY: do u like what you c?
> VOLPONE814: Yes.
> LEXXY: what turns u on?
> VOLPONE814: Everything. Touch your breasts.

She does, unenthusiastically, mechanically, shimmying up to the pinhole camera until her semisoft nipple occupies the majority of my screen.

> VOLPONE814: I'm rock hard.
> LEXXY: i want u in my mouth
> VOLPONE814: This is going to sound strange, and I apologize, but could you not abbreviate words?

Her fingers pause over her clit. She purses her lips and, with her free hand, types back.

> LEXXY: ?
> VOLPONE814: Again, sorry. For example: u instead of you.
> LEXXY: im playing with my wet pussy
> VOLPONE814: That's terrific. Really hot. Please, just type to me normal.

Her brow furrows. I can see the lines through the caked-on makeup. She takes both hands off herself and leans forward to the screen. Now it's her bloodshot eyes an inch from my face.

> LEXXY: Like this? Proper grammar and spelling? Punctuation and everything?
> VOLPONE814: Yes! Thank you! I'm going to come so hard now.

She shrugs, a little smile, a genuine smile at the corner of her lip.

> LEXXY: Your cute. Sorry! You're cute.
> VOLPONE814: Your cute two. (☺)
> LEXXY: I'm going to put my vibrator inside of me and pretend it's your hard cock. Do you want that?
> VOLPONE814: God yes.

She leans back, her hand crossing to her nightstand, and the largest vibrator I have ever seen comes into the frame for a split second—it's as thick as a flashlight—before the bedroom door opens and Jenny sticks her head in.

I look up from the screen, casually, clicking the tab for Playbill. Jenny isn't interested, though; she barely looks at me on her way to the dresser. She strips off her sailor-striped shirt and unhooks her bra, laying it on top of the dresser before turning to face me. There's no self-consciousness to her nudity, never has been. Her ribs jut out like whalebones. She's lost too much weight. She takes out a fresh bra and clips it on, throwing her shirt on over it. Then she's gone again. It's this wonderful strange thing she does—deciding that an article of clothing she's wearing is stale and swapping out just that one. Socks, bras, underwear.

To spend a day inside that brain, to spend even an hour. I stare at the door she just walked through and look lovingly at Jenny's vapor, my heart too full for one small chest.

If I click back on to Girlcam, I may not get Lexxy. She may have moved on to her next gentleman caller. Something was stirring beneath the sheets and now it's not. I could go into the bathroom and run the shower while I get myself off, but the mood has passed. I could go back on to the parenting boards and live vicariously through my imaginary child's first few years, but my heart's not in that either. He's been everything from a newborn to a toddler, has started potty training and teething biscuits, and loves mashed bananas and his stuffed manatee. He's had illnesses and ailments and injuries, but nothing too serious. He's been my fella and champ and buddy and wiggly worm—dozens of names that aren't names. My actual son never got a name. He left the hospital as anonymous ashes.

I click off the Girlcam and the parenting board for the day, scrub my browser history, and delete all cookies.

Jenny sticks her head back in. Instinctively, my finger runs over the mouse pad to clear the history again, even though I'm only looking at the audition boards.

"What time is he coming?" she asks.

"It's tomorrow."

"I know it's tomorrow. What time?"

"I think around eleven. Last I spoke to him he was going to wait until rush hour cleared up and then come."

"Is he driving?"

"No, but he said he's bringing some wood samples for you to look at."

"So I have to be here?"

I open my arms to invite her in, but she remains standing in the doorway, her hip now cocked. When I don't answer she rolls her eyes and leaves again. A minute later, the time it takes for me to absorb this latest wave of animosity, she walks back into the room. "Can you take off work tomorrow?"

"I can't. I'm over my days as is."

"Fenn!"

"I'm sorry. I missed a lot of work."

"So what time will you be home?"

And here's the part she's forgotten, though I've told her. I say quietly, "I have an audition tomorrow night."

Her eyes narrow in response. "*That* you have time for?"

"Jenny, please."

"Fine. Do whatever it is you want to do, Fenn." She doesn't elaborate on that, doesn't crucify me further, which indicates to me that she doesn't feel as strongly as she pretends to. I know her anger like a dog whistle, tone clusters only I can accurately perceive.

Unfresh once again, she strips to her underwear and walks into our bathroom. The water starts up. Her second shower of the day will lessen the tension, she'll come back out slightly chastened at her own hostility, more ready to talk to me, to hear about the audition, maybe even to run lines. Or, she may come out and resent me for still being here, for impinging upon her remorse. I shut my laptop, leave it on the nightstand, and step out for a walk. I'll pick up some mushrooms from the fancy market on Manhattan Avenue, some portobellos to slice up and roast with rosemary. That's one of Jenny's top five favorite side dishes. It'll be okay. Michael will come tomorrow and build her an office where she can write the great novel I know she has in her. And when she's ready we'll start trying again, for all of the right reasons, and we'll have a healthy baby that will shatter the walls Jenny builds around herself. And with those walls crumbled, I'll finally get in as well.

Michael Gould

Present Day: July 19, 2010

10:35 AM

It's crested one hundred degrees, according to the radio. Or, rather, it's ninety-five degrees, but it "feels like" one hundred degrees. I've trudged down twenty blocks, bobbing and weaving my way through crowds.

In the past fifteen minutes, I've overheard snippets of conversation that describe what's going on in midtown as a full-scale riot, complete with the National Guard. It's also been a plane crash, or a helicopter crash, smack in the middle of Times Square, like the ball dropping directly onto the tourists. I've heard dirty bomb, subway derailment, mayoral assassination, even coup d'état. Everything sounds equally implausible but still provides fodder for debate among the sweaty horde.

My bottle of water is empty but I hold on to it anyway, in case I can fill it up somewhere. The fluid I've put in my body has already leaked out, droplets of sweat sting my eyes. I look to the other side of the street, to see if that's the side in the shade, but it's as bright as the side I'm on. Only scaffolding offers intermittent relief, a few seconds of respite from direct sunlight.

At the corner of 140th I stop for traffic and see a man sitting in the front seat of his black town car. The license plate has the $T\ C$ parentheses and I look around, as if this could be a hidden camera trick. No one but me seems to notice that there is a car for hire waiting here, one that can take me home in air-conditioned luxury. Even if we hit a wall of traffic, better to do so sitting in a backseat and paying an agreed-upon price, right? And I could have him zip me over one of the uptown bridges, avoiding midtown altogether. I'd be in Greenpoint before noon.

I knock on the passenger-side window and he lolls his turban-wrapped head over slowly. I wave and smile, cheerful and chipper, a good passenger, a happy passenger, one who will pay and not complain about loud music. Finally he rolls down the window. A puff of Freon runs over my body, a shudder from top to tail that I close my eyes to appreciate. "What?" he says roughly.

"How much to get me back to Brooklyn?"

"No cars," he replies. He starts to roll the window back up, his index finger controlling it. I put my hands in the way and he stirs, a flash of anger.

"This is a car," I point out.

"I can't go anywhere." He waves his arms. "Everything is closed south of the park."

"Not a problem," I purr. "Just take me over the Kennedy and we'll go through Queens. Nowhere near whatever is going on."

He gestures to the other side of the street, the gridlocked traffic going north. "All of that is also trying to get off the island. No cars right now."

There's no point in trying to argue with him, so I take out my wallet and make as if I'm counting a stack of twenties thick as my forearm. "How much?"

He sits up in his seat. Now he's considering. "This would be my only ride today."

"Charge me accordingly."

He scans, as if weighing me with his eyes. Measuring my worth, calculating the value of my clothes and the cost of my haircut, then multiplying from there. It's the street hustler math of New York, a well-honed practice I can't help but admire, even if I'm the marble in his shell game. "Two hundred," he tosses off lazily.

I'd pay two hundred dollars to get home. I'd pay two hundred dollars to get to Greenpoint on the hottest day of the year. It's a plane ticket, essentially. I can justify it to myself, even if I don't have two hundred in the couch cushions for moments like these. The rainy day fund is a couple of twenties at best.

"I need to run into the deli and use the ATM. Will you wait?"

He responds by rolling up the window, sucking the air-conditioning back into his car. I feel like I've leaped back into an oven.

In the nearest bodega a line has formed six deep at the ATM machine in the back. The person currently poking it looks increasingly frustrated, then irate. "It's not working," he yells at the cashier.

"It's all down," the cashier yells back. He holds up his credit card reader seemingly as evidence. "This doesn't work. My phone doesn't work. ATM doesn't work. No communication with the bank." Three people in front of me groan and curse and shuffle off, but the remaining person waits her turn, then scans her card and punches in her code, glancing back at me, checking my thieving credentials. When she looks back at the machine something about it perplexes her. She scans her card and again keeps an eye on me as she punches in four digits. It all seems too much for her to handle. That's when the tears start and this woman, my mother's age, breaks down in the middle of the store. "It doesn't work," she weeps to me.

"Are you far from home?" I ask.

"No. I live nearby. But I have cats. I need to buy cat food."

The cashier shouts from behind the counter, "I know you!" Both the lady and I turn to him. "You are in here all the time," he's shouting at her. She takes it as an accusation, shrinks back, wails louder. "No," he reassures. "Show me how much you are taking and you can pay me next time. I know you."

"Thank you," she says, under her breath, then again more forcefully, grabbing cans of cat food off the shelf and getting a pre-receipt from the cashier. He tells her the total and jots it down on a slip of paper. At that she weeps even louder, in gratitude, in the sacred relief that something has gone right amid the chaos.

Though I know it won't work I swipe my card and punch in my PIN, Rebecca's birthday, only to get an error message in response.

This machine is currently not dispensing funds. We are working to resolve the situation. I nod to the cashier on my way out, holding up my empty water bottle as a gesture that I'm not stealing from him, that I brought it in with me. He waves me past; his eyes miss nothing—not his regular customers, not the strangers.

The black cab is still there when I come back out and he rolls the window down, this time just a sliver. "Listen, the ATM is down. It's a citywide thing. All of the computers are down, the guy in there said so. I can give you my credit card numbers, or we can try some ATMs in Queens or Brooklyn, but I don't have two hundred in cash right now."

"I don't take IOUs," he replies. Then he closes the sliver. I wait a three count, staring at him, then knock. I knock with my keys so it resonates. Click, click, click. The sliver reopens. "Fuck off," he instructs.

"Listen, I'll pay you. I'll let you hold my wallet until I can get to a working ATM. I just need you to take me home. Come on, it's fucking crazy up here, it's insanely hot, and I'm willing to pay you two hundred dollars, *plus tip,* to get me home. Please take me home."

He mulls this over. Actually strokes his chin. Then he straddles the center console, sliding himself over to the passenger side of the car, so that we're talking a little closer, like in a confessional booth. "You know what's going on down there?" he asks me.

"No. Have they said on the radio?"

"No. I've scanned every station, but no one knows what's up. Just that midtown is closed off, and that no one should be out if they don't have to be."

"We'll avoid all of it, take the Kennedy to Queens. Please."

"You think it's terrorism?"

"I don't know," I admit. I don't want to talk to someone with his skin tone about terrorism. Come on, dude. "Maybe."

"See, you don't know, and I don't know. Probably nobody knows. And once they say what happened, it'll take a while for everyone to find out, and even then, some people will still think it's terrorism. Some people, no matter what you tell them or what you show them, will insist that it's terrorism. And if I stop at a red light, in Manhattan, or Queens, or Brooklyn, and some asshole thinks that I'm a terrorist, then I'm going to get the shit kicked out of me, or my car is going to get all fucked up."

"That's not going to happen," I try to reassure, my voice sounding more desperate now.

"Maybe not." He taps his turban. "I'm a Sikh. Al-Qaeda's just as happy to blow me up. Grew up in Oklahoma. Went to school at Grinnell. You believe that? Grinnell. So now you know, and you don't think I'm a terrorist. But how fast do you think I could explain that to a group of assholes who spent the day drinking beer on their stoop and looking for brown people to fuck up?"

"Three hundred," I offer.

"Forget it. I'm sorry," he says. "I sympathize, I do. But I've got a kid. Not worth the risk. No cars today. Not until this shit is over."

I straighten up. He slides back over to the driver's seat. Something strikes me and I lean back down and say through the slit, "If you're not driving anywhere, how come you're just sitting in your car?"

"Rolling brownouts." He shakes his head. "Funny how it always seems to roll up here first."

Fuck. What would losing power mean for Rebecca and Jackson? What does he need daily that requires electricity? "Are you sure?"

"Positive. Rolling brownouts. That much the news can report. Everyone smart enough to stay inside is stressing out the grid. Power went out in my apartment an hour ago," he replies simply. "No air-conditioning." Then he shuts me out once more.

Michael Gould

Eleven Months Ago: August 28, 2009

Rebecca says good-bye with solemnity, clutching me close for the kiss, first on the lips (*"I love you"*), then on the forehead. She never kisses me on the forehead—it's creepy, horror-movie maternal to me. She's packed a batch of cookies and a loaf of zucchini bread in my bag alongside my tools and the wood samples, her baked goods talismans against a house that Death has visited, I suppose. Jackson grumpily twitches in his papoose chair so I peck him on the bean before venturing out, ruminating on how long I'll do that. How old will my son be before I stop kissing him every time one of us goes out or comes home? With Rebecca, it's an obligation. Once those planes hit those buildings, couples the world over insisted on the good-bye kiss and the restoration kiss. If I tried to leave without kissing Rebecca, even if I had to wake her up to do so, she'd chase me outside. But Jackson? How long until kissing my son embarrasses him?

We haven't spoken about Paul and Jennifer since the dinner, though they interfere with our lives nevertheless. In the middle of baking cookies, Rebecca will count, then pause, lost in thought, and I've known her long enough to know exactly what she's thinking, that she's tied these cookies she's made to the child that Paul and Jennifer have lost, and she absorbs the guilt, believing herself not only a designated mourner, but also somehow culpable, equal to the same untenable blame that Jennifer hoists upon herself. Rebecca accepts that fault on behalf of all womanhood, wombs of every land.

When I think back to the dinner, I imagine Jennifer as a series of tiny, unattended packages left in the subway. Each one explodes, not catastrophically enough to evacuate the premises, just enough to wound the person closest by—a limb blown to smithereens, ears ringing, skin scorched. And then another. And then another. All too small to get the city to shield the public from the danger, just large enough to do some damage.

I kiss Rebecca once more. Once more she mutters her victory love.

It's the first gorgeous day in months. The first day that won't find me sweating while waiting for the bus. The air blows cool off the rivers and the sun casts those tail-end-of-summer shadows, that gorgeous, horizontal light, over everything. I decide to walk to the subway. I'm in no rush to get to Greenpoint.

I'm in no rush to return to Red Hook, either, I think as I climb the steps to the subway. The dinner with Paul and Jennifer caught me on unguarded terrain, left me with an envy for something I'd never fully want.

Everyone talks about the bond a parent forms with a child, immediately ironclad. To fail at that bond is the purview of sociopaths. And to a cynical mind it all becomes alarmist, that my parents, and Rebecca, and all of her parenting books have united in this effort to convince me of something that I accept without controversy. Yes, I've bonded with my son. I love my son. You don't need to keep telling me how much I love my son—there aren't chalk marks rising up a wall to note that new level. I love my son. The end.

It doesn't mean that I don't look at Paul and Jennifer, the first couple I've managed to see in seemingly forever, and feel a pang of jealousy that they can venture outside without strapping on thirty pounds. Or even that they get to leave their house as they please. That they are beholden to each other, but mostly to themselves. That's nonsense from a manchild cliché, sure. Not every thought has to be stitched onto a throw pillow. That's why they're thoughts.

I know Rebecca, and I know that she looks at life as a massive checklist. She's checked off husband—she doesn't need to worry about that anymore. She's checked off child, and whether she has a second as yet empty box, for a second as yet unconceived child, is information I'm not privy to. Rebecca checks her boxes and with each one a flood of endorphins rushes through her brain. As the train takes me from one obligation to the next, I wonder if a reset button exists to make my brain work the same. I'm a very comfortable man, and that comfort makes my skin itch like shingles.

Jennifer Sayles opens her door and stares at me, vexed. She wears flannel pants and a purple T-shirt pockmarked with holes. Her hair flies in all directions. The stench of cigarettes wafts off her in waves. She's not getting out of the way, or inviting me in. "Where are your tools?" she asks.

Hopefully she didn't see me take a step back. I tamp down my subway thoughts. They wax less philosophical and more idiotic when greeted on a front stoop by a refugee from the death camps.

"Just taking measurements and doing some drawings today. Everything I need is in my bag."

"Paul is at work," she says absently.

"Shouldn't take long. May I come in?"

She squints at me and leans on the doorjamb. "Do you want a drink?"

I can't just barrel past her, right? That would be the simplest solution, to physically move her, charge upstairs, lay some wood samples out in the kitchen while I deal with the room, and if she doesn't choose one, I will.

"It's a really nice day," I posit. I'm not certain what dormant humanist instinct in me prompts this next offer, but I propose, "How about I finish what I need to get done and then we take a walk somewhere, hit up a happy hour." Happy hours start at four. Or three. It's eleven thirty.

She shakes her head. "I don't want to go out today."

I try raffish on for size. "Well fuck it, then."

Jennifer blinks at the brightness of the sun, as if her brain has finally registered it. She looks confused, but also irritated. Her hands shake in tiny tremors as she knocks a cigarette out of the pack and lights it. She holds the pack up to my face. "I'd like one, but after I get a little work done. I'm going to go take some measurements and then I'll join you for a smoke. Cool?" She takes two quick drags. I can't tell if she's ignoring me or not, so I add, "I'm going to keep the door closed if that works for you."

It works like a password. She steps aside.

Paul broke the room down, gave away the crib and the glider. I'll need to strip the walls of the robin's egg paint. That will be step one. Interior decoration isn't my strong suit—I build furniture; I don't design rooms—but there's a psychology with which I approach this project. The goal is to exorcise all latent spirits from the bedroom of their dead child, so that when they walk in, it's an entirely new experience, a room they've never entered, charged with none of its old rotting emotions.

I open the closet doors and find garbage bags stacked up to my chest. A quick squeeze tells me it's clothing. I glance upward to see enough ceiling space that I could create a nook, a place to tuck things out of sight if not out of mind, let them use this closet for more pressing matters.

A half hour later I'm kneeling on the floor, running a tape measure from wall to wall, envisioning the built-in bookcase I'm going to build for them. My pad is filling with notes and numbers, calculating how much wood. It's easy to get lost in the work; it happens every time I start a painting too. It's a running downhill feeling, control at the willing mercy of momentum. With each snap of the tape measure I crave another, notching length and width and depth like brushstrokes. I sense a presence behind me and spin to see Jennifer standing in the open doorway. She doesn't look upset, her face isn't any different from when she greeted me at the door. She's stock-still, taking in the room like a prospective buyer. "I thought you were going to close this door."

I straighten. "It slipped my mind. I'm really sorry."

"That's an inhumanely cruel thing for you to do," she says, but without an accusatory edge to her voice; it's just her casual observation.

"Again, I'm sorry."

"You don't have to be such a fucking monster," she says, in the same detached monotone.

I don't know what makes me stand my ground. I'm not an aggressive person. I don't seek out confrontation. And yet I say, "I would be if I left it open intentionally, but I didn't. It was an accident. It was a careless mistake, and I apologized. Would you like me to tell you what I plan to do in here?"

After a spell, she nods.

"Come in and I'll show you," and then I turn away, take a measurement of the window frame even though there's nothing I plan to do with it whatsoever. I feel her stepping into the room. When I turn around she's right in the middle, hands at her sides, fingers tugging down the hem of her shirt. "You get great light," I explain. "So I'm going to build you built-in bookshelves along that wall and you can put a desk underneath. I'll make sure you have a ton of space. I'll run track lighting across the ceiling, put that on a dimmer. That wall is also going to have some shelving on it, not built-in though, so you can make this room a little more personal if you'd like. I'm also going to strip the walls and the floor, repaint and revarnish, so we should discuss what colors and shades you might want for those, whenever you're feeling up to it. Do you want to have that cigarette now?"

If she's listened to a word of what I've said she hides it like stolen fruit. She says, "I'm going to take a shower."

"All right."

"I like your plans."

"I have a few more measurements to take."

"Can you let yourself out?"

She doesn't wait for my answer, just turns and leaves. I go back to taking actual measurements, noting where to put a small mirrored bar into the bookshelf, another step to render this room childproof. I hear a shower start up, the angry coughing fits of old building pipes sputtering to life, then a steady stream of water and the slither of a shower curtain drawn aside. The hum of an exhaust fan.

My phone chirps a marimba sound: a text from Rebecca.

How is it going?

I type back:

Almost done.

A moment later:

How is Jennifer?

And from me:

Quiet. Weird. This is uncomfortable.

I tuck the phone back, but it chirps again. That's Rebecca following up; I can predict the text. She's asking me, *Uncomfortable how?* When I explain that, she'll keep the conversation going by poking and prodding. *Weird how? Has she said anything to you? Did she go in the room?* It's all stuff I'll answer later when I see her, later as in an hour from now, so there's no need to prep her via text. After jotting down some final notes, I tuck everything back into my backpack and step into the hall, closing the door behind me.

Their bathroom is at the end of the hall, and the door to it is wide-open. My mind rushes to Rebecca, who gets annoyed with me when I leave the bathroom door open a crack, so that the mirror gets less steamy and I can see when I shave. She passive-aggressively shuts it on me when I'm already in the shower, so I step out into fog and shave a soft-focus version of myself.

That's not the case here. I can see directly into the bathroom, the silhouette of Jennifer behind a translucent plastic shower curtain, soaping up an arm.

Clever lady, I think to myself. The cynic (or realist) in me suspects this is a trap, that she wants me to invade her privacy, saunter into the bathroom and talk to her while she showers, even if it's to tell her I'm going, just to get close to her while she's vulnerable. Naked, no less. Then when Paul gets home she'll tiptoe around my visit, piquing his interest, hinting at some transgression, until she spills in a torrent of tears and self-recriminations. *I shouldn't have left the bathroom door open. I thought he was already gone.*

I don't know what kind of man Paul Fenniger is when his needle goes into the red. Maybe he's the type to come to my home and beat the everloving shit out of me in front of my family. Maybe he's the silky type to draw me out, invite me for a drink to talk about the project, and then put my face through a bathroom mirror. Real mob shit, or what I think is real mob shit from movies, keeping dirty business out of the home. Maybe he's just a screamer, and I'd get an irate phone call from him demanding that I keep away from his wife. End result: room stays the same. The strongest vibe I get thus far is that this is Paul's pet project; Jenny feels nowhere near as keen.

The open bathroom door: the line. The naked woman behind a diaphanous scrim: the hook. And me: a little fishy, distracted in the hallway by a shiny object.

I'm curious. So curious I almost want to ask her, shouted from a safe and respectable distance in the hall. Or, I could go back into the room, wait until she's out of the shower, and then confront her once she's dressed. If entrapment was her plan all along, I want to ask, couldn't she accuse me regardless? Tell Paul I did whatever pervy bullshit she needs to concoct to get me fired. It'd be her word against mine.

Somewhere in all this contemplation, in all this chess of clever, I process that Jenny has a very nice silhouette. My face flushes, a spark of arousal slides its way down from the lizard part of my brain. That doorway stands open to me, that threshold mine to cross, but I make my way outside, back into the blinding sun, the afternoon heat enough to make me sweat while standing still.

Michael Gould

Eleven Months Ago: August 28, 2009

I'm a block from home when it dawns on me that I forgot to give Jenny the baked goods. I forgot to show her the wood samples as well. I'm not usually the type to let things slip my mind—everything is in working order up there, and I leave my workroom only after notching every item off a mental list of tasks accomplished. But I've forgotten to hand off the cookies and the zucchini bread, and now if I bring it home and insist to Rebecca that I can bring it tomorrow, she'll be furious with me at even the suggestion, since tomorrow they won't be as fresh, and then Paul and Jenny will think less of her as a baker. Rebecca would rather be thought of as borderline genocidal than as less of a baker. So I double back to my shop, the empty shop, and place the baked goods in the fridge. In my best-case scenario, I grab them on my way tomorrow and no one is the wiser.

Home carries the scent of brown sugar and maple bacon, greeting me at the bottom of the stairs, faithful and inviting. I call these blow job cookies, privately, to Rebecca, because she only makes them for special occasions—my birthday or the anniversary of our first date. Today I'm being rewarded for starting this project, for my discount work for a grieving couple, a noble deed Rebecca deems maple-bacon-sugar-cookie-worthy.

Aha. When I open the door I see who is holding my son, and I realize the cookies aren't for my work. They're to calm me down or, barring that, distract me. The woman holding my son looks just like Rebecca after a few hundred catastrophic choices. Her hair is stringier, dirty-looking, if not actually dirty. Her skin shimmers, with a gleam like plastic, as if permanently under the fluorescent lights of a hospital. She has Rebecca's face with the warmth sucked out of it, her body minus a few pounds too many, Rebecca's curves planed down to angry, ramshackle bones. And when she holds Jackson, she looks like Rebecca holding Jackson, only with the added element of risk, as if she'd drop him, or trade him for opiates.

"Hi, Jolie," I say, my hand instinctively moving to protect my wallet.

"Michael Gould." Her voice is even more gutted out than the last time I saw her. I can't imagine how she achieves that hoarseness. She could drink bleach, I suppose, or have an infinite supply of lit cigarettes sticking out of her mouth. Otherwise, it's another mystery from the Agatha Christie of sisters-in-law. She cracks a smile, as jagged as the rest of her. "How the devil are you?"

"Where's Rebecca?"

She emerges from the bathroom, kisses me hello, squeezes my arm, and gives the least subtle *behave yourself* look possible. "How was the job?"

I recount the day, layering in as much boring craftsman detail to lard the story. By the time I get to the end they regret asking me in the first place. No follow-up questions to tease out details I don't want to give. I hunker down on the couch next to Jolie and motion for my son, coo and cuddle with him like a good dad should, get him the hell away from my sister-in-law until I know what she has coursing through her veins at the moment.

"We had a very interesting day," Rebecca singsongs. The bell goes off on the timer and she clicks the button to stop it, then takes a batch of perfectly browned cookies out of the oven. "I got a call from Dawn. She's closing Riziki."

"Oh shit. That was fast."

"It was, but not to worry, she says, because she's opening up a new restaurant called Mavuno. It means harvest."

"Also in Bed-Stuy?"

"Oh no," Rebecca explains. "Mavuno is going to open up in the up-and-coming neighborhood of Brownsville."

"I don't think I have ever set foot in Brownsville."

"Finally, one for my bingo card." She laughs at her joke. Jolie does too, and it sounds like shaking broken glass. "I called a car service and dropped Jackson off with your mom for a few hours, and went to see the space."

"You went to Brownsville?" I ask, incredulous. Jolie reaches over and pokes a crone's crooked finger into the soft folds of Jackson's thighs. "Why does she need you to see the space?"

"Because"—Rebecca trumpets her news—"Dawn de la Puente wants to bring me on as a partner. Five whole percent."

Rebecca Gould, restaurateur. My mind spasms through a litany of emotions. Husband Michael cheers hooray and tells her how proud I am of her. Accountant Michael reminds her how in debt we are to my parents, and 5 percent of a restaurant, even way the fuck out in Brownsville, is still too rich for our blood. Artist Michael rants against corporate selling out, that she's the Becky of Becky's Bites, dammit, and that's her canvas. She shouldn't be stuck figuring out inventory and hiring. Father Michael shakes his head, dismissively, because Jackson needs the flexibility our current schedules offer. Otherwise, we may as well leave him with Jolie and hope he doesn't learn how to tie off from watching her.

"That's an honor," I say. Praise first. Now I've been supportive and can ask, "How do you feel about that?"

She brushes it off. "I gave it some thought. I have no interest in owning a restaurant. Not with Dawn, and not in Brownsville, and not right now. Right now is no risk and modest profit instead of plenty of risk for potential profit. Was a fun thought to entertain for an afternoon, but I like what I have going."

Attagirl.

Rebecca goes on. "When I left the restaurant space, I told the driver to wait for me, but he didn't. So I was standing on a corner in Brownsville waiting ten minutes for him. And I couldn't go back in and face Dawn again, because I'd already told her I wouldn't be investing, so she was pissy with me. I started walking."

"In Brownsville."

"In Brownsville. I get maybe one block and I still can't find the car and, trust me, it would stick out, but guess who I run into?"

Jolie throws up her arms, smiles broadly, revealing a mouth full of reconstructed teeth. "Me!"

"How fortuitous." I ask the obvious question. "What brought you to the welcoming climes of Brownsville, Jolie?"

She triumphantly slaps a coin down on our coffee table. I shift Jackson and look. It's a three-month chip, from AA or NA or one of those church basements Jolie has frequented over the years. Whether this is a fresh chip or something she earned years ago from some rare ninety-day stint of sobriety, and now brings out to grift people like her sister I don't know. TO THINE OWN SELF BE TRUE, it reads. A better phrase would be Try to Not Fuck Up Quite So Much.

"It's actually a few months old. I've five months clean." She puffs out her chest. "And I'm going to meetings every day, and I have an apartment, and a job, and a boyfriend." Oh those nouns, how they shapeshift into cot, corner, and pimp.

"Tell us about all three," I say and hold Jackson up. Bubbles come out of his mouth in response. He's on the descent into a nap, so I lay the warm baby on my chest and hope he drifts off. I can't be tense with this lump of doughy love lazing against my heartbeat.

"Well, the apartment is in Jackson Heights. It's small, but I live with a couple other addicts, so it's good, because we keep each other level, you know? And the job is through the city, so I have insurance and everything. I go to schools and do student outreach."

"How does that work?"

Jolie's eyes go everywhere when she talks. She addresses a roomful of giants and dwarves. "Like, I go and talk about the choices I've made, and the people I've hurt, and how young I was when I started on drugs and alcohol and blahdy blahdy blah. It's boring talking about yourself all day. And they only want to hear the really bad shit, you know? And then I sit around in some vacant office for the rest of the day and students can come and talk to me one-on-one, like I'm their counselor. Sometimes I make shit up, because if I'm trying to scare them straight, I want to really scare the fucking shit out of them, you know? So I tell them that my first boyfriend told me he loved me, so we didn't use condoms and then when I got pregnant he and his friends gang-raped me so I'd mis-carry. Never happened, but those little eyes turn into dinner plates."

"You're doing God's work," I drawl. "And the boyfriend?"

"And the boyfriend," she echoes. "It's new, so I'm going to keep that one to myself for the time being, if that's all right."

"You minx. You vixen. You outdoor cat."

"Meow."

"Jolie waited with me until I finally found the car," Rebecca pipes in, "and since she hadn't met Jackson yet, I thought today would be the perfect opportunity."

"Oh. Did my mom meet Jolie?" I try to keep the weight out of the question but fail.

"I waited in the car," Jolie rasps.

"I thought we'd have dinner and then you could drive Jolie back to Queens."

Yeah, that's not happening. I'm not sitting in a car with Jolie for an hour and hauling ass back and forth to Queens. Rebecca knows this, she's just putting up a token effort, but she'll reach into her purse and give Jolie eighty bucks to cover a car back with enough left over for what will hopefully go toward food. It's not that I don't like Jolie—she's an intriguing guest star—but seeing how my wife looks at Jolie as she spins her ninety-day chip, a mix of pride and trepidation across Rebecca's trusting face, I hear the future phone call, made from a police station, or a hospital. Jolie is a story that doesn't end well. Jackson turns his garbanzo bean head toward her, blinks a few times as if he can see her future, and elects to nap instead. Take her in, son, every wrecked inch of her. She's your family. She's your cautionary tale.

Paul Fenniger

Present Day: July 19, 2010

11:13 AM

I skulk forward, step by cautious step. There should be emergency lights, but there aren't. That's what Perry told me. He said these tunnels are lined with emergency lights, for construction, and track work, and that they run on a different line than the third rail. They can keep the tracks cold but light the way for us. Only they haven't.

Or they can't. The glow I had seen from the train was the train itself, its taillights illuminating the ten feet directly behind. We're past that now. That light is gone. The train itself let out a last hiss before whatever gave it power also shut down. It's near pitch-black in the tunnel, and I hear the whimpering of the people in front of me. These are the slow, the terminally slow. Old people, people who probably should have stayed on the train and waited for guides had that been an option, but also a few dozen enduring their own personal hell. Afraid of the dark, of rats, of enclosed spaces, these are the petrified, walking stiff and gasping for air.

After we helped everyone off the train, the conductor intro-duced himself. Perry shook my hand and thanked me while chastising me that they don't need heroes down here today. "Like putting your own mask on first before helping someone else," he explained, "like on a plane. Just get yourself out of the tunnel." He doesn't know what's going on. Or he's not telling me. Are we buried alive? Is that what he isn't saying?

Standing behind the train with Perry, I considered for the first time that I may die today. There were people who died on impact when the planes hit the towers. And then there was the exodus. And from that there were those who never got out. I can't be the only one thinking about this in the tunnel. I can't be the only person waiting for our sky to fall. It would be a watery grave—a rumble, a fissure, a drip, and then the flood.

I cannot die today. I cannot do that to Jenny. Not under tons of cement in the new bottom of the East River.

After repeating that they do not need heroes, don't want heroes, the conductor asks me to hang back and help people through. Keep them calm. "You're a big guy." He assesses me. He had to run ahead with his flashlight, give people a sense of where to go. I watched his light bounce forward, a single firefly in the tunnel, until it became a pinprick off in the distance and I was left behind with the elderly and the terrified.

My eyes have adjusted enough that I can see my own feet, one in front of the other, stepping in the well between the tracks, lifting every few steps to get over the ties. I look down for a few paces, then up to mark myself against the half form in front of me, working a slow rhythm. I don't want to get ahead of the people I've been charged to guide.

"Not much farther," I say under my breath, loud enough for the people around me to hear. Whispers carry in the tunnel.

A man's voice, about twenty yards ahead, yells "Enough," like a battle cry, and then what follows roars in response. There are the grunts of bodies being knocked to the side and falling onto the tracks, the wails of bruises and cuts, the slapping of footfalls as this man charges forward, no longer buying into the social contract of calm and steady walking. Screams echo through the tunnel, both at the chaos he's unleashed, and at the fear of what might follow, that if one guy plowing everyone over isn't punished, then there's nothing to stop might from making right as even more people knock the weak aside, leaving them in the tunnel as rat food.

There comes silence like a knife's edge, three camps making a collective decision. Those who think they could run forward and get out of the tunnel sooner are deciding whether the risk involved is too great, whether running blindly through a darkened tunnel is more likely to lead to injury than to freedom. Those who know they can't run—the people around me, for instance—are deciding whether to stand stock-still against the walls, to wait out the storm of people, to take their chances with the rats and the dimming of the flashlights, to hope that after the first swell of people emerges first responders will flood into the tunnel and carry them out.

Then there are those on the fence, people who have no intention of standing one second longer in the tunnel than they need to but are no more willing to increase their level of danger. They are waiting to see what the other camps will do.

The footfalls of the running man end in a loud clang and a yelp. He's run into something larger or more solid than himself, or tripped on a tie and fallen. He moans, "My leg!" It's all the cue the three camps need.

The risk is too great. There's nothing to be gained from pushing. We sally forth, one step at a time. I expect to pass him, to see some darkened version of him hunkered down on the track, waiting for medical help. But I never do. Even he continues onward.

Michael Gould

Present Day: July 19, 2010

11:15 AM

Every car in Manhattan is leaving the island. The roads leading to the GW Bridge, up Riverside and the Henry Hudson, up Broadway and Amsterdam, are gridlocked. More than gridlocked—they stand still, drivers wearing out their horns trying to jailbreak through intersections. A green Hyundai climbs onto the sidewalk to make its way across town, the driver at least having the wherewithal to slow to an idle roll as pedestrians part the sea to let it through, slapping the hood angrily. I step out of its way and look in, see a man with his tie still perfectly knotted, his sleeves still buttoned, eyes tense as he hunches over his steering wheel. He clicks on his emergency blinkers and attempts to slide back into traffic at the end of the street. There isn't a cop around to stop him.

Cabs, as I learned, aren't taking passengers. The drivers line up in every illegal spot they can find, flipping the switch for their not-in-service lights, idling in front of fire hydrants and driveways.

I've passed a few subway stations, which, by this point, have caution tape across the entrances. People hold out their phones, spinning in circles, still trying to get a signal. Everyone I pass is holding a water bottle and a phone, the two last tools of this apocalypse. There's still no information as to what is happening in midtown. This boggles the mind, this information blackout. Everyone becomes a conspiracy theorist, sharing tales of foreign invasions or a series of car bombs. An alien invasion gets posited with a *y'know, fuck it* insouciance. This prompts another favorite New York pastime: if that's the case then why this? If it's aliens—a woman shakes

115

her head, taking offense at the very thought—then why would the buses be shut down? *Why don't aliens want me riding the bus?* I just keep walking forward, sliding in and out of foot traffic, a step faster than the people around me, making my way toward the very bad place that everyone else flees.

The crowds grow sparse as I move farther south. The heat and lack of public transport are enough to keep the lookie-loos at home. So as long as the electrical grid doesn't crap out entirely, people can sit in the relative comfort of air-conditioned rooms and watch the tragedy unfold. There's no need to scurry toward it for the *I was there* factor.

At 138th a squat pecan of a man sits in front of his store on a lawn chair, sipping a bottle of High Life with a hose across his lap like a dead snake. His wares stacked behind him, some sort of hybrid bodega and junk shop. He's got Hula-Hoops and flower pots out front, a cooler of soda, rags and bones and forgotten things. He smiles at my approach. "Spray you with a hose?" he asks.

I contemplate his offer. I really can't get any more wet, my body drenched in its own sweat. "Please."

"Two dollars." He grins wide.

"Two bucks to spray me with a hose?"

"Very hot. Will cool you off. Good deal."

Fucked if he doesn't make a good case. "How long?"

"Long as you want."

"You'll spray me until I say to stop?"

"Two dollars."

"Right. And can I fill my water bottle from the hose too? Still only two dollars?"

This he contemplates. "Okay."

I hand him my remaining five and he peels three ones off a roll and hands them back to me. He readies the hose, takes aim at me, but I give him the universal signal for one second. I take my shoes off, no need to get those soaked. And my socks, ball them up and put them to the side. I tuck my iPhone into the toe of my right shoe, my wallet into the toe of my left. These I set out of the splash zone, closer to him than me. This requires a degree of trust I could not fathom when the day began.

I stand six feet from him, strike a Vitruvian Man pose, with arms and legs spread. "Wait. What's your name?" I ask.

"Luis."

"Luis?"

"Yes."

"Please don't spray me in the balls."

"You got it." In an instant, I'm soaked head to toe in glorious, New York hose water. It smells of pennies on sidewalks, smells the way a dog does on a hot day, but it's cool and cascades down my body, every drop a gift. I run my hands through my hair, gather the water in my palms and soak my face. Luis laughs as I spin and let him coat me from head to toe. Then I drop to my knees and Luis stops. I shake like a dog.

"I didn't say stop." He shrugs and sprays me some more, and I absorb it through every pore. "Thank you," I repeat. "Thank you thank you thank you thank you." I wipe the water from my eyes and laugh with Luis, the hose once more across his lap. I collect my water bottle and hold it underneath the nozzle, let him fill it with this disgusting water.

When we're done I sit next to him in the shade and drip dry a little. Luis offers everyone who walks by a turn with the hose but is refused, even with this advertisement for bliss sitting next to him. Don't you people know what you're missing? Being sprayed with a hose is the only antidote for today. "I wish more pretty girls," he remarks, then mimics spraying their ample chests with a hose, somehow making their breasts grow as he soaks them.

"You know what's happening down there?" I point to our left.

He considers my query. "Nine Eleven," he replies.

"Really? You think terrorist attack?"

"I know this. Yes."

"How do you know this?"

"I know." Ah, so he doesn't. The man with the hose doesn't free-lance for Reuters.

"Were you here for Nine Eleven?" I ask. Not usually a conversa-tion New Yorkers like to have, but he did bring it up . . .

He laughs softly in response. "I was right here." He points to the ground upon which he sits.

"I was at college. I was born and raised in Brooklyn, but I went to school in California. I woke up because my parents were calling me to let me know that they were all right, and then I watched the news with everyone else, sitting on a dorm couch that reeked of bong water and stale pizza."

"Very sad." He finishes his beer, reaches into the cooler for an-other. He offers me one. "A dollar."

I pass. "I couldn't escape news that day. Between the television and my classmates and my parents calling every hour, I couldn't not know every last detail of everything that was happening. And everyone in my dorm knew I was from New York, so they kept ask-ing me for updates, like I had a different news feed, like Giuliani was calling me to give me inside information. I didn't know anyone who died. I didn't even know people who knew people, but every-one kept treating me like my entire family was buried. One guy on my floor had a family friend who worked at Cantor Fitzgerald. He had a closer tie to the human cost than I did. But he was from Allentown, Pennsylvania. And I was from Brooklyn."

Luis offers to spray a man in a suit with the hose and the man gladly accepts, handing over three dollars for the privilege. He doesn't even remove his sport coat, just gratefully takes ten seconds of hosing down, and continues on his way. Luis adds the bills to his roll, smiles again at me. My feet have already dried, so I roll back on my stiff socks and lace back up my shoes. My pockets are even dry enough to replace my wallet and phone.

A man wearing loose-fitting clothing steps out of a van and gets on a train somewhere in Manhattan. He wouldn't want to be in public longer than he has to. He waits until he is underneath one of the major stations in midtown, major because of the assembled humanity there at every given second of the day, major because of how integral the station is to how people move about the city. There he presses a button, or flips a switch, or whatever one does to set off a vest. The people around him don't even hear death before it vaporizes them. And out and out it travels, concentric circles of impact, until the last people at the very edge of the blast zone sustain those minor cuts and bruises.

They shut down transit in case the man with the vest isn't the only one. Because the loss of human life will get digested in think pieces, but the city has to run the cold calculations of fixing a bombed-out train station, of replacing subway cars and buses, of convincing people that Manhattan is not an island that can support anxiety traffic, that if people don't readily take mass transit daily, a stone will lodge in the city's throat, choking off a terrifying amount of the world's economy.

A moment of clarity while I'm drip-drying. My city got attacked again. I'm positive. What's left is for the details to leak, then get explained, then get muddied, first by conjecture, then by conspiracy.

I rise and nod to Luis. "Thank you."

"No problem, good luck!" he calls out cheerfully.

The sun instantly wicks away the last droplets of water from my body and a block later I'm once again cooking. I contemplate going back and sitting by Luis in the shade for as long as he'll let me, offer to be his assistant, someone trustworthy to hold on to the valuables of people he sprays. I won't even charge him, just as much time with the hose and as many refills of water as I can drink while the trains are being held. It could be days, for all I know, like during that September, when I heard about entire sections of the city being shut down, only those with proof of residency being allowed below Fourteenth Street.

This radio silence is maddening. Yesterday there wasn't a scintilla of information the tiny computer in my pocket couldn't access.

I have the Library at Alexandria in the palm of my hand dozens of times a day. But not today, when it can't even call home. I've stepped back a decade, into the morass of confusion and unease that is unknowing, that is speculation over even halfheartedly gathered facts.

As I crest 135th the next ten blocks roll out before me. People in California think of Manhattan as being flat but it's not, especially up in Harlem, where the city rolls in hills only shades less steep than those of San Francisco. I've climbed to the top of a precipice and now I gaze upon a new vista, one that reveals nothing so far as midtown, but instead the elevated tracks of the 1 train. A train sits on the tracks, silver and still, like a dead caterpillar. My perspective makes it look small enough that I could pick it up like a toy, hold it in my hands, and slide it back and forth along the tracks.

I continue south, downhill until the next ascent.

Michael Gould

Eleven Months Ago: August 30, 2009

I've decided that if Jennifer doesn't bring up the shower, then I won't, either. Maybe she's the type who showers with the door open and doesn't care who is around, or maybe she thought I had already left. On the train ride over, I come up with dozens of explanations, cataloged and dismissed or considered, ranked by plausibility.

Jennifer opens the door and walks back into her apartment, smoking a cigarette. "I made you cookies," she says over her shoulder by way of greeting.

"You made me cookies?" I parrot back.

She points to a plate on the counter. Standard chocolate chip disks, by the look of them. I take the smallest one and bite into it. It's a little like hardtack; she didn't use enough butter, inevitably by following some flawed recipe, but she doesn't pick up on the hard crunch my teeth make. She still looks at me expectantly. "These are delicious," I say through crumbs.

She rolls her eyes and takes the rest of the cookie out of my hand, chucks it in the trash. "I'm going to go work unless you need me."

"Actually." I lay my backpack on the counter. "Today is all about you. I have some wood samples for the shelves and some paint samples for the walls."

"Just ask Paul. Whatever he wants is fine with me."

"He said to ask you, and whatever you want is fine with him."

"Then we leave it up to you." She turns away from me and I grab her wrist. Gently. This is the first time I've touched her; we didn't shake hands when Rebecca and I came for dinner. She came into the room late. This wrist in my hand is the first moment. She doesn't break away from me, but she doesn't seem upset by this transgression either, merely turns and looks down at my hand curiously, as if it has detached itself from my body, or she put on a gaudy bangle in the shape of a human hand. I take it back and we let the room settle. "Go ahead, then," she prompts. Jennifer cocks a hip petulantly, still smoking, such a ridiculous image I smirk while opening my backpack. "Shouldn't we do this in there?" she asks.

"That would make more sense. Is it okay with you if we do?" She flips the faucet on and rinses off her cigarette, throws it in the trash, then motions for me to follow.

I open the door and step aside. Light spreads buttery across the floor. We've picked the perfect day for sample testing; this is the exact light I hope the room will get, that I hope it will absorb. "After you," she says gruffly. I walk to the window, stare out, give her the space to cross her personal Rubicon in her own time. When I turn around she has both feet in. The light catches her dry eyes;

she's prettier than I've given her credit for, whatever this unsolicited, internal, wolf-whistle praise is worth.

We sit on the floor and I set all of the wood samples out before us, and then lay the paint samples over them, like a giant fan. There's oak and birch and pine, in different finishes, matte and gloss, made to look slick with oil or burned. My color samples avoid the studious and austere. The room draws in too much free sun to make deep maroons or rich greens make sense. This room's original purpose for Jennifer and Paul was to house a child, and nothing I can splatter on the walls is going to change that. The best I can do is keep it happy and inviting, a good place to curl up with a book, or to write one.

While she paws at the samples, getting incrementally more involved, taping some swatches up to the wall to stand back and envision, I inquire, "What kind of writing do you do?"

"The kind that doesn't get published," she finally replies. "What kind of painting do you do?"

"The kind that doesn't get hung." That garners a smile.

She sits down across from me, the samples between us. The light follows her, reveals the lines on her face, the pale translucence of her skin, veins prominent on her neck and jaw, like tributaries off an unseen river. "What is this costing us?" she asks.

"Very little," I reply. "You'll pay for the materials."

"Because you pity me?"

I don't know how to answer in a way that isn't pitying. "Paul is a nice guy. Seemed like he could use a break."

"And some shelves and a paint job is going to make up for his wife killing their child?"

"Not sure how he has this budgeted out."

"Not sure that's the right place for a joke."

I roll my eyes, straight out of the frosty teenager playbook. "How many people have fallen for this routine?"

She sits up. "Excuse me?"

And then immediately, I retreat, chastened. The line to not

cross with Jennifer Sayles sits a few feet behind where I'm standing. "Forget it," I mumble. "Not my place."

"To passive-aggressively judge me and then be a fucking coward about it? No, it's not."

I pause, study the wood samples intently. "You know," I finally say, "normal people don't seek out confrontation. That's not cowardice."

"All the fucking same," she spits.

"Same what?"

"Forget it," she sneers. "Not my place."

"Rebecca does this too. When she's just aching for a fight."

"Glad you menfolk are past such adolescent tantrums."

I throw up my hands. "It's just such bullshit. It's tragic enough, you losing a child. That's what I meant. You don't need to season it with additional tragedy. This is so clearly not your fault unless there's something you're not telling us. Maybe when you were pregnant you did enough cocaine to kill a horse."

"I . . . No," she sputters.

"Yeah, everyone knows that and no one assumes otherwise. So saying that you killed your kid—it's finding a way to make it worse. It's already the worst. What happened to you and Paul is the worst thing that can happen to people. There is no lower point. And it doesn't need you"—I search for the metaphor—"rubbing salt on your own wounds."

I think she's going to yell at me to get out, or slap me, or cry. But while her jaw is set, her face has lost its fight. "You're very perceptive, Michael Gould. I'm crying inside. Inside of that, I'm screaming. Then wailing. Then shouting. I'm a Matryoshka doll of emotion."

"You're joking by not joking."

"I . . ." Her gears spin. "I'm tired of talking about this." She adds, as a happy discovery, "I don't need to talk about this with you."

"No, you definitely don't."

She stands up. "Fuck it. Come have a drink with me."

"It's early."

"I know. Come have a drink with me. I've seen all your samples and I want a minute to think. I'll be nice. I won't be crazy. Come on. Have a drink with me and I'll pick samples after."

"I don't think you're crazy."

"You don't even know me."

"Very true," I concede, following her out of the room. She instructs in a small voice, one that leaks out from someplace buried deep and dark within her, to leave the door open.

Jennifer plucks a bottle of Campari from a cabinet under the sink. She takes out two glasses and drops ice cubes into each. "I buy a bottle of Campari every year in June and for the entire summer I drink Campari and soda. It's all I drink. Usually I go through three or four bottles but this year, because I was pregnant, this is still the June bottle. Paul had to get it because I was embarrassed to be showing and in a liquor store. We're drinking the last Campari and sodas of the year."

"The bottle still has about a third left," I point out.

"Then we can't stop at one." She layers the red, syrupy liqueur over the ice and slowly unscrews the cap on a fresh bottle of club soda. It still bubbles over and she rushes to get most of it into the sink. "What's being a father like?"

I lean on her island and assess, both the question and the questioner. After she makes our drinks, she hoists herself onto the counter, cheers me from a distance, and lights another cigarette, ashing into the drain. What's the answer I could give her that sounds honest but not banal, or hurtful, or bragging. Being a father is great, and it's terrifying, and it's frequently boring, because Jackson spends most of his day sleeping and all of his day needing. He needs one thing or another, and one of us always has to be with him, so it's like house arrest whenever Rebecca goes out. And if one of us is going out, it has to be for work, or on an errand. It's never to go out just to have a drink, even the last Campari and soda of the summer, because you don't leave the other person shackled to the kid for selfish reasons. So I don't see friends anymore, and I relish the time I spend on the subway, or in my workshop. It's my time. I didn't anticipate that I'd stop living my life by my early thirties. That it would no longer be mine to live. If they could distill that and find a way to puncture a thick adolescent skull, that's how they'd keep kids from getting knocked up.

"I thought I would be happier," I admit. It leaves my mouth like vomit.

But she takes it in stride. "Happier how?"

"That's a weird thing to say. I guess I mean I thought every day would be family portrait day. It's just a slog."

"Imagine how it must be for Rebecca."

"Oh, I'm not comparing. She has to keep the restaurant open twenty-four seven. She has the harder job. If you asked her you'd probably get a different answer."

"Maybe not one as honest, though."

I sip my Campari. It tastes of liquid rind, or the syrup they make orange soda with. But it does pair nicely with summer. "No, maybe not."

"You deserve to be happy," Jennifer says.

"I'm not not happy. How did this become me bitching to you about being a parent?"

"I don't mind. It's like you said—I'm already dealing with the worst."

"I'm happy. I promise, I'm happy. It just feels preordained." She doesn't prompt me, but I explain anyway. "Like when Rebecca buys fifty pounds of sugar, she knows how long that will go for. Whatever else happens, barring something unforeseen like . . . flooding, like a flood coming through our apartment and dissolving all the sugar, she knows how long it'll last. She's comforted by reassuring thoughts. That's not how my mind works. I like the uncertainty. For me, it's like cigarettes. You buy a pack of cigarettes, and unless you are super disciplined and only have x number of cigarettes a day, you don't really know how long that pack will last you. Maybe it'll only last you a really hard day, or it could last a month until that last cigarette is plain disgusting. But I like the unknowing, of having to make that decision with each cigarette whether you have enough to get you through before you have to buy another pack. Having a kid is like buying enough sugar for the rest of your life. I was hoping it would be more like cigarettes. And maybe it will. Just not yet. I'm just not there yet."

Jennifer hops down from the counter and puts her cigarette out in a coffee cup. She pushes our glasses aside and leans forward, wraps her arms around my neck. Her body pressed against mine, chest against my chest, thighs against my thighs. My pelvis instinctively shifts back, an *I'm hiding my erection* maneuver learned and perfected in sixth grade. Something flickers on for me, this closeness, the feel of a woman mashed against me, her hands clutching my shoulders. But it's reflex. Or it's the blind old lech in my pants, ready to get it up for anyone worth whistling at. I'm downgrading this hug, even as it extends itself, as it goes longer than a friendly, jovial, or commiserating hug should go. Jennifer asked me a question and I sounded pathetic answering, so childish with my complaints. So she's hugging me in a *there there* way, her version of a weary pat on the head for my whiny existential crisis. Right now, she's thinking better a dead kid with Paul than a live one with this sad sack. It occurs to me that I'm not hugging her back, that her arms still break around my shoulders, pulling me into her, and mine are at my sides, stiffly, like hers were when Rebecca hugged her. So I lower my arms, make the hug easier on us both, and hold her around her waist, keeping my hands light and firmly on her sides, at the north end of her hips.

For an eternity, we stand like that, crushed against one another. "Jenny?"

She crooks her head back and kisses me. Her lips brush mine, testing, before coming back full. At first I'm being polite, keeping my mouth where it was, not pulling away, moving my lips in a reasonable facsimile of how she is moving hers. Then I'm not being polite anymore. I respond, my hands gathering thin fabric and my mouth on hers, now pressing her against the island in her kitchen. The whole time, however long the kiss lasts, I'm piecing together the past ten minutes, trying to determine where this started, whether I did something wrong, how this ties back to the shower. But another woman's tongue is in my mouth, reminding me that Rebecca doesn't kiss this way unless it's a precursor to sex, unless it's a kiss with intention. It's gravity and momentum and undertow and a river's unceasing current, dragging moment by moment.

I turn aggressor, slipping my tongue into her mouth, committing to this kiss without equivocation. Her lips feel so different from Rebecca's, more nimble for starters. Jennifer's lips move side to side while she kisses me, strafing my mouth, her tongue lingering whereas Rebecca's tends to dart. And this, this moment of analysis walks in front of the motion sensor in a dormant part of my brain and triggers the floodlights. I know exactly how Rebecca will respond when I slide a hand to her breast, but I don't yet know what this new person will do.

And I want to know. While I'm already here, I have the half-formed thought, I should discover everything that I can.

I move my hand to her breast and Jennifer bites down on my lower lip, hard enough to elicit a flinch. So there's a discovery. I pull my head back and our eyes meet. It's a dumbstruck moment, no longer than an intake of breath, when we stare into one another. If I'm supposed to see my wife and child, my comfortable life, my future all the way to death, I don't. If I'm supposed to see a button marked either RESET or SELF-DESTRUCT, I don't see that, either. I see two eyes looking back at me, and my brain doesn't form any thought more complex than noticing that her eyes are blue, without producing an adjective to narrow the description from there. The thought of what she must see in my eyes at that moment never crosses my mind. After that moment passes, we move our heads toward each other once more, both complicit, in percentages to be determined later.

We end up horizontal in her bed, still clinging and kissing, hands everywhere. She's worked my shirt over my head and I've yanked her skirt down by its elastic waist. Clothing piles up on the floor, some articles we take off ourselves, some off each other. She demands the whole time that I look her in the eye as she tugs my pants and boxers off in one motion; as I unhook her bra, she grabs my jaw and forces me to look her in the eye, as if committing to the act, acknowledging that this is not an accident, that I am not pasting another face onto hers.

"Look me in the eye," she hisses, one hand gripping my face, the other hand lower, the first hand on my cock that hasn't belonged to either my wife or myself in longer than I can calculate right now. Her eyes are closed, her head tilted back, exposing her neck. One of my hands is partially inside of her, and I realize that I did this without asking (was I supposed to ask?). "Look me in my eyes," she says again, snapping me to attention. I grab her hand off my face and clutch it; the pressure on her fingers makes her wince.

"You look me in my eyes," I hiss back.

The sin is ours, Jennifer Sayles. Neither one of us gets to say later that this happened while I had my eyes closed.

The sex itself is furtive, passion not begetting coordination. I fall back on a few standard moves, she grips my hair and bites my nipple, which no one has ever done to me before, so that's new. Her body is different from Rebecca's, more light, more lissome; the feeling is less like being enmeshed than being swallowed. I'm falling back on dorm room etiquette, touching gently to see if I'm encouraged to touch more, entering her slowly and waiting for her to request a more furious effort. She's drier than Rebecca, and that comparison, more than any other moral aspect of this, makes me go momentarily soft. But we rally, we have sex, actual sex, vanilla save for the rings on our fingers that we didn't give to each other. Jenny arches her back and groans in huffed grunts, like she's climbing stairs and enjoying it. I can't tell if she came or not, and I'm too tense to go over the falls myself. Rebecca likes to talk a bit during, to check in with one another and ask tiny, almost silly questions. *Do you like this? How does this feel? Where are you ticklish?* Jenny is all business, silent save for the sex noises, and the slapping of her hands on my chest.

Finally, by letting my mind go vacant, I come, shuddering, so hard I take myself aback. I will never love any feeling more than that. We catch our breaths, Jenny underneath me, sweat from my forehead dripping onto her neck. "Did you just come inside of me?"

Jesus Christ, I did. Not a condom ever considered. Rebecca and I stopped using them years ago and it simply never occurred to me, and now my mind floods with all the ramifications, as if I'm back in college, the reality of repercussions cutting through an alcohol haze. "I'm sorry."

She pauses, then bursts out laughing. "You look so terrified!" She throws her head back and laughs until tears are streaming from the corners of her eyes. I spill out of her, limp, and assess the stain on the sheets. "I have to wash these anyways." She sits up. Again, she grips my jaw and makes me look her in the eye. "I'm not going to get pregnant. I'm just not. You can trust me on that."

Seems poor manners to bring up diseases. Instead, I lay next to her on the bed, expect some further discussion, but Jenny springs up and pats my stomach; she goes off and the pipes mimic our noises a second later so I wait while Jenny does whatever mysterious things women do in the bathroom after sex. When she comes out she stands unself-consciously before me and I see her body in full for the first time. Her breasts are smaller than Rebecca's, the left slightly fuller than the right, but her stomach is a flat plane, still taut. She's assessing me back as I sit up on her bed. Her eyes dwell around my fleshy parts, my bony parts, my doughy parts, the rim of fat around my middle, the dead snail exhaustion of my post-coital cock.

She throws on shorts and a T-shirt and instructs me to get dressed, then meet her outside. I'm left alone in her room, on wobbly legs, and I buttress myself against the dresser while I gather up what the fuck I just did, what these discoveries bought me. I'm fairly certain any favors I was doing for Paul have been nullified by the past twenty minutes. There aren't any pictures of him, of him or of them, in their bedroom. It's reassuring to know that he wasn't watching us on the bed he will later sleep on.

I sit back down on the bed, next to the telltale puddle. Has Rebecca ever fucked another guy on our bed? I don't think she has. I don't think she's ever made a stain like this with anyone but me since we started dating. And now I have. There isn't the electricity of anxiety in my body, in my mind. Not yet. If it comes later, it comes later. Right now my body slowly reassembles itself while my mind assesses from a respectful distance, surprised at the turn the married-and-a-parent-in-my-early-thirties experiment has taken.

She's laid two fresh Campari and sodas out on the front steps next to the empty bottle. "The last of the summer." She smiles, handing me my glass. "I think I'll go with the birch natural oiled and the top color on that lighter blue one. Do you know which one I'm talking about?"

"Fog. I think it's called fog. If that's the one you picked."

"Maybe. Go with bright colors. If you think something else would work better, go with it."

"But it's your choice," I point out.

"And I've made it, but I respect your opinion."

We look at each other knowingly, though what it is we now know I'm not sure. Jenny offers me a cigarette and I accept it. I haven't smoked in a while. It's foreign and familiar, inhaling and choking. Jenny and I sit and stare at the park across from her house while sipping the last Campari and soda of the year. "What's your drink for fall?" I ask.

My phone rings before she can answer. I take it out of my pocket and see Rebecca's and Jackson's faces pop up, and every movie and TV show I've ever seen says that seeing their faces should fill me with immeasurable self-loathing, because I am that guy. I'm that guy, only less handsome. Still, I don't feel any differently about it than I would have two hours ago. This is my wife and son; my wife is calling me. I don't separate out a before from an after, at least not yet, though I grant that I may change how I feel, without any self-inflicted penalties. I'm giving myself grace, the methadone to the heroin of forgiveness.

"Hey, pretty lady," I answer. Her voice responds tight, tearful, as if she already knows what I've done. I can hear shrieking in the background.

"I need you to come home right now."

"I'm on my way," I reassure her; always reassure her first. Jenny picks up both glasses from the step. I ask into my phone, "What's the matter?"

"It's Jackson," she says. "Something is wrong."

Michael Gould

Eleven Months Ago: August 30, 2009

I sprint to the train, leaving my backpack holding all the samples back with Jenny. She didn't require an explanation, waved me off from her front step like dismissing a jester who no longer amused her, or as if I had planted the phone call to extricate myself, that while I was putting on my clothes I quickly texted my wife, "Hey, I just fucked Jennifer Sayles. Super awkward convo coming up. Can you bail me out in five? Say it has to do with our son."

The first cab I have ever seen in Greenpoint rolls down Manhattan Avenue and stops at the intersection in front of the subway entrance. I take it as a sign from God that if this is an emergency, I should not take the hour-long trip from the train to the bus.

Sitting in the backseat, my address shouted twice, I have another moment to process what I just did. I'm not weighing it yet on a spiritual level, whether I just broke a solemn vow or compromised my morals—I did and I have, there's no going back on that. I had sex with a woman who is, to put it mildly, unstable, and I don't know if this is a revenge ploy she's using against her husband, whether she's going to lord this over me, whether she intends to let Rebecca know. I sniff my arms, my shirt, inhale deep in the back of the cab to see if I can scent her on my body. If this is truly an emergency, even my creepily perceptive wife isn't going to notice, but that doesn't relax me as we wend our way through midday traffic on the BQE.

I burst in to find Rebecca cradling Jackson on the couch, and they're both sobbing. It's incongruous and yet oddly comforting that the apartment still smells of cookies. "He won't stop crying," she explains. "He woke up from his nap and he won't eat and now he won't stop crying."

I take him from her arms and he continues to howl, his little fists balled over his head, quaking. Rebecca has handed him to me because I'm the guy who fixes things, things like pipes and burned-out lightbulbs. I crave the day when Jackson will be able to calmly point to his leg and say, "See how the bone juts out of the skin? It's clearly broken." For now, all he can do is make noise and give me and his mother a collective heart attack.

His open mouth also reveals white patches, like leftover milk. He opens wide to unleash another unholy scream and I see the blotches all over the inside of his cheeks and lips. "It's thrush," I say. Rebecca stands next to me and double-checks my work, disbelieving that I've come up with an answer so quickly.

"But he won't eat."

"Yeah, he's got, like, a yeast infection in his mouth."

Her eyes go wide. "Did I get him sick?"

"No! Jesus, how do I know more about this than you do?"

"Don't talk down to me, Michael," she chides. "What do we do?"

I conjure up a plan, suddenly Dr. Spock. "Go pump. We'll need to bottle-feed him until we get him to a doctor. If it's really bad, she might give us something to rub on those white patches and your nipples. Maybe some Tylenol. It's not bad, Becks. This is one of those things babies get all the time."

"So we need to go to the hospital?"

"It's thrush," I repeat, but it doesn't permeate.

"How serious is that?"

"He doesn't like it. His mouth hurts. It's not fatal. It's not even that harmful. He'll still make *Law Review*."

Rebecca stops crying. Now she's whimpering, her arms across her chest, holding herself. Jackson is slowly winding himself down, cried out. "Go pump."

"He's crying."

"Put him in the shaken baby chair." It's the chair that vibrates. I regret giving it that joke name now.

"But it's not time for his nap. He'll go off schedule."

"Fuck his schedule. I'm going to reserve a Zipcar and then we'll take him to the doctor, see what she says."

"He's going to be all right?" It's heartwrenching how plaintively she asks. I hand him back to her and he lolls his heavy head onto her shoulder. Poor boy is exhausted, overwhelmed by the past hour. It's such a huge portion of his life, even an hour. He doesn't remember a time his mouth didn't hurt. My son is, hopefully only for the time being, like a goldfish.

I reserve us the next available Zipcar and then clean up the past two hours of my own life. While Rebecca pumps I strip off my clothes and throw them into the bottom of the hamper, slip into the bathroom to give myself a quick scrubbing in the shower. I rub soap on my cock hard enough to strip paint.

She's packed his bags and is ready to go when I come out ten minutes later, freshly washed. She's giving me a puzzled look, bordering on disappointed, probably because I just showered instead of kicking down doors until I found the one our doctor is behind. I head off her ire at the pass. "I swear, Rebecca, I'm an only child. You have a sister."

"What does that have to do with anything?"

"Shouldn't you know about shit like this?"

"Jolie is older," she says coldly, vulnerable to my unwise pressing of the matter. "If Jackson ever needs to get off Oxy, I'll know what to do."

"I'm sorry."

"I thought I hurt our son."

"You didn't."

"I was worried I had really hurt him."

"But you didn't."

She's crying again, "I kept hearing Jenny Sayles in my head talking about how she feels like she hurt her baby. I thought she was being dramatic, but now I get it. I thought I hurt our baby."

"Jenny is being dramatic," I reassure. It clicks to me, and maybe I'm just repeating after Rebecca, but somewhere along this day she metamorphosed from Jennifer to Jenny. "Let's go get him to a doctor." Jackson stirs when I take him from the shaken baby chair and put him in his car seat, so I rock it back and forth, surprisingly heavy, and gather Rebecca in with my free arm. Freshly washed, I collect my family and keep them close, corral them in and grip them tight, the day crashing over me like waves breaking, finally over the falls, plummeting toward the rocks below.

Paul Fenniger

Eleven Months Ago: August 30, 2009

First I poke my head into Jeff's office. Jeff is the office manager whose job consists primarily of ordering a variety of folders. He also handles time sheets, including mine, which I fill out every Friday.

"Jeff." He looks up from a supply catalog. "Just a reminder that I have to go early today for an audition."

This does not please him. He makes an exaggerated frown. *Disappointed.* "I thought you did that the other day."

"I did. This is a callback."

"Oh." Now his face contorts into a grin. *Joyful.* Jeff has a face a social psychologist would love. Other lawyers joke that if you can't tell exactly what emotion he is projecting, you're probably a sociopath. "Congratulations."

"Don't have the role yet."

"What's the show?"

"It's called *The Country Wife.*"

He furrows his brow. *Confused.* "Never heard of it."

"By a guy named William Wycherly."

"Is it a musical?"

"No, it's really old."

Mouth into an excited O. *Enthusiastic.* "Like a Greek tragedy?"

"Later than that. I just have to leave an hour early."

Mouth back into a flat line. Eyes dead. *Professionally solemn.* "Clear it with Gregg and it's fine with me."

Gregg is an associate. Like Jeff, he's four years younger than I am, working seventy-hour weeks until he makes partner, which he hopes to do in the next two years. He's decorated his office with as much USC memorabilia as will fit. As the senior associate, he's also in charge of the paralegals, myself included. He is, though he disdains the term, my direct supervisor. Gregg's face doesn't move, at least not in the office. Whether listening to a client or giving me instructions or discussing his weekend, Gregg's face neither twitches nor betrays any emotion whatsoever. Other lawyers joke that he'd be a great poker player. Or a serial killer.

"Gregg, Jeff told me to come see you. I have an audition today so I need to leave an hour early. That okay with you?"

"Second time this week."

"Yeah, it's a callback."

"I don't know what that is."

"It's a second audition. I'm closer to getting the role."

"Is that good?"

"Yes."

He thinks on this, gives it due consideration. The other paralegals are terrified of him, but Gregg and I have a good relationship. He knows I'm not here for the long haul, sees my intrinsic value. In Gregg's mind, at some near point in the future, he'll need to woo a client by taking him to a Broadway show, and I'll be the call he makes to get backstage. "Let Toni know and tell her I cleared it."

Toni sits at the desk in the front of the office, directs phone calls and fetches beverages for clients. "I'm leaving an hour early, Gregg and Jeff both cleared it," I say hastily on my way out the door. She doesn't look up from *Vogue*, but she does wave to indicate she heard me.

A week back, for the first auditions, Ted rented out studio space on the Lower East Side for two hours, a fifth-floor walkup leading to a hallway with doors at opposite ends: one a dance studio with thin walls, and the other a black box theater. While an introduction to tap class took place next door, I read my classical monologue from *The Princess of Elis* for Teddy Gilles, artistic director of the Beehive Theater Company, so named for the London pub he drank in when he first conceived of starting a theater company in the already oversaturated market of New York. For the callbacks, Ted texts me the address, which I recognize as his own. He is going to have me read scenes from the play in his one-bedroom apartment in Alphabet City.

Ted opens the door, greets me with applause. "There you are."

"Am I late?"

"No, just there you are. Come in, come in." He shoos me into his den. The coffee table has been turned sideways, leaving a three-by-three patch of rug upon which he expects Thespis to visit. I glance around—the bathroom door is open, so is his bedroom door. Unless he's hiding someone else, I'm going to be reading scenes with him, which immediately raises my bile. Reading with the person auditioning you is the actor equivalent of performing your own surgery.

"Just us tonight?" I ask.

"Sit down, Paul. Can I get you a drink?" He grabs a beer out of his fridge, twists off the cap, takes a sip, then extends it to me. I decline. "Let's talk about *The Country Wife*. You like the play?"

"I do."

"So do I. Very funny. Still relevant today. Or resonant. Which word do I mean?"

". . . I don't know. I guess either."

"Irregardless, you're fantastic. Your audition was Oliviers ahead of the pack. Long way of saying you're my Horner. If you want to be, of course. I hope you want to be."

Yes, I want to be. A role is a role. Stage time is stage time. Acting in New York means accepting a series of tautologies, but a love of theater is a love of theater.

He continues, "You'll also be a few other people."

"Oh. But . . . Horner is the lead."

"In the regular production, absolutely. But I've decided to do something a little more avant-garde. About a year ago, I saw a production by the Wooster Group, and they employed videography and other metatextual elements to create a more immersive experience."

I'm fairly certain he just used between four and six words incorrectly, but I stay silent and let him continue.

"Why do a regular production of *The Country Wife*? Who wants to come and see that? Instead, Beehive is going to do an innovative three-person production. I'm going to have to chop the text some, but you'll be playing most of the male roles, Elspeth Piery is going to play most of the female roles, and I'm going to find someone totally androgynous to be the third person in any scene where we need a third person. And then, there's also going to be computer monitors onstage, and we're going to make YouTube videos, and those will have prerecorded scene partners, so this play that's about seduction is going to feature different forms that take place in the present day. Isn't that an amazing idea?"

My shoulders sink. Translation: barely anyone auditioned, he can't afford to costume us, so he's going to improvise. A part of me respects the hell out of Ted Gilles. That part isn't being asked to memorize an entire play for a cut of the house. Jenny has been picking up freelance gigs left and right, so at least it won't mean dipping into savings.

"Who else would I be playing?" my weary tongue asks.

This question flusters and irritates him. He shakes his head like scrubbing away a bad idea. "I don't know yet, Paul. But let's do this. I'll try to find some weird space to stage it. It'll be like the Wooster Group, but much cooler."

It's a show. It's a line on a résumé. Always a chance that a blogger will cover it and a junior agent will see it and it could lead to bigger things. When I came to New York, starting small and working my way up to bigger things seemed like a preordained path, the way a student would apprentice under a glassblower until gradually he learned every aspect of the trade and became a renowned glassblower in his own right. Such was my path for acting. Ten years later and I'm still looking for that place to apprentice.

Suddenly I miss my son. It hits me sideways when I don't expect it. I'd like to leave now and be with Jenny.

"Let's do this." I shake Ted's hand.

He leaps off his couch and hugs me, then escorts me out the door, promising to be in touch with a rehearsal schedule and all the other important details, like who I would be playing beyond Horner, as soon as possible. On the steps outside his building, I spot Elspeth Piery smoking a cigarette. I like Elspeth, she's young and blond and hopeful and set a semiserious goal of playing a corpse on one of the *Law & Orders* before she turned thirty. Ted spoke as if she'd already agreed to the role(s), but my guess is that was wishful thinking that he now intends to make a reality, with my name dangled as her opposite. Not my place to blow up his spot, so I make twenty seconds of small talk with Elspeth and jog to the subway.

The apartment smells like a cookout, and two plates of kielbasa and beans steam on the table. My heart swells to see it. I haven't gone to the Polish butcher in weeks, there hasn't been time and Jenny hasn't had the appetite. She must have gone out today, left the apartment and walked the blocks to get this meal.

I move toward our bedroom to get changed but stop at the open door to the nameless room. Formerly the nursery, in time the office. Now it's a project, one I'm paying another man to do, and Jenny stands in the middle of it, the last light of the day sinking through the windows. She has wooden boards in a semicircle around her feet. I wrap my arms around her and she exhales. I kiss her cheeks to find they're dry, and when she turns to me and I see her in half-light, she looks more like the Jenny I remember from a year ago. From years ago.

"You got us kielbasa," I marvel. "Thank you."

"How did the audition go?"

"I got the part."

She vibrates in my arms. "Yay! Fenn, that's awesome. Where is it going to be?"

"Downtown somewhere."

"How downtown is downtown?"

Staten Island? New Jersey? "I don't know. Ted will figure that out. I'll tell you about it over dinner. How did it go with Michael today?"

"He's really good at this." She turns back to the wood samples. "He left these for us to decide. I think we should go with the natural oiled birch for the wood and the fog color for the paint."

"That sounds great." I kiss her lips. She doesn't pull back. She doesn't tense. We're in the very sad room kissing and she's picking wood samples, and it's all going so well that I decide to try something. I decide to push my luck by placing my right hand on her hip, low, enough that my fingers curl around to the top of her bum (she calls it that and I love her for it). She sighs into my mouth and kisses me harder. This is the Jenny I know, and I've missed her so very badly for so very long. The past two months have been the worst of my life, and with one kiss she's dangled the rope down the well to pull me back out.

We break the kiss, and she brushes my hair out of my face. "I want you to fuck the daylights out of me," she says, and laughs. And I laugh, because it's an old line between us, an inside joke, a catch-phrase, a password and song lyric and psalm and antidote.

"I can do that," I say my line back. Then I carry Jenny Sayles into our bedroom, where she's laid fresh sheets and lit vanilla-scented candles; she's been three steps ahead of me this entire time. And I place her on the bed, a starring role and cold kielbasa and the home of my heart coming back to me in one fell swoop.

Paul Fenniger

Present Day: July 19, 2010

11:59 AM

It finally sinks in what the surface must be like. No one in the East River tunnel speaks above a whisper, but their voices carry, and only the most delusional still think track fire or some other innocuous inconvenience. Above our heads we see buildings falling and fires spreading. We see our city laid to waste. Even the small footprint of a dirty bomb or a downed helicopter is cause for mass casualties. In our mind's ears we hear sirens, drones swarming to the hive, to recover and stitch and save what can be salvaged. And tonight, there will be a chasm of sadness and grateful relief for those who survived. The knowledge of what has happened above us shortens our steps on this cautious walk.

Whatever apprehension I feel is mitigated by the security that Jenny's on the right side of the river. There's simply no way she made it to Manhattan and I didn't, short of stealing a car or hijacking a boat. If they have routed us back toward the Bedford Avenue stop then the danger must be behind, not ahead of us.

Jenny must be scared that something has happened to me. Or she isn't, and I've earned that. I understand why she'd be on the fence about me still. If she's worried, my Jenny drowns her guilt in morning cigarettes and breakfast screwdrivers.

Can't say for certain where Michael is at this point. He may be back in Red Hook, standing on the roof of his studio, watching pandemonium from afar. Or he may be flattened under a very large piece of building, splattered and wafer-thin like a cartoon character. I can't decide which I'm hoping for.

A wiry, shirtless man does a backward weave through the stragglers to the rear of the pack, where I keep a slow pace. "Think we can smoke down here?" he asks me.

"Probably shouldn't. In case it's a gas leak." My voice takes on the tone of authority. I have no idea what put the ramrod straight spine into my throat.

"It's not a gas leak. This is some false flag bullshit. It's something designed so that they can restrict civil liberties and no one will complain because we don't want another July Nineteenth. I'm Carl." He extends his hand out across his body. It hits me in the chest, like a branch, until I find it and shake it once. "I saw you helping people off the train."

"Yep."

"What made you do that?"

"I don't know." I try to size him up in the gloom, whether or not he has muscle tone, whether he looks dangerous. From what I can tell, he's barely three-dimensional, but to reassure myself that I'm not about to get shivved by someone who thinks I'm on the "inside,"

I take a misstep and stumble into him, gentle enough to not send him sprawling, but enough that he would have to deal with my weight. I jostle his shoulder and he goes into the wall of the tunnel, kicking the third rail along the way. He's waifishly thin, so he's less of a threat. "I'm so sorry," I say, offering my hand to the darkness.

"It's okay, I can't see shit down here either."

Carl falls back in step with me. "Listen, I don't mean to come off like I'm crazy. About the conspiracy stuff." I don't reply, still walking forward, keeping pace, the old and infirm in front of me, following the waving flashlight some quarter mile in the distance. People turn to look at us, but we're practically invisible to them, just two inky blobs floating in the blackness. "I think I'm just stressed about not knowing."

"Bothers me too," I try to soothe.

"I have three different devices in my apartment that can tell me almost anything. My boyfriend and I were debating this the other night, the limits to what information is out there. And I asked him to name a celebrity, any celebrity. He said Kevin Costner. And I bet him that I could find out, from our couch, what Kevin Costner had to eat within the past week. Maybe not for breakfast that morning, but some meal within the last seven days. So I do a search and it takes me thirty seconds to find someone tweeting that they sat next to Kevin Costner in some restaurant in Los Angeles. And then they followed it with a tweet about what he ate. I can find all sorts of shit like that and I don't even know what's going on above my head right now."

"We'll find out soon enough."

"How fucking crazy is that, though? There has to be a condition for this, that we can't deal with less than total information. It doesn't even need to be good information, I'd take eyewitnesses who know somebody who saw something. It's even more pronounced in kids. We need to know everything at all times, or our skeletons will leap out of our skin."

The people in front of us pause, but I don't realize this until I crash into the back of an older man, redeem myself by catching him before he falls flat on his face. There's a low, angry rumble above us. Everyone pauses, holding breath in our chests in case it's the last breath we take. Carl reaches out and grips my shoulder. I clutch the man in front of me, who grips my forearm back. We're trying to fuse ourselves together, assemble into something terrifying and powerful, be mightier by size than whatever is making that sound, like the vibrations of the lowest note on a piano.

This is it. This is it.

The growl of the space around us grows louder. People moan and heave sound, too scrambled even to scream, or the scream is starting in the bowels and working its way up to peak volume.

The tunnel is collapsing. I clench my eyes shut, brace myself, hope that the water somehow spits me out at Bedford. I think of Jenny. I make sure my last thought is of Jenny. I think of my parents, see flashes of their faces, a checklist of the people in my life that I've loved. That I've truly loved. My mother. My father. My son. Jenny. And Jenny. I come back to Jenny. I see her face, laughing. Head back, laughing from the throat, biting my ear on the couch because she's bored. Then laughing. That's the image to die on. The rumble rises to its fever pitch. Now the screams start. A thousand of us in the tunnel yell, and cry, and wail, but no one runs. Not a single person runs from what comes next. Given fight or flight, we accept fate.

And the rumbling stops. The only water I feel is the sweat pouring off my face. Shrieks give way to tears. The feet start up again. I open my eyes. Jenny's face dissolves and the blackness of the tunnel returns. Carl takes his hand back. I let the man in front of me go.

Then a voice, from a hundred feet ahead, says, "Let's keep moving."

No, it's just the echo that makes it seem so far away. It's my voice, carrying over everyone, stage-trained to reach the cheap seats. I can't see whether people are listening, but I can hear it, starting with a shuffle forward from Carl.

One foot in front of the other. A fresh stench of urine now wafts through the air. Images flit through the mind's eye: people screaming, people running, helicopters descending into the middle of intersections, police in riot gear, the National Guard carrying AK-47s down Broadway and Madison and Delancey Street in Humvees. One foot in front of the other, back to Brooklyn. The rumbling has stopped. Safe in the tunnel. Jenny is okay. Jenny is okay. Jenny is okay.

"Your boyfriend back in Brooklyn?" I make small talk to get out of my head. The words still don't feel like they're coming from my mouth.

"No." Carl sighs. "He goes into work at seven every day. He works on Wall Street. When I get to the surface the first thing I'll try to find out is whether or not the old jerk's still alive."

I can't make out Carl's expression in the dark, so I don't try.

Michael Gould

Present Day: July 19, 2010

11:50 AM

I'm a dying animal, panting and lumbering toward a cool, dark corner in which to die. I squint under the ridiculous sun and sniff the air for the silvery scent of water. I don't even have the energy to lash out at people standing in the way of my zombie shuffle through Morningside Heights. I fantasize about bowls of chilled soup, cold lunch meats, salads slathered in dressing, the cubed ham like life rafts.

Still north of the park, my energy stores are running critically low. All that's gone into my face today are two bottles of water and the granola bar I ate a hundred blocks ago. Rebecca keeps logs of cookie dough in the freezer, and more than anything right now I would like to saw off two thick slabs and use them as the bread for a peanut butter and jelly sandwich, to be devoured without shame. Let her film me if she wants to, this disgusting sweaty shitpig eating a raw cookie dough hoagie. I'm that starving.

But I'm also down to four dollars. The ATMs, and I've tried a bunch, still don't work. Stores haven't yet hit their charitable place, wherein they respond to mass tragedy by handing out Luna Bars and Naked Juice in Dixie cups to people passing by. I duck into a bagel store north of Columbia, on Amsterdam. I've been drifting eastward when the lights oblige, trimming time and distance whenever possible. I scan the menu and realize the only thing I can buy that will leave me with enough money left over to buy another bottle of water is a bagel with nothing on it. I want to mash my face into the cream cheese, hold it there for the sheer relief against my skin, but I'd settle for a dozen of those doughy motherfuckers.

With the sun glowing through the windows, it also takes me a tick to realize that all of the lights are out. All of the cream cheeses in the dim display cases are gray, with a sheen skimming the top. The lightboards behind the counter are down as well. I peer back out the windows and see the lights are on across the street, but there's no food on that side and I need to eat now.

The young cashier behind the counter waits for my approach, distaste on his permasneer. He's fashioned a sign reading ONLY CASH from receipts and taped it to the register. "What bagel has the most calories?" I ask him. He raises a pierced eyebrow and turns to look at the bins. Plain. Egg. Sesame seed. Do sesame seeds have more calories than poppy seeds? A seven-grain bagel is essentially a plain bagel with oats glued to it; will that provide a bigger meal than cinnamon raisin?

To his credit, he takes my question seriously. "Probably jalepeño cheddar."

"Can I get one of those, please?"

"What would you like on it?"

"Nothing, just by itself."

He huffs, aggrieved, as if paid on commission, as he yanks a slip of wax paper from a box and grabs a bagel from the bin, throws it into a paper bag. "Eighty-five cents," he says. I hand over one of my last four dollars and hold up my empty bottle of water.

"Listen, I've got a long walk ahead of me and I'm out of water. Can you please refill this?"

He points at the darkened refrigerators behind me. "We have bottled water."

"I know, but I only have three dollars left and I have to walk to Brooklyn. All of the subways have stopped. Can you do me a solid and fill it from the tap?"

"I can't, my manager won't let me. I'm sorry." He shakes his head but a smirk finds its way to the corner of his mouth. He looks behind me, but there's no one else in line, no one else in the store.

I'm bigger than this man. I'm bigger than he is and I can take what I want. Might makes right in an emergency, and this qualifies. There's a camera over his head; we both glance at it at the same time. If the power is out, then the camera is out. My veins pump adrenaline in coughing spurts, workstrong hands clench and unclench at my sides.

"How long has the power been out?" I ask.

"Comes and goes."

"Do you know what's going on downtown?"

"Nope. Wi-fi is down. I keep hearing shit, though. People coming in with theories and shit. Classes got canceled, so that's all I know."

"Classes?"

"At Columbia?"

"Do you go there?"

"Yeah." He turns his jaw up to me at that. Slave to chasing the round doughy dragon today, a titan of industry tomorrow. Someday, I'll work for this philosophy major, his sneer tells me, and meanwhile I can take my empty water bottle and unadorned bagel and fuck myself.

I take three deep breaths, right in front of him. He looks past me again but it is still just me and him and an entire police force dealing with a level of fuck we cannot begin to fathom a hundred blocks south of here. Everything I do, I could get away with.

Short of murder. I cannot murder this man. "Must be really bad."

"The entire subway system is shut down?" he asks.

"And the buses. Probably a terrorist attack. That's why everywhere that people can congregate is shut down. That's why cell phones aren't working. They turn off the towers to prevent people from detonating bombs with cell phones." I've never met the man who spoke through my mouth just now, but he sounds like he'd be intense at a party. I add, more in my own voice, "Only way to get around is on foot."

"Shit."

"You live around here?"

"Like, ten blocks away."

"How much longer is your shift?"

He checks his watch with the same placid disdain he's done everything else since I set foot. "Another hour. I've been here since six."

"Maybe it'll be fixed by then," I offer. He nods, seems to appreciate that glimmer of hope. One more deep breath. One more attempt at the standards and practices of civil society. Then, I decide, glaring at him, I am going to get into my first physical altercation since puberty. "Come on," I implore. "Fill up my water for me. Everything is fucked everywhere today. Please, help me out."

He takes my bottle from me, looks at it dolefully. Then he hands it back, leans across the counter, and lowers his voice. "Can't let you back here, but we have a bathroom, you can fill it up from the tap." He's slides a key attached to a block of wood across the counter to me.

In the cramped bathroom, next to the cleaning supplies, in pitch-blackness, I feel my way around the sink and angle the bottle until I've filled it halfway, then cup my hands as a makeshift funnel until my bottle is full again. After that, I crack the door enough to give myself light to see the toilet. I manage to pee a little as well, glad that I'm not so dehydrated my body can't spare a bit. There's a terrified moment as I flush, questioning whether I will, at some point today, need to drink my own pee to survive. Is that what today will come to?

I thank him by dropping a dime and nickel into the tip jar, getting the desired huff of dissatisfaction as gratitude. On the street outside, with the sun beating down on me, I chew half the bagel slowly, savoring as much as I can while the peppers scald my tongue and make me gulp water to work the lump of bread down my throat. Half does nothing for me; I don't have the willpower to stop there. Cramming the remaining half into my mouth, I add as little water as I can spare. I am a wild animal uncaged. I am stronger than this city, and I will step over its ruins to take what is mine and ford the East River with the bodies of those who oppose me. Fortified by boiled dough and lukewarm water, my hunger temporarily sated and my thirst slaked for the time being, I continue my strange pilgrimage with a hulking ursine gait.

Michael Gould

Ten Months Ago: September 4, 2009

I plan to be married to Rebecca for the next fifty to sixty years. Barring unfathomable tragedy, we will grow old together. In that time, we will cook and eat tens of thousands of meals together. We will tell each other innumerable jokes, comfort each other as our parents die off, tend to each other as our bodies fail. It's mapped out in front of us, this future, like a well-tended path, void of cracks. At the end of those sixty years—because let's be optimistic and anticipate sixty—only one of us will have been faithful for the entirety of the marriage. I can't see that blemish tainting the entire portrait.

As of right now, I've slept with a woman who is not my wife. Once. That's the semantic argument I make to myself over a donut and coffee, sitting legs tucked under in a booth at a Polish bakery five minutes from Jenny's place. The bars aren't open this early, or the two I passed were not. But I couldn't go straight to the apartment, so instead I've bought a donut that is the best fucking donut I think I've ever eaten, from a grim woman with broad Slavic features and an air of contempt for me, as if she could hear my internal monologue and judged me for it.

Admittedly, I should have called. Or texted. But I haven't. I'm going to walk to Jenny's (and Paul's—I keep leaving him out of the equation, as if he's the variable, not me) apartment, and I'm going to knock, and Jenny and I are going to address what we did. Because we did it. I did not seduce her. I definitely did not force myself on her. I slept with another woman, and she slept with another man, and that merits further discussion. I finish the donut, but I have half a cup of coffee left, so I get up and buy another.

"Was so good I'd like a second," I tell the woman, who still doesn't smile at me. When I pay I smile at her, broad and bright, locking it in place as she hands me my change, and I don't move from the counter until she finally gives me a perfunctory grimace back, but it feels like a victory. I take the first bite of my second donut and contemplate a third.

It's intensely stupid to think that a couple will remain monogamous for the duration of the relationship. Every argument for that involves comparing humans to swans, or exalting boilerplate vows. The only reason people stop fucking outside of the marriage, I believe, is that the hassle is greater than the payoff. If I had to flirt with Jenny, and go on dates, and charm my way into her bed, like I had to do with Rebecca, there's no way I would ever have slept with her. Pressing a new body against mine triggered all the usual responses, the responses I'm supposed to have, or at least the ones I'd otherwise have to go to great lengths to suppress, and I did a human thing. I get that, presented with the same scenario, Rebecca wouldn't have gone to bed with Paul. She'd have brushed him off, politely at first and forcefully a moment later. Her math has a stronger moral element than mine.

I break the donut into three remaining pieces and contemplate the next step.

Scenario A: Jenny, irate that I didn't get in touch with her after mashing my boy parts into her girl parts, kicks me out and fires me, but as she too committed adultery (what a stupid, biblical term—if we committed *adultery* then it's because we had *intercourse*), she keeps her mouth shut. I claim to Rebecca that they decided not to change the room or realized they couldn't afford me even at a steeply discounted rate; Jenny tells Paul that she fired me because she wants the room to stay the same and to save their money, and what happened five days ago evaporates over time. I never see her again, Rebecca never knows, and I don't need to worry about it until I'm old and demented and making deathbed confessions. *On the plus side:* My marriage stays intact and my crime goes unreported, victimless. *On the minus side:* Well . . . put a pushpin in there.

I set the first piece of donut aside.

Scenario B: Jenny, again irate, decides that she doesn't mind assured destruction so long as it's mutual, tells Paul, tells Rebecca, and now it's a known known. Rebecca is crushed. But it happened once, and I own up to it. Rebecca makes me get tested for the suite of STDs, then I absorb the scorn of a marriage counselor, and we move on, though with past indiscretions hanging over my head during every future fight. *On the plus side:* Rebecca is in too much debt to my parents to leave me, she's not going to raise Jackson on her own, and given her history with Jolie, a one-time mistake is far preferable to a pathology of atrocious decision making. *On the minus side:* I might get the shit kicked out of me by a larger man, my wife will hate me for a while, and I'll get to hear chestnuts like "once a cheater, always a cheater" in my head, in Rebecca's voice, long after I stop hearing it in my ears.

That piece of donut joins the first.

Scenario C: Jenny, not irate, nevertheless realizes that while what we did wasn't a mistake—we didn't stumble, we weren't drunk—it cannot happen again. I finish the room, awkwardly tiptoeing around Jenny and Paul, and then, because we're already united by this fucking writing office, we continue to hang out as couples, so I see every few months the woman I cheated on my wife with, and she sees the man she cheated on her husband with. Or her partner, whatever bullshit term they co-opted. *On the plus side:* Again, I get away with it, more or less. *On the minus side:* An itch was scratched. Something happened five days ago, something I stayed awake struggling to process after we got back from the pharmacy, after Jackson finished his bottle and Rebecca collapsed into a motionless sleep. Fucking Jenny didn't make me feel young—that line of thinking is too stupid to dignify. But she did make me feel unformed again, and I hadn't realized how much I missed that feeling. Standing still means that for the rest of my life I'm a husband and a father and a guy who makes furniture while painting on the side, and that all I'll have to navigate from here on out are the small catastrophes like the deaths of my parents, or the inevitable fights about where to send Jackson to school, when to finally move out of New York, or how to finance a car while saving for retirement. Jenny threw a twist into my story, and now I'm reinvested in the plot. That's a . . . minus. Another bite of donut. Another sip of coffee. That's a minus.

I'm all out of donut. I set the cup of coffee in front of me, swirl around the dregs.

Scenario D: I take my phone out and scroll to her number. I tap my finger on the little word bubble icon, a conversation icon, though I may end up "talking" to myself.

> I should have called. I'm sorry. I should
> have called.

I put the phone down and drink the coffee-soaked crumbs from the bottom of the cup. This somehow makes perfection even better. My phone beeps.

Yes, you should have. Or texted.

> I'm in the neighborhood. I was going to
> come by and show you sketches.

OK?

> Is it?

Is it what?

> OK?

Is what OK?

> That I'm going to come by.

Yes, come by. I'll be here.

I stop by the counter one last time before strolling purposefully to Jenny's apartment door. That's where I stand for a few minutes, staring at it, wondering if she's waiting on the other side. I take my phone out again, reread the conversation, try to pick up inflection.

Is she casual, like what happened didn't matter? Or is she rancorous, that I fucked up and she wants to yell at me in person?

Or is she flirting? What am I walking into? I type another message.

I brought donuts.

From Peter Pan?

Is that the bakery on Manhattan Avenue?

With the vaguely hostile waitresses.

Yes, from there.

Good move.

And a deep breath. On the plus side. On the minus side.

Hey, you mind if I try something bold?

. . . ?

It may just be cheesy, or stupid, and it
might be entirely unwelcome, but it's
bold.

You have good text etiquette. The editrix
in me appreciates it.

Is that a yes?

It's a go ahead and be bold. The worst
you can do is embarrass yourself and
you've already done that.

153

Are you any good at math?

Oh I can already tell what comes next is
going to be bananapants ridiculous.

Then play along. Are you good at math?

Yes, I'm good at writing and editing and I
know how to use a semicolon; I'm also
quite skilled at math.

I have an equation for you.

You + Me = Happiness?

Not that one.

Go ahead. Let's hear it, as it were.

Clothing < what you are wearing when I
ring the doorbell.

Oh. My.

And now there's proof. And if it comes out, if the nuclear scenario happens and Jenny spills, then I can show this to Rebecca, after she knows, well after she knows, and show her that this was about sex. I didn't love Jenny, or want her more than I want Rebecca. This was me as a horny adolescent, doing something unconscionable that I will never do again, and that I'm so, so sorry. With bag in hand, I ring the bell and wait.

The buzzer lingers, lets me in. I push open the door and walk upstairs to the second floor, past her unseen neighbors. When I get to her door it opens slowly, but she's not standing in front of me.

She's standing behind the door, because she's wearing less than clothing. The first thing she does is take the bag of donuts from my hand and place it on the table behind her. The second thing she does is lock the door and put the chain on.

The third thing she does is start an affair with a married man.

Michael Gould

Nine Months Ago: October 31, 2009

There exists, because I have seen it with my own eyes, a photograph of Rebecca and Jolie, both plump as rabbits, in matching white lace dresses, sitting in a red, rusty-handled wagon, crammed in next to a well-packed bale of hay, holding hands and grinning with every Chiclet tooth on display. Their parents bought them a session of child glamour shots, and so the two girls were primped and buffed and later airbrushed into what resembles a glossy shampoo ad for WASP children. Rebecca doesn't like to acknowledge that she loves this shit. The changing of diapers, the successful tuck-in, the tutoring, the sex talk, the advice giving, the college move, walking him down the aisle—all of that gets to be more or less public pride. She'll win Mother of the Year from whatever committee decides it, but only if they don't discover her abiding love for the uncomfortably staged shot. She buries this part of herself in a drawer next to all affections she deems shameful, like corn chips and Southern Comfort and carnival games and swallowing. I know her dark secret though, that a teaspoon of her glee in motherhood centers around dressing up a living doll and taking pictures of it. Jackson's first Halloween finds him glowering, uncomfortably stuffed into a costume Rebecca stitched together from patterns she downloaded, sewing yellow window after yellow window onto gray fabric deep into the night so that her son could spend his first Halloween as the Empire State Building, a landmark we have never visited and have no intention of ever visiting.

"He looks like a penis," Jolie comments. Rebecca slaps her arm. She insists, "He doesn't. The hat part is pointy."

"He looks like an uncircumcised penis. Trust me, I've seen a lot of dick. The resemblance is uncanny." Jolie looks to me for confirmation. Of what? That I too have seen a lot of dick? Or that my wife has dressed our son up like one? Now Rebecca is looking at me as well, so this is no longer rhetorical.

"The windows make it look more like a building," I offer.

"A diseased dick," Jolie counters. Rebecca clicks her tongue at both of us, snaps away as Jackson struggles mightily to get the spire hat off his head. My phone vibrates in my pocket.

> We just got trick or treaters dressed as
> sexy Klansmen. Seriously.

> Pointy hats and . . .

> . . . Garters.

"Who are you texting?" Rebecca asks.

"Jenny Sayles," I reply, nonchalant, nothing to hide.

Rebecca absorbs the world's pain into her eyes. I should admire her empathy more than I do. "I'll bet Halloween is hard for them."

"Yeah."

I saw Jenny yesterday. I'll see her again in two days. We've managed to stretch out the design process three sessions longer than the one it required, claiming Jenny's discerning and fickle eye. Once the drawings were settled, the painting began. I've been painting the same walls for the past two weeks, double-primed and two coats of fog.

She makes me wait after I come, wants to feel me going soft inside of her, retreating slowly. Rebecca doesn't expect me to flee as if her vagina is on fire but makes no similar requests, so after a few times of finishing and exiting, Jenny forced the issue by grabbing my hips and yanking me back into her. "Stay for a minute," she purred. "I just had an orgasm."

I'm learning her demands. Her etiquette. Does she expect me to speak?

"Good," I venture.

"Could you tell?"

"No."

"No?"

"Not for certain. I never can," I admit. "I just assume if you have sex with me again then I must do something right, so I kind of do my thing and see how you respond and go from there. But it worked?"

She laughs. "It worked." She strokes the side of my head, running a fingernail through my hair, down my ears, tweaking my earlobes. She says, "I knew girls in college who bragged about how well they could fake an orgasm. Like it was an acquired skill, akin to making a pie crust or mastering the double stitch. My roommate brought it up once and a bunch of girls nodded their heads like she spoke truth to power, like a passcode for this sisterhood of forced moans. Some claimed they didn't fake the orgasm, per se, but their enthusiasm, that they turned *la petite mort* into *le grand mal*, thrashing and shrieking. Others confessed to faking orgasms whole cloth."

"And what did you say?"

"Nothing. I kept my mouth shut. I listened and pretended to be passively in on the conversation. I've never faked an orgasm in my life. Fuck that. My body responds. I don't have mental hang-ups and I'm not sexually blocked from some meddlesome uncle. Everything works if you're competent. Obviously. I'm supposed to offer positive reinforcement when you don't deserve it? I'm supposed to pat you on the head for a mediocre job? Who does that benefit? Stupid fucking girls. Can't even figure out the right things to lie about."

Rebecca snaps pictures while Jolie props my son up in her lap. He enjoys none of this. "Michael, you hold him," Rebecca instructs. I tuck my phone away and cuddle my boy close. He starts crying, and it's not his hungry cry, nor his dirty diaper cry, nor his exhaustion cry. This is a pure *fuck you* howl, so I grin as wide as my cheeks go for Rebecca to take one for framing. *Click.*

It isn't just sex, I remind myself. It's not a Douglas Sirk movie come to life, with bored housewives and jaunty charmers. For the first few weeks it was the safe space where we dwelled, a green zone in the vicinity of the bed. We talked but avoided topics, listening to the notes we weren't playing. She didn't mention Paul; I didn't mention Rebecca or Jackson. I told her stories of growing up in Brooklyn and how it's changed—that filled hours. She talked incessantly about her editorial work.

"How did you get into that?"

"Just something I know how to do," she mulls. "I like correcting the way other people speak and write."

"Seriously."

"I like rules."

"Clearly."

She rolls over onto her stomach, lays her chin on my shoulder. "I used to cook. I used to be a very good cook, actually. And then Paul said *you must be tired, let me cook,* and I said sure enough times that he took over all the cooking, and I'd wash the dishes. Then he'd say *I cooked, I should have to clean up after myself* and I didn't argue, so soon he both cooked and washed the dishes. I thought I'd married a progressive man, so I'd sit and watch him. Who knows? Had it not been for Paul, I might have my own show on the cooking channel. If I keep you around long enough I reckon you'll stifle my dreams of becoming a carpenter."

"What does that have to do with being an editor?"

"I'm really good at it. No one else I know is as good. So it's mine. All mine."

"That wasn't so hard."

"Is our time up, doctor?"

"Almost. Tell me about your novel."

She kicked her legs behind her. "I'm hungry."

"Let's get lunch."

". . . out?"

"Sure. Come on, I'll take you out for pierogies. Fried or boiled."

Jenny chewed me up and spat me out with a look. "You don't need to do that."

"Take you to lunch?"

"Pretend we're a couple. I know we're not a couple." She sounded hurt, and I stammered to buy time, replayed the conversation at warp speed, determine whether I'd actually said anything hurtful.

Finally, I run my hand over her nipple and say, "Just because we're not making more of this than it is doesn't mean we need to make less of it. I like you. Let's get lunch."

This happened. I was there when this happened. When I stopped being able to think of Jenny Sayles as the mistake, early-midlife-crisis-variety-other-woman with whom I was living out some Mr. Bovary fantasy. I saw that door shut and lock and blend invisible into the wall, trapping me on the inside. I was there, in her bed, and I knew it the instant after, a realization so blunt and heavy it should have set off a puff of smoke.

Twins dressed as mice! Twins dressed as mice!

How old?

No clue. Soooooo cute!

"You text like an adolescent girl. My girls at the school, that's how they peck out love notes." Jolie mimics me, unwraps another bite-size Snickers bar. Rebecca can't stand that we give out mass-produced candy instead of her cookies on Halloween, but it turns out all the PSAs we grew up with about random strangers sticking razor blades in anything and everything has birthed a generation of new parents who practically check the candy in front of us.

Rebecca stayed inside with Jackson. Jolie and I sit on the front step, mostly to prevent anyone from ringing the bell, and we hand out candy to the trick-or-treaters of Red Hook. In deference to the troop of monkeys that hang from Jolie's slender back, we sip herbal tea from a thermos. She wears thigh-high tights, cargo shorts, and a T-shirt that says I GAVE MY WORD TO STOP AT THIRD, promoting Abstinence Day. She's got temporary tattoos supplementing actual tattoos, and has drawn a thick, expertly curled mustache on her face. She is, in a manner of speaking, a sexy hipster. She's not going out later, she insists, this is just what she wore to see her nephew, then sit on our front step and hand out candy to our neighbors. Parents have been, for the most part, standing back at the sidewalk and sending their kids forward like panhandlers. More than a few solo fathers have approached, though.

She nudges me again. "Who are you texting? Does Michael have a giiiiirrrrrrrrrrrllllllfriend?"

"Of course. Nothing makes girls wetter than a guy who smells of baby formula and fresh-baked cookies." This either placates her or she grows bored, walking (on spiked heels) to the curb, looking in both directions. "Where the fuck are your neighbors?"

"We've given out a lot of candy. We may be done for the night."

"It's so boring here, Michael. How can you live in such a boring place?"

"Red Hook isn't boring." I bristle. "There's a lot of crime, and it's the first neighborhood to flood in a storm."

"How is my little sister so old? Where was I when that happened?"

Court-ordered rehab? Court-ordered prison? A litany of snotty, mostly truthful answers scroll through. "How are things going with the boyfriend?" She shoots me a nasty look. "Sorry I asked."

"All right, I'm heading to Bushwick. Tell Rebecca I'm off, please. I'll call her."

"You don't want to come up?"

She's shivering, though it's not cold. "Nope. Jackson's probably asleep. Have a spooktacular Halloween." With that, she scampers off and into the night, leaving me perplexed but alone on the front step. I chomp into a Snickers and pull out my phone.

I see you in two days.

I know!

I'm counting the minutes.

That must be very time-consuming.

Let's go somewhere.

Like where?

Like a museum. Or a movie at the very least.

OK.

I want to go somewhere with you.

I'd like that.

I like every minute I spend with you.

No response. I work caramel out of my teeth with my tongue.

> I'm being a cheeseball and thinking about
> you. I think about thinking about you and
> then I think about you some more.

I jam another bite-size candy bar into my mouth as acid roils in my stomach.

> No response? No witty comebacks?

Response bubbles don't appear. My notes sit there like brackish puddles.

> Hate to sound like a high schooler here,
> Jenny, but if you feel the same, could you
> let me know?

I wait. I wait a full five minutes.

Oh God! I was in the shower! Ooooooh nooooo! I could hear my phone going nuts but I was all naked and soapy and missing you. Yes, yes all the same and more. Two days. Two days too long, harrumph.

> Harrumph.

Stay away from ghouls and goblins, Mickey.

She calls me Mickey Gould, like a 1940s gangster. I'm her Mickey Gould. I can't get enough of that name. It's more my name than my own name, I respond to it more readily, with all of my being.

I climb the stairs back inside and leave the half-filled bowl of Snickers on the counter. Jenny might boil them all down and make scrap-heap cookies out of them. I mean Rebecca. Rebecca, who bakes. My wife. Rebecca. Jesus.

Upstairs, Rebecca stands over Jackson's crib. He's back in his pajamas, wrapped up and shaking his little fist in his sleep. His face is the most perfect thing in all of the world. Its shape, its size. My son's face is the reason art was invented. He reminds me that I need to get back to painting. His room is entirely void of abstract expressionism—what kind of Thomas Kinkade bullshit will he get into if I'm not guiding him?

Rebecca wraps her arms around me from behind, stands and spoons me at Jackson's crib, rubs my chest as my breath seeps out in a grateful hiss. She kisses the spot between my shoulder blades. Kisses it over and over and over again until I turn around and kiss her back. And kiss her back. And kiss her back. Her faithful husband, wearing his costume.

Paul Fenniger

Present Day: July 19, 2010

12:50 PM

The noises behind me sound almost like frightened dogs. Sharp, shrill yips. It's the rats retaking the tunnel behind the crowd. They grow bolder, and their scurrying is more audible than our footsteps. Though I see a bit more than shapes, I don't spot the man as I pass him. It's his labored breathing that draws my attention. He's rowed himself to the banks from farther ahead, let the current go past. Now he sits in a carved nook on the side, some dug-out area possibly for the track workers to tuck themselves into when trains pass. He pants. I'm reminded of a Saint Bernard my parents had when I was young, when he was old. When he was dying.

"You okay?" I ask loudly. It reverberates through the tunnel.

"Just need to rest for a minute." His words come out staccato. I put my hands on his chest and he flinches, the social contract among New Yorkers—to be constantly in each other's space yet not deliberately breach it—now broken. I feel along to unbutton the top two buttons of his shirt, constrict his considerable bulk less. He doesn't stop me. While the masses shuffle forward, following that strafing flashlight, I remain back with this man. When he notices that I'm not moving, he pats me on the arm. "You go ahead. I'll be fine."

"I can wait. What if you needed help? No one could find you."

"Someone will be through. It's procedure. They'll look for stragglers. Trust me, I drive a bus." Does he say this for my benefit, or for his own? He hunches over, conserving what strength he has. He mutters, "People will be down here soon enough."

His face is obscured by darkness, nearly invisible. He continues to pat my arm. "Go," he repeats.

"My dad is a bus driver."

He laughs, hacking and sputtering. "No kidding? What's his route?"

"Not here. In Cadott."

"Where the hell is Cadott?"

"Wisconsin. It's small."

"No kidding."

"Yeah, the whole town is like fifteen hundred people."

"My apartment building is fifteen hundred people."

"My dad is the bus driver. The only one. He takes kids to school in the morning, and he does a little route for old folks. He's more like a taxi driver most days."

A bright light catches my eye. Some people have camera phones, complete with flash, and they've been giving the intermittent instant of vision to the crowd. The light hurts like hell and shows nothing new, but still there's a flash every few minutes.

His hand comes to rest on my forearm and he leans farther forward, dragging me down with his weight. He smells sweet, like burned sugar. "Give me a minute," he whispers. I don't know if I can carry him. The alternative is to run ahead, to navigate my way through the sea of people, jostling them in the dark, to get help more quickly. If it's another major disaster in Manhattan, though, every EMT will be on location there. A team of volunteers will be waiting for us on the platform with ice packs. "What does the son of a bus driver do?"

"I'm an actor," I apologize. He rasps out another laugh. Down the tunnel the flashlight beam seems to grow closer, a buzzing of voices making its way back to us. "Look, I'll stay with you. When they come to find you, they'll find me too." My mouth is so dry. I strip off my dress shirt all the way and let it fall to the tracks. I've passed articles of clothing, stepped on jackets and shirts, hats and bags on my way through already. People move into survival mode silently, like slipping into sleep, discarding their vanities and their possessions along the way. No one takes off shoes, though. Even the women in heels. Any layer between feet and ground or feet and rat remains a necessity.

The man no longer argues with me, just leans with both hands on my arm, reaching for his next breath. That he's not clutching his chest seems like the best of signs at the moment.

"What do you think happened?" I ask. Keep him talking.

"I know what happened. Train on train." He coughs and spits to the side. "That's why they're making us walk. Signal failure, two trains get a green light and boom. Terrible thing."

The beam of light works its way back to us and shines in my face. "Come on, hero, you both need to keep moving." It's Perry, the subway worker.

"This guy can't keep going. He needs medical attention."

"A lot of people do. We need to clear the tunnel first." Perry shines the light on the man and I see him for the first time. Swollen and clay red, he doesn't look anything like my father. He looks stitched together and stuffed, his dark skin slick, a puddle of sweat at his feet. "Come on."

"He can't go."

"But you can." Perry takes a step toward me. "Come on. Get out of the tunnel, buddy."

I put my hand on the beam, lower it as gently as I can. This is not the best place to start a fight. Perry hisses, "Hey, asshole, I can't get out of the tunnel until everyone else gets out of the tunnel. That includes you. I'm not going to be held up because your daily Bible verse told you to help those less fortunate. Now get the fuck out of the tunnel and I'll deal with this guy once we're on the platform." He shines the beam into his own face so I can see how far he is from messing around. The man stops leaning on me, takes a wet breath, and leans back into the cubbyhole. I glare at Perry but keep moving forward. A few moments later, he passes me with the flashlight, making his way back to the front, a beacon. He mutters "fucking hero" as he goes by. I look back in the tunnel and the darkness has swallowed the man whole. He's gone.

Paul Fenniger

Eight Months Ago: November 2, 2009

Foh, you filthy Toad, nay now I've done jesting.

"Let's pause there." The three of us turn to Ted Gilles, who stares at his vibrating phone, contemplating his next move. "Break for a cigarette. I need to take this."

Elspeth flops down onto the floor as if dropped by the puppeteer. A thin, flat-chested woman named Marie rounds out the cast, playing all the roles that Elspeth and I cannot. She leans against the exposed brick wall and whips her phone out as well. Anything beyond what the three of us can handle has been cut, characters have been amalgamated, and Ted keeps trying to set up time to film us for the YouTube videos, requesting random, inconvenient times like early Sunday morning. Credit to Ted for one ingenious work-around to our meager budget—his day job is as a real estate agent, so he knows which apartments are empty and has keys to all of them. Every day we get a text message on where to go, and once he's done showing empty spaces, the three of us congregate and rehearse. Tonight we're in an obscenely expensive waterfront condo on the edges of Williamsburg, a new construction that's been halted, waiting for the economy. The lower floors have already taken a more or less final form, as if built by a lazy child with an Erector set. All of the most expensive apartments and all of the cheapest apartments are taken. The unleased midrange is where we strut and fret our hour upon the stage.

Foh, you filthy Toad, nay now I've done jesting. Elspeth turns her face up to me. "Do you think I should do this with an accent?"

"Ask Ted."

"I'm asking you."

I give her my best slow-churn cockney, replete with Johnny Rotten sneer. "Cor blimey."

Marie slinks off to the balcony to smoke. Her view of Manhattan runs panoramic from its southern tip all the way up to Harlem, with only a bridge or two in the way. Elspeth stretches her hamstrings, raising her legs and tugging them back, holding her pose, looking at me catlike and satisfied. I've seen her onstage a couple times, mostly the experimental work she did at NYU and continues to do. She has a perfectly ovoid face, a platonic ideal of symmetry. I assess her as I run my lines, project her career over the next ten years. She already has Ophelia somewhere on the back of her headshot, probably Laura Wingfield as well.

Elspeth and I are getting along well, playfully teasing each other when one of us screws up a line, which happens often, since we've had to memorize the majority of a play. Over cigarette breaks she's been talking about how fluid female sexuality is, building up to the casual admission that she's now dating a woman. Marie remains a tough nut to crack. I haven't had a conversation with her in the past two weeks that has gone longer than three sentences. She lives in Queens. She was born in New Mexico. She likes pizza. I shared these factoids with Jenny and she quipped, "Two truths and a lie."

Ted rallies us back and restarts the scene. Elspeth and I stand opposite one another. I'm playing Horner in this scene, she's Mrs. Squeamish, a woman I am seducing by pretending to be impotent and, evidently, therefore harmless. Marie plays Old Mrs. Squeamish, as well as Sir Jasper Fidget. Ted reads the lines that will be prerecorded, reciting them in a droll monotone that Elspeth says makes her feel like we're acting, for a brief moment, in porn.

"Prythee kiss her," Marie instructs, "and I'le give you her Picture / in little, that you admir'd so last night, prythee do."

"Well," I say, taking a step toward a prim Elspeth, "nothing but that could bribe me, I love a woman / only in Effigie, and good Painting as much as I hate / them—I'le do't, for I cou'd adore the Devil well painted."

I lean forward and kiss her. Ted directs me to sustain it, that I'm kissing her with intent, a rake who is, in the gray areas of Restoration comedy, sexually assaulting a series of semiwilling women. So I kiss Elspeth, who has remarkably soft lips, who holds the kiss and doesn't stiffen when my hands go to her hair, to the back of her neck, pulling her toward me. And then we break.

Something suddenly feels terribly wrong. The room has gone silent, airless, like I've overstepped all professional bounds. I swallow back a wave of nausea, a rush of bile into my throat. Elspeth meets my eyes, but only flicks her eyelashes at me, like erasing a bad memory.

"Foh, you filthy Toad, nay now I've done jesting."

Michael Gould

Eight Months Ago: November 10, 2009

Our code word is *ice cream*. If either of us brings up ice cream at any point, that's a signal to the other that a spouse knows. Rejected code words included *pineapple, narwhal,* and *conjunctivitis.* We decided this a week ago, walking hand in hand through the old site of the World's Fair in Flushing Meadows, Queens, hinterlands where moral laws do not apply.

Hand in hand is something new. We're playacting at couplehood, classing up our movie by giving it a plot, rather than just framework dialogue around sex scenes. I called us fuck buddies and Jenny got genuinely offended, insisted that we were, at the very least, sexual chums.

"What do we do if one of our significant others finds out?" I broached the subject first. Jenny strolled blithely onward, ever closer to the steel globe. I had to ask her twice so that she knew this topic needed some addressing.

"If Fenn finds out, I'll tell him you raped me. If Rebecca finds out, I'll tell her you raped me."

"I'm serious."

"I can tell. You have your serious voice on. It's very monotone. It's your beige voice."

"So take me seriously, and then we can go back to debating what animal you think you could take in a fight."

Her lightbulbs strobe. "We'll pick a code word," she chirps. "And I could fuck up a bear. Kick it right in the face."

That eventually led to *ice cream.* And Jenny demonstrating for me that she could kick a six-foot bear in the face.

I can't envision the scenario in which Jenny tells me she has a strange craving for *ice cream* and I'm not hearing this from underneath Paul's fists, or wherein I tell her that a new *ice cream* place opened up near me and she's not distracted by a howling, sobbing Rebecca, but in the event that we are all together and one of us brings up *ice cream,* the other person has been duly alerted.

Rebecca looks up from the counter. "Do you like ice cream?" She spreads homemade vanilla ice cream between two peanut butter chocolate chip cookies. Homemade cookiewiches. She's making dessert. Always making dessert. Hearing the words, though, registering her question, I'm momentarily taken aback. Does she know? Does she know everything? Is my wife omniscient? "What?" I shoot back, a tad too clipped.

"I can't remember you ever eating ice cream. That's all. Some people don't like cold."

"No. I like ice cream. There are just always cookies."

She smiles. "If you ate ice cream you'd feel like you were cheating on my cookies?"

For fuck's sake, Rebecca. We'd laugh about this if we were capable of laughing about this. Instead I smirk and continue to Swiffer the floor. Jackson kicks his legs in his Pack 'n Play, grunting to himself. He's pooping, the grunts a convenient timer to let me know I have about ten minutes before he'll need changing.

Rebecca strides over, shoves a bite of peanut butter cookie in my mouth. "Tell me if this tastes weird."

I roll the masticated ball around on my tongue. "No. Why?"

"I changed peanut butters. The collective I was buying from raised its prices. I asked if I could be kept at the old price given the volume I buy, and they said no, so I went with a different collective."

"How cutthroat. Gimme more cookie." She obliges me with the rest.

She goes back to spreading, to shaping perfect hockey pucks. "Three years with the same supplier. They thought I would pay it because . . . I don't know. I worked it out. Depending on orders, I'll save between six and eight hundred dollars a year. But it adds up. And . . ." She pauses, gathers herself. For an endless second I think she's about to tell me she's pregnant again. "I'm thinking long-term. Five-year plans and hiring delivery people and expansion."

Rebecca smiles to herself, not wanting to share something so immodest, so gauche, with me, but wanting me to see it nevertheless. It's the look she gave me the first time she ever wore fancy lingerie for me, my cotton-brief girlfriend trying on something with straps because that was what I was supposed to like. It's the look I catch her giving when I'm holding Jackson, proud of herself for forming a perfect baby in her own body. "What changed?" I ask her.

"What do you mean?"

"You've been doing this since you were a teenager. Why now are you thinking big?"

"Not big, just bigger," she corrects. "Some of it is Jolie. She's on her feet now. But a lot of it is you. You and your parents. You've invested time and money in me, and I don't want anyone to think they've just been supporting a hobby. If I have investors, then this is a business, and I should treat it like one." She punctuates with a nod.

"A baking empire," I assess. "You'll be bigger than Mrs. Fields someday very soon."

"I'm going to take that bitch down," Rebecca says. "Now leave me alone, I have to finish these before they get here."

We have company coming. Rebecca insisted, given the amount of time I spend over there, that we invite Jenny and Paul to our house for dinner. She wrote an invitation in cursive on thick paper stock, put it in my hand to give directly to Jenny, who accepted it from me like it was a dead mouse. When Jenny read it, with her face pinched tight, I thought she'd cry, but that's not Jenny's mode. Her eyes go liquid, but they don't spill over, or at least not in front of me. Instead she stared at the invitation, almost sounding out each word, studying it. "I'll need a night to think this over," she told me, like I had offered her a job.

It's not lost on me how difficult this must be for her. For Paul, as well. It's strange how little I consider his feelings now, as if he's her butler. For the both of them, seeing the kids of strangers has to be difficult enough, but Jackson was born the same day in the same hospital, and he's going to be in the same room.

I'm being insensitive by not being reverent the way Rebecca is. Rebecca pumped so that Jenny would not need to see her breast-feed, and so that she can drink with Jenny. Rebecca's goal is to have Jackson asleep and in the next room minutes after Jenny and Paul come in, treading the line between hiding him and appearing like we're hiding him, as if we're worried that they'll abscond with our son. I watch my wife mash dessert together, scrape off the sides, and I'm ashamed of myself, because she is perfect every second and on my best day I'm the sum of my flaws. The doorbell rings, Rebecca shoves the adultery code sandwiches into the freezer and tosses Jackson into the shaken baby chair.

"Welcome." I take Paul's and Jenny's coats, lead them into our apartment. Paul hangs shyly behind Jenny, looking every bit the bed wetter at summer camp. His eyes watch Jenny while her eyes search out my son. Rebecca moved him and his chair to the kitchen counter. His chin glistens with drool, his eyes droop at half-mast, well on his way to his next dream about breasts. Jenny offers a perfunctory smile to Rebecca as she walks past, walks right up to Jackson. He doesn't register her presence, just continues to do his infant thing, build synaptic bridges and ignore the profound moments around him. The room holds its collective breath.

Jenny turns to us. "He's beautiful," she says, and then wipes her cheek where a tear is supposed to go. Paul gives her a hug and they stand over Jackson, cooing at him, making those soft sounds. Rebecca sidles up to me, curling her arm around mine, mirroring Paul's pose.

"I think his diaper is full." Jenny laughs through the crying. Rebecca's crying. My wife, tears already streaming down both cheeks, the world's pain her own, laughs along and picks up Jackson. He fusses in his tiny voice, no longer vibrating, not asleep, and not pressed against a boob. "Can I go change him with you?" Jenny asks.

Rebecca nods gratefully, and the two women go into Jackson's room to wipe away tears and feces. Relieved we're past that, I turn to Paul, "How about a drink?"

"Yes, please." I pour us both bourbon, seems fitting.

While I'm standing over the glasses he strides up to me, his body looming over mine. An arm with definition comes into frame on my left and I lean back and right, dormant playground instincts return at once. He gets close, so red alarms flash in my mind. *Ice cream. Ice cream. Ice cream. Man pummeled as his son has diaper changed in the next room.* But he leans in and says low, "After dinner, could we go get a drink?"

"Just you and me?"

"Yeah, got something I want to talk with you about," he whispers.

". . . okay." *Ice cream. Ice cream. Ice cream. My body found by the warehouses.*

"Thanks. Just make it sound like your idea."

"Is everything all right?" *Ice cream. Ice cream. Ice cream. Arms detached from torso, used as cudgels to beat man to death.*

"Yeah, I don't mean to be so weird. Just—I need some advice."

Advice. Like on whether to castrate you before or after I crush your windpipe. Ice cream. Ice cream. Ice cream.

The women come back. My women, in a manner of speaking. Jenny holding my son. She's got him awkwardly cradled, holding him the way you would a small dog. But she's grinning from ear to ear. And Jackson is fast asleep. "He's going to watch us eat," she announces. "Sort of." Jackson is once more laid in the low hum of his chair while Rebecca, tears dry and jaw set, launches into hostess mode.

Dinner, in two informal courses

FIRST COURSE

Sangria-marinated hanger steak, rosemary potatoes, honey-and-tangerine-glazed carrots. Served with an apology by the hostess for being so "informal," summarily brushed off by the guests as being unnecessary, further apology presented and disregarded, with praise in response that everything smells amazing, finished with heartfelt platitude at just being glad to get together with friends and agreed to with the perfunctory raising of glasses.

WINE PAIRING

An entire bottle of Beaujolais, split between two women

Unlike our first dinner, the conversation moves in fits and starts. I've been cutting and semiassembling the shelves in my studio, bringing them piecemeal to Greenpoint, installing them against the wall and screwing them together, having sex with Jenny, and following it up with a drink at one of Greenpoint's many wonderful bars, but none of these topics seem appropriate dinner conversation. Jenny nudges Paul into talking about the play he's doing, which I could feign interest in, but he balks at discussing it. Evidently experimental theater operates on a code of silence. Rebecca gives an update on the cookie business that occupies three minutes, and then we're silent again, only the soporific buzz of Jackson's chair filling in the empty space. Rebecca has sucked her lips as far back as they'll go; this is her horrified face. I recognize a portion of it in her realization that she doesn't know these two people very well, that she's overestimated their friendship, and a portion that she did not come to the table prepped with a litany of topics to discuss and feels herself to be an inadequate hostess, even though she spent most of the morning with her breasts in a machine.

Rebecca refills the wineglasses once they hit the halfway point. A drunk guest is a chatty guest.

"What made you decide to have a child?" Jenny slices into her steak, asks with her head down. I defer to Rebecca on the answer, it's inevitably hers to give. I would say, were I put on the spot, that having a child, or at least trying to have a child, feels like one of those assignments you're given at the beginning of the semester that you can get done at any time, but it will be due and it counts for 60 percent of your grade. I married the woman; I got the steady income; I built the nest. From there all it took was minimal pressure. Rebecca never made passive-aggressive comments or sighed loudly at other children, just stated plainly that she'd like to try to have a child, and it made sense. I couldn't think of a good reason not to. And I love my wife fiercely and have wide tracts of fertile land in my heart upon which a child can roam. That as well.

And she got pregnant. In sum, I got my shit together, love my wife, couldn't think of a reason to pressure her into an abortion. Hence why I stare at Rebecca for her answer, something more palatable that I can ape.

"I . . . can't remember," Rebecca says, to my surprise. I'm aghast. I actually have to put down my utensil, stare at her like she just made a rape joke. "Don't give me that look of horror, Michael. I grew up taking care of my sister, and I guess I'm just such a homemaker."

"Don't say *homemaker* like it's a dirty word," Jenny chides.

"Sorry. I don't mean it pejoratively. I guess I just couldn't complete that picture I've had in my head until there was a Jackson involved. Baby to teenager, even when he's surly and hates me, it still feels right."

"He won't hate you," I comment.

"He'll hate you more," she replies. "I'm sorry. I wish I could explain it better than that."

Jenny sighs. "Truth be told, once I was pregnant, I wanted a baby for this one. Fenn is just a beautiful man. I wanted to make a smaller version of him, even if it was diluted with a little of me." She reaches across the table and grips Paul's hand. "God, how do you have skin like that? Didn't you have a single zit as an adolescent?"

"I had many." His perfect skin reddens, as does mine.

"So yeah, that's what I liked about the idea of a child. A little Fenn, making the same embarrassed faces at my torrential love." Quick as a snakebite, Jenny flicks her eyes over my way, relishing the mixture of confusion and jealousy and sneering superiority passing like storm clouds across my face.

That's right, handsome man, you have marvelous bone structure. Your genetics sparkle and shimmer. And I'm fucking your wife in your bed. Hang that from the smooth planes of your perfect cheekbones.

DESSERT COURSE
Cookiewiches

WINE PAIRING
An entire bottle of rosé, split between two women. Men share a look and retire to nearby bar for after-dinner beers before evening devolves into drunken shitshow.

It falls to me to find a reason to get Paul out of my apartment and over to a beer. "I'm going to show Paul my studio," I announce. Both Jenny and Rebecca look skeptical. "He'll get a kick out of it." He follows my lead, grabbing our jackets, kissing Jenny good-bye, promising to be back in a bit.

"Are you two going to smoke?" Jenny asks.

"I don't smoke," I reply, raising the involuntary eye roll from Jenny. Rebecca, on the other hand, gives me a knowing look. In her world, guys sometimes need guy time, and Paul and I are leaving so we can talk about our anxieties and fears without censoring ourselves because of women. Conversely, gals need gal time, and Jenny has no idea the penetrative thoroughness of the heart-to-heart she is about to engage in the minute the men leave.

When Paul and I are outside, walking away from my apartment, he glances behind him and asks, "Where are we going?"

"I'm taking you to a bar called Fort Defiance."

"Are we stopping by your studio?"

"No."

"What will I tell Jenny about it?"

I roll my eyes. "Say I forgot my key, so we got a beer instead."

"Oh." Paul takes quick steps to keep up with me. "I'm not good at lying to her. She usually sees right through it. I'm shit at hiding her birthday presents or keeping surprises from her."

I stop and assess this milquetoast man. "This isn't espionage. We're getting a beer. You wanted to talk, right?"

He bites his lip. His entire demeanor says this isn't the ice cream conversation. If he were going to beat the shit out of me, he would have been more excited to get out of the house; he wouldn't have to rush to keep up with me. "Right," he says eventually.

At the bar, I order an IPA and Paul gets a stout. He turns and looks around the space, at the people eating dinner, at the other people sitting at the bar, gives a long look at the bartender. For a brief, horrified moment, I think he's about to make an announcement, and is sizing up the room for how it will be received. But no, he's checking for familiar faces. This is clandestine Paul. I sit, amused, watching him squirm. Did he lose his job? Is that what this is about? Or, it hits me: Is Jenny pregnant again? Oh no no no no no. No. And how long, I sidebar my own internal monologue, will I assume that every pause precedes a pregnancy announcement? When the fuck did that start?

"So what's up, Paul?" my voice strains.

He gives one last pan of the room and tilts toward me. "So I'm in this show." *It's going to Broadway, but I'm worried I can't do it because Jenny is pregnant.*

I nod, deaf to the noise of the bar, numb to everything but Paul's next few sentences.

"It's a Restoration-era sex comedy called *The Country Wife*. And it's this avant-garde production, so I'm playing every male character." *So my masculinity is feeling pretty good now, as evidenced by Jenny's nascent pregnancy.*

"I'm opposite an actress that I haven't worked with before, but I know her, and she's okay. She's a good actress. And I have to kiss her, like, the entire play . . ." He trails off, pushing my train of thought off its rails. Jenny's not pregnant, Paul just has . . . I don't know what.

"So you have to kiss an actress," I goad him on.

"I'm attracted to her," he says quietly. I wait for the next sentence, the gavel sentence, before realizing that's my sentence. I'm the one with sins that turn less jaded heads. Paul has admitted his shameful confession. He's attracted to another woman.

"Are you sleeping with her?"

"No!"

I shake my head incredulously. "Are you kissing her outside of rehearsal?"

"No."

"So you're in a froth because the person you're pretending to be has to kiss another person pretending to be someone else and you like it and you think that's cheating on your wife."

"My partner," he corrects automatically. Again, I roll my eyes, but he's looking everywhere but at me, too embarrassed now that he has dragged me into the actress-kissing closet with him. "I don't think that I'm cheating. Like you said, I'm pretending. It's not Paul Fenniger up there in the holistic sense, right? And I've kissed other women onstage, but this feels different. I'm just not usually attracted to other women like that. It feels unfaithful. That's the word, I feel unfaithful to my partner."

Ice cream. Ice cream. Ice cream. You know nothing of ice cream.

"Paul, look around the room." We take inventory. The yoga-thin blonde poking a fork into duck breast, the brunette two tables down from her who wears slimming black and is showing ample cleavage, the Asian maître d' with the pert calves, the redhead at the bar who looks like she's spent a lot of time at spoken word poetry nights, the waitress who has listened to every indie band of the past five years and has the RCA dog tattooed on the nape of her neck, even the woman sitting next to Paul, behind his sloped back, periodically glancing at the incredibly handsome, ferociously jittery man sitting next to her—I point all of these women out to Paul, making his eyes settle on them. Then I get to my point. "Paul, take consequence out of the equation and add consent, and I would fuck any one of these women."

"That's not the same. We don't know these women. These women are avatars to us. She's a person. The actress. She's an actual person."

I wave his nonsense off. Shut up, Paul. "And by consequence, I don't even mean the whole wife-and-child thing. I mean that at this point in my life, it is too much fucking trouble to even try with any of these women. I know Rebecca's brand of crazy, and I know her brand of difficult, and I've grown so used to both brands that if you changed them up on me, I'd be like *'What the fuck is this? Mr. Pibb?'* I don't have the energy for sneaking around and covering up and all the other bullshit. That's what I mean by consequence. But, much as I love my wife, if any of these women came up to me and offered NSA sex in the bathroom here, and it was *guaranteed* that no one would find out ever, and the only issue I'd have to deal with is realigning my own moral compass . . . I'm going in that bathroom, Paul. The wanting isn't cheating. It's not even infidelity, unless you want to be all batshit Fundamentalist Christian about it. The wanting isn't anything more than seeing something new on the shelves and thinking about how you always buy the same peanut butter and wouldn't it be nice to try something else, before buying another jar of the same fucking peanut butter."

He contemplates this, looking at each of the women again. He's thinking it's about looks, because he's simple, but it's not a looks thing. I like the way Rebecca looks, I like her body, and my desire hasn't waned since she popped out a kid. I am still turned on by my wife.

But the unknown. It's the reason we hate spoilers and read mysteries. Not knowing what comes next spares us the crushing monotony of our quotidian existence. That sounds a little too undergrad existentialist for me, so I bite my tongue rather than convey it to Paul. "I think we're just different," Paul concludes.

"Yes, yes we are," I agree. "Still, it's not infidelity. It's your character kissing her character, and however Paul Fenniger feels about that, it's not de facto, de jure, or any other type of infidelity."

He finishes his beer. I didn't even see him drink it, but it's gone, as if he poured it out when I wasn't looking. I'm still three-quarters full. He starts looking toward the exit, the lie of seeing my studio weighing on him. I take one last gulp and leave it half-full on the bar. On the way back Paul walks ahead of me, agitated steps. As we turn the corner to get back to our wives (or "partners"), he spins on me. "Can this stay between us?"

"Of course," I say, and add in my head *save for Jenny, who I'll tell at some point in the near future.*

"Thank you. You're a friend. A new friend. That's a good thing to have." He laughs weakly. Then his head drops, his chin bangs into his chest. "I can be a bad person sometimes."

"This doesn't make you a bad person."

"Not just this. With Jenny, I . . ." He chokes back the rest of the sentence, like a deathbed confession cut short. It devolves into hiccupped babble. Whatever admission is weighing him down, he can't unburden himself of it here and now. Instead, defeated, he repeats glumly, "I am a bad person."

"No you're not," I reassure. "You only want to be to justify how bad you feel about this thing you don't need to feel bad about." I add in my head *and also because it might finally give you something that makes you interesting, you brittle gelding.* He claps my shoulder and walks on. Behind him, I scan him head to toe, really look at this kindhearted, decent man, and I think that I'm going to take Jenny from him. I'm not a competitive man, and I don't love his wife. But I'm going to amputate this feeble limb from her body. My only challenge is finding a way to keep Rebecca as well, but it's on this night, in this moment, that I decide. She's going to be mine. Mine and not his. Just mine.

Michael Gould

Present Day: July 19, 2010

12:16 PM

I cut across 112th Street, walking in between car lanes. They aren't going anywhere, sitting and honking, trying to get to Riverside Drive, where they'll sit and honk some more. The parking attendants of Manhattan must have had the busiest morning of all, pulling cars out from the bowels of garages for every long-term resident seeking shelter off the island. I pick up snippets of radio as I walk between stalled drivers. The mayor encourages calm, has announced a press conference for six tonight. He asks that New Yorkers avoid going south of the park and above Fourteenth, which means that the police halo is forty blocks large and encompasses literally millions of people living and working in midtown. There's still no information on what is causing the issue—I can't see that far south from where I'm standing—but talk radio has speculated a bank heist, which sounds to me like wishful thinking, the old nobility of cracking the safe and making your getaway through the warrens underneath Manhattan. The screenplay practically writes itself.

It's the semantics of having no additional information to report that leaves me more wry than annoyed. Of course the mayor knows more than he's saying. If a sinkhole swallowed two blocks, he could say that. But instead he has nothing to report, because truth has consequences.

My father told me this moment would come, when the liberal in me would compete with the realist and the realist would put the liberal on the canvas. The mayor isn't reporting anything because the security cameras show a guy in a long linen robe climbing aboard the train. The mayor is letting all the good Muslims of New York get behind any fortifications they can find before making the announcement and putting every single one of them at risk. Today is why my father votes for repugnant men and smugly insists that I will too someday.

A few enterprising boys walk shirtless through traffic, coolers strapped to their shoulders, bottled water dripping from each hand. Only five dollars. It's funny to see drivers beckon them over and then watch their expressions change when they hear the price. It's capitalism at its most Darwinian. My bottle is still half-full of bathroom water. All I accomplish by drinking from it is manufacturing more sweat, feeding coal into an overburdened train engine. I stopped checking my phone for the temperature as soon as I saw the pop-up alert that I'm down to 10 percent battery, with the ominous red button underneath asking me to dismiss. I know it's over a hundred degrees. I can feel it's over a hundred, and even hotter with the blistering humidity and the lack of a breeze.

On the corner of 112th and Malcom X some virgin-worthy hero has taken a wrench to the fire hydrant, sending gallons of water pouring out onto the pavement, providing a makeshift shower and wading pool. Dozens of kids in bathing suits splash each other, shin deep, bent over and flinging their arms to the heavens to rinse off their fellow bathers and the idling cars. I strip my shoes off and tuck one apiece into my back pockets, then dive into the middle of it, seeking some short but exalted relief, the baptism of bacteria-laden water from the sewers soothing my skin as it soaks my clothing through.

Once more quenched, I slip my shoes back on and start the few blocks down to the park. The radio on a stalled Hyundai tells me the mayor isn't taking questions at this time. The reporter speculates that it's a dirty bomb and advises we all get inside immediately.

Michael Gould

Eight Months Ago: November 18, 2009

Jenny dips her toes in conversational waters. She likes to ask me questions after sex, interviewing me while I'm languid and midday sleepy, curled in blankets keeping out the chill of her apartment, her leg draped over my thigh. She always starts out with softballs. She asks me New York questions.

Where's the best Indian food?
Jackson Diner, in Queens.

Where's the best Thai food?
SriPraPhai, also in Queens.

Where's the best Mexican?
Mexican Mexican? Like Oaxacan? Or Tex-Mex?

. . . Both.

And I answer, let my raised eyebrows remind her that I know what she's doing. Rebecca also beats dough into compliance before she carves it up. But Jenny charges ahead, setting her Rube Goldberg machine up for the next volley, one answer a coin that buys the next question. The questions get more personal from there. She dances around the topic of Rebecca and Jackson, shuffling her feet to leave no identifying footprints. I answer whatever she asks because it's easier that way. It's easier to be honest, less effort than to come up with some equivocation or to pretend I'm someone else.

Rebecca takes a half answer as full, doesn't press issues, picking up on discomfort with emotional antennae, and she retreats. "What's Jenny like when you're over there?" she asked me. Jenny is affectionate, she touches me all the time while I'm working, as we smoke out the bedroom window. "She's quiet, sort of does her own thing," I reply tersely, and Rebecca lets it drop. Jenny, conversely, pokes and prods, an evaded answer her cue to pick at the scab until she's exposed the wound underneath.

She bites and scratches me when we have sex. I've asked her not to, and she apologizes, but I question the sincerity, since she does it again. She claims that she's in the moment. "I get a little lost during, you know? Don't you?" she says, mock casual. I speak tone, Jenny. I'm fluent in intonation. And no, the answer is I don't. I don't get so lost that I'm not in control of where I put my teeth. Call me a chilly lover. But I can't answer with that, I can't tell her how in control I am. So I clam up. "Don't you?" she repeats. "Don't you?" she pokes my ribs with her fingers, teases my neck with her lips. "Don't you?"

"Fair enough," I reply. Conceding her point, that's my best victory.

When Paul comes home, he looks in on the room, but it's only to be polite. He's not measuring my progress, and I'm not charging him virtually anything for my time, so he harbors no concerns about how long it's taking me to build shelves. The glory of a generation raised with little to no knowledge of home repair. I could spin the knob behind his toilet and Paul would assume he'd have to move, that once it's busted it can never be repaired. Paul looks in on the room so he can give me empty praise with his happy, sheepdog look. He kisses Jenny and she kisses him back and acid corrodes my throat, but he cooks us dinner, and we sit and eat and discuss our days, a three-person family, cast less traditionally than the one I will rejoin hours later in Red Hook.

Paul's play has been put on hiatus while the director trolls for funds, taking him out of the immediate vicinity of the actress who set him all aflutter. I didn't tell this to Jenny. I kept Paul's secret, not out of loyalty to Paul, but because there's no gain yet in causing strife where there doesn't need to be. Nothing gets better for me by tearing a rift between Jenny and Paul. Let her ruffle his hair and call him Fenn and peck his lips on her way to and from a room. She told me that they have sex about once a month. Once a month. I sit across from him at the dinner table, eating the meal he prepared for me, drinking the wine he bought, and I know this about him. This beautiful, sexless man, like a prized eunuch. He makes jokes to me across the table, speaks to me in bro-tones, because we're buddies. In my head I refer to him as Cuck Finn. *Cuckold*, what an antiquated word, so perfect for right now. He's a cuckold, and I feel equal parts pity and disgust for him that he doesn't realize his seemingly only friend has given him his horns. I gave him his horns. What a silly, olde-timey thing to believe. I mentally dress myself in a doublet and codpiece when I think it, but I did it. I did it to you, Paul. You *boy*. I gave you your horns.

His blank, lineless face recounts a day at a law firm and I sit across, cutting into a delicious piece of chicken almondine. Spooning up a bouillabaisse. Actually enjoying tofu for the first time. Dinners start to blend together. The boy can cook. The three of us sitting around a table, chattering away like pigeons, me sinking my teeth into the food he's made while Jenny strokes my leg under the table with her bare foot. Paul ambles on, oblivious to it all.

I wonder if I hate Paul Fenniger, if though I laugh with him genuinely, though I like talking with him, hanging out with him, though he and I have started going to postdinner drinks without

Jenny, whether the whole time I look at him with a false, solicitous smile.

There are points when I watch him watching Jenny, or striving to connect with me, and I'm swallowed whole into the gaping maw of self-loathing. He'd make this easier if he were malevolent.

When I work, installing the shelves, Jenny chooses the music we listen to: the Replacements, Pavement, other bands that make me wonder if she regrets not being cooler in the 1980s. I don't mind it, watching Jenny bop around the apartment, bounce to the Pixies and Morphine, periodically grab me for a spin around the room. When Paul comes home, Jenny cedes the music selection to him, the cook choosing the soundtrack, and Paul likes classical. I'm using that as a general, catchall term because I couldn't give a flying fuck about any of it. Yes, it's beautiful. But Jenny and I share aggrieved looks, silent groans, as another piano sonata starts, turning the apartment into a cat food commercial.

A week of dinners and now Erik Satie plays for us. Not Erik Satie himself, per se, but whomever is actually banging away on the piano to his composition. I had to check the iPod to even know that it's Erik Satie, a man I can safely say never made it into the Gould household in Midwood—Woodstock was ground zero for my parents' record collection. Satie wrote pleasant music to watch a rainstorm to. Paul runs his fingers over the counter, inelegantly playing along. Jenny and I are sex tired, jelly-legged, lazing around on the couch. She reads, I close my eyes and rub her foot. We've grown more brazen, through apathy or adolescent petulance I can't tell—the peck on the cheek when I say good night, a hand running along my shoulders when she passes me, her feet in my lap. It goes unnoticed, or unremarked.

"Let's dance," Jenny says. I open my eyes to see her inches from my face.

"To this?"

"Dance with me," she orders. Paul and I share a look across the room. He stirs a pot.

"I'll dance with you," he offers.

"You're cooking. Michael will be an excellent understudy." She yanks me up off the couch, manipulates my hands like I'm her automaton, one on her hip, one gripped in hers, fingers interlaced, and we sway. We twirl. We shuffle back and forth in rough rhythm, her head on my chest, her arms encircling me, fingers pressing into my shoulder blade. This song is beautiful. I've never noticed how beautiful before, how elegiac, how bittersweet and tender. When it ends, barely three minutes and a lifetime later, I look up, and Paul has a scrim over his face, his own sinking sense of comprehension finally permeating.

And I don't care. Let him know. What does it matter? I bow gallantly to Jenny. She curtsys back. We all laugh, because it's funny. Get in on the joke, Paul. It's funny.

Paul is uncharacteristically quiet over dinner, brusque though still amiable. He doesn't have the muscle to be less friendly, only less enthusiastic, like a dog who can keep his tail from wagging. After dinner Jenny says she'll walk me to the train, that she wants the air, even though it's starting to actually get cold at night and today a slick mist hangs in the air, just short of a drizzle. As we turn the corner on Greenpoint Avenue she reaches over and clutches my hand, squeezes it for an instant before letting it go. We reach the subway and she stops me.

She says plainly, "If you could, I think you would tell me you love me."

I see her attempt to shock, and I raise her. "You don't need to dare me to say that I love you. I do. I love you. I'm in love with you. So what do we do about that?"

I don't even know if I mean it. It certainly didn't emerge as a lie, and it got a stammer out of her. It robbed her of her words. For only a moment, though. Jenny Sayles is never far from her next sentence. "To be discussed." She breathes out. To be discussed.

Back at home an hour later, I rock Jackson while Rebecca prepares cookie dough. Jackson babbles, so I babble back, mimicking and riffing, his babababab morphing into my bababadada. When Rebecca comes up from behind and hugs me, it's her arms I feel. When she whispers that she loves me, it's her voice I hear. And when we lay together that night, it's her body pressed against mine. But a part of me remains in Greenpoint—a part I have yet to define, but I can feel its absence. I can't yet tell if it's the hole of a donut, whether it's supposed to be there, or a cake without eggs, destined to break apart and crumble, no matter how enticing it may appear.

Michael Gould

Eight Months Ago: November 24, 2009

Coming back from Greenpoint, I kiss Rebecca and Jackson and immediately step into the shower. Jenny doesn't wear perfume, I don't worry that her scent has somehow imprinted onto my body, but there's a rinsing and scrubbing that needs to occur before I can be comfortable again in front of my wife and son. That moment I kiss Rebecca hello tightens every sinew, my body rebelling against the infidelity as surely as it will succumb to it again. Kissing Jackson is easier, he's a beautiful and ignorant lump, happily dwelling in his own world, fat and solipsistic.

To make this shower routine seem more routine I've been, for the past month, leaping into the shower after coming home from the studio as well. I didn't used to, the fine grains of sawdust would appear on my pillow the next morning, to Rebecca's chagrin. That memory exists somewhere in the bottom of my bag of excuses in case she brings this up, to say that I'm showering for her and— here's the perpetual trump card—so as to not shake sawdust off onto Jackson. So helpless is he that his father could do irreparable damage dandruffing tree dust onto his vulnerable face.

Within the tiles of the shower I separate out my emotions, divide them into Venn diagrams and determine which need to be sequestered. That a bewildered fuck with Jenny turned into an affair and has now developed into some scratched-and-dented relationship requires cupboard space in my mind. Guilt has to go somewhere where the drawers won't rattle. So does pride. Me 'n' Jenny, since the I-love-you's, have escalated what we once could get out of clean. We've taken each other as willing hostages.

Jenny's boyfriend is the part of me that sluices down the drain. By the time I dry off, all that's left of me is Rebecca's husband. I go through the process in reverse on the trip to Greenpoint.

I'm not two people. That's an asinine thought. I'm one person sleeping with two women, there's nothing more cinematic about that. Common as muck the world over, the cheating husband. I'm a cliché. It's still difficult to negotiate. I'm doing it to myself, and were it not so very worth it, it wouldn't be worth it at all.

Today has been a normal day. I spent a few hours at the shop, handling the rent-paying business—a chest of drawers and another coffee table. Then I trained to Greenpoint, put in an hour of work while Jenny copyedited a dissertation. After I came to a logical stopping point, I knocked gently on her bedroom door and veered off to rinse my face in the bathroom while she pranced through the house and slipped on the chain. Then we had sex on her bed because she needed to wash the sheets anyway. Otherwise we would have had sex in her shower. I'm making it sound quotidian, but it's still lovely. There's still passion and need. But we've hit a comfortable place where there isn't as much tentative groping, where we can talk before and during, even laugh at positions tried and failed.

We've reached a point where either one of us can say I love you first, and the other person can parrot it back—not breathlessly, like in a Brontë novel, but effortlessly, like it's a given, a question already asked and answered. We hit that today. Before today, I said "I love you" with a quarter note of a question mark. Today I just said it, tossed it off and she caught it, threw it right back to me. Mickey Gould and his moll, Jenny.

In the shower at home I process and compartmentalize while I duck my head under the nozzle and let warm water run down my spine, loosening the tension in my lower back. The door opens and there's the sound of clothing hitting the floor. "Hello?"

Rebecca steps into the shower with me. "Thought I'd join you." She gives me a wet hug complete with a grin. "That okay?"

"Oh, are you a . . . dirty girl?" I say in my creepy, deep, pedophile voice. She hates this voice, so for my troubles I'm slapped on the chest. "Where's the wee one?"

"Sleeping."

"Chair or crib?"

"Crib. He's been taking longer naps lately." She throws it out there, a statement like a question, see what I think of this ongoing development.

"Do you think he's entering middle age?"

She charges on, "I mean he might be down for an hour. Ninety minutes. We have plenty of time before he's awake." Rebecca doesn't initiate sex. We've discussed this ad infinitum that if she's forever making me initiate then it makes me feel coercive, if not downright rapey. So she's started dropping hints, innocuous statements said with what she thinks is a sultry voice but sound vaguely like a cartoon character attempting seduction. Still, hearing that intonation triggers me, even more than her nudity, even more than her stepping into the shower with me, that I'm now free to touch her, to commence foreplay. It makes me feel less like a guy rubbing up against her on a subway and hoping that, because I've watched too much porn, she'll just fucking love it.

I place her under the water and run my hands along the swell of her breasts. They've been turned into a restaurant for four months now, so I feel like I'm doing a good deed reminding her that they are still sexualized body parts to me. She arches her back and hums. Her hands travel southward. My body doesn't respond the way I want it to, and I kiss her hard, pin her hands up against the tile wall as if this is how we're going to do this, this is how she'll be taken today, but in reality I'm struggling to buy myself some time. I'm past a refractory period, there's no reason for me not to get hard for Rebecca, but it's not coming alive. I delay with fingers. There's still no response in my downbelows. Oh good gravychrist, I do not want to fail to get it up for her: just the thought of a conversation about impotence has me silently hollering at my cock to do its damn job. We make out for a while, I try dry humping my wife against a shower wall, which she enjoys in tiny vocalizations. Finally, the conductor in my brain finishes his coffee break and I start to get erect.

Rebecca pulls back from me with a jolt, her face confused. "Oh baby," she pities, "how did you cut yourself?" Her hand goes to the back of my shoulder. When she takes it away, I angle myself in the shaving mirror, contort myself to see behind, and there I find the bite mark Jenny left there earlier, one she assured me hadn't broken skin. It's two near-perfect parabolas, bright red in color. "It looks like a bite mark," Rebecca remarks, but not in accusation. I'm almost offended that she's not asking me with an accusatory tone, that she's giving me the leeway to lie my way out of this.

The doorbell rings. Rebecca hops out of the shower without another thought, a mother's protective instinct immediately kicking in that her child is sleeping and doorbells are loud. I rub the bite mark with soap and water, start running through a catalog of tools that could have fallen on me that would have made such a mark. I settle on a board, just a large board from a high shelf that I should have been more careful taking down. More embarrassed than anything else. Didn't think it hit me hard enough to leave a mark. Goddamit, Michael. And goddamit, Jenny.

Rebecca shrieks. This inhuman sound flies like upward lightning from downstairs and I leap out of the shower, wrap a towel around my waist. When I open the door she's still howling, and Jackson, now awake, wails angry cries. The house is a cacophony, and all I can make out through the sound of screaming in both ears is the crackle of walkie-talkies and the name, over again and again, coming from my wife's body like it was being ripped from her in strips.

Jolie. Jolie. Jolie.

Paul Fenniger

Present Day: July 19, 2010

1:26 PM

The crowd blobs together in front of me, already slow and now ossifying, standing still in the tunnel. People ask each other whether this bottleneck is because we've reached the platform at Bedford, whether we've made it through to the end. There's hope in their voices, strained and quivering, exhausted and overheated. We can't see that far ahead from the back of the pack, and the mass shuffles forward as if we're being pulled down a giant drain. Gradually, the word works its way back to us.

Train. Said over a shoulder, then over a shoulder, then over a shoulder. Grumbled from person to person to person, all the way back to me. Train.

We left at rush hour. It would make sense for another train to pull in right behind ours, collect the next sea of people. Would make sense for that train to go through the same procedures as ours: the evacuation, the mass exodus from the tunnel, the fear, the drenching sweat. I'm oddly relieved that others endured what I've endured today, the thought that straphangers throughout the city may have had to leave trains in the middle of tunnels, even on raised platforms, and walk where we aren't meant to walk. It'll give us all some common ground in bars, looking back on that nineteenth of July when we were the tunnel people. The moles—that's how we'll come to be known.

I'm hot, bordering on delirious. I stopped sweating ten minutes ago. My body expels dry heat.

The crowd stumbles forward. No one has the energy to push, all fears about leaving the first train now supplanted by weary resignation, degradation even. The tunnel still isn't wide enough to walk around this other stalled train. The conductor with the flashlight and our officer stand at the doorway to the front, helping people up. We'll pass through the train as through the belly of a snake.

"Step forward. Wait. Wait. Step forward. Wait. Wait. Wait." The commands repeat for another half hour before I reach the train. "Are you the last?" Perry waves his flashlight beam over us. Grumbles of assent. "This is the damn hero," he says to the cop. "Everyone behind him needs evac." The cop nods. Both hoist people up. "Walk through the train, some people will be at the back to help you down." Perry then loudly adds, "The platform isn't much farther." Whether or not it's true, I'm grateful to him for cutting through all of the confusion with a dose of hope.

In the train itself the lights are out, and Perry and the cop walk behind me, helping people up from the benches where they sit or lie down. This must be the makeshift trauma unit, the place where people who can go no farther can wait for medical care. I think back to the man in the tunnel, measure out how much longer he would have had to walk and wait before he could be among the others. Only a few people come up from behind me, raising themselves off the seats with hoarse groans, stumbling onward with Perry's help.

When I get to the last car, still in single file, I'm helped down by a man and a woman. I turn to help the next person down but instead I'm roughly shoved forward. "Keep moving. We've got this," a voice says. I've been digested by another L train. Hanging back from the rear of the crowd, I hear the rumble of a generator and soon I can make out lights up ahead, glowing like Vegas in the desert night.

Paul Fenniger

Seven Months Ago: December 14, 2009

Every day closer to Christmas brings less oversight to my corner of the office. A last gasp for the year's billable hours has everyone coming in early and staying late, sequestered behind closed-off doors.

I keep three windows open on my computer. The first window is a template for a thank-you note. Gregg asked me to start plugging in the addresses for a boilerplate thank-you-for-your-Christmas-gift letter that we'll mail to clients who sent boxes of Godiva and dried fruit platters. Transferring the addresses from one database to the letters takes, and I'm being charitably slow here, fifteen minutes. That's what the other two windows are for.

> Signed in as NYPeach (12:04pm)
> Hardguy8in joined the chat (12:06pm)
>
> HARDGUY8IN: Hey
> NYPEACH: Hi there! How are you?
> HARDGUY8IN: Horny.
> NYPEACH: Oh yeah, me too. What should we do about that?
> HARDGUY8IN: Tell me abut yrslf.
> NYPEACH: Pardon?
> HARDGUY8IN: ?
> NYPEACH: I didn't understand that.
> HARDGUY8IN: R U a fuckin computer?

NYPEACH: No, I'm definitely a real girl. What should I do?

HARDGUY8IN: Tell me about yourself.

NYPEACH: Oh! Absolutely. I'm nineteen, and I just came to New York to be a model.

HARDGUY8IN: U should suck my dick. R U hot?

NYPEACH: I've been told I'm hot. I have 36C breasts and long blond hair that hangs all the way down to my ass.

HARDGUY8IN: S#n pix.

NYPEACH: I'll bet you have a monster cock, and I want to do all sorts of things to it, but do you think you could type so I can understand you better? You know, spell words out?

HARDGUY8IN: WTF?????

NYPEACH: Smart guys get me so wet!

HARDGUY8IN: Fuk u bitch.

NYPeach left chat (12:13pm)

I have been men and women, gay and straight. For the first year of this, every encounter tied to sex. I was a wife looking to cheat on her husband. I was a husband seeking someone to film him and his wife. I discovered that if it can be conceived, it can be a fetish. But at some point the sex talk grew rote. So I mixed it up. I'm an accountant looking for a gently used car. I'm a parent seeking information about the schools in Ames, Iowa.

At first it was silly, then funny, then kinky, then intriguing, then absorbing, then necessary. At first I thought I would share it with Jenny, because I want to share everything with Jenny, and at some point between kinky and intriguing, at some point when I found the boards for child loss, I realized that this had to stay inside of me.

At its best, it hurts no one and becomes a rehearsal for life. When nimble, I can sidestep conflict with Jenny because I gamed out a resolution as someone else hours or days earlier. Or if she is already burdened, I can take my problems elsewhere, like a virtual bar I can sidle up to and bend an ear.

No one can tell from your font whether you are crying, or raging. Being a grieving father gets significantly easier when it's a skin you can shed every time you log off. You work it out as someone else, then get to be your best self for the person who needs you.

I close out of the second window and open the third. This is the Gmail account where pgvj7-3843277948@pers.craigslist.org goes to. I posted on Craigslist three days ago, an ad that advertised my bodily dimensions (38C-24-38, taken from Sophia Loren's Wikipedia page) and invited the right man to come meet me for a drink, maybe more. Send a pic, and if I like it, you get a pic back.

Fifty-three different men have responded, some of them more than once. Fifty-three, craving the possibility that I'll send the picture I've promised. Do they solely want sex? I want to write each one of them back and ask them that: Do you solely want sex from me, or do you believe that sex is the map from which we'll discover love, that you will meet a stranger on Craigslist for a hookup and it'll become the story you tell your grandkids?

Click the six new ones, new from the last time I checked. I don't even bother to read whatever they've written, it's either bold predictions for what they'll do to me or offers of cash. Six new ones, four dick pics. Two are close-ups, one guy self-shot from the neck down. One open, honest gentleman took a whole body shot, face and all, in the mirror of his bathroom. Two toothbrushes on the sink.

We live with the assumption that everyone is on the level, because if we didn't, we would be too paranoid to exist.

Every time I sign on as someone else, every time I continue a conversation, drawing myself in deeper, I feel what I have been told I'm supposed to feel every time I go "method" as an actor—my brain becomes convinced that I am who I claim to be. No one ever believes us with the fervor we believe in ourselves.

Jeff whistles Cat Stevens as he walks down the hall, giving me ample time to shift back to the thank-you notes. He pokes his head into my cube. "Paul." His mouth forms a straight line. *Concerned.* "I'm sure you have Christmas shopping to do. Finish whatever

Gregg has you working on and get out of here early today." Broad smile. *Beatific.* "Put in for the full time when you do your time sheet." I thank him and he chuckles, ever magnanimous. I think I just received my Christmas bonus.

I go back and click through the fifty-three replies, including the thirty-eight men who have sent me a picture of themselves, thirty-six of them electing to share their penises, as if I'm doing a study. I suppose I am. I clear my browser history and close out. I stroll down the hall into the men's room, where I check under the dividers in the stalls, looking for feet. Seeing none, I lock the door behind me and furiously rub one out into a wad of toilet paper.

It also turns me on. Not the grieving-by-proxy, but the rest of it, even being someone as banal as a man seeking a hypoallergenic rescue dog. Even that. I wish it didn't, I really do. I wish I were just a troll, someone who hates the world and wants to lob bombs at it from the safety of anonymity, but no matter who I pretend to be, before I have that method moment, I get hard. It's never happened for me this way while acting. Only online. It's not me, I tell myself. It's me playing the role of not-me. I cast myself. Some aspects of the characters just hew closer to Paul Fenniger than others.

The instant I come waves of disgust crash over me. I flush, and wash my hands in the sink, staring into the mirror, slowly reclaiming the man I recognize.

Michael Gould

Present Day: July 19, 2010

12:43 PM

My father holds all subjective things Brooklyn over all subjective things Manhattan. The tallest buildings are in Manhattan and he cannot argue this, because they dominate the skyline and we don't need a ruler to measure. But the most beautiful buildings are in Brooklyn, as are the best slices, the prettier streets, the nicer people, even the better weather. (All those buildings create wind tunnels.) Queens doesn't get a horse in this race, though my father concedes most non-European ethnic food to it. The subways run better in Brooklyn, he proclaims. The air is cleaner in Brooklyn, he sniffs deep. And Brooklyn has the most beautiful park—Prospect Park.

Over Central Park, you might argue? Absolutely, he states unequivocally, offended to even consider. Designed by the same man, Olmsted, you point out. Pshaw, he actually says out loud. Pshaw. Olmsted had to design Central Park, manicure it and carve it into a chunk of land so that rich Manhattanites could have their playground. Prospect Park simply *exists*, the way nature is intended to exist, with the grass and the water and the hills and the cement all living in harmony. Central Park is much bigger, you offer up, though by this point you're also seeking an exit to the conversation. And there are cemeteries bigger than both, and landfills that would dwarf all of it, he counters. Still, give me a nice day and I'll wander through Prospect Park, scaled to a more human size. And, he adds, there's maybe two square feet of space in Central Park where you forget where you are, where you don't have the shadows of office buildings or condos where Vanderbilts and Astors live. You take five steps into Prospect Park and the world disappears but for the green. All the glorious green, says my father, Marty Gould, the belligerent tour guide.

I've finally hit Central Park, the very northern edge of it, having walked almost a hundred blocks thus far. I am Lewis and Clark seeing the Pacific for the first time. This park, this is recognizable to me. I've been here before. My internal map spreads out. If I turn right, there is the K2 of hills.

A runner approaches on my left, and I stand and watch him go past, staring as if at a centaur. His nylon shorts show almost every inch of his sinewy legs, and he wheezes a chanted huff as he passes, sweat following his body like a trail. Assuming he hasn't been running since this morning, this man saw that something major was happening downtown, something big and terrifying enough to shut down a massive chunk of the city, as well as all public transport and phone lines and God knows what else, and he still decided to go out on his run. On the hottest day of the year. I think of him as resilient, a gloriously crazy variety of resilient. My father would dig shallow for a Yiddish pejorative to mutter.

I'm sure my parents are both worrying about me. The first thing they would do is try my cell phone, then Rebecca's. When that didn't work, they'd get in their car and come to Red Hook. My father has just enough Papa Bear in him to believe that his presence will protect us. If Rebecca has explained to them my whereabouts, either or both of them (likely my mother) would drive to Greenpoint and confront Jenny. If she explained the situation to them, eventually they'd realize that I'm on the island where the trouble is, and I rue the years I could be taking off their lives.

Kites float back and forth in the sky, picking up wind that I cannot feel, launched from the Great Lawn some forty blocks south of where I stand. Kites, on a day like today, weather and mayhem be damned. Again I reach down, take off my shoes, and walk barefoot in the grass, my clothes sticking to my skin, my ankles and shins and knees and the arches of my feet and the meat of my calves all burning, my hamstrings tightening, starved for water. My bottle is running low, but if I'm in the park I'll find a water fountain before long. I can't think about that now. Now is for appreciating the grass that pokes the pads of my feet, that wends its way between my toes, tickles me like carpet. I sit. I sit down for a minute. I'm going to sweat no matter what I do, I'm going to pant and burn and my eyes are going to sting with the salt from my brow running down my face no matter what I do, so I sit and rest. Another runner goes by. Then another. Kites and runners in a boiling Central Park—emergency vehicles and mayhem far away. This, even more than Christmas, is when New York feels to me like a snow globe, a city that remains the same no matter how hard you shake it. All you can really do is shift the debris around.

From the park I'll walk down Fifth Avenue to get to Fifty-ninth, from Fifty-ninth I'll cross the Queensboro Bridge, from Queens I'll walk south across the Pulaski Bridge, over the fetid canal that separates it from Brooklyn. And from there I'll walk to Franklin Street, right up to Jenny's door, and she will look at my blistered face and my cracked lips and there will be an accounting for decisions we made together.

There I'll call my parents if the phones work. There I'll call Rebecca.

It's difficult to stand up, but I do, rickety and quivering, my skeleton rebuilding the scaffolding of my body. Then I walk forward, across the scorching pavement and onto the edge of the Harlem Meer, and step into the brackish water, the ducks and geese swimming away from me. Standing for a soothing moment, I feel the moss beneath my feet now, a calm resolve steeling my nerves, and stepping out, I slide on my shoes and continue onward.

Michael Gould

Seven Months Ago: December 12, 2009

We six walk slowly through Central Park, coming in from the Seventy-second Street side, past the tourists standing over Strawberry Fields. John Lennon was shot on a December 8, so the memorial overflows with decaying flowers and eight-by-tens of him in his New York City shirt.

Seven. There are seven of us. Counting Jackson, wrapped and padded in layer upon layer upon layer, sleeping in his stroller. My parents walk behind us, pushing him slowly through the park, my mother pointing out birdies and trees and squirrels in a quiet sing-song voice. My father walks solemnly alongside, a designated mourner.

Eight. Eight of us, if I'm entering the spiritual realm. Rebecca leads the vanguard, holding a wine bag with an urn inside of it. Inside of the urn is Jolie.

Paul hangs back, like he's tailing Rebecca. I speak sidemouthed to Jenny, "Is there a reason he's walking by himself?"

"He doesn't like funerals."

"Does anyone?"

Her head tilts away from me. "I don't mind them."

When we got the news, my parents came to stay with Jackson while Rebecca and I were driven in an unmarked police car to the morgue on the other side of Prospect Park. I soothed Jackson while Rebecca got dressed, then I fixed the police officers a pot of coffee, the entire time still clad in only a towel. I even gave each officer a cookie. We both resented waiting. My parents have a key. We could leave Jackson in his vibrating chair or his crib and he wouldn't go anywhere. He wasn't even hungry at the moment. We could have left, but suggesting that to the cops would only have opened up a whole new set of issues.

We pass the *Falconer* statue. My mother points it out to Jackson, who has awoken but remains immobilized in his Gore-Tex cocoon. His cow-mittened fists clutch and release, clutch and release.

Jenny says quietly, "Who has the worse loss, me or Rebecca?"

"Jesus, Jenny."

"On one hand, losing a child is worse than losing a sibling. And Jolie probably cheated death plenty of times, so on some level, Rebecca had to have been preparing for this day for years. On the other hand, I can always have another child, whereas Rebecca is all out of sisters."

"The gallows math of tragedy," I remark.

Rebecca called her parents from our house later that night, after seeing the body. After nodding her head and declaring, "That's Jolie." After signing papers and receiving gruff condolences from the police. After my parents left. She waited until they were gone, checked with me that they had gotten back into their car and driven off. She knew how the phone call would go and didn't want good parents to see how bad parents acted, in case they thought less of her, thought neglect and apathy could be passed down through the genes. My mother cried when she heard the news about Jolie. She wept softly in the bathroom, against all of her louder instincts. I know my mother. My mother handles bad news, truly bad news, by wailing. But a sleeping baby alters every response. My father sat on the couch and steeled his soft, aged jaw— a blame-the-world posture. Ten years ago he would have blamed the blacks, tried to justify his accusation with some statistic or flimsy bit of anecdotal evidence. Call him on his bullshit and he would have insisted that he's not a racist, that he worked for the MTA with hundreds of black guys during his career. That he keeps his mouth shut and holds back the tidewaters of blame counts for Marty as late-in-life growth.

Rebecca called her parents and apologized for the late hour, told them Jolie was dead, then apologized again for calling them so late at night. The whole call took two minutes from start to finish. They paid the cremation fees because they didn't want Rebecca to, but they insisted that they buried their daughter years ago and that they wouldn't be attending a second funeral for Jolene McMahon.

"I want you to promise me," Rebecca seethed, "promise me that if I die, you will do everything in your power to make sure Jackson sees as little of those two people as possible, and never without you present."

"I promise."

"Not for a minute. You have to pee, you take him with you."

We cross the Bow Bridge and start our way into the Ramble, searching for a quiet, secluded spot to scatter Jolie. This is illegal, I'm sure. Unhygienic at the very least. But Rebecca insisted, tears and tight mouth, that Jackson come as well, that he got to hear about his aunt even if he'd never remember today. "You can't scatter Jolie while holding Jackson," I pleaded, and finally she relented. So as long as he was there, my parents could come as well to take care of him.

How Jenny and Paul came along makes less sense to me. Jenny called Rebecca to offer condolences, then Paul did the same, and both asked if there would be a service. Rebecca invited them along. It occurs to me that this couple constitutes our best friends. I haven't been back to Greenpoint since we found out; Jenny and I steal lemur-eyed glances, confused and upset at our interruption, tethered to lives that feel less and less like the central plot, more like the place where we visit with the supporting cast.

So let's say we tried something absolutely fucking crazy and formed some unholy polyamorous relationship wherein we all sort of lived together and raised Jackson. I mean, with a number of variables falling the right way—that wouldn't be the worst idea, right? Like a hippie commune. Or a cult. This doesn't strike me as the right line of thinking at a funeral. I should place my hand somewhere on Rebecca now. But if it made us all happy . . .

"Do you think about trying again?" I ask Jenny.

"All the time," she replies. "There are complications to that, though."

"Oh yeah?"

She looks at me, the conversation suddenly more serious, more sad, more funereal. "Yeah, Mickey."

The paved path starts to get bumpy, and my mother struggles to push the stroller. I stop the convoy and pick Jackson up, hold him against me, and tell my parents to wait here, that we'll be back soon. Jackson fidgets in my arms, but I quiet him with a binky. Every book I've read tells me that a binky will be the root of tens of thousands of dollars' worth of orthodontic work later, but I'll pay it to keep him quiet for now. A pacifier is to babies what cigarettes are to adults—a necessary salve, damn the consequences.

Rebecca leads us off the path, into the woods, where a few hardier tourists smile at us as they pass, especially at Jackson. When I started taking the subway alone, and coming into Manhattan on the weekend with my friends, my father told me never to go into the Ramble. He described it as a place where "men make love to men for money." I think about that now and stifle a giggle.

Finally Rebecca stops. We gather around her, encased in bare trees, stiff dirt beneath our shoes. She starts to unscrew the urn and it's Paul who stops her. "Do you want to say anything?" he asks.

She kneels down, sprinkles a bit of Jolie on the ground to see how it plays, to see where it will go. We wait for the wind to blow while a pile of human cremains sits in a small pyramid on a dead leaf. Rebecca sighs to analyze it. "When Jolie first came to the city she told me that her favorite place was Central Park. She wasn't a nature girl when we were growing up, so I assumed this was where she scored, but when I came to see her the park was the first place she took me. She acted like my sister when she was in the park. My sister from when we were growing up. I have no idea why this park, and I didn't ask her and now I can't, but this is where she was her most Jolie. And I loved that person, so here's where she'll stay."

A small breeze blows the ashes already poured across the

ground, mixing like seed. Rebecca gets low and tips the urn over in the direction the wind is going, blowing Jolie away from us. Jenny and Paul huddle together. I cradle Jackson tight to my chest.

Jolie was found with her throat cut in a vacant apartment in Flushing. Ligature marks on her wrists led the police to believe she had been tied down with an electrical cord.

Rebecca holds her head high, tears streaming down her face, watching her sister's ashes mix with the leaves and dirt of the Ramble.

The coroner found no traces of either drugs or alcohol in Jolie's body. Jolie died clean, Rebecca asserted, heartsick and defiant in the face of overwhelming grief. She says it again, the last of the ashes spilling from the urn, the last of Jolie scattered in the park. Jolie died clean.

Michael Gould

Seven Months Ago: December 22, 2009

Adam Cavendish can ogle the span of the Williamsburg Bridge from his living room. He's earned such a view, his tech start-up performing better than anyone could have anticipated. He saw a piece of my furniture—I don't know which—at a dinner party, and he likes my work. Wants to start out commissioning a coffee table, something he can put his feet on. The first few sessions have been mostly philosophical, Cavendish sitting me down on a couch that costs more than a car and talking me through his maxims of life, all twenty-eight years of it, while I take notes and shape them into coffee table details. What does his upbringing tell me about how to stain the wood?

Rebecca ooooohs and ahhhhhs as I describe the opulence. The

best thing she does is not press the issue. She asks no questions that I cannot answer or plausibly plead ignorance to. And thank God for that.

I created Adam Cavendish from whole cloth. I planed him down into shape and sanded away his edges. I am building a coffee table, though it's for a man in Chelsea who is buying it for his son, who lives in Providence. If Rebecca visits my studio, she will indeed see sketches and pieces of a coffee table strewn about. In creating Adam Cavendish, I chose tech work because anyone over thirty who understands Web start-ups is also a billionaire and not likely to associate with my wife and me. And Williamsburg because Williamsburg is a stop away from Greenpoint, and that's where I spend my days, figuring out how to extricate myself from portions of one life without salting the earth.

Jenny kneels over a plastic Christmas tree, pulling tiny decorations from a box. "I think that's the cutest slash saddest thing I've ever seen," I declare. She locks the door behind me and slips on the chain. "You and Paul don't get a real tree? You strike me as the real-tree type of gal."

"Not this year."

"Ah."

"Big days are harder this year." I spread my legs and pull her to me while she rotates the tree to decorate it evenly. "I've had this tree since college. My roommate got it for us because she wanted a tree but was going home for Christmas, and I wasn't willing to water it and pick up all the needles. So she bought this, and we got drunk and decorated it, and when I moved in with Fenn I just took it."

We're a treeless family this year, plastic or otherwise. Rebecca had a tree growing up but connects it to emotionally absent parents and now to her sister, so she didn't want one. I offered three times to go out and get one. Fairway had them stacked like dead soldiers in the parking lot. First she demurred, then refused, then cried. I'm Jewish, too Jewish for a tree at least, and Jackson was born five months ago and hasn't made his wishes known yet. When she at last emerged from our bedroom, dry-eyed and composed, Rebecca asked to table the tree discussion for another year (or two), and I agreed without hesitation.

"What did you get me for Christmas?" Jenny asks. Her hands free of ornaments, she tugs my cuffs up to my knees and rubs my shins. I love this, how she can fixate on parts of my body I never thought could be charged.

"It's not Christmas yet."

"I know, that's why I'm asking. I hate surprises. Come on." She turns and crinkles her nose. The cute pout can turn into the real pout on a dime.

"What did I get you publicly, or privately?"

"Oooooh, you got me two gifts?"

"I did."

"Tell me both."

"Nopeeeees."

"Harrrumph." Then, "What did you get Rebecca?"

"Lingerie."

She repays my joke with a look that reminds me I'm too dumb for buttons. I amend, "A gift card to the King Arthur Flour Company and a catalog." Now she seems offended on behalf of my wife. I protest, "What?"

"That's not romantic at all."

"Rebecca and I both hate getting gifts."

"No! Everybody likes getting presents! What sort of monsters are you?"

I laugh. "We used to buy ourselves gifts, that's how opposed we were. For my birthday, I would buy myself art supplies or something and show it off to Rebecca that I had spent money on myself and some whim I had. She'd do the same. Now we buy each other gifts, but we don't like it. There's way more stress than joy."

I pluck an ornament off the tree over Jenny's half-hearted protests. It feels delicate in my hand, like a robin's egg, trailing glitter across my fingertips. I hate getting gifts. Can't explain it. Have ever since I was a kid. Seeing a wrapped box and knowing it's for me prompts a physical revulsion that settles in my throat and sits there until I've opened the fucking thing and faked enthusiasm. Doesn't matter what it's for. That's been a huge fear of fatherhood, to be reckoned with at some later date. I think I'll be okay with Jackson making me things in school, with him sticking his hand in some clay and calling it a paperweight. But God help the boy if he spends a cent of his allowance on a gift for Dad.

Every year I tell Rebecca that there's nothing I need, nothing I want. Birthday, anniversary, whatever. She's just ambivalent, as happy with a bottle of wine as a gift card. She hasn't appreciated a gift enthusiastically since her engagement ring, which counted more as a contract than a gift. Call it a martyr complex and I'll agree. In my head there's a point far into the future when I'm destitute, when Rebecca and Jackson and I warm ourselves by the heat of a barrel fire, and at that point I will resent the digital camera they bought me that I barely used. We have perfectly good phones on our cameras. And yes, I know my parents are rich, and that once they die I in turn will be rich.

"I think it's that nothing is ever good enough," Jenny accuses, taking the ornament back, hanging it carefully from a plastic branch.

"That's not true."

"I'll bet that when you open a gift, there's a hitch in your face between surprise and delight, a skittish horse unable to leap the steeple fluidly. And in that moment anyone looking can spot the real justification—that no gift is ever the right gift for Michael Gould. You open every box hoping that someone will give you the gift that shows how well someone knows the core of who you are as a person, and that's why you're always disappointed."

I lean back, taking her with me, kiss her on her floor. "You've cut to the very marrow of me, Jenny."

Jenny needed to take a shower, so we multitasked and had sex while she washed herself. She leaves me in her bathroom, and by the time I'm done drying myself with her towel (so as to not transfer my scent to Paul's towel, or Paul's to me), she's sitting in her new office, at her computer, one knee crooked up, foot tucked underneath her, the author-as-flamingo pose, contemplative, with a pen tapping a rhythm on her lower lip. "What did you get Paul?" she asks.

"Why do you want to know?"

"I'm materialistic," she whines. "I'm an awful person. I'm going to judge how you really feel about me based on where I deem my gift to rank."

"That would be funny if now I didn't think it might be true."

Her eyes frost over. "Ouch, Mickey."

"I'm kidding."

"Kid your ass back to Red Hook if you're going to be an asshole."

"A bottle of bourbon. I got Paul a bottle of Blanton's." I explain the night at the hospital, delicately, testing the waters of mentioning that day to her. Jenny's expression doesn't change with the reference, she hears it like she hears everything else. I recount how Paul and I shared a nip from my flask, celebrating impending fatherhood in front of a church. I cringe, realizing the sense memory I may trigger with Paul by giving him a bottle of that bourbon. He'll be polite about it, Paul is too bloodlessly Midwestern to be anything but; still a sip of Blanton's may be a smooth reminder of the worst day of his life. Maybe this is why I hate getting gifts.

"What did you get Jackson?" She's working her way back to me.

"I am only moderately embarrassed to admit that I didn't get a single thing for Jackson. I don't think Rebecca has, either. Wouldn't make sense for us to get him separate gifts, right?"

"I don't know how it's supposed to work."

"Right. Well, I'll probably take one of his stuffed animals, hide it from him for a day so he forgets he ever had it, then give it to him again and his love will spring anew."

"Just tell me what you got me," she snaps. "I told you I don't like surprises. I'd like to think you'd understand why. So if you're giving me a gift because you think it would make me happy, you're ruining that."

There she is, I think. I sit down to show that I'm taking this conversation seriously, that I'm present and in the moment and consider her feelings valid, even though everything going on behind that facade is wondering what is causing her to act like a complete fucking lunatic about this. She's in the office that I built for her, ten minutes after we just went down on each other in her shower, and this has turned into a fight.

"I got you a subscription to *Harper's*," I say slowly. "And I carved you curtain rods."

A stunned ellipsis of a stare.

"What is confusing you? Curtain rods. Like for the curtains in here. I made you, physically *made you* fancy curtain rods." Still nothing. "So that you can write in here. And see them. And think of me. And they're long and hard and fancy, so you'll think about my penis."

"Shut up. Just shut up." She shakes her hands. "Fucking curtain rods? Really, Mickey?"

Our first fight. Click. For posterity.

"What's the matter with curtain rods?"

"Nothing, Michael. Nothing. Curtain rods are a perfectly appropriate gift to get the girl you're fucking on the side. I'm touched by the gesture." She shoots up out of the chair and stands over me. "You know what I got you? For our first Christmas?" The question sounds rhetorical, but it's not.

I try to speak calmly, to defuse, but that only makes it worse. "What did you get me?"

"I got you a watch," she spits at me. "I engraved a fucking watch for you."

We both glance at my bare wrists. I haven't worn a watch since I was a little kid. My upper lip starts to sweat and tuck in, my mouth goes dry. This is the bile of knowing that I'm getting a gift, of enduring the hassle of obligation that comes with someone giving you something. This is why people trade coins for knives. Jenny stands over me, ready to kill, as every reason against a watch jostles in my mind.

First, my phone is a perfectly adequate watch. Second, there's no point in my day when I'm desperate to know the time and unable to find it out thanks to my phone, or the millions of other people around me also with phones (some with watches) or any number of other sources. Third, if I were the type to wear a watch, I could get a watch. They aren't difficult to locate. Obviously, I don't wear a watch by choice. Maybe I'm just such a free spirit that I can't be shackled to time. Or maybe I work with machines that have giant, spinning discs of metal teeth and you're not supposed to wear any jewelry around them, in the interest of keeping limbs attached.

But I don't give any of those reasons. Because I'm too stupid for my own good. Instead, I say to Jenny, the incredulity sliding into my voice like blood into the well, "I can't wear a watch from you."

"And why is that?"

"Because I'd think Rebecca would be curious as to where the watch I'm now wearing came from, and even if I lied and said I bought it for myself, or said you and Paul bought it for me, or just that you bought it for me, I think she'd be a little confused that our friends got me an engraved watch. It's a little personal, Jenny, isn't it?"

She folds her arms across her chest and glares at me. Then she explodes, "Fuck you!" She yells. "You don't even know what it says, but I'm glad you've let me know where I rank. I'm just good enough to fuck but God forbid you make me feel like I'm a human being."

"That's not fair, Jenny."

"Fuck you!" She flicks her head forward when she says this, flinging it at me, shaking her hair out. "Fuck you!"

"What does it say?" I raise my voice. "What did you have engraved?" Then I stand up, and suddenly the room changes perspective, and I'm bigger than Jennifer Sayles. My arms twitch at their sides. I'm done being yelled at.

"It just says *with love*. I left it vague, you asshole. So it could mean anything, and you can tell your precious wife that it's from me and Paul," she sneers.

"How does that make sense? Why would Paul write *with love*?"

"Because you were a good person when our child died, you ignorant, selfish fucking asshole."

The room deflates. "I'm sorry," I say. Quick math tells me the balance of this fight is my fault, but I can't apologize in full. I can't absorb all the blame. Too much ground to cede. "I overreacted. That's a beautiful thing to write. I was going to carve something like that into the curtain rods, just for you to see." I hadn't, but the idea seems good now.

I take a step toward Jenny and she doesn't retreat, so I take another one until I'm right up next to her and have gathered her into my arms, kissing the top of her head and waiting for her arms to uncross. They finally do, and she tucks her head into my chest and hugs me back. This is how we put ourselves back together again. Here is the point where we could have ended, in our first fight, realizing that going halfway on an affair leaves too much hanging over us, that watches and curtain rods will end up being the most romantic, personal things we'll exchange other than words and the well-hidden note. She's given me a few of those, and they felt like loaded guns, so I hid them in a locked cabinet in my studio, in a drawer where I keep my awls. "I love you," I tell her. In a muffled, withdrawn voice, she says it back.

"I've never cheated on my wife before," I say. "And I know that I love you, I do, and I want us to work out, but I don't know what that looks like, and I don't know that I can trust myself to make the right decisions or say the right thing all the time. Does that make sense? These are uncharted waters for me, Jenny. You're my first."

She eyes me curiously, like I've just revealed a hitherto hidden talent. Then she says, "Well, Mickey Gould, you're my fifth. So if you can't trust yourself, you can try trusting me."

We're interrupted by the sound of a door opening, or trying to open, but hitting the chain instead. Jenny's eyes goes wide, but for just a second. Just a second of inattention, half a breath of regrouping. Then it's back to a placid normalcy. "The cabinet broke," she says under her breath, a meaningful look, then tapping her desk on the way out, as if getting it in on the grift as well.

"Hello?" Paul's voice calls. I hear the door close and then the chain slide off.

"You're home early," Jenny says.

"They let me go home. Did you write today?"

"I did write today."

"Good. Why was the chain on?"

She laughs, loud and breezily. "It's silly girl at work. Ever since Jolie, I'm just paranoid."

"Oh," Paul says. "Okay." He starts down the hall to his bedroom, but stops to see me standing in the office. If I didn't know any better, I'd say he knew immediately why I was there, and it's all I can do to not check my head to see if my hair is still wet.

"The cabinet broke because our builder turned out to be crap," Jenny drawls. "But he came by to fix it."

"Good as new," I remark. "But now I've got to run. Everything I build seems to be falling apart. Can't get anything right on the first try."

Jenny walks me to the door, mouths the words *I love you* as she shuts me out, even slides the chain back on to sell the lie. *I can get out of this clean*, I think as I walk back to the subway, to go home and pretend Adam Cavendish exists. I can end things with Jenny even with this new information, even knowing that she's done this before.

There's a clean exit. The door will open, and then I just have to slide through it before it closes again. Right?

Paul Fenniger

Twenty-one Months Ago: October 5, 2008

In every relationship, one person loves more. In my own relationship, that person is Jenny. She loves me more than I love her. It gives me something to strive for every day, to balance the scales.

I started college knowing one inalienable truth: everyone would be able to tell that I was a virgin. On a fundamental level, I could reconcile being an eighteen-year-old who had never had sex. My high school had 128 girls total. That was the pool from which the sex I would be having would spring, and when you take the freshmen out of the equation, and then take out the girls who were already dating one of the 133 boys, I was left with a smaller pond of, by my count, 49 girls. Forty-nine devout Lutherans. I starred in the school plays, and won the senior superlative of best-looking, but I never profited from it. With the few girls I dated, out of what puddles were left from the pool, we never progressed beyond kissing or groping through sweaters.

I knew in my bones that I could not hide my virginity when I got to college. The way I thought it would happen is that a group of guys would be talking one day about sex, just sitting around on a couch and discoursing, and one of them would turn to me and ask, "Paul, what can you tell us about pussy?" And there would be nothing that I didn't get from Mrs. Mitchell's quick and flustered reproductive unit in biology. "There are two holes, and I'm terrified that I am going to try to put my dick in the wrong one," would be my most honest answer.

The opportunity didn't present itself my freshman or sophomore year. That makes it sound like it was everyone else's fault. It was mine. The opportunity presented itself dozens of times, I'll bet, but I was too stupid to notice it or too shy to act on it.

The first thing I loved about Jenny was how she took control.

She brought me to a bed and sat me down. She took her clothes off. Then she took my clothes off. And everything that followed was gentle instruction and encouragement. Do that. Keep doing that. Move a little more like that. Every *that* punctuated by a small gasp, a reassuring clutch. I lasted through tracks five to seven of *Pleased to Meet Me* before I shuddered and came into a condom that she had rolled onto me.

Afterward, we lay next to each other for the rest of the album. She had been so kind, so supportive through the whole process that I felt it only right to trust her with my secret.

"You were my first," I said quietly. If she didn't hear me, I wouldn't repeat it. But she did, and she rolled over onto her side and ran her finger over my jaw.

"Then we should celebrate with whiskey drinks. Now that you're a real manly man."

The question that meant to come out of my mouth was how did I do. I meant to ask for a critique, but it spewed out instead as, "Was I your first too?"

The second thing I loved about Jenny was how she takes everything in stride. Her eyebrows raised, but she laughed and told me, "A lady never tells."

"I'm sorry."

"It's okay."

"No, I'm really sorry."

"I'll tell you this much: if you were my first, then I have been missing out on this whole sex thing." She sized me up with a look, then ran her hand down to my balls. I was twenty-one, so everything was more or less ready to go again. Jenny paused. "What does your family call you?" she asked.

"My name. I don't have a nickname."

"Okay . . . but what do they call you?"

"Paul."

"Paul," she repeats. "Paul Paul Paul. Virginal no more. Paul. You're not going to imprint on me, little duckling, are you?"

I didn't know what she meant, but she shook her head as she asked, so I shook my head in response. That earned me more sex.

One part of determining who loves more is to decide who knows the other person better. Jenny knows me so well that she knows I will be waiting up for her, waiting for her to return home. She knows that I'll have cleaned the apartment to give my hands an activity to do. She knows that I'll be on the couch, rather than in the chair by the window, and I'll be reading a magazine, rather than a book. She knows all of this about me, whereas I don't even know where she is.

We moved to Lefferts Gardens because it was still cheap, by Brooklyn standards. And it's next to a corner of Prospect Park, even though it's the corner where the homeless camp out, not the one where indie bands play concerts. But we can afford it without dipping into our savings, on the money we take in while we pursue what Jenny calls our "Love Careers." For now. Our lease is up in two months and both of us tremble at the rent hike. Jenny finds it not-ha-ha-hilarious that gentrification is going to push two white kids out of a predominantly Caribbean neighborhood.

She started working with a writing group four weeks ago. She's been a writer for as long as I've known her. I asked to read something by her once and she politely declined. "But I let you see me in plays," I protested.

"But I don't come see the rehearsals," she countered. "You can see results, not process." Over the years, though, process has never begat results. I blend patience with encouragement, certain that a stack of pages will greet me one day, and that the brilliant brain I love will have produced her masterpiece, maybe even dedicated it to me.

The writing group meets in the basement of a bookstore in Carroll Gardens and reads each other's work. I don't take offense that they get let in to rooms I'm locked out of; feedback from peers is part of the process. Still, Jenny says that most of her group mates are kind of clueless and think idle praise counts as helpful, but then there is Jonah.

I heard about Jonah for days after the first meeting. He's a great writer ("He already has an agent, Fenn"), and he really engages with her work. After the second meeting, she again couldn't stop speaking about him, circling back to Jonah no matter where the conversation meandered, but his name didn't linger as long afterward. After her last meeting, she barely mentioned him at all, instead complaining about a cabal of men who dispense opinions liberally and all write pieces "they hope Philip Roth will have his last orgasm across."

There's a way that Jenny says Jonah's name, a Morse code signal she gives with her eyes. When she tells me that she's going to meet for coffee to talk through a chapter, I offer to go with her and hang out. "I won't be able to work if you're there," she counters, then floats out the door with a sheaf of papers rolled up, jutting out of her purse. She comes home four hours later, no coffee on her breath, veers immediately toward the shower. "Wash this day off of me," she mutters as she brushes past. They meet for coffee a couple of times that week, each time for around four hours.

Tonight is the latest Jenny's ever stayed out. The sky has started to reform itself. I've positioned my body so that I can't see any clocks. Watching time pass would drive me insane, make me say something I would regret when Jenny gets home. Jonah only has one name so far; I wouldn't even know where to look for her.

I did the very thing she told me not to. I imprinted on Jennifer Sayles. If she doesn't come home, I will float away until my legs grow too weary, and then I will drown. This is why Jenny loves more in our relationship, because she doesn't conflate love and need. All of my verbs are under the same umbrella when it comes to her: need, want, hope, trust, live.

The key grinds into the lock and I leap from the couch. Like a dog, it doesn't matter whether Jenny has been gone for ten minutes or ten hours, my heart races to see her again. She comes in and puts her bag down next to the doorway, notices the lights are still on, and then notices me, standing there. She assesses, her eyes blinking another Morse message easily read.

"You didn't need to wait up," she rasps.

"Where were you?"

"I was with Jonah." She walks past me to the kitchen, fixes herself a glass of water. "We were working on his novel. He really values my take, Fenn. I like editing him, because you tell authors to do something and they just nod their head and then they don't even try, or they do but they fuck it up. Jonah just takes a note and runs with it and makes the piece better. I also picked up two freelance gigs today, so you can keep your plasma another month."

"It's almost morning." My voice sharpens to an edge I don't like, and neither does she.

"We lost track of time."

Jenny stares into her glass, so I wait until she raises her head again and looks me in the eye. Then, I tell her, "I'm not stupid, Jenny."

She puts the glass down, places both palms flat on the counter, grounding herself to brace for a storm. "Do you want to know?"

I stammer, "Just stop treating me like I'm an idiot."

"Do you want to know, Fenn? Do you want me to tell you?"

"Stop it."

"I can give it words. Is that what you want?"

This is supposed to escalate further. We're supposed to shout here. I'm supposed to get very, very angry and make demands. Threats are supposed to be made. Doors are supposed to be slammed.

That's not what I want. Jenny came home late tonight. She was helping a fellow writer. Not even a friend, just another writer. I turn and go to bed. Jenny showers and then joins me, and we sleep, her spooning me, until noon the same day.

Jenny loves me more because she chooses to love me. Every day, she goes against the instincts in her being and chooses to love me. For me, there's no choice in the matter. I have as much control over loving Jenny as I do over breathing—to stop would mean death.

Five nights later, Jenny comes home early, crying. It's not full tears, just a hiccupping, short-breath sort of crying. I try to find out what's wrong, but she locks herself in the bathroom for twenty minutes and sobs. When she comes out she is composed once again, not even a trace of puffiness under her eyes. "I'm so unhappy," she says plaintively.

"How do we make you happy again?" I toss that off casual, a gentle smile. I don't expect there to be an answer, but Jenny gives two.

"I want us to move," she starts.

"Our lease is up next month. Done." Easy fix. We'll find somewhere equally affordable or we'll dip into savings a bit. We don't need to buy a house, no need to have savings if there's nothing big we're saving for. "We'll start looking for a new place tonight."

"Thank you. And I want something else."

"Anything."

"I want it to just be us for a while. Please don't audition for anything. I'm not going to join any more writing groups. I just want to spend my time with you, all of it. Just us together."

Christmas comes early this year. "I'd love that."

"Thank you."

I stroke her hair for a while. She presses her head to my stomach. She loves more in our relationship, and my love for her is legion. Hers must be strong enough to melt the world.

Jenny finds a third thing that will make her happy. She lays it out for me like spreading blueprints across a drafting table. "After we move into a new place, we should have a baby."

Paul Fenniger

Present Day: July 19, 2010

1:43 PM

When I finally reach the Bedford Street platform, I regard it with awe, like the first time I rode the New York City subway. From Port Authority, fresh off the bus, a cliché in a plaid shirt and jeans. Jenny and I descended at Forty-second Street, and she vamped the one line from the song that she remembered.

On the avenue I'm taking you to . . .

Over and over again, first under her breath, timorous humming, then brassier and brassier. Jenny will immerse herself in anything; nothing intimidates her.

I had never seen so many people, and this was an average Wednesday in Port Authority, a typical day with people coming and going. The entire population of Cadott standing in one room; it boggled my mind. Every minute a new superlative—this building I'm in is taller than any in Cadott. This street is longer than any highway in Cadott. It was like Madison, the big, bustling, dangerous city, with its office buildings. Only more so. This, this is a city. New York is a *metropolis,* a word I connected only to *Superman* comics.

We bought fare cards. Jenny sulked over that, her first disappointment in New York. She wanted a subway token, but they had discontinued them. I learned that later. That first day I didn't want to seem like a tourist, or like the rube I was, so: no questions. Narrow my eyes. Act like I've been here before. Pound the "aw jeez" out of my accent. Jenny already had. She adapted before we came, studying stereotypes of New Yorkers and then gradually working them into her personality, like taking on an acting role for a show that never shuttered. Walking faster, speaking at a harsher, speedier clip in a voice so distant from what I knew that she sounded almost British. I got her drunk in the first few months to hear her old voice, that's how far she took it, until gradually all the levels evened out and Jenny became Jenny again.

That first subway ride we stood on the platform and waited for the A train. It seemed famous, as if we should ask the train itself for its autograph. I stood back from the platform edge, but Jenny put the tips of her toes on the pebbled warning strip, looking at me over her shoulder and poking her tongue through her teeth.

On the ave-eh-nue I'm taking you to . . .

The train scared the show out of her. She took three quick steps back, ran into me. It came in so fast, I couldn't imagine how it would stop, but it did. It slowed with a squeal and stopped, fitting the length of the platform perfectly. The doors opened. Jenny hesitated. "Let's get on," I said to her, reverently, as if the greatest adventure was beyond those doors. Truth be told, I was worried that if we were waiting on the platform when the train pulled away, our tickets would be invalid and I'd have to buy two more. God bless the verdant, they keep New York young.

The A train was packed, and once it started Jenny and I were both thrown back, nearly off our feet. She grabbed on to a man's shirt and he caught her, chuckled at her clumsiness. "So sorry," she said in her odd Mary Poppins voice. We gripped a metal pole until our knuckles were white, our bags tucked between our feet, shifting our hips whenever the door opened and people got off, or people came in, nudged us in one direction or another, stared at us because we didn't belong yet.

It took weeks before the subway lost its magic for me. Go down some stairs at any time of day or night and you can go anywhere. Even after they raised the rates, and when they raised them again, and again after that, I didn't begrudge them their money. *Anywhere.*

Even to Brooklyn. Especially to and from Brooklyn, shuttling across the river, day in and day out.

. . .

At Bedford I climb the steps to get off the tracks, set just off to the side in the gully. A giant fan roars next to the turnstiles, so I stand in front of it for a minute, let the hot air dry me off. At street level people have been enlisted to steer me up Bedford Avenue and into McCarren Park. These are the helpers, and I thank every person who moves me along, reciting their instructions and then giving me a gentle shove. The entire street has been shut down to traffic—we can walk in the middle of it, and we do, like zombies, blinking hard against the sun, all the brighter for our having been in the tunnel. It doesn't feel any cooler up here. I stare to my left, toward the city, seeking out some sign, some mushroom cloud or giant lizard, but I can't see anything in the sky. Everything above me is a blue so blue it hurts.

I'm welcomed at the park entrance by a man with coolers of bottled water. He puts one in each of my hands. "If you need medical attention, walk behind me about twenty yards." He gestures with a bottle where some tents have been set up, providing shade for people lying down underneath.

"What's going on?" I ask.

He shrugs. "You're the thousandth person to ask me. I've heard flooding."

That seems unlikely. "It hasn't rained."

"We had a volunteer EMT here earlier, and he told me that there are these pockets underground that collect seawater, like behind cement walls, even really far inland, because it *seeps,* and today one of them just burst. They're supposed to be everywhere. These pockets. But that's just what I've heard. Mayor is giving a press conference at six."

"It's not terrorism, though?"

He squints back at the city, surveying a field. "Maybe. Lots of people leaving the city for a flood. Whole lot of guesses, that's all. Electricity has been all come and go, and cell service is down."

I take out my phone, forgot I had it this entire time. Not that it was much use in the tunnel. Couldn't call Jenny from the tunnel. Couldn't text. All it would have been good for down there was to play Sudoku while I walked. This thought is so funny to me that I start laughing. I raise my phone into the air and start laughing and the water guy starts laughing with me, but I keep laughing long after he stops, and then some more after that, big heaving belly laughs that I keep laughing and laughing and laughing until my head hits the ground and this bright sunny world goes black.

Michael Gould

Seven Months Ago: December 30, 2009

While Jackson speaks in an alphabet comprised entirely of shrieks, Rebecca answers him with the utmost seriousness. Everything in agreement. "We *are* going to Fairway. You're very observant to pick that up." She sounds like she's speaking to a hair-trigger dictator.

When we pass the liquor store, a few blocks before the supermarket, I ask Rebecca, "What would you think of serving mulled wine?" She thinks it's a splendid idea but elects to wait outside, in the winter chill, with our son in his stroller, while I run in to get something red. While the clerk rings me up, Rebecca sits on the front step, rocking Jackson back and forth, holding a conversation. She doesn't see me through the window watching her bond with him, watching her solidify those emotional ties. It swells the heart, but there's a tinge of jealousy as well. There are a thousand reasons he'll want to kill me and marry her, but the main one is that he simply loves her more.

I cringe at the Fairway lot. It's full, which means bringing a stroller into the market will be like packing a Saint Bernard onto an elevator. Jackson, of course, doesn't care. It's his father who will get the looks of scorn. "Hey." I get out that much and only that much of protest before Rebecca hands off the stroller and yanks out a cart. She relinquishes parenting duties to me from produce to checkout. Along with the kitchen, the supermarket is Mommy's office and she has work to do.

Tomorrow night she plans to cook a festive meal for Jenny and Paul. She hummed with energy last week at the idea of having them over for New Year's Eve. I thought we had friends in the plural sense, but when we sat to make a list she dismissed everyone we used to know. The single were too single ("I don't want to play matchmaker"), and the couples had one or two members that Rebecca didn't want to deal with. Some people she rejected because she simply hadn't seen them in so long and was hoping they had forgotten she ever existed. Our guest list ended up being Dawn de la Puente, who declined by text without explanation, and Paul and Jenny, the last survivors on Friend Island. She genuinely likes both Jenny and Paul, but there's a tablespoon of compassion in the invite. It's a topic not worth open debate whether it's better for her to forever look at Jenny as tragedy wrapped in skin or to see her as the woman her husband might be in love with.

Rebecca charges ahead, leaving me and Jackson to get out of the way as best we can. "Everyone *is* an asshole the day before New Year's. You are very perceptive," I mutter. Today's trip will consist almost entirely of recon. Rebecca aims to plan the meal around what looks good, and then to have me come back tomorrow and pick it all up. Today we test the fish; tomorrow we buy and cook the fish. There's a limit to what bearing me a child will induce me to put up with, and Rebecca edges ever closer to that threshold.

But we buy the dry goods today, so as to ensure that we don't forget anything. It's safety net shopping. That's a thing to my wife. Rebecca, when we get home, will line up everything we've purchased on the counter, posing the meal for a before picture, and she'll check off the ingredients on each recipe card. Anything that remains unchecked either should be bought the day of or was forgotten but can still be acquired, since we've given ourselves a buffer.

I cannot express how numb I have become to this. This passes for normal when my wife entertains guests. My journey has gone from bemused to endeared to annoyed to totally compliant. While Rebecca molests squash to judge ripeness, Jackson and I keep strolling, up and down produce aisles, the colors capturing his attention and keeping him happily babbling.

"I agree," I tell him. "People here are spending too much for asparagus because they think it grants them social status. That is very sad. You're astute to pick up on that."

My phone vibrates, and I stop pushing Jackson to check it.

I wish you were here today.

I'm at Fairway instead. Rebecca is going to great lengths. I think she may be trying to get you into bed.

Wasn't being sweet. I mean it. Wish you weren't somewhere else today.

Everything okay?

Rebecca shows up at my elbow and I tuck my phone back into my pocket. It vibrates against my thigh, insisting that I give it attention. "Should I do a soup?" Rebecca asks.

"Yes," I reply. Go. Go and get your ingredients for soup. Or just note what ingredients I should get tomorrow. The phone vibrates again. Go.

"Are you saying that because you think soup is a good idea, or are you saying that because you're already annoyed to be here?"

"I'm saying that because if they're boring and we want to poison them, it's easiest to hide that in soup."

Rebecca giggles, then checks her list again. "I reserve the right to send you back here later to pick up soup makings. I'm going to go research cheese."

My thigh tingles once more. "We'll be out of the way somewhere." Rebecca charges over to the cheesemonger, who's dressed head to toe in white: apron and toque. He slides around an egregiously expansive display of cheese for a private consultation.

Jackson has discovered his left foot, one of his main sources of entertainment these days, so I push him out of the way and get my phone back out.

> Today is a hard day.

> I just needed you and you're not around.

> It's not anybody's fault. Bye.

It's that *bye* that gets me. I don't know why Jenny's having a hard day, I don't know why she needs me, I don't know whose fault it should be, would be, could be, but evidently it's not anybody's, which in my experience means it's going to be thought of at least somewhat as mine. And then this *bye,* like a high school poet's suicide threat, the sign-off of jaded youth.

> What's going on?

I hit send and immediately cringe. Connotation doesn't come through in text form. Those three words can be read as disinterested, or aggressive. I should have written *I'm really concerned about you. Please tell me what's upsetting you,* but that scans to me as trying to talk a robot down off a ledge. I hold my phone at my side, waiting for it to vibrate, to see whether I'm getting an answer, or hostility, or both in response. Rebecca stands on the other side of the room, and the cheesemonger stands very close to her.

"Curious," I say to Jackson. He babbles his reply. "That's true. The cheese guy is all up in Mommy's personal space. Let's go bail her out."

I push Jackson forward but stop when I get a little closer. Rebecca is laughing at something the cheese guy said, and then she puts her hand on his forearm. It's covered by his white coat, it's not skin to skin, but it's still personal. He's got a knife in the other hand, one he keeps slicing her whisper-thin wedges of cheese with, wiping the blade down on his thigh, and then another joke, and then another laugh. Cheese, joke, laugh.

She's not wearing her wedding ring. This isn't unusual, she takes it off all the time when she maniacally cleans the apartment because people will be coming over. She just forgot to put it back on and now the cheese guy thinks this pretty lady is (a) single and (b) not lactose intolerant. I stand ten feet away watching this mating ritual, enthralled, and not jealous in the least.

I'm not jealous, or angry, or possessive, or any of those things. I don't want to beat that man to death with a wheel of cheese, only in part because he's holding a twelve-inch blade in his hand.

Maybe this is how my mind works. That nothing belongs to anybody, from neighborhoods to families. The normal is always new, ever-evolving; only the bitter and disenfranchised try to dispute this. Better to envision your wife flirting with a cheesemonger and not let your blood pressure crest 120. "You're right, Jackson," I say, watching Rebecca accept another small wedge of cheese, soft and formless, as if painted by Dalí. "You're one hundred percent spot-on. Everything can be taken or given freely." His foot has reached his mouth. He wiggles pea-shaped toes against his gums. "Except for you," I amend. "You belong to me."

Rebecca comes back with a sampling of cheeses. I look over her shoulder and the cheese guy has moved to another customer. Still, I give her a kiss there in the store. She tickles Jackson underneath his glistening chin and ambles off to the olive bar for more recon. We follow at a distance, trying to stay out of the way of the crowds and failing miserably with every turn. My thigh vibrates again and I yank my phone out like a gunslinger.

> Don't worry about it. You wouldn't
> understand.

No, Jenny. No, I probably wouldn't.

Paul Fenniger

Seven Months Ago: December 30, 2009

Jenny has been slow walking around the apartment all morning. She slides in and out of rooms, confused as to how she got there and where she should go next. I made us pancakes for breakfast and she ate half of one, left the other half on her plate in a puddle of syrup, shuffling off back into her office, then the bathroom, then the bedroom. I watched from the table. One right after the other.

I walk in on her changing her shirt in the bedroom. She sits down on the edge of the bed, hums words to herself closed-lipped. Her eyes have that pre-cry storm brewing in them, a tightness and tremor at the edges. Fingers dance in her lap, interdependent of her body. She doesn't realize she's scratching angry welts into the backs of her hands. I hunch over in front of her and gently separate her from herself.

If I ask her if something is wrong, she'll drift inward, because something obviously is wrong. If I ask her what is wrong, she'll throw up a barricade, because I should know, or at least be able to guess. She's not wrong about that. When she does tell me what's bothering her it will seem like a twist in a movie I should have been able to see coming from an hour away. The path into Jenny is to orbit. Bide my time circling and eventually she'll pity my ignorance and tell me what's wrong.

"Do you want to see a movie?" I ask. Something with explosions. A bright and loud distraction. Popcorn.

She shakes her head. I say, "Good. I didn't want to see a movie either." She smiles a little at that. Then, in her quietest voice, she whispers, "Please go and get him."

It's a twist I should have seen coming when we woke up this morning, and it still clubs me sideways. Him is our son. Jenny's distracted because she's thinking about our son and now is talking about our son. She means our son. She means his remains. He was a living child. For a short window of time, our son was the youngest child on the planet. Then, for a flicker, he was the closest to death. In between were mere hours, most of them spent apart from us, on the other side of a glass wall, where all we could see was the green shapeless mass of doctors and nurses hovering over him. When one of the doctors came out to tell us that our son had died and they could not revive him, I felt, amid all of the crushing weight, a sense of relief, because now I finally would be able to see him.

And I did. Jenny did as well. We got to spend as much time as we needed with him—Dr. Mulitz put us in a private room and no one bothered us for an hour. A full hour. I checked the clock on the wall when we sat down, because if someone had come in, needing the room, needing us to leave or give our son back, I wanted to be able to point at that clock and say, "We have only had twenty-three minutes!" After eighty-four minutes a nurse came in and asked us if she could get us anything. Jenny shook her head and said we were ready to go, and so we did. We each gave our son a kiss on his tiny, perfect, dead face, and handed him to the nurse. That was the last time either of us saw him. We never got a picture. I don't know how to feel about that, not having a picture of him.

I stand up and leave Jenny in the bedroom, walking back to her office. They gave us our son in a canister, no larger than a cheese shaker at a pizza restaurant. We brought his ashes home and Jenny said that we should put them away. She said I should throw them out first. I couldn't do that then. She yelled at me for hours, on and off, while I clutched my son in my fist, making sure to not hold him so tightly that I would have dented the thin metal. She yelled at me so much I had to go down and apologize to the neighbors, to explain all the screaming. They spoke only Polish, and they were horrified by what I was holding in my hands, but they understood.

Jenny finally told me to hide the canister, and to not tell her where it is. She went to the nearest bodega to buy her first pack of cigarettes in nine months. Before she left I made her promise me that if she ever found the canister, she wouldn't throw it out. She wouldn't do anything to it. I made her promise twice.

Emotions aside, it's difficult to scramble around in the fifteen minutes it takes Jenny to buy a pack of cigarettes and smoke one to find a hiding spot in the apartment. The cap on the canister was screwed on tightly, so I didn't worry that I was going to spill him out, but there didn't seem to be an appropriate room. The bathroom was out of the question. The kitchen seemed intensely cruel, where I would hide him in an absurdist comedy were he the cremains of a curmudgeonly miser and not my barely born son. I sought a spot in our bedroom, tucked away in a drawer, but the truth there was that I didn't want his presence in that room with us all the time. The weight of our loss was oppressive enough—I didn't want to go to bed at night knowing he was literally five feet away from me and there was nothing I could do as his father.

We created a nursery for him. We had every intention of bringing him home and putting him in this nursery, so I opened the closet and dug around until I found my box in the back. I had brought it from my bedroom in Cadott, a collection of knickknacks from my childhood. Baseball cards, magic tricks, a photo album of Polaroids—there's no way Jenny would ever throw this out. I laid my son gently into that box, devastated to realize that he will never have a box like this of his own, the sum of a young life, but instead be laid to rest for the time being next to all the joys of my boyhood.

I closed the box, went to the kitchen, got a Sharpie from the crap drawer, and wrote on the lid VERY IMPORTANT—DO NOT DISCARD.

That is where, five months later, I find our son. I cradle him in the palm of my hand, willing myself to stay steady. When I get back into the bedroom Jenny still sits on the edge of the bed, texting on her phone. She looks up and sees what I'm holding. "It's time," she says.

"Okay."

"I don't want to carry this loss into the new year. And tomorrow there's this fucking party, and I can't do this and that in the same day. And I want to do that. I want us to do that so we're not sitting by ourselves and grieving, Fenn. Do you want to do this?"

"It's a good idea."

"Are you sure?"

"It's a good idea," I repeat, numb. I'm holding my son. This I can do for him.

"Okay. Let's get this over with."

"Where do you want to scatter him?"

She hadn't thought about that. Once we release him he is everywhere and nowhere, but we remain somewhere. If ever we were to move from New York, he would remain behind, at least the way Jenny and I think about him. She shakes her head. "I don't know."

"I think we should go to the water, and scatter him in the East River. Because it's not going anywhere, and then we'll think about him every time we go into Manhattan."

She considers this. Then she starts crying. "That's real good, Fenn," she sobs out.

Jenny composes herself in the bathroom—for whom, I don't know. Herself, I suppose. I gather our jackets, tucking our son in my pocket. On our front stoop she pauses, lights a cigarette, sends another text, and wraps her arm in mine. We walk purposefully, in silence, grim and unyielding against a wind coming off of the river.

We reach a patch of green off Kent Avenue, something set aside for the residents of all the new construction popping up along the water. We may have witnesses to this ceremony, which doesn't bother me, but I know Jenny would not want to be watched. At the end of a pier we find a bench and sit for a spell, the canister in my hand, in my pocket. Jenny curls herself into my side.

"You would have been a great mom to him," I tell her. Her chuckle comes out corrosively bitter, but she clutches me tighter.

She replies, "Best thing I did for this kid was pick the right father." I rub my fingers against the canister, stroking his sleeping head, his cheeks, his stomach rising and falling with each breath. I stroke the metal that holds his ashes and wait for Jenny to tell me what to do next.

"You remember how much I used to drink in college?" she asks. I can't tell from her tone whether I should answer.

"You didn't drink any more than the rest of us."

"I did, and not by a small margin. I was a grand old pickle."

"You don't drink too much now."

"I know. Listen. It didn't worry me, because I thought that I was getting it out of my system. I remember thinking that when I added a job and a family then there wouldn't be the time to drink, so I'm just getting it out of my system while I can. Get my fill in, and then I won't miss it when it's gone. Thought I'd do the same thing with cigarettes—just get it out of my system."

"You can quit smoking. I've seen you do it before."

She furrows her brow. "No, I . . . Yeah, I guess I can. Sure. Listen to me."

"I'm listening."

"My point is that my system may be my system. No matter how much I think I'm getting things out of it, I can always make more. That's how my system works."

"We can try again when you're ready."

Her eyes snap into slits, but then she takes a long breath, lets it out with curls of steam, nuzzles her face into my shoulder instead. We sit like that, watching a tugboat go past, absurd and antiquated.

It comforts me that our son will be in this river. It's a timeless place. I'm doing something right for him.

"I want you to know how I love you, Fenn. I never get that out of my system, either," Jenny says slowly, deliberately.

"I love you too."

"I want you to know how. Listen to me." But she doesn't say anything after that. I wait and wait to learn how, but she stares out at the river, tight-lipped. The canister feels cold beneath my fingertips. I can reassure myself on an intellectual level, but a visceral part of me wants to get our son out of the chill.

"Can we give him a name, please?" I ask. Jenny sniffs hard.

"I don't want to, Fenn. We lost him. He didn't live long enough to get a name. It's easier for me to think of him as our son."

"I really want to name him, Jenny."

I brace myself for anger, but she rubs my forehead with a soft hand. "Can you name him and not tell me?" she asks. I can do that. "I'll say good-bye, and then you'll say good-bye, and you can call him whatever name you would have wanted to give him, and then we'll say good-bye together. But you can't ever tell me the name you were going to give him, okay?"

I can do that. She takes the canister from my hand and walks to the railing at the end of the pier. She's out of earshot, and it kills me to not know what she's saying to him. Jenny would have been the most brilliant of mothers. She still may be. But not for this child. All she can do for him is pass along whatever it is she's passing along now. I know enough to not ask her what she said when she comes back to the bench and hands him back to me. She'll never tell.

At the railing it occurs to me that I don't know what name I would have given our son. For the small fuss I just made over it, I didn't have a name picked out. Jenny wanted those super-literary names, and I was happy to go along. Left to name him on my own, I can't think of anything. A quiver starts at my knee, a shaking I can't control. I'm wasting my last moments with him trying to think of what to call him.

Paul Jr. doesn't sound right. I couldn't do anything for my son; it's not right to give him my name. There's no historical figure I feel enough admiration for to name my son after. I run through all the names of my friends growing up, my baseball heroes, names of men at the firm, a Rolodex in baby book form racing through my head. What would I have wanted to call him for the rest of my life? How would I have wanted to introduce him?

This is my son, his name is . . . and I am so proud to be his father.

My dad's name is Hank Fenniger. He drives a bus in Cadott, Wisconsin, and when I told him I was moving to New York with Jenny, he whistled and told me I was going to have quite the adventure. When I called my dad to tell him he was only a grandfather for a very little while, I said that one of the saddest parts about this was that I would have raised my son the way Hank Fenniger had raised me. That's the highest praise, I suppose, a son can pay, to view his own dad as a fatherhood manual.

Hank isn't his actual name, of course. It's Henry, and so that's what I name our son. Henry Fenniger. I say hello and good-bye in the same speech. In between I fit a lifetime of hopes and advice and dreams and warnings and love and love and love for this child I barely met. The quiver spreads. "Jenny, come here," I yell. I can't move from the railing. I can't move or I'm going to break down. I'm going to crumble and drop him and then he'll roll off the pier and into the water and stay sealed and never get to grow up and move away from us and find his own way. "Jenny, come here please."

She puts her hands over mine and together we open the canister. Jenny doesn't want to look in but I do. I see Henry's ashes. Hello and good-bye.

We wait until the wind dies down, then we tilt Henry up and out over the railing and into the East River, where our son is carried away in the air and water like smoke.

Paul Fenniger

Seven Months Ago: December 31, 2009

"Let's dress up," Jenny proclaimed. She leaped out of bed this morning, actually bounced herself off the mattress, and declared her desire, even adding that she had a "capital idea." I naturally agreed and picked out a suit from my closet. Dressing up for me bears many similarities to dressing for work. Rather than being aggrieved at having to wear a suit on a day off, I like this idea, dressing up for a party. Jenny escaped after breakfast to shop the tiny boutiques along our street. She found a green dress she says is too thin for winter but she'll wear a big coat over it. She waved the bag around, spinning and dancing through the apartment, holding the dress up against her body, using my adoring eyes as her mirror.

The pendulum of her moods, capricious in general, swings a wider arc of late. She must have thought she'd have to oversell the dressing-up idea, because her voice immediately launched into that breathless speed, a torrent amped up to shock and awe. She needn't have wasted the energy, though it was a sight to behold. I'm not used to seeing Jenny snap back to a good place so fast; I thought she'd swing low for a while after yesterday.

These past few weeks, she's retreated into her new office to read or write and ignore me for hours, which is unusual for her. She loves to shout her thoughts to me as I walk by, draw me into whatever room she's in to recount the story she just read. Or, she barnacles herself to me while I cook or read, touching me, as if to make sure I haven't disappeared. That part I love, her nearness and affection, how she rubs my back or just runs her hand along my shoulders as she walks by me at the stove. When we went grocery shopping last night, I left her in the produce aisle for a minute while she turned over every head of romaine to find the most pristine one, with the fewest sullied leaves. I left her to that for a moment, so I could grab vinegar. One aisle over. When I came back she hugged me, wrapped her arms around my waist and held me tightly, in the middle of the store. "Put a bell around your neck, Fenn, so I always know you're near," she swooned wistfully.

Armchair-psychologist me wants to attribute this to the weight lifted after yesterday. Jenny is ready to start anew. All of this recent scattershot emotion was the buildup, and yesterday she flushed it out. This is what I keep telling myself, crowding out other voices, other explanations.

Jenny's behavior strikes me as simultaneously erratic and familiar. I've seen her eyes move independently of her head before, like she's checking around corners that aren't there. I've seen her monitor my movement in and out of a room. I've seen her look at me before as if I'm a stranger, a lodger renting a room.

I think she's had a fight with Michael. Whenever I bring him up, usually in the context of the job he's done on the room, she brushes it off or says something small and cutting about him, about his personality. "Do you want to skip their party?" I asked her again last night. "We can say I'm sick."

"No." She gazed off to the side. "We may as well go."

"We can tell them what we did," I said gently.

Her eyes narrow. I'm a stranger again. "Let's have some things be our things, okay?"

December crams metaphors into perspective. The only thing for me that changes tomorrow is the number I put on a check, but Jenny gives this day greater heft. Or December just brings with it a vague sense of time passing, while Jenny's growing dissatisfaction with her life gets compounded exponentially twice every year—once on her birthday and once tonight. I'm her only constant, and when she gets melancholic and withdrawn, I wonder if the reason—or rather how much a part of the reason—is her disappointment in that stability.

But it's okay. January will bring with it the old Jenny, somewhere in between clingy and sullen, making future plans and discussing celebrity marriages at length.

New Year's Eve. Getting ready to go to a party. Noisemakers and champagne. While I'm leaning over the end of the bed, tying my shoes, she comes into our room wearing her green dress. She still drops my jaw, every damn time.

She points at my chest and cocks her head. "Is that really the tie you're going to wear?" She doesn't wait for my answer, just turns and waits by the front door, impatient.

On the subway ride over, most revelers behave at least three drinks in. The couple next to us talks loudly, critiquing each other's resolutions. Jenny gathers herself into me, burrows into the fabric of my coat. "Do you remember New Year's 2006?" she asks.

Oh I do. I grin at the memory. "I'm afraid I don't," I say slow enough that she knows it's a joke, that she knows I remember every second of it. "Refresh my memory. Did we spend that year together?"

"We did. I forget how we spent it, but I do recall making lots and lots of awful puns about balls dropping."

"Oh Jenny, you are a card."

"Shut up! They were funny at the time."

I kiss the top of her head. "Grow old with me, Jennifer Sayles." Please.

"I will, Fenn." She sighs. "I envision us wrinkled and mute, sitting next to each other at a bar, cradling medicinal whiskey drinks, something to help us get to sleep that night. We'll look like two derelicts, strangers who wandered in off the street and gravitated toward each other, as if to section off a tiny fragment of the bar for the aged. For the experienced." She savors that last word. "Our postures stooped, our eyes fixed forward. And you'll turn to me, lock your rheumy eyes with mine, and say, 'I love the fucking Christ out of you.' You'll say it without preamble or prompting, just a declarative statement, heavy with the weight of shared time. I think about that when I think about us growing old together, Fenn, and it counts as romantic."

Jenny can joke, but when I first saw her across the room at a college party, time did stop and music did play. That orchestra still picks back up every time she crosses my mind.

"I love the fucking Christ out of you," I say, and kiss the top of her head again.

Jenny ambushes Jackson when we get to their house. I love Jenny for her unbendable resilience. After dinner, Michael insists on taking us to the roof of his studio. I look to Rebecca to shoot this idea down on Jackson's behalf, but she seems more excited than he is by the prospect. She still retains a shred of sobriety, though my head is wrapped in a warm blanket of the mulled wine Michael has been ladling into our glasses all night. We bundle into jackets and hats, Rebecca straps a sleeping Jackson into a BabyBjörn, and we set out. "When he's out, he's out," she says, proudly.

When Michael mentioned his studio I thought to myself that I had been there before, then realized that was a lie I had told Jenny. But I have the vague recollection that Michael was going to say that he forgot his key, so we went to a bar instead that night. It's possible that in both the real and duplicitous worlds I still have not been inside his studio. Lies within lies—it's exhausting. In this hazy, drunken state, I'm rigid with anxiety that someone will ask me a question, and when we start walking, I make sure Michael leads the way, bending to retie my shoe as he sets out.

His studio looks how I pictured it, with sections of the floor taped off, tools strapped to the walls, and half-finished projects lying around. Michael gives us a grand tour. Tony's section has metal shelving stacked with ceramic plates and bowls, a potter's wheel and a kiln, a picture of a bearded man with a wife and children, and a basketball. Regina's section is all jagged splinters of wood and rolls of canvas. "I think she's building a boat," Michael tosses off. Marc's section has a funhouse-of-terror vibe to it, metal spikes pointing in every which way, like the rays of the sun. "He's on a fence-building jag," Michael explains. He finishes by showing us his section, the ornately carved table legs and pictures of projects finished. At the bottom right he's taped a photograph of Jenny's office. She's immensely tickled by this, that he kept a picture, but I'm strangely possessive. It rubs me in a way I can't define that he has this, that he displays Jenny's room like a pinup.

I'm very drunk. Some attentive secretary in my mind makes a note that everything I think, say, and especially do for the rest of the evening must now be monitored more closely, because I am very, very drunk.

The roof offers the panoramic view of lower Manhattan I'd expect. Fireworks go off somewhere over New Jersey, small pinpricks on the distant horizon, oddly cute in their minuscule state. Michael says that we're technically not supposed to be on the roof, but that the landlord has to keep it accessible as a fire escape and so instructed his tenants to use it only during an emergency. The small crowd up here makes clear that this rule is widely disregarded. Tony and his wife sip from a flask and greet us all with hugs, his red, bearded face stinking of some brown liquor, but his eyes kind. Michael introduces me as an actor and Tony reacts with starstruck wonder. Regina introduces herself and her girlfriend, whose name is German and flees my head as soon as she says it. "I like what you're building," I say cordially, and she gives me a small, patronizing smile in response. Her girlfriend immediately takes to Jackson, chatting away at him in German.

Michael has brought bottles of wine and glasses to the roof, so we continue the party up there. Tony regales us with his first New Year's in New York, which he spent in an emergency room because he'd been hit by a cab. At midnight, the doctors and nurses gathered at the desk and toasted with sparkling cider.

Jenny slips away from the rest of us to smoke, and Michael looks beseechingly to Rebecca. "It's a holiday," he whines. She shoots him a half-convincing look of disappointment, but then waves her hand dismissively.

"Go ahead." And Michael scampers over to Jenny to join her. "He thinks he hides it better than he does," she tells me. Jackson, as if to confirm, let's out a tiny squeak of protest. He's woken up, not quite out once he was out, but he doesn't seem to mind the cold, the noise, the disorientation, the people. He is not aware that my head swims upstream.

I wonder if my son would have been so chill on New Year's. Nope. Can't cry. Can't cry here.

"Wow, he really doesn't cry much, does he?" I ask Rebecca. Jackson lies against her breast, his stumpy legs kicking air.

"Certain things bother him," Rebecca explains. "He doesn't like baths, and he makes a lot of noise when he wakes up hungry from a nap." She stares at him dreamily.

I look over at Michael and Jenny, who sit huddled next to each other, passing a cigarette back and forth. Thin plumes of smoke rise off them, these two bundled close together. He tilts his head toward her, saying something too low for us to hear, like two kids scheming.

Jenny's behavior now strikes me as less erratic, more familiar. I know this song, verse and chorus.

I've been blind—this intimacy they share goes beyond offices and casual friendship. I love Jenny, and I trust Jenny, but I also know Jenny, and I've seen what it means when she shuffles herself closer to another man, presses her shoulder to his, as if willing their two bodies together.

It's happening again, in front of my face.

I'm not sober, but I'm clear as still water. They exhale at the same time, turned away from one another, and on this windless night the smoke rises to the side, like two horns from the same beast.

I turn to Rebecca, to see if she's watching the show I'm watching, and discover her face coming toward mine. With a hand guarding her son from being crushed between us, Rebecca's mouth veers off at the last second and pecks me on the cheek. "Happy

New Year," she coos. I spin around the roof, looking at everyone kissing everyone else. Michael comes up to me and shakes my hand, transforms it into a hug. "Happy New Year, brother," he says to me.

I was facing Rebecca when the ball dropped. When it hit midnight. I completely missed how Michael and Jenny rang in the new year. It happened ten feet from where I'm standing, but I was looking the other way.

Paul Fenniger

Five Months Ago: February 2, 2010

> *Vain Fopps, but court, and dress, and keep a puther,*
> *To pass for Womens men, with one another.*
> *But he who aimes by women to be priz'd,*
> *First by the men you see must be despis'd.*

Those are my last lines onstage. I walk off to some piped-in harpsichord, because Ted connects harpsichord to anything before 1900, and the monitor onstage plays a final speech we recorded two weeks ago—me as Mr. Hart, recapping everything in iambs.

Marie hands me a bottle of High Life once I'm offstage, our nightly tradition for the past week. Elspeth sits on an overturned black wooden box, already halfway through hers. We have another thirty seconds before the curtain call to roll our eyes and thank good Christ another night of this is over. Ted called us back four weeks ago, right after the new year, to tell us that he'd secured a space for us to perform in. Show goes up in twenty-four days. Rehearsals start back up tomorrow.

The first time he told us about the performance space, he spoke rhapsodically about its technical capabilities and location, and slipped in that it would cost $3,000 for the week. Each subsequent time he spoke about the space he downplayed its West Village location and emphasized the cost. The three members of the cast discussed this over drinks after rehearsal one night, after we separated from Ted.

"You know we're not getting paid," Elspeth said before the drinks arrived. My attraction for her has waned almost as powerfully as it arose, like getting over a nagging cold. Now what I feel for her is mostly revulsion, on a personal level at least. As a scene partner, I like her more now than when Ted cast her. She's on time, doesn't step on my lines, and engages with the material. But I've projected enough of a cold front to her offstage that she's confused, wondering if she offended me somehow.

Marie can't turn her androgyny off, and Elspeth and I suspect she doesn't want to, that reading as either male or female is a role she carries offstage with her hair cropped and buttoned shirts billowy enough to hide the breasts I wouldn't be surprised if she taped down. And it works for her, she draws the eye. She's the only one of us with her next gig already lined up. There's something intimate about her conscious ungendering that forces an audience to engage with her to glean basic information. She shook her hands in front of her and said, "Whoa. Since when are we not getting paid?"

"Ted's in the hole at least three grand," I agreed with Elspeth. "He's done this before."

"Not pay you?"

"It's not that we don't get paid," I hemmed and hawed. "It's that we don't get paid first. Ted will recoup what he's put out first, then pay us from the box office. No more than what we were originally going to get. We'll get paid something," I reassured Marie. Elspeth blew the bangs from her face. "It's not as guaranteed as before."

The audience starts clapping, they're so small an audience we can hear individual sets of hands, so we put our bottles down and walk out to bow. At quick count, about two dozen people came to see our final performance. Jenny sits house left; I found her immediately upon my first entrance. She doesn't sit in the front row because she worries she'll distract me, and in a theater this small, she would—I'd be able to see her beneath the lights. I can't see anything but silhouettes past the third row, but it would be difficult to kiss another woman in front of her, even in character. She applauds, beaming at me. There's a warmth in that, this public display of support. Michael claps and hoots next to her. Rebecca sits politely next to him on the other side, clapping as if she doesn't want to hurt her hands.

I bow and bow again, hold hands with my costars and we gesture toward the back to show our gratitude, to demand the audience's gratitude for our tech crew, which comprises Ted and another friend he roped in to run the lighting board. The audience can only respond so far before the clapping becomes more sporadic, thins out like a fire slowly dying. After some more harpsichord, we exit.

Our single dressing room is crowded even when only one of us is in it. Elspeth has already signed the wall, next to hundreds of other illegible signatures of actors, interspersed with photographs of past productions taped, captioned, defaced.

As I sip my beer backstage and slowly get out of costume, I wipe my makeup off and stare at the lines on my face. They weren't there the last time I checked, or they were and I simply hadn't noticed them. Hadn't thought to look.

Dressing room mirrors speak in declarative sentences. I'm thirty-two years old. I'm acting, potentially for free, in obscure productions for audiences that consist mainly of friends and family. The production basically extorts the money we are too proud to ask our loved ones for directly, not that my parents would travel from Cadott to see a show I'm in. I don't begrudge them that—dropping my parents into New York would be akin to dropping them into the

Serengeti. They'd go wide-eyed and slack-jawed for ten minutes, like being teleported into the movies, before some small pinprick—getting jostled on the sidewalk, seeing the price of breakfast, confronting homelessness—would start the polite, passive-aggressive Midwestern questions like "Are you sure this street is safe?" or "You wouldn't come here when it's dark out, right?"

This is how it goes when I think about my acting career. My mind, in desperate self-preservation, darts wildly down some other path. I went to school for acting. I trained. I'm no dilettante. And I live and work in the most theater-conscious city in the world. Every week there are hundreds of auditions for student films and off-off-Broadway shows and corporate gigs and productions in the parks. Every week opportunities are laid before me, have been for a decade, and yet here I am, no further along than when I was young and unlined, when I could play the male ingénue, the beautiful object any director could find the flimsiest excuse to put onstage without a shirt.

Oh my God those days are done. Oh my God I'm thirty-two and one set of doors has closed without another set opening. Physically I'm still the same body type—the salt can be dyed out of my hair, makeup will cover these few shallow ridges—but those days are done. A new generation of chorus boys has stepped off the bus to answer the callbacks I used to get.

I own a career that never belonged to me.

Jenny kisses me on the cheek when I step outside, kisses me on the cheek the way she kisses Michael on the cheek when he leaves our house. She's drawn the equivalency between us. Now that I have my evenings back, Jenny and I should spend more time together. We should reconnect as a couple. Being in this play, pursuing this farcical dream, wearing failure as some noble badge, has hurt my marriage. When we decide on an East Village bar for my celebratory drink, Michael and Jenny fall into step next to one another. They separate from Rebecca and me as naturally as oil from water, forging on ahead, talking and laughing and ignoring the silent partners who walk like spies behind them.

This is my fault, I think. This division. Through my negligence, I've let this in. This presence in my marriage, this widening rift.

I had nothing to do with it, and it's all my fault.

Michael Gould

Present Day: July 19, 2010

1:17 PM

The ambulance bay outside of Mount Sinai curves eerily empty away from an equally empty lobby. Only a few security guards stand by the door, craning their necks to see in both directions down the street, like restaurateurs eager to goad passersby into dining tonight. The ambulances must be out on calls, concentrated in midtown, in makeshift field hospitals. I was told once by an EMT friend (now downgraded to an EMT acquaintance) that the back of an ambulance is equipped to handle most procedures, just under significantly worse conditions than an operating theater.

I've bounced to the perimeter of the park, the straight line of Fifth Avenue, only intermittently broken by cross streets that connect the Upper East Side to the Upper West Side. This has to be faster than the meandering running path. In quick succession I pass the Guggenheim and the Met, both closed. Crowds mill outside, confused tourists standing one foot in the street with a hand raised to hail one of the cabs their guidebooks promised them are as common as ants. Entire families huddle over maps spread out on the sidewalk, penciling a route back to the hotel. Phones are consulted and shaken. People scream into them to no avail. But mostly, people loiter, waiting for instructions, waiting for the voice from on high to tell them to run for their lives. At the Met, about a dozen people stand in the fountains, cooling off, and the guards don't even bother to chase them away. They're busier trying to clear the steps, so crowded it looks like a protest.

I grow increasingly certain of a subway bombing. The question then becomes who, and from where did he come, so we know where to start demanding retribution, though we never get that comfort of the past, of having a sanctioned attack from a country. Saudi Arabia's official military is never going to attack us. Iraq according to Rand McNally is never going to attack us. What country both hates New York enough and has the resources to launch a ground attack? All I can come up with off the top of my head is Texas.

After 9/11, my father worried about looting, about opportunistic rioters coming into the neighborhood at night on the assumption that the police were too busy manning the bucket brigades in lower Manhattan or drowning their sorrows over fallen colleagues. He worried that reports of a break-in down in the Jewish section of Brooklyn would be met with a shrug and a "they police their own" mentality. "Chaos begets chaos," he warned. He barricaded the doors of the house each night, continued to do so even when I came home two weeks later, demanded I help him shift a wardrobe against the front door and the oven against the back. He was willing to trade the obstacles that would likely kill us in the event of a fire for the inconvenient delay it would cause a robber before he simply smashed glass and came in through a window.

Nothing happened, of course. Just as nothing is going to happen to these apartments along Fifth Avenue, which have locked their doors. New York operates (for the paler hued, at least) on the skullcracker theory of policing during times of citywide calamity. Getting caught stealing on a regular day will earn you a beating from the shop owner and a smack from the cops if you aren't unfailingly contrite and cooperative. Get caught using mass hysteria as a distraction and the cops will look the other way if you happened to run full speed into a baseball bat a half-dozen times before they arrived. The doormen stand guard, legs spread shoulder width, hands clasped in front of them, receptionists turned mercenaries, eyeing the passersby from posts on the opposite side of glass-doored entryways, sentries unlocking the ramparts only to let in residents. With the power still coming and going, and the air-conditioning out with it, they glisten like glazed donuts in their uniforms.

Crowds pick up at about Seventieth. There's a noticeable shortening of steps, a slow congealing of the crowd. These aren't just the tourists. A Central Park vendor loudly protests getting kicked out of the park today without being given a reason. At Sixty-fifth forward movement stops altogether. At first I assume that I'm standing at the back of a crowd of rubberneckers, that something is happening in front of us as people watch enrapt. Heads tilt up, mesmerized by the fleet of helicopters droning over midtown like black mosquitoes. As we trudge forward, I realize that this is foot traffic headed off the island, backed up to the park, five blocks north and roughly six long blocks west of the Queensboro Bridge.

As a crowd forms behind me, I start to get sucked into the mass. I bail before I become a part of the amoeba, dart off down Sixty-fourth, map the route that will jump my place in line, get me on the bridge faster. Etiquette cedes its place, the largest and most powerful cutting a swath through the crowd that enables the slower, the older, the weaker to follow. We all misquote the same tenets of Darwin in our heads, waiting for the alpha males to lead us to safety.

Foot traffic moves even as it approaches the corkscrew entrance to the footpath of the Queensboro Bridge. Someone must be directing people at the other end, in Queens, getting the crowds to disperse, otherwise we'd be as stalled as the cars are on the bridge. We press on under the midday heat, last reported as 103 officially, "feels like" 109, inhaling the exhaust fumes of idling cars, the guttural growl of stalled trucks drowning out all other sounds. People around me keep checking their phones to see if there's service once

247

off the island. We are the Israelites in Exodus, heads bowed in prayer to our phones.

A man stands fifty feet past the entrance of the bridge, pressed nearly flat against the guard fence. He's dressed like I am, like any rational human being would dress on a day like today. He's shaved his face and combed his hair and wouldn't warrant a second glance on an ordinary day. But today he stands at the entrance of the Queensboro Bridge and he shrieks at the top of his lungs, "What are they not telling us?" Every word gets its own exclamation point. His eyes aren't even wide. "What aren't they telling us?" he shouts over and over again. After three or four times his voice recedes to an uneasy place, gravel rubbing in the backs of our minds.

I'm surrounded by thousands of people, yet none of us seem to know what has happened in midtown today. New York is not a secretive place, not for most of us. We share information. Trains are running express instead of local and you'll hear about it from a dozen people before you swipe your card through. That no one has any idea paints the day with an artificiality, all of us extras on a giant set.

Of course, there's a far scarier explanation: no one crossing the bridge knows what's happened because no one who knows what's happened made it out of midtown.

We walk with urgency. Many of the women walk in pinched, pained steps, heels in hand, still striding forth as fast as their cut and blistered feet will take them. When a woman collapses about two hundred feet onto the bridge, she's immediately lifted up by fellow New Yorkers, carried arm over shoulder, a wounded comrade being dragged to the nearest medical tent, should one even exist. On the other side of the fence, separating feet from tires, horns honk and people yell back.

I catch glimpses through the steel girders. The footpath is on the north side of the bridge, but I see parts of Brooklyn to the south. The subway map makes the boroughs look more geometrically elegant than they actually are. In reality, the rivers wend through and Brooklyn hooks underneath Manhattan, spooning the island. The phallic spire of the Williamsburgh Savings Bank in downtown Brooklyn situates me like a beacon. Walk toward that and I can find my way home.

Halfway across the bridge, people in front of me start turning around, walking backward for a few steps, snapping pictures on their phones. I spin with them and see Manhattan from a distance for the first time. I'm blocked by steel and cars, by the unending crowd of people, but I can make out some of the buildings of midtown. In the vicinity of Times Square, a thin plume of smoke rises, as if the island were casually smoking a cigarette. It bends and trails off south, carried along the invisible currents of a breeze too faint to detect. Something is on fire.

As we approach Queensboro Plaza, we pass over hundreds of people tucked below the bridge, those who walked across before us but couldn't stop on the bridge, so they retreated down toward the banks of the East River. They now look across, waiting for a sign of what to fear, what to run from, so I turn around one last time as well. No shower of ash this time, no buildings collapsing inward. It's our shining city, unbroken if not unbreakable, the only change to the skyline that slender wisp of smoke, rising steadily until it dissipates into a grainy haze.

Michael Gould

Five Months Ago: February 19, 2010

Adam Cavendish loves his table. Will definitely call me for all of his future custom furniture needs. "Did you tell him you paint?" Rebecca asks. "Not in the market for art right now," I reply. Not in the practice, either. It's been months since I've picked up a brush.

Whatever time I would have been dedicating to it has been channeled elsewhere. Or I've outgrown the artistic ambitions I once held sacrosanct. I don't have the mental bandwidth to contemplate why I've stopped painting. Rebecca, politely, hasn't asked.

Next up is a set of kitchen chairs for a family that lives in Hell's Kitchen in reality and in Prospect Heights in the narrative I've spun. It's a neighborhood down from Williamsburg, but in sort of the same direction from here. Rebecca congratulates me on the new gig, claims a whole set of anything sounds expensive, but her voice has a strain to it, her joy for me doesn't reach her eyes. When we're in bed later that night, when I'm the ladle and she's the teaspoon and my arms are draped around her middle and I warn her that if she falls asleep before I do, then I'm going to swallow her up whole and she'll live inside my tummy, she laughs only to be genial. I ask her what's wrong.

"You're never here," she says.

Pause. Breath. Pause. Brace. "It only feels that way because you're always here."

"Maybe." She elongates the word; I feel her shift and fluster, casting doubt. "It seems like you're always either in your shop or working with a client and when you're not you're hanging out with Jenny."

"And Paul," I amend.

"And Paul. I'm glad you have friends—"

"We have friends—"

"—yes, we're friends. I mean, our friends." She exhales, shrinks in my arms. "I'm being clingy. Sorry. Can we blame mommy hormones?"

"Nothing to be sorry for," I reassure her. "But if you fall asleep, I'm first going to bite your face off, chew it up. Then I'm going to bite off each of your fingers, one at a time, suck the meat out. Then I'll move on to your sweetmeats . . ."

Devour you whole, Rebecca Gould. Keep you inside of me forever.

. . .

Two days later, unseasonably warm in late February, Jenny and I decide to venture out into our city. There's been a sexual segue in our relationship, one in which we don't feel the need to make sex either the thing we get out of the way the instant I arrive, or the culmination of our day together, a figurative and physical climax to shared time. Lately, I come over and we go out from there. Less wear and tear on the sheets. Like today. When it's time to leave Jenny scrunches her face and retraces her steps through the apartment. "Where are my keys?"

I spin around, looking at countertops. "Thank you, Mickey. Very helpful." Then she reaches into her purse and plucks them out by a ring. "You goose." I laugh at her until she joins in and then I can laugh with her.

"I used to hide Paul's keys from him. He'd leave them on the counter and I'd slip them into his jacket pocket, and he'd go nuts trying to remember where he'd left them. I'd act exasperated and then reach into his pocket, or wherever else I'd hidden them, and hand them over."

"Why'd you do that?"

"So that he'd remember how much he needs me," she says as she locks the door behind us.

Jenny's head goes on a swivel when we're in her neighborhood. I've never seen her with a friend, she and Paul seem like a supremely insular couple, so I'm not sure who she's worried might see us together. Today it's particularly bad—she's checking behind her so often that I begin to get paranoid that she's in deep to the mob. "What's going on?"

"Nothing. What do you mean?"

"You keep checking your six."

"My six?"

"Behind you."

"Why are you using hipster lingo?"

"Because you're behaving like we're in a seventies cop movie. What's going on?"

She stops us from walking. We're two blocks away from her house, on our way to the subway. It's the middle of the day. We're alone save for the not unpleasant stench of smoked fish wafting off of the Acme warehouse. Alone but for the sound of trucks rumbling in the deep background. Alone but for eyes at windows, the street bare before us in both directions. "I want to try something new." She composes herself, then reaches out and grasps my hand in hers. We commence walking, in her neighborhood, hand in hand. Thus begins our Young Lovers Tour of New York.

February 28

The American Museum of Natural History
(Central Park West, at Seventy-ninth Street)

We museum shuffle from skeleton to skeleton. At first I worried that Jenny would be skittish here. When we pass babies in carriages it often sends her into reboot mode. She goes silent for a few seconds, then slowly works herself back into whatever conversation we were having. I worried that this museum, where every hour of every day there is a different school group, would be a hornet's nest of triggers for her. But it's not. She smiles plainly at the kids pressing their faces against glass and the stupid things they say about the whale ("That thing is bigger than a car!") but otherwise ignores them. It's possible she never visualized her baby as a child. Or maybe, in the throes of grief, she walled a psychological cutoff somewhere around toddler lest she stroke out every time she sees any boy younger than herself and thinks of her son.

Jenny falls in love with a South American sloth because it's called the Robber Tooth. "That's my new favorite thing in this museum," she chirps proudly. Two rooms after that Jenny turns away from the medieval weaponry. I'm not particularly interested in it, either. She says, "You know where I've never been?"

"The Cloisters," I reply.

"How did you know?"

"Is that seriously it?"

"Yes, I've always wanted to go and I've never been."

"No one has. It's forever away. I've never been either."

She tugs my arms, gives me doe eyes, not because she needs to, but because she knows how I love it so. "Can we go, please?"

"Anytime."

Today is the first time our talk hasn't been about the us-ness of us, the first time we haven't had a meta-relationship conversation. It's not that we've avoided it, just that it hasn't come up. Hand in hand, today felt blissfully normal, right up to the point when I took a different subway home.

March 5

Jackson Diner (37-47 Seventy-fourth Street, Queens)

We're a milky island in a sea of darker faces. We are the gentrification of this restaurant. It's built like it was made for weddings: high ceilings, wide-open spaces, a seating plan that can accommodate at least two hundred Indian men. And us. I joke, "I'll bet we could get a ride home pretty easily." Jenny groans, because my ironic racism still counts in her world. Whatever. She's just upset she didn't think up the line first.

"This is fucking delicious," Jenny says. She has an obscene amount of red sauce on her chin—I think it's from bhindi masala, but I wasn't looking at what she loaded up on her plate.

"I want to stick my cock in this." I'm on my third trip to the buffet. Go easy on the rice, that's the secret. Go easy on the rice, go easy on the naan. That's how I've worked three helpings of chicken kadai down my gullet.

She finally draws a napkin across her face, no longer looks like she went down on a jelly donut. She asks, "Where do you want to go?"

"Back to your place?"

"Then where?"

"What are my options?"

She smiles. "Anywhere in the world. For two weeks."

I swallow. "A nice place." I cringe. I'm usually better at hypotheticals. My honest first thought was convenience. Where can we take Jackson? I don't think that's what Jenny asks me.

"What makes a place nice?"

"It isn't likely to explode."

"That's smart thinking. Where would you go? Name three places."

First one is easy. "Paris."

"Cliché."

Okay, there are correct answers. "Morocco."

"I like."

"Montreal."

"Canada? That's like America's sideline."

"A weekend trip then. On the way to Prague."

"Oooooh, Prague. Yes, please."

I put down my fork. "Where would you go?"

Jenny closes her eyes to think. "Paris, Morocco, and Montreal. And Prague."

"All good places."

"I have a longer list, but I'd start there."

"Are you a good flier?"

"Never flown."

"Never?"

"Neverdy ever."

"You'll get the hang of it in no time."

She scratches the back of my hand with a fingernail. "Do you want to travel the world with me?"

We'd pack light, wouldn't need to check a stroller. "I do, Jenny."

"I'm serious."

"I am too, Jenny."

A beat. "I love you."

"I love you."

". . . you want to get back in line at the buffet?"

"Lead the way."

March 12

Paris Theater (4 West Fifty-eighth Street)

We bought our tickets from the usher in the glassed-in vestibule on
Fifty-eighth. We climbed the crooked staircase. We took our seats
and waited for the lights to dim, for the curtain to part, for the
tommy gun percussion of the projector to perforate the hushed
murmuring of the sparse midday crowd.

We make out in the balcony like teenagers. We make out until
our lips are swollen. We don't even pay attention to the movie, can't
kiss and read the subtitles at the same time. Neither of us speaks
a syllable beyond emergency French.

Jenny texts Paul afterward, when we're walking past the Plaza
and into the park. She tells him that she's in the mood for cassoulet. "He says he's chomping at the bit to cook it."

"It's 'champing at the bit.' The expression."

"I know."

"He's only chomping because he doesn't know I'm joining."

"It's possible."

"Does he know about us?"

Jenny gives a half smile. "Knows about us or know he knows
about us?"

"Either."

"He hasn't said anything to me," she relays, and her smile cur-
dles bittersweet. I may have grimaced at this point; it's difficult to

control every facial tic. Paul and I have a friendship built on sand and broken glass, unified at the very least by our love for Jenny—his open, mine less so. But it is a friendship, which makes it an even stranger relationship than the one I'm in with Jenny. Would that he openly and nakedly wanted to crush my skull—I'd know better what to do with that.

Later, when Paul opens the door, his face falls to see me standing behind Jenny, grinning and holding a bottle of wine. I'm everybody's friend, Paul. I'm coming for dinner, and you and I are going to get along and have a nice conversation. When I ask you about your day, as I do while you confit a duck leg, I care about the answer. Jenny smokes out the window, we sip wine, and you get to recount your life to someone who wants to hear about it. Accept this new stasis, bury your suspicions deep—not because they aren't valid, but because no good can come of them.

Jenny checks the recipe and whines to Paul, "Where's the bacon?" He glances over the printout. "There's no bacon," he protests, more confused than assertive.

"No! You're making a Castelnaudary cassoulet instead of a Toulouse cassoulet. The Toulouse one has meaty happy bacon joy." Paul and I share a look over Jenny's head. "I'm serious." She jostles him, grabs his arms, and shakes him back and forth. "This should have bacon. It makes such a difference."

Paul shrugs and throws on his jacket. "I'll be right back."

She watches Paul from the window, then leaps onto my lap. "You'll have to explain what just happened."

"I knew what recipe he was going to use. If we had bacon, I would have sent him out for carrots, or leeks, or celery."

"You looked up varieties of cassoulet?"

She bites her lip. "Yes, goose, I wanted to give us more time alone."

"He'll be back in ten minutes." I actually feel annoyed on Paul's behalf.

Then she kisses me on my swollen mouth and I don't feel anything toward Paul. "I want more time." Another kiss. "I want as much time as I can get." Another kiss. Her mouth on mine before I can come up for air. "I want all of the time."

March 19

Museum of Modern Art (11 West Fifty-third Street)

"The painting on the left is called *Man with a Guitar* and it's by a French artist named Georges Braque. He was one of the founders of the school of cubism. What do you see?"

"You know that I know all of this already."

"Humor me. Pretend someday I'll teach art."

"Okay, but only if you pretend I'm really young and ignorant. That gets me wet. Now tell my lady brain about the mishy-mashy paint wall."

I'm practicing for when I give this lesson to Jackson, Jenny. That's what I'm hoping you don't hear in my tone. She goes wide-eyed, cupping her chin in two fists. It's a cuteness designed to let me know I'm not really offending her. "In cubism, the subject is simultaneously broken down into parts but also analyzed from multiple angles, so as to see it in its actual entirety, even on a two-dimensional plane. Braque takes a man with a guitar and shows him from every conceivable viewpoint, rendering the subject abstract but more truthfully represented. Now the painting on the right"—I take her hand and drag her two feet over—"Is called *Ma Jolie*, or *My Pretty*. It's by Pablo Picasso. This painting combines both a depiction of a woman Picasso was in love with, or at least sleeping with, and a song that was popular at the time. So it shows both the musical notation that would indicate the song but also an abstract portrait of . . . let's call her his love."

"Rounding up?" Jenny cocks an eyebrow. She walks up to the side, looks at the brushwork to see how thick Braque or Picasso laid it on, peers as close as she can get to the canvas itself before the guard asks her to step back. We've seen all the greatest hits today, all the furious lines and big ideas.

She turns to me and whispers, "What do you notice about this room?" I look around and see that everyone else has his or her phone out and is taking pictures of the paintings, seeing the masterworks of the modern era through iPhone screens. "Exactly," Jenny remarks.

She turns back from *Ma Jolie* to face me. "Is this what your painting looks like?"

"Sort of. I'm a bigger fan of abstract expressionism. Think Jackson Pollock."

"Only less so?"

"Only more so."

She turns back to the painting to sound casual. "I want to see what you paint."

"I want to read what you write," I retort. Her spine straightens as she considers this. "Like a hostage swap?" she asks.

"I'll trust you if you trust me."

"I trust you." She takes my hand again. It feels empty now without hers tucked into it. I walk on her right because my left arm and her right arm are the perfect hand-holding length. We tried the other way but it left either our shoulders or our wrists in an awkward crook. My left and her right fit together perfectly, as if our arms and wrists and hands and fingers were designed for this love. "Come on, professor. Show me this art only more so."

At home, Rebecca bakes cookies for Dawn de la Puente, who has trimmed her order but still keeps the ovens perpetually warm at Becky's Bites. Rebecca added a few other restaurants in the past month, her reach spreading, her reputation growing. I catch her bent over accounting software as often as bent over a mixing bowl now.

"Empire building?" I ask to be cute.

"Empire building." Serious as a librarian in her reply.

She goes to sleep earlier, often before I get home. I soft-shoe into our room and she doesn't stir for me. I had never gone a full day without speaking to my wife. I've done so three times in the past month. These statistics trouble me, ominous as an engine rattle, as a dark spot on an X-ray.

April 2

Staten Island Ferry (alight at 4 South Street)

Cold snap snapped, warm weather abounds, spring has sprung. Saltwater scent envelops us, wind blows her hair into curtains. We lean against the railing and watch the Statue pass us. We tip our hats and wave.

"I can't believe I've never done this before," Jenny yells over the noise of wake. "Do you think we're going to hit that boat?"

"Probably not." I squint into the horizon. It's a party boat, running a tour. "It's been years since I've been on this. Rebecca and I took a trip the first week we lived here. She wanted to set foot on all five boroughs to feel like a real New Yorker. The terminal was as far as she wanted to go into Staten Island, and I think we got out of the subway in the Bronx, had a slice of pizza at the first place we saw, and got back on. Five boroughs, one week." It's a pleasant memory and I share it, casually, speaking of my wife with the same tone I speak about my mother and father.

Jenny tilts on her hip, though, before she gets quiet. Her whole body reacts when she's upset. It shuts down, locks up. Every joint sets itself with a click. "I don't like it when you talk about Rebecca," she says. She means to say it quietly but has to shout to be heard. "I know that's unfair, but I don't like it."

I don't know what to say to that, how to respond to something so patently ludicrous, so I don't respond at all. I lean against the railing next to her. Jenny usually keeps up a patter the entire time we're together, but we chug along the rest of the way to Staten Island in silence. On a typical day, when she's not angry with me, when the conversation lulls, she pulls a question out from her bag of dinner party games, asks me something that she herself wants to answer. To shut down the conversation is tantamount to arguing; I fight my loudest with Jenny in absolute silence. At the terminal in Staten Island, we stand there and regard each other with a challenge. What did you expect? How did you think this would go?

We look into each other's eyes and see the affair that we've dressed up in finery, and we're each, in our own way, mortified that we convinced ourselves it rose above the hoi polloi, that we had an ounce of class.

And we hated each other, in the Staten Island Terminal, for sharing in the costuming, and in the sham.

Then we get on the same ferry, because we're in Staten Island. Because there isn't a separate subway for us to take. Had we had this fight in Brooklyn, or Queens, or Manhattan, or the Bronx, we could have broken up and gone our separate ways then and there. By the grace or the curse of the disfigured Kennedy child of boroughs were we forced to board the same boat back. On that boat, we simultaneously noticed how many people had done exactly what we had just done. It was like no one actually lived in Staten Island—we had just shared an experience with a few hundred other tourists too cheap to get tickets for a cruise tour. Jenny and I share this joke silently. Then I put my hand on her thigh. She turns to me and asks, "If you could own any exotic pet, what would it be?"

And I reply, "What would you choose?"

Right on cue, "I'm glad you asked . . ."

Later in the evening I sit across from Paul, having dinner away from Rebecca and Jackson, because I'm in love with another woman and that beast needs to be fed. But I sit across from him and make pleasant conversation and then, after the bottle of wine is finished and I've helped clear the table and maybe even washed the dishes, I go home. I go home and leave her with Paul, who I hear plenty about. It wouldn't be out of line to have brought that up on the ferry, to throw a little elbow back at Jenny, show that I can get angry as well, to call her out on hypocritical bullshit. It could double as a test, see how fast we throw the brakes, see if we can slow it down before it even devolves into a fight.

On the boat ride back, after we've made up, after she gave a half apology and I gave a half apology in response, we stand on the bow of the ferry and gaze out over lower Manhattan. The sky runs blue in every direction, sailboats dot the distance. It's short-sleeve weather. What would winning an argument accomplish?

April 5

Deno's Wonder Wheel Amusement Park
(3059 Denos Vourderis Place, Brooklyn)

Around and around we go. Who are these other people in the other cars on the Ferris wheel? Don't they have jobs? I do. I finished the third of four chairs this morning. Jenny indexed a book about the Louisiana Purchase. Hearing that she actually did tangible work surprises me a little. Something about Jenny smacks of the idle rich, like she has hobbies rather than employment. She's always claiming to be writing a novel, or revising a novel, but I never hear about a publisher or an agent. Or any specifics about the novel itself. And there's the editorial work she does, which is real enough that I see the checks "for editorial services" on her counter. Then we meet and come to Coney Island, where she gets a ridiculously large lollipop for the visual effect it provides.

The man running the ride lets us spin as long as we want. He has no line, no one waits, so why not keep it going—let the cars that slide keep sliding back and forth, let the couples in the station-ary cars keep staring out over the ocean at the toy boat tankers before going back to kissing. When it's busier he'll short a couple cars on their turn. The New York economy evens everything out.

After this we'll get funnel cake and walk the boardwalk. Maybe we'll stop into the aquarium, or sit on the sand for the afternoon. Maybe the freak show. Or maybe we'll head back to Greenpoint, with a quick stop in Midwood to show her a sliver of where I grew up and get a slice at Di Fara's.

In the meantime, around and around we go.

April 15

Brooklyn Bridge

I make a mental list of all the torturous walks in history: the Trail of Tears, the Bataan Death March. There were death marches at the end of the Holocaust, but those don't have catchy names. I relate this to Jenny as we crest the Williamsburg Bridge and she tells me to grow some balls. Then she takes a Nalgene bottle from her bag that looks like it's filled with red Gatorade.

"I'm not thirsty."

"Drink it anyway," she insists. I open it up and tilt my head back. It's Campari and soda. She's mixed us a giant batch of Campari and soda for our long walk. "First of the year," she says proudly.

We wend our way through the Lower East Side, through Chinatown. We eat donuts on Grand Street, steamed buns on Mott. We write caloric checks and hope our long walks can cash them.

On the Brooklyn Bridge, we hang to the right, avoiding the bikes that zip down the wooden slats at compound-fracture speed. Hordes of German tourists stand still and point and take photographs with digital cameras, lenses telescopic, getting in our way and occasionally drifting into the bike lane. Jenny and I admittedly take up more space than we should, walking side by side with our hands interwoven rather than in single file. We've put a dent in our thirty-two ounces of aperitif and both of us ride a nice buzz.

"Would you ever live anywhere other than New York?" I ask.

"I have lived elsewhere already."

"Where did you grow up?" This question has been asked in the past. It's in the first dozen questions of any bar pickup. But Jenny dodges it like she's in witness protection.

She starts to answer, then catches herself. "Is that Governor's Island?"

"Yep." We walk in silence until the bridge levels out. "Can I ask you a personal question?"

She squeezes my hand. "You are entitled."

"Has it really been five other guys?" It's taken me weeks to work up the nerve to ask her this, and I don't think I would if I weren't mildly drunk right now, but I want to know. I want to know how many others she's been with since Paul and how she can do it. I want to know her secrets, how she made that work.

I've built this up in my mind as being the most offensive thing I could ask her, an accusation dressed up as an interrogative. If she turned the other way and walked away from me, if she yelled at me or slapped me across my face, if she pushed me off the footpath into fucking traffic it would make sense to me. But Jenny lets out a light laugh, as if she had been waiting to be asked as long as I've waited to ask her. "Paul was number eight in my roster," she says. "You're lucky number thirteen. So it's actually four others."

"How are you counting them?"

"What do you mean?"

"What earns someone a number?"

She gives me a look that I deserve for a dumb question. "His penis has been inside my vagina, Mickey. I don't count blow jobs as half. I'm not a guy."

"How many of those?" In for a penny . . .

The look easily transforms into a glare, weary of this grief. "Focus on your own penis. Nothing else belongs to you."

"Fair enough." In for a pound . . . "Follow-up question."

"I expected as much." She sighs. "Go ahead."

"How did you do it?"

"Do what?"

". . . can I use the C word?"

Now she bristles. "Are you going to call me a cunt?"

"No! Cheat. How did you cheat?"

"Oh." She takes another swig from the Nalgene bottle, turns her face to the sun. "It's a pretty standard procedure, Mickey. I have sex with men other than Paul. That's how I cheat."

I monotone a droll, "Ha."

"Oh, you mean morally? How do I make peace with my God over breaking His commandment?"

"It's not an unreasonable question."

"The first one happened because Paul was out of town doing a show for a month. Met someone at a bar, took him home, and we had a thing for a month. Paul came back and it ended. He went away quietly. I liked that about him. Numbers two through four just sort of happened. One-night stands that stayed on their feet. Paul suspected all of them, whether during or in retrospect. I'm sure he suspects us, but I keep doing it because he keeps letting me get away with it." She nods her head. "I made him a victim only once. After that, he gets what he deserves."

"Why did the others end?"

This she mulls over as we walk downhill back into Brooklyn. Our plan is to get a pie at Grimaldi's, because Jenny has never been. We'll wait in line with the tourists. "They ended because all of them wanted to push things forward. Or two of them did. The other one ended because these things end. But two of them wanted me to leave Paul, or threatened to out us. I told them they were welcome to and broke it off. Neither of them did. They were both much smaller than Paul and I think they worried he'd beat them to death."

And then the crux. All my chips to the center. "How am I different?"

This she laughs at. Loudly. "You're Mickey. You just are." The deep furrow of my brow tells her this answer does not satisfy. "I love you, for starters. I didn't love the others. And you haven't pressured me, and while I know some of that is about your own situation, I still appreciate it. You treat me like a grown-up, which I am, so that's a point in your favor. I mean, why do we love anyone, Mickey Gould?" She gives up when she sees the line for Grimaldi's, skipping ahead, waving me on.

It's a good question. Why do we love anyone? Because we choose to. And then we do because we no longer have the choice.

And then what happens?

April 20

Economy Candy (108 Rivington Street)

She picks out gummy lobsters and gummy butterflies and gummy strawberries and gummy root beer bottles and gummy worms and gummy dinosaurs and gummy letters. Everything but gummy bears. "I don't like the taste," she claims.

I get a quarter pound of licorice jelly beans. "The fuck is wrong with you, Mickey."

"I like licorice."

"I don't."

"Well then I won't have to share with you."

"Or I won't kiss you because you'll taste of licorice."

". . . you'll still kiss me."

"Harrumph. I will, but I won't like it. And I'll probably pinch you as well."

I grab a box of Junior Mints on my way to the register.

May 4

Belvedere Castle
(Central Park above the Seventy-ninth Street Transverse)

On the ramparts of the castle we have a treetop view of Manhattan. Such an unusual perspective, to see the roof of the Met and feel like you are eye level with some of the lower buildings surrounding the park. We both appreciate the fairy-tale kitsch of it, the silliness of a faux castle in the middle of Central Park, overlooking a murky pond. Hardly worth invading unless you're a tourist. Wander south a few hundred yards and we'd hike through Jolie's final resting place, or her initial final resting place. But Jenny people-watches from her perch, eyes the even more absurd turret to determine how high we are able to go before it's trespassing.

I hadn't seen her in over two weeks. Circumstance gets the blame for the absence, though Jenny thinks that I could stand to shoulder some of it as well. I've missed her terribly, a cavernous ache swelled inside of me that my thoughts kept getting sucked into. But I and my father took Jackson to his first baseball game, minor league at Coney Island. It underwhelmed him, but I lived out a long dormant paternal dream, spreading the gospel to the next generation. While he chewed on a cold rubber ring to sooth his broken gums, I taught him about the infield shift.

Rebecca and I celebrated our anniversary a week ago. After seven consecutive days at home, fully present, fully attentive, she's warmed to me again. Jackson spent his first night away from home so that Rebecca and I could have the place to ourselves. That was the euphemism we all used, my parents and my wife and I, each one of us speaking in code to avoid saying that my wife and I wanted to have sex without keening our ears to a baby monitor, and that Rebecca wanted to make the guinea pig squeak she makes when she gets close to coming. We did and she did, and afterward we lay facing each other, and she ran her hands over my body as if in disbelief that it was there, that I'm still solid, flesh and bone, and not the aching pain of the phantom husband she lost.

I got her further on my good side with the work I did. In my workshop I felt comfortable taking my phone out and texting Jenny, though she responded brusquely, because my obligations are personal failings whereas her obligations are somehow noble. I built two goddamn tables over the past three weeks. One I sold to a family in Midwood, another gig my father threw me. The other one I carried the few blocks home, even hoisted it up the stairs, and dropped it where the old table used to be. All the while Rebecca had been in the sad little park by our house, letting Jackson play on a patch of grass lest he become weird. She came home and made the same guinea pig squeak. That's Rebecca's sound of full approval.

She spread her arms out and, with utter bliss, hugged our new table. I had made her happy, and this in turn made me happy. It was at this point I realized I had entered the friend zone with my own wife. Making a table for Rebecca was neither an audition nor something to barter for sex. I planed and sanded and screwed it all together because she wanted one and there was no good reason not to make her one. What a passionless experience.

I want the mountains of a relationship; I'm too young to move to the plains.

Back at the castle I lay my forehead between Jenny's shoulder blades. We haven't put ourselves back together again. She didn't even want to meet me in Greenpoint to travel together. We took separate trains to the park, texting horrible directions back and forth until we found each other. She told me that she was near a big tree at one point. It's really big. I replied that I'm next to a squirrel, then not anymore. We haven't yet had the sex that's supposed to bond this relationship together. That's one of the advantages of starting from that animalistic, physical place. We have a safe space to which we can return. My head on her back, her breath even, standing in a castle, we simply haven't found our way back there yet.

Jenny says to me, "I missed you every minute."

"You read my mind," I reply. She nudges me off.

She says, "Would seem there might be an easy solution for this."

"And what would that be?"

Jennifer Sayles rolls her eyes at me. Oh you petulant girl. You need to make me say it? You need me to be the first to leap so you can see how badly I might dash my body on the rocks below? Fine. Fine then. Parachute off. Here I go.

"If you will, I will," I say. Her chest rises and falls, respirating this offer. "I can't give up Jackson—"

She cuts me off with a wave. "I'm not asking you to."

"I know. And I'm saying I can't. But for all the other stuff, if you will, I will."

I just said that. I just said that and I meant it. While Jenny considers my life-altering offer, I look down into Turtle Pond, a dark puddle made charming by its location. If she says no, I'm going to leap over this stone wall and swan-dive into it.

But she doesn't. She says yes. She says yes and okay and I'd like that and I love you and everything else I want to hear. And we gather our hands once more to get ourselves back into bed in Greenpoint, in a wagon, careening down a steep hill with the brakes missing and the cliff's edge rushing to meet us and it looks to me exactly like unhinged, glorious freedom.

June 2

Jenny and Paul's Apartment
(114 Franklin Street, Brooklyn, New York)

The leap stalls. We both seek the seismic event that will make this exit strategy from our current relationships either impossible or inevitable. Some great calamity must befall us to sweep away all obstacles. I root for Paul to die. I don't like myself for doing so. Meanwhile, we've exhausted ourselves on New York, on fighting the rising flotsam of tourists. We stay in.

Jenny and I laze, indecisive about what to get for lunch. Any restaurant is fine by me— there's nothing she'd suggest that I'd say no to. Certain cuisines may not be as appetizing on a humid, heat-wretched day like today, when New York is in day two of what promises to be a full week of early height-of-summer anguish, but if Jenny were to suggest our favorite Polish restaurant, I'd endure the cement in my stomach and sweat potato flour.

Nothing, on the other hand, appeals to Jenny, who sprawls out on top of the sheets in jeans and a bra. She shoots down restaurant after restaurant, picking reasons as if plucking petals off flowers. Too far. Too expensive. Bathrooms are always gross. The servers are hipster assholes.

"What about Greek?" I present it wearily, still in my boxers, halfway to a nap. The afternoon heat hangs in her room, weighs us down. If I closed my eyes I could doze for an hour, easily.

"I don't like phyllo dough," she replies. "It makes me feel like I'm eating an animal's shell."

"*You racist.*"

She slaps my side, not entirely playfully. "Don't call me a racist."

"Munf." I grunt my assent.

"How about Enid's?" she suggests. I've walked by Enid's innumerable times, on its cozy corner, and I've never been in. "What kind of food is that?"

"It's . . . food. American? Go look at the menu. I'm peckish." She puts a hand on my hips and shoves, rolling me out of bed. I get my feet underneath me at the last minute and shuffle toward her office. "Grab Paul's computer," she calls out after me. "My battery is dead."

She boots up Paul's laptop, her laptop's twin, save for the distinguishing birthmark of a comedy and tragedy mask sticker taped to the top ("My contribution," Jenny points, pleased with herself). While it loads up I kiss her side and she giggles, playing with my hair and tickling the small of my back. I buck and shudder, as ticklish as a toddler, amusing Jenny to no end. The menu looks pretty straightforward, things stuck between buns, every dish has one extra artisanal ingredient to placate the clientele. "Let's do it," I decide.

"Lemme check the weather." Jenny starts to type it into the browser.

"It's hot."

"I know, I want to know how hot."

"What difference does it make?"

"None, I just like to know." She screws up the Web address a few times in her haste. Wether.com, then weahter.com.

"How come it doesn't autofill?" I point this out, not because I genuinely care, but because I'm so heat-weary that I get punchy, asking questions just to provoke, licking the soft flesh of her belly until she bats my head like chastising a dog.

"Paul's computer has a glitch. It never autofills."

"Give it here." I turn it my way, click on a few tabs. "Paul has it set to clear his page history when he logs off. Once he clicks out of his browser, it's like wiping the blackboard."

"Oh," Jenny says, because what else is one supposed to say at this revelation. She doesn't seem disturbed by this, more confused, even a little annoyed. She clicks a few buttons and changes Paul's settings. Now he'll retain. She closes his laptop, a punctuation mark to the conversation. Full stop. "All fixed." Then, sharp enough to be considered an order, "Get dressed, I'm starving."

Paul Fenniger

Present Day: July 19, 2010

2:33 PM

I come to underneath the shade of a makeshift tent, lying on my back on a yoga mat. I turn my head left and right, on both sides of me are people in states of semiconsciousness. The person next to me appears near death save for the gentle flutter of her eyelids. She lies on top of a towel.

When I shift my weight I realize I'm covered in wet paper towels, affixed to my body like leeches. Someone has stuck a couple on my chest and neck, wedged a few into my armpits. I'm a papier-mâché man.

I roll first onto my side to see how that plays. When I don't immediately black out again I prop myself up on an elbow, then onto my hand, finally sitting upright. There's a thick wedge of watermelon and a bottle of water just off the mat. Small sips, a few bites, see if it stays down. I probe my head with my fingertips, gently, working my way front to back, first along the sides, then over the top. Slowly, carefully, like a scalp massage. There's no dried blood, no sore patches. I'm okay. Had I hit my head, were I here for a concussion, some evidence would present itself. I'm in the tent for dehydration—I must have passed out. Last thing I remember was coming up the stairs from the subway.

A while later, when my stomach keeps down the watermelon and bottle of water, my strength slowly returns. I try to stand on jellied legs, looking for my shirt. A man my father's age, salt-and-pepper beard neatly trimmed, strides from across the tent to me. "Feeling better?" he asks.

There was a man selling water at the park entrance. Or giving it out, not selling it. I spoke to him. The thought interrupts, uninvited. It comes back piecemeal. "What happened?"

"You passed out." He hands me another bottle of water, takes my empty. "We can't transport to hospitals for another couple hours, but if you want to rest here, we'll keep giving you fluids until we can."

"What happened?"

"You were hot and thirsty and you passed out," he says slower, louder.

"Sorry. I mean what happened in New York today?"

He looks toward the city and shrugs. "There's smoke, so there's fire. Beyond that, mayor is speaking in about three hours." I guide my arm over his shoulders and he helps me walk out of the tent.

By the time I reach its perimeter someone else has taken the yoga mat. "I live near here. Am I okay to walk?"

"I guess," he replies.

"Are you a doctor?" He shakes his head. "An EMT?" No.

"Community organizer." He shakes my limp hand. "I'm trained in first aid, though. There's a doctor around here somewhere. If you're walking, do you want another bottle of water?"

Grateful, I take two more from him, tucking them into my pockets. The cool wetness against my thighs provides relief for the trip. I look around at the makeshift medical area. There was a man in the tunnel who could go no farther. He pressed himself into a wall and waited for help. There was Carl, waiting to hear if his boyfriend is okay. There were people who stayed on the trains, because they were too old or infirm to move in that heat. I look for them, in the hopes we'd recognize each other by scent, by common experience.

My legs can barely stay vertical. It's time to go. Paul Fenniger survived.

It takes a few moments to situate myself in the park, to find my polestar and steer myself home. Thoughts still move soupy through my head. I look for familiarity, be it a landmark or a person. A guide. Jenny, at the park to help and, after finding me, taking me back home.

McCarren Pool to my right. Tennis courts off a hundred yards to the left. Internal compass aligned. Has it really been this hot up here this entire day? Where is Jenny? One foot in front of the other, Paul. Come on. You got out of the tunnel. Come on. You're okay. It's okay. There. There you go.

At the north end of the park, I walk past a group of hipsters, tossing a Frisbee. I walk past people tending to an illegal home-made grill, essentially a cinder block fire pit dug into the dirt of McCarren Park. Drum and bass thump through speakers, though no one is dancing. Everyone, however, is drinking, raising bottles of IPA to their lips, toasting to being on the other side of the river from the end of the world.

Paul Fenniger

One Month Ago: June 17, 2010

I close the lid of my laptop and leave it on the nightstand, then go to brush my teeth. Jenny slinks in behind me and motions for the toothpaste. We brush our teeth together in quiet, happy domesticity. These are the small moments that make up the brunt of a successful lifetime, brushing your teeth next to someone you love.

Jenny challenges me, as she always does, to see who can brush the longest. It's the look in her eye that throws down the gauntlet, and the slowing of her concentric circles, working her molars like she's trying to gradually sandblast concrete. But I'm game. We brush and brush, spitting and continuing, until I have a goatee of foam and my mouth burns from menthol and I have to quit. She wins again. Jenny raises her toothbrush in triumph and her spit follows mine down the drain.

We get into bed and I spoon her. She digs herself back into me.

Before I turn the lights out, she startles. "Can I check your computer? I forgot to send an e-mail." I roll over and grab it, hand it over. She boots it back up.

I passed up an audition today. A slightly bigger company working on a marginally bigger stage. An Arthur Miller play I had never heard of. Measuring the benefits of gaining exposure against being present in my marriage made this no choice whatsoever. Jenny must sniff this secret on me; she's been side-eyeing me all night, bobbing and weaving. I'll have to tell her eventually.

She pokes me in between my shoulder blades. "Fenn? What's this?"

I prop up on an elbow. She turns the screen to show me a site for an escort agency in Ottawa. Above it I can see tabs for other pages, for parenting chat rooms and Craigslist ads. But right now she's focused on the prostitutes in Ottawa.

"I don't know."

"What do you mean you don't know? You don't know how a Web site for an escort service got into your browser history?"

"Oh." My stomach lurches and I fear throwing up in our bed. "It's for work," I mumble, as casually as I can manage. Heat rushes to my face—I flush and my throat closes up. She clicks through the site in front of me, muttering about *reasonable rates* and *zodiac sign, how thorough.* "Jeff is going to Canada and he wants to get a prostitute," I say with a thin laugh.

"Jeff . . . from work?"

"Jeff from work."

"Really Fenn? Let's help him, then. This one is nice." Jenny clicks through thumbnail photographs. "Her head is cut off, but her body is very well airbrushed. Do you think Jeff would like her?"

"I don't know what kind Jeff would like."

"Should I click over to the chat rooms or—"

"I'm a terrible person," I blurt out. My cable snaps. I'm free-falling, watching the ground rise up, bracing myself for the last impact of my life. "I'm a terrible person." Jenny clicks over to the chat rooms anyway, starts perusing my shame. "I'm a terrible person."

"Yeah, looks like you kind of are. What the fuck is all this?"

"It's stupid," I explain. "It's nothing. I'm just looking at stuff. It doesn't even turn me on." One more lie on top of all of the others is rancid icing on a bitter cake, but I tell it. "It's stupid. It's so stupid. I'm so stupid. No one could think less of me than I do of myself."

Jenny keeps clicking, keeps uncovering. "I have a puncher's chance, Fenn."

She stands up, can't even be next to me in our bed anymore, taking the laptop with her. Jenny parades around in the room, holding our annihilation in her hands. I want to explain to her that she's the only one I'm attracted to, that all the online stuff is tourism, like going to a bookstore and checking out guidebooks for places you know you'll never go. It's harmless voyeurism. My mouth opens to say these words but they die in my chest. She paces, reading, scrolling through whichever page she's on. "Password," she says, now icy. I already know what she means. Oh God this gets worse.

"IloveJen. Capital *I*, capital *J*. All one word. No spaces."

If looks could maim before they killed.

I sit up on the edge of the bed, feet on the floor. My hope is that she's going to read over the last couple, but Jenny isn't stupid like I am. And she's not careless. Her eyes scan the page and I know she's working her way back in time, back ten months, back to July of last year.

I know what she's going to find.

When she does, she winces like a wounded animal. "You told strangers?" I did. I couldn't talk with her about the hospital, she needed to be the one to talk and get through it. I had to be strong to deal with grief in my own way. So I created a person who resembled me solely in that I am a man who just lost a child. No other connecting details. Then I picked a someone. An anyone out of a support group for child loss. "You told strangers about our dead baby." She speaks so small, her voice so crushed. "And then . . . two hours later . . . you asked Cobrajaws18 what he'd do after he tied you up."

"I'm a terrible person." I shake my head back and forth. Tears well up. I don't want to cry in front of Jenny. Strength is what she needs. I am her rock. "I'm not even human."

"Shut up, Fenn. Is this what you want?"

"I want you!" I shout.

"Evidently I'm not enough."

"You're more than enough. But you're not . . ." I can explain this. It's okay. We can get through this. "We have sex maybe twice a month since . . ."

"Since . . ." Her eyes flash wide and dangerous. "Since our child died? Is that when you started cheating on me, you fucking ass-hole?"

"It's not sex," I plead. "I'm not actually meeting these people. It's . . ."

She fills in the blank, "It's you jerking off to other women. *And men.* Jesus, Fenn, who the fuck are you? Men too?"

"It's not a sex thing. It is but it's not. There's a lot of innocuous stuff there as well. I'm just pretending. It's like method acting," I blurt. She stops pacing and then, merciful God in heaven, she closes my laptop and sets it down behind her. Maybe I just found the right key, that this is masturbation. I get myself hard from strangers and kinks and all this other nonsense goes in one eye and out the other and doesn't matter to me. And then I masturbate. I masturbated before I met Jenny, she knows that because she met me after I was twelve. It's natural. Should I try to explain this to her, or would that respark the fire?

Jenny stands stock-still, her legs planted, challenging me to jus-tify. And I could, but for where it would take us. I tread up to my line in the sand, the one I drew there years before. On the other side are straight accusations, conversations we can never come back from. On the line itself are hints and cowardice. And on my side is the unknowing, of simply not knowing what she hasn't told me, and that's where I live. I don't want to go where I don't live. In the end I say to her, gently as I can, "I miss sex, Jenny. I miss sex with you. Don't you miss sex?"

And while the fight in her doesn't flare up again, while her face is no longer a mask of rage, I've nevertheless said the wrong thing. Jenny looks me in the eye and says, "Get out."

I stay seated, because my first thought is baffling stupidity: *my name is on the lease here and she can't really kick me out of my own home.* She says again, louder, "Get out. Now."

"Why?"

"Because you sicken me. You sanctimonious, hypocritical pervert."

"I'm sorry."

"Shut up and get out, Fenn."

I look around. "Where can I go, Jenny?"

"I don't care. Maybe one of your online friends has a spare room. Pack a bag and go."

"Why don't I sleep on the couch?" I try to reason.

And then she plays her trump card. "Paul, one of us is leaving this apartment tonight. If it's me, you will never see me again. Do you understand?"

I do. I do understand. Repairing the damage I've done begins here, with me on my knees, tears running down my face, throwing a few outfits into a suitcase on the floor of our closet.

Paul Fenniger

One Month Ago: June 17, 2010

I roll my suitcase through the revolving door as smoothly as I can. Manuel sits behind the desk in the lobby, his radio tuned to NPR. He and I have spoken about soccer when I work late—or rather, he's tried to engage me in a conversation about soccer, especially soccer in Honduras, and I've smiled and nodded along.

I can try to walk by Manuel with a smile and wave, scan my keycard, and take the elevator up to the inevitably empty office.

Or I can walk up to Manuel, tell him I've forgotten my keycard, get him to let me in as unspoken approval that I'm bringing a suitcase into the office at one in the morning, which is rarely a work-related act.

Or I can ask Manuel for his permission to camp out in the office, making him a full accomplice.

Of course, he could refuse, tell me that people cannot sleep in the office, or report me in an e-mail to Gregg. I tread an egg-shell path across the office lobby. He's watching me the whole way, his mouth smiling under curious eyes. "Hello, Mr. Fenniger," he says.

I hybridize my three options. "Hello, Manuel," I bellow cheerfully. That my eyes are still puffy from crying on the subway is probably a giveaway that not everything is all right. "Is it okay if I go up to the office?"

"Of course! Do you need a keycard?"

"No, I've got it." I look at my suitcase until he does too. "So, when do the first people usually arrive on my floor?"

He holds up a single finger and I think he's telling me one, as in they should already be arriving, or he's being cute, and he means that it's now one, and I'm here, so there's my answer. But he's checking his computer. "Most days, Ms. Blaine is the first one in, around six forty-five." Emily Blaine. One of the partners.

"Does that sort of thing get checked? When people come and go?"

Manuel steeples his fingers pensively. "I don't really know." He comes around from behind the desk. "I think I heard a noise on your floor about a half hour ago," he says. "Why don't you follow me up and we'll check on it." With that, he sweeps me through the main gate and into my office, his keycard logged in the system, leaving me alone with only the motion sensors on the lights keeping me company.

She watched me pack a suitcase, arms crossed the entire time. Cigarette in one hand, drink in the other, she seethed while I chose my clothing as slowly as possible. The only thing she said to me, when I started to zip up, was, "You'll need more than that."

Jacob Weinstock comes into the office once a week, if that. Other partners joke that he's senile, but I've seen the man quote case law from decades ago verbatim from memory. Mostly when he comes in he reads the newspaper behind his desk and throws in his two cents on matters too complex for the associates. Given his tenure with the firm, however, he gets his own large office, furnished with two couches. He doesn't bother to lock the door, so I roll my suitcase in and plug my phone into his wall. Then I take off my shoes, set my phone's alarm to wake me at five forty-five, and lay still as I can until the motion sensor forgets about me and clicks off the lights.

Michael Gould

Present Day: July 19, 2010

3:15 PM

I wend my way through back streets of Queens. Whoever landed here got monopoly and built warehouses, tucked shipping containers in alleyways, as if a giant child spilled his toys and didn't bother to pick them up. This is an empty place, and I walk quickly through it.

I cross Pulaski Bridge, venturing over the stinking canal, acres of toxic sludge buried belowground, the mistakes of generations poisoning the water table and raising a sulfurous stench. The bridge rumbles beneath me with every passing truck. And when I step off, I am in Brooklyn. I am back in my borough.

I hold my breath past the onion tanks of the sewage treatment plant, alien and silver reflecting the glare of the afternoon sun. My bottle is empty but doesn't worry me. It doesn't bother me at all. My thirst will be slaked soon.

I don't slow, just turn my head to the right, check the plume of smoke across the river. It still rises, now twinned, constant and steady, neither expanding nor sputtering away. Somewhere in Manhattan, something burns, whether a building or an entire block. But I'm on this side of the river. I gaze across, safely buffered by the barrier of slow, deep water.

I march, one step in front of the other, ignoring the anguish in my heels each time I step down.

I drip sweat from every pore. Still. This goddamn day.

I am on my way home, along the river, all the way to Red Hook.

I have a stop to make first.

I will be your reckoning, Jennifer Sayles. I will be your choice. You cannot have ended us in a text message, Jenny—that's not how rational adults act. If you need us to be tragic, we can be tragic. We can be the lamentable pair at the mercy of brooding gods. I'll rend my garments and wail next to you. But it has to mean something. I didn't just cheat on my wife. I didn't build everything I've built for thirty-three years and then tear it down like some sweaty salesman at the hotel bar, falling into a honey trap to stave off the boredom of living on a plateau. It's more important than that. It has to be. I'm not acting entitled, but it simply has to be.

Michael Gould

One Month Ago: June 18, 2010

More than six months have passed since Jolie's death and Rebecca still mourns in waves. Most days she goes about her routine, walks Jackson to the end of the pier and back, trying to teach him to wave to the Statue of Liberty, in preparation for what is beyond my ken. Some days she wanders around the apartment as if she'd been cruelly blindfolded, spun around, and she now has to reacclimate using an entirely different sense. She'll bump into the counter, forget how to open the oven, let her buzzer beep shrill while she takes her cookies out, then go to turn it off. These are cataclysms in the world of Rebecca Gould.

I've grown skilled in reading the spillage of rocks to detect the avalanche. When Dawn had to stop carrying Rebecca's cookies, because Dawn's restaurants were folding one by one in spite of a tidal wave of gentrification, it cut Rebecca deeply. Financially, we were fine, but her empire sputtered in fits and starts. I made myself present at these strange, fragile times, even helping in the kitchen as much as Rebecca would allow, taking every chore she'd let me take off of her shoulders.

The steepest drop came after Detective Lewis's last call. Jolie's case stays open. I like Detective Lewis. She doesn't bullshit. Jolie ran in dangerous circles, and those circles tended to be closed off from the rest of the world. Detective Lewis will continue to investigate, but she braced Rebecca for the possibility that Jolie's murder will go unsolved. That led to the Jolie-yard stare, the Jolie tremens, and Jolie alcohol syndrome. I pulled a sobbing Rebecca off the toilet and put half an Ambien under her tongue, stroked her head until she passed out. In sickness and in health. We never spoke of that afternoon again.

I felt the tremors early yesterday, Rebecca coming down again with a case of the Jolies. She forgot the word *chip*. As in, "Could you check to see if I have enough chocolate?" Then pointing at the bin. At the bin, jabbing her finger. "Chocolate . . ." She formed the word and spat it out of her mouth like it was lukewarm. "Chocolate . . ."

"Chips?" I helped.

She looked crestfallen, sprayed a sterile counter with vinegar solution, and said, "Yes, chocolate chips."

So tonight I'm home, having bathed my son and tucked him in, giving Rebecca a chance to catch up on anything she could possibly want to catch up on. Read a book, watch television, drink herself into a stupor—all on the menu. I grabbed us dinner from the only Chinese food storefront within walking distance.

"This is the absolute middle of the road for Chinese food," I comment after a few bites of the house fried rice. "It's not bad, but it's not good. I can't even think of adjectives I'd use to describe it."

"Not too greasy," Rebecca remarks. She's ordered orange beef, her go-to dish.

"Also not too dry," I counter.

"It's passable." She smiles a little. This is how she comes back, in tentative steps to the land of the living, where her life goes on.

"It's tolerable."

"I would eat it again if we really wanted Chinese food and were too lazy to walk to somewhere we like." And with that assessment final, we eat in amiable silence until the doorbell rings.

Rebecca bolts down the steps. I hone my ears to the monitor, hear nothing out of Jackson's room but contented baby breath whooshing loud-soft-loud. Two sets of footsteps come back up and, suddenly, wholly unexpectedly, there's Jenny in my apartment. Jenny walking in front of Rebecca, whose face has changed completely. Rebecca's face, that is. She's gone from mousy to steel magnolia in a flight of stairs, because she once again has someone to take care of. This is the truest shortcut out of grand mal Jolie, replacing one wounded animal with another.

Oh, Jenny is crying. That's why Rebecca has her arms on Jenny's shoulders. That's why Rebecca has gone into octopus-caregiver mode, with arms reaching for glasses of water and a box of tissues and turning the volume down on the monitor and putting cookies on a plate while offering words of encouragement. Jenny turns to me while Rebecca's head is in the fridge and mouths *Sorry*. I shrug, because I have no idea what she is sorry for.

Hands steady, voice plangent, Jenny sits on our couch and tells the tale about that low-down, no-good man of hers. She calls him that, grins ruefully to say it, like this is a performance and we're her audience, or this is a sales pitch and we're her customers. I catch this moment, this feeling of being hoodwinked, and it nags at me, makes me want to roll my eyes and ask Jenny for more matter and less art, but Rebecca's hand is on Jenny's knee and her eyes are limpid, bottomless pools of empathy. That strange rictus grin Jenny musters fishhooks my wife completely. And so I sit back and silence my phone, because the show is about to begin.

She starts with the premise: she's found some things on Paul's computer. A bit of elaboration and red flags go flying for me, because I am currently in a sexual relationship with two women and I still find time every week to take care of myself. Explaining why would involve a long treatise on the nature of male sexuality that I'm flaccid even considering. My point is that if Jenny has shown up on our doorstep because Paul ogled some models, I'll need to start prepping damage control for when she finds out where I've been when I'm "checking my e-mail."

Nope. It goes much deeper than that. Red flags retracted. Interest piqued.

Paul's porn habit takes all sorts of forms, from role-playing to gathering cock shots, as if he has been trying to collect the whole set. Jenny has spent the day going through his computer after demanding the passwords from a spectacularly booted and banished Paul. She makes it clear to us that she has no problem with Paul looking at porn, gives the pat speech about how it's natural. We nod along, Rebecca more sympathetically, though, when Jenny explains the betrayal she feels here is in how personal he got with strangers. She found long exchanges in chat rooms about Jenny, about their marriage, about their baby. "He should have been talking with me," Jenny strains. "He's got, like, a dozen different online personalities, and they hold no resemblance to my husband. One minute he's telling people about what I'm going through, and the next minute he's on a different board pretending to be a sophomore at Columbia trolling for dick. Literally the next minute. Everything is time stamped."

My eyebrows are arched in a frozen expression of solidarity, but my thoughts are twofold.

First, that motherfucker. That phony motherfucker whining passive-aggressive commentary and staring at us with self-righteous, heavy-lidded looks, wielding his weapons from the moral high ground, as if to say that he knows what we're doing; he knows and he disapproves. Fuck him.

Second, I relish in his weakness. I bask in how even in his cheating Paul maintained a fidelity, that he couldn't even allow himself the thrill of human contact. Maybe this is just what's been discovered, the smoke and mirrors on stage right while he bangs away at that actress on stage left. I contemplate bringing that up here, but it's information best kept in reserve. Paul doesn't need a stronger push. I suspect, from everything Jenny is saying, that this is as far as Paul has gone, this is all this fucking actor can muster.

"How can we help?" Rebecca asks, her voice tight.

Jenny takes the question in, gives her answer serious thought. It's right here, at this very moment, that I understand why she has come here and told us all of this. The sympathetic ear, the cookies, the looks of deep and terrible understanding, all of those are gravy. She's here to let me know that Paul is, for the time being, out of the picture, which means the picture now has a Michael-size gap in it. Whether she's asking me to fill it or expecting me to fill it is another matter. "I want someone to say this out loud to, make sure I'm not being crazy, or unreasonable for kicking him out," she says, finally.

When Rebecca has reassured her that she's not, and a few placating cookies have been consumed, Jenny asks me to walk her back to the subway. Not the bus, that would be one block outside my apartment, but the subway, fifteen minutes away. Right before I leave I take one last look at Rebecca, see her tidying up, turning the monitor back to jet engine volume, once again troubled, deep in the throes of the Jolies.

We're not even to the end of the block when Jenny confirms all of my suspicions. She turns to me and says, "I need you to step up your game, Mickey Gould."

And I ask, like an interviewer bewitched by a starlet's meteoric rise, "What do you think the future holds for you and Paul?"

"I don't ever want to see Paul again," she replies. "I get that what I'm doing is worse than what he's doing. I'm not going to pretend it's just *different*; it's fundamentally worse. So I can't explain why I feel so betrayed, but I can't even look at him."

This is the lesson my father never taught me. This is the lesson my mother left unlearned. If I knew how it all worked, the sheer logistics of extricating myself from one relationship to become fully involved in another, doing so without Rebecca thinking I'm a villain, without making it hard for me to see Jackson, I could commit to that course of action. I could amend the parts where Rebecca blames me for her unhappiness, or where Jackson grows up thinking I abandoned him. My parents never sat me down and instructed me on the finer points of how to not destroy lives. They never gave me the guidance to know what choices were the right choices, how to know if I had a good thing going.

If I knew for certain that my life would be happier with Jenny than it's been with Rebecca I could get on the train with her now and come back later to pick up my razor.

"Mickey, I want to be yours. If you let me, I will be your choice. If this is something you're not sure about, and you want me to fight for us, I'll do it. I'll fight you for us. I'll prove how right I am for you. But if you've made up your mind, and you just don't want to be the person who ends the relationship, then I can't fight. I can't fight nothing, Mickey. But I will fight."

I stand with her at the entrance to the subway. "I need time," I say.

"I know. I know you do." She strokes my face. "Don't take too long."

Walking back, it eludes me why this is important, but I need to remember how I met Rebecca. I need to have that first moment in my head. It doesn't come to me, though. All I remember is the moment we cemented, when in my heart and in my gut, turning back was no longer an option.

I introduced her as Rebecca. Just Rebecca, like a celebrity famous enough to forgo a last name. She wore white to further darken her complexion, bury deep the Irish flush. Marty and Miriam, ever polite and passive-aggressive, didn't address the matter directly. Instead, my mother served kreplach for dinner.

"Have you ever had these before, dear?" Miriam asked, her voice lined with honey.

And Rebecca, poor little shiksa lamb, said, "Of course I have. My mom made ravioli all the time." I let out a noise like a death rattle while my mother stood, triumphant, and ladled applesauce onto my plate. I'd brought a gentile girl home. A McMahon at that. My parents would be nice to her, they would be welcoming and even charming, but they would never accept her. I could slap a ring on her finger and a baby in her belly and my parents would still refer to her as "Michael's girl," a tentative label for a temporary distraction.

After dinner, my parents employed the divide-and-conquer strategy, my mother grabbing me to help her clean up while my father took Rebecca around the living room, showing her photos in cheap gilt frames of me as a boy, pictures worn as the carpet. He closed the tour at the mantelpiece, where a giant curved objet d'art dominated the space. It had the gloss of plastic. I dried dishes and watched Rebecca motion to touch it, seeking permission from my father. "Are you helping or are you watching?" my mother asked.

My father smiled warmly and put it in her hands. "That"—he tightened her grip—"is a shofar from Krasnystaw. Do you know where that is?"

"I don't," Rebecca admitted. She admits when she doesn't know something. I love that about her.

"It's in a part of Poland that used to be called Galicia. It's where my family is from, both the parts of it that survived and the parts that didn't. The whole town was a welcome mat for the rest of Poland. Russians wiped their feet on us, Germans stamped their boots. You've heard of the Warsaw Ghetto, yes?"

"Yes."

"Lodz?" he tested.

"Yes." Atta girl.

"Krasnystaw was another place where the Jewish people were rounded up before being sent to the camps. Not so famous as the others." He leaned forward and confided, "I don't think Michael's mother could tell you where Krasnystaw is, and she's been dusting this shofar for over thirty years."

"I most certainly could." My mother didn't break her scrubbing rhythm to shout. She can shout through anything.

Rebecca held it in her hands firmly, but gently, like she would a baby. My father laughed to see how unnatural it looked. He lifted it from her grasp, held it in one hand, and raised it to his mouth, heralding a piercing, flatulent sound that resonated through the house. Soft laughter emanated from my mother.

"It's a ram's horn, Rebecca. You couldn't break it if you tried. It survived annexation, the ghetto, the camps, the purges, forced marches, the weight of history, and found its way across the sea to the mantel of a privileged lowercase-*J* Jew here in Brooklyn. Take a town by strategy or force, salt the land underneath, but history not only survives, it roars to be heard." She covered her ears in time as he blew on it again, louder than before.

"L'shana tovah!" comes from my mother. Her voice, loud and cheerful. A boisterous code, bellowed to separate and unify, like a gate between those who belong and their tagalong guests.

Now seemed as good a time as any, so I put down the bowl I had been drying, strode into the living room, and took Rebecca's hand. "We came here to make an announcement." My mother turned, ashen, still elbow deep in soapy dishwater. My father laid the shofar back into its place, then faced us, reared himself up to his full height. He's shorter than I am, but he wears his dignity like a well-cut suit. He made the trains run on time, dammit, and nothing I say could cow him.

"Not now," Rebecca said under her breath.

"If not now, when?"

"Yes, Michael, if not now, then when?" my father seconded. "Tell us your news."

"Rebecca and I are engaged."

My parents share a look, don't even bother with subtlety. My mother finally dries off her forearms, comes and takes my father's arm. Now it's two united fronts, weather patterns clashing in the living room. I expect my mother to get loud from word one, my father to speak hyperbolically or tell some long-winded parable about our family's time fleeing west, but they both surprise me. A calm seems to waft off them, and even Rebecca loosens her claw grip on my hand.

This is what the money has bought them, I realize. They kept the same house, the same cheap car and threadbare appliances, all the familiar rattles and leaks to remind them that this is their home, from which they will not be moved. When they put the money in the bank, they were buying peace of mind. What could be more random than your family being slaughtered as enemies of the state, even the children? What could be more random than investing in a stock that pays you more in a year than you earned in a lifetime of hard work? When everything is so chaotic, what's the real harm of having your son marry goyim? My mother shrugged a bit, perhaps reconciling herself to the thought that Rebecca's heritage translates to a lower risk for Tay-Sachs and all the other illnesses that target Jews like purse snatchers.

Man makes plan, and God laughs. They'd stitch a sampler of that and hang it on the wall were that not such a gentile thing to do.

"If this is the woman our son is to marry, why have we not met her before tonight?" My father speaks evenly when he's struggling to maintain control. I've heard this voice with incompetent waiters and cabdrivers who can't find their way to Midwood.

"Rebecca isn't Jewish."

"Yes. That much we can tell."

"I didn't think you'd approve."

"That's not giving us much credit."

"Still. I wanted to wait until we were certain. I love Rebecca McMahon." My voice stumbles over her last name, adding a hitched syllable that causes her to flinch. "And she is going to be my family. It's important to me that you both also want to be a part of this family, and welcome her into ours, but it's not necessary. I'm going to marry her regardless."

My parents consider my speech, whether it was respectful or

coherent, and Rebecca gives my palm a double squeeze, a small show of appreciation for whatever it is I just said.

My father takes a deep breath. He looks at us both, and then smiles kindly at Rebecca. My dad has a gentle smile. Mine is two shades too wolfish; I hope it softens with age and I inherit his later in life. "I can't speak for your mother," he begins, "but if you give me time, and perhaps indulge me a stupid question or an indelicate statement or two, I can put my son's happiness over my God and welcome his wife into my family."

"He can speak for me." My mother sighs.

Six months later, my mother bought Rebecca silicone baking sheets, rolled up and wrapped in Christmas-themed wrapping paper. Santa and reindeer, red and green, no mistaking it for happy holidays. My parents opened up our family to a small external influence, a person who knew all of the verses of "Silent Night" and could make eggnog from scratch.

Not that it mattered. We got married in City Hall, with a clerk as our only witness and photographer. Our choice, to make that day solely about us. My father, with all of his money, went to the corner store and bought another eight-by-ten gilt frame, and my mother stuck it on the mantel, me and Rebecca, arm in arm, at the far end, the first thing that would fall off if someone were to bump into it, while vacuuming, say.

Once I made that announcement, I was marrying Rebecca. Good as signing the papers and twisting the ring onto her finger. I would rise and fall with her, for the rest of our lives. That was the plan. That was always the best-laid plan.

I'm back home, standing outside, staring up.

When I get upstairs Rebecca has laid a suitcase out on our bedroom floor. It's wide-open but empty. She comes out of the bathroom with her hair tied back, her face freshly washed and rosy. She wraps a spindly hand around the back of my neck and draws me in for a long kiss. "I love you," she says, the instant we break, absent her triumphant smirk.

"Going somewhere?"

"I know that you two have a relationship that you shouldn't. If it's just sex, I can understand that." She composes herself, inhales and exhales like an actress in the wings. She locates her center while I watch, wide-eyed and anxious. "You look at my saggy breasts and wobbly arms and giant ass and you're turned off. I'm turned off, Michael. I think I'm disgusting."

"That's not what this is."

"Shut up. Shut up. Shut up." She burrows her nails into her scalp. "A baby came out of me, and my body disgusts me. That's what I think about when I think about my own body, so I can only imagine how you must look at it. Maybe Jenny just snapped back a little more quickly. So if you two are just fucking, I can understand that. That makes sense to me. I can explain that to myself."

I sit down. Rebecca doesn't.

"If it's something deeper than that, I can make sense of that too. Is this an emotional affair? Do those even exist? Do you even like cookies?" She pauses. "Not rhetorical. Do you even like cookies?"

"I like your cookies."

Rebecca laughs mirthlessly. "I applaud you, Michael. Falling in love with another woman and I can't even say I feel neglected. You're a good dad to Jackson, you're attentive to me. Living two lives agrees with you."

I raise my voice to protest, "I'm not living two lives."

"Oh, just shut up. I am not done with you. If this is something else entirely, if I've completely misread the past months, then it's still something, and I'm grateful you've at least been discreet and not shoved my nose in it. I wonder if Paul can't say the same. Every little niggling thought I've had I've brushed off as my own paranoia. Until tonight. You made it easy for me to think I'm just being a silly, jealous woman."

"If this is how you've felt, why can't you keep feeling this way?" I don't mean to sound flip when I ask this, but Rebecca takes my question like a cold slap.

"The problem"—she recoils—"is that I can't explain this to Jackson. For all I know, I'm now in an open marriage. You've dragged me into something, and now, what, I get you when you're not with her? I'm the South Brooklyn wife?"

"That's not what this is," I repeat.

"Shut up! I didn't sign Jackson up for an open family. We didn't bring him into this so that he could navigate your needs, your wants."

"Please don't bring Jackson into this."

She shakes her head, banishing an ugly thought. "I'm going to bed. You can join me and we can discuss this further in the morning. Or you can pack and leave. And yes, it is an either-me-or-her choice you face, so whatever this is that you don't have the balls to acknowledge, there are going to be consequences either way."

This is where I could eloquently lay out the grand design of a semiopen relationship, monogamy an unrealistic concept, a village raising a child, our needs met in full, all of us, happier than we were before, continuing on, growing.

The words mash together in my head. So when I open my mouth, instead I admit, "I don't know what it is."

And Rebecca shakes her head at me slowly, in sheer revulsion. "Then I have even less respect for you than I did five minutes ago."

Rebecca climbs into bed, pulls the covers over herself, sets an alarm, and turns away from me. It's as final a punctuation mark to her ultimatum as she can deliver. When she hears me throw some T-shirts into the suitcase, she starts to sob quietly. "I'm going to sleep at the shop," I say. We have a cot folded up against the wall. Tony uses it when he needs to work long nights firing pottery. He won't mind if I crash on it. A few pairs of socks, some underwear. It's not until I have to press down on the top of the suitcase to get it to zip back up that I realize I've packed for longer than a short stay next to the table saw. I don't kiss Rebecca good-bye, because that feels intensely cruel. But I do slip into Jackson's room and kiss my sleeping son. I stand over his crib, try to read his future in the tea leaves of an unlined face.

Someday, Jackson, you're going to be in your thirties, and you're going to realize that your life is essentially done being built and now all you can do is live inside of it or raze it and hope to find greater satisfaction in the rebuilding. You're the untouchable structure to me. You're the landmark I will protect from the bulldozer and the wrecking ball. Right now you're too young to realize this, but when you are old enough, someday, I hope at least a small part of you forgives, or at least understands.

Then I carry my suitcase out the door, past my shop, back across the expressway.

Paul Fenniger

Present Day: July 19, 2010

3:12 PM

I'm moderately more lucid than I was before. Ten minutes ago I saw black spots as big as cicadas floating before my eyes—I tried to swat a few of them away before realizing they followed me wherever I looked. Now I see clearly, if through the sweaty haze of this still sweltering day. Memories of the tunnel feel as if they happened yesterday, or last week. My connection to them is tenuous at best.

At Meserole Avenue it finally clicks for me that I'm back on my street. I'm back on Franklin Street, where Jenny and I live. I'm almost home. I have the apartment keys in my pocket, but I'll ring the buzzer. I'll press my ear against the door and listen for footsteps, and when she opens it and sees that I'm still alive, that I'm okay, that I came back to her as soon as I could, I'll know that we're stitched back together, that I'm still her everyday.

I reach the park across from my house, see if I can spot her in the window, maybe looking for me, waiting for my return. My head goes light again, flutters, and then the sensation passes. My legs go liquid before resetting themselves beneath me. That's when I look left, as I lurch and catch myself on the sycamore tree across the street from the apartment. That's when I see a figure walking toward me, walking toward my house with the same heat-exhausted gait. And he looks familiar. In my fug, I try to place where I've seen Michael Gould before.

Michael Gould

Present Day: July 19, 2010

3:16 PM

Is he here to fight me?

Paul and I stand a block apart, staring at each other. I'm unsteady on my feet, hazy-headed—even my teeth feel wobbly. If I am not currently in the throes of sunstroke, I may be a superhero.

Paul, on the other hand, drifts side to side, punch-drunk, completely bare from the waist up but business casual from the waist down: sensible slacks and outlet mall Eccos. Shirtless and glistening, he looks like a cover model for a Harlequin office romance. It makes no sense for him to be coming from inside the apartment, he didn't put on half an outfit to meet me in the middle of Franklin Street.

If I have to fight this man, the strategy will be to aim for the balls, early and often. I'm too exhausted to grapple. We approach each other slowly, cautiously.

"Fancy seeing you here." I give him my jauntiest smile. He's looking at me horrified; I assume because my raspberry-shaded face peels before his eyes.

"Where are you coming from?" His voice slurs the question.

"Hither and yon. You?"

"The tunnel. What happened?"

We both turn to the city, to the same plumes of smoke, to the same unanswered questions. "Terrorism," I answer simply.

"Jesus. What happened?"

"I'm guessing a subway bombing."

"You don't know?"

"Do you?"

Paul shakes his head and sits down. He's here, but not entirely. I hunker down next to him—it feels magnificent to sit, stabbing pain the entire way down and then pure relief. We lean against a spiked iron fence, the border cage of the playground, our feet digging into chipped dirt and our asses sore on stone bricks, under the barest shade. He turns to me, squinting dumbly. "Do you want a beer?"

"Now?"

He points down the block. "Get a couple from that bodega and sit here."

I count the money in my wallet. Paul lays a twenty across my wrist. "Gemme one." He smiles.

In the bodega, I grab two beers, two Xtreme grape electrolyte drinks, and three Clif Bars to tide me over. The electricity works, so I open the fridge door and stand before the mist of Freon until the clerk yells at me. Paul still waits under the sycamore tree in front of the park, gazing up at the apartment, breathing steadily. His hands lay limp across his lap. I twist the top off his beer and hand it to him with the coins of his change. If he notices, he doesn't comment, merely shoves it into his pocket.

He holds up his bottle. "What are we toasting to?" I ask. I expect a platitude like *We're alive,* some reference to having survived whatever is going on. I'd even accept some crazy connective tissue, toasting *To Jenny,* two teenagers at the end of summer camp raising a glass to their unrequited collective crush. Paul surprises me by winking, actually winking, as if he knows and I know what we're toasting to and it need not be spoken aloud. We bump bottles and sip. The beer hits my tongue cold and sour and perfect. I tear open a Clif Bar, offering some to Paul. He takes it gratefully, and we eat like animals to avoid getting drunk off a thimble's worth of watery beer.

He presses the bottle to his throat, sighs appreciation for the small mercies of the day. I'm sure a part of him thinks he will walk across the street and shower, change into fresh clothes, sit across from the air conditioner while Jenny frets over the news. It's not going to happen. He's not coming back into her life; she said as much. He can grab a change of clothes, but this isn't his stop anymore.

If it comes down to a fight, an actual fight, I'd imagine he would win. Even in his kittenish state. He's larger, and with his shirt off I can confirm that he is more defined than I am, that he has muscle tone from more than carrying table legs to a truck. My New York upbringing somehow didn't include enough formative playground scraps. Somewhere my father failed in not enabling me to get my ass kicked by a series of kids in Midwood so that I could someday be battle-hardened enough to beat up a Wisconsin farm boy trying to steal back his wife.

"You know Jenny and I have been fucking." The words leave my lips and I brace myself for him to lunge at me, but he sits still, facing forward, no sign of emotion.

"I don't believe you."

"Since last August."

His face doesn't even twitch. He pulls off his bottle. "I don't believe you," he repeats stoically.

"I came up with a nickname for you. Cuck Fenn. Like Huck Finn. Get it? Jenny laughs when I call you that."

"It's pretty creative."

"And I told her I was amazed that you could get her pregnant in the first place, because all evidence tells me you have no balls."

That elicits teeth, whether a smile, a grimace, or a misshapen sneer I can't tell, but the line has been crossed, and now we can at least get down to what needs to happen. One of us needs to be victorious. Jenny needs one of us vanquished. Even if he breaks a beer bottle over my head, it'll still be cold comfort on a hot day when he has to keep walking. But he laughs softly. "You know some good one-liners, Michael."

"I know you like pictures. I can get you pictures next time. Or we can just ask Jenny if you want. She'll tell you."

"Let's finish our beers first."

"I'm not the first person she's cheated on you with. There have been at least four others. She told me that, which means there could be plenty of others she's not telling either of us about."

"So. You. Say."

"I'm in love with her too," I admit. He nods.

"Now that I believe completely."

His joyous face widens, smile stretched beatifically ear to ear. He looks like a saint in the throes of ecstasy, but it's not until he lifts his hand to wave that I understand why. I follow his adoring gaze to the window of the apartment, where Jenny has appeared, looking down upon us across the street, smiling right back.

Paul Fenniger

Present Day: July 19, 2010

3:16 PM

Why is Michael wearing face paint?

I had readied myself to shuffle my way across Franklin Street and ring the bell. I'd stand strong and upright before Jenny. Shirtless, but that's okay. At the other end of my block, I spy my first hallucination of the day: Michael, striding toward me. His clothes hang ragged from his body, sweat stained and matted. Where has he come from? He's not coming from Red Hook, not from that direction. I'm lucid enough to grasp that. Did he go out to get lunch and wander in from the apocalypse? Has he been across the river, a survivor of whatever calamity befell Manhattan?

As he gets closer I flinch to see his face. He's the shade of red kids get when they hang upside down for five minutes. Flecks of skin like broken shards of potato chips have already started to flake from his ruined cheeks and nose. Whatever other feelings I have toward him right now are cut through with horror. Today will inevitably leave multiple people scarred. It will leave Michael Gould scarred and leathery.

He tries to be insouciant with me, aims for gallows humor, but I'm too exhausted to laugh. He doesn't know what's happened today any more than I do, but he thinks he does. Michael Gould is that subspecies of New Yorker who knows everything, even when he doesn't. I'm glad for his uncertainty, though. To hear terrible news from Michael Gould's mouth would sit sour in my gut, to have to remember hearing about a bomb or a crash with Michael would render the moment all the more grotesque.

I can't stand up anymore. My legs are scaffolding, about to collapse. There's a spot in the shade against the park's fence so I sit there. Michael sits down next to me, and after I take a moment to collect and situate myself, it sinks in that something will need to be done. I may need to summon the strength to cave his skull in. The fence I'm leaning against is tipped in spikes and I consider from my seated, vacant-eyed position whether it's been built sharp enough to impale. "Do you want a beer?" I say. It comes out polite; I'm pleased with my tone, but in truth I want him away long enough to either get Jenny to spot me across the street or to give me an alternative to beating this man to death.

Death is a strong word. Probably an exaggeration.

He scampers off while I stare at the windows in our front room, wonder if Jenny sits in her office typing away or lazing about our bedroom, the only air-conditioned room in the place, reading on our bed. I wonder if she's worried. Who she's worried about. In what proportions. Michael comes back a few minutes later; he's spent almost every cent I gave him, but he brought me a beer so I raise the bottle to him. "What are we toasting to?" he asks. To me not shattering every one of your bones with my hands. I think I've kept that thought inside of my head so I wink in response.

It's still so hot. I can't remember a day this hot in my entire life. Not in Cadott. Our summers were mild. Our winters were brutal, winds rattling the house, snowdrifts taller than I was until puberty hit. I close my eyes and bask in those memories, make future plans to take Jenny back to Cadott, demand that she go with me, to see a piece of my past. She won't need to share hers to see mine, I'll take her as she is, but I want her to see the pot of dirt from which I grew.

Michael says something obscene. He's goading me, aiming to poke the bear into doing something I'll regret. Maybe he thinks this is the way to Jenny, for her to see me as a savage and him as the enlightened victim. I don't care. My body relaxes, the sinews in my hands and wrists and arms unclench. I'm not going to give Michael Gould the satisfaction.

We had a barn on our property in Cadott. Most families did, and most families used their barn for barnlike purposes. Housing livestock, storing farming implements. Not my father. He kept the bus parked in there. And my mother worried, because every winter the roof of the barn would sag under the weight of the snow, and the wind would whistle through the slats, and she worried that it would collapse on the bus, or on my father. But he reassured her that the barn was built true, and it would hold. Year in and year out, the barn withstood all storms.

And so would I. There may have been people before Michael Gould, and there very well may be people after him. I'm not blind, nor oblivious, nor stupid. But I'm steadfast, and if I stand in one spot and don't move, not an inch, Jenny will cleave to me as her barn, a safe spot even in the worst of storms.

"I'm in love with her too," he says in his mewling, pathetic voice. My role needs no understudy. You will not take her from me. Not today and not ever. I do not need to beat you senseless to crush you; I do not need to lower myself to vanquish you completely.

"Now that I believe completely," I reply, because I do believe him. Jenny is someone I can't imagine anyone not loving, not being in love with. If the world truly saw her through my eyes, she'd be an earthly deity we were lucky to merely exist alongside.

As if I called her with my thoughts, like the lady in the tower, Jenny appears at the window. There you are. I came home to you. I walked through the veins of New York to rest outside of your window, under a sycamore tree.

I wave. She waves back. And I am home.

Michael Gould

Two Weeks Ago: July 5, 2010

These floors are not my floors. But I can walk on them barefoot all the same. Some minutes go by where I stare dumbly at the walls, or I tiptoe my way to furniture, like a dog brought home from the shelter, testing his owner's patience. Can I sit here? What about here? Here too?

The only room I'm completely comfortable in is the office. I don't own any of this, but it all seems to belong to me now.

Jenny snaps me back to the present. "What are you looking for?"

"A spatula."

"To your left. It's in there."

I lift it triumphantly. Jenny applauds. "I couldn't see it because it's flat."

This morning I make us eggs. Yesterday morning she got bagels and tofu cream cheese that was better than I ever anticipated it being. Rebecca is all full-fat, lecturing on how there's no healthy way to eat butter and cheese so you might as well enjoy it sparingly. Jenny likes her gin mixed with diet tonic water, her milk skim, her cream cheese tofu'd. I catch myself comparing the two of them again, column A and column B. I shouldn't do that, and luckily haven't done so out loud. This time it happens while I'm cracking shells, working the yolk back and forth for egg-white omelets. My mind wanders, and that dangerous little dwelling is where it wanders to, like an unforgivably stupid child who keeps falling down the same well. If Jenny notices, she hasn't called me on it yet. Her mind may be on a similar walkabout, circling the same well.

Rebecca's name doesn't come up most days. Neither does Paul's. Most days, Jenny and I snuggle in our cocoon, phones turned silent, happily sequestered.

On our first night, we discovered that the act of actually sleeping together involved choreography neither of us practiced for. Our sleep habits never came up, because they never needed to. Napping lacks the formal, Bauhaus structure of sleep for me. I have trouble powering down, so I swaddle myself until my body and mind finally give way and I pass out. Once that point has been reached, I can be molded into any position and comfortably used as one would a stuffed animal. Jenny, on the other hand, can't sleep unless she is being spooned, enmeshed in arms. After that point, she'll wake up at any shift in weight, any rustle of a blanket, even a stiff breeze. So far we're compromising, but I see trouble on that horizon.

Groggy though we may be, the rest of our relationship hasn't appreciably changed, only grown more ordinary. She hates cleaning bathrooms. I've never been allowed to clean the kitchen. So, I scrub the toilet while she scrubs the stovetop. We didn't used to clean at all when our time was centered around sex. We still do that as well, and Jenny still puts the chain on the door, though she tries to do so behind my back now, quietly, once I'm in the bedroom, leaving as if she had forgotten something in the heat of the moment, and then the telltale clink of metal on metal, of Jenny once again protecting the fortress of our deceit.

I still see Jackson, usually every other day. Rebecca goes for a long walk while I spend time with our son. He ironically has chosen this time to develop his sense of humor. Daddy making fart noises with his mouth kills as a reliable closer. Rebecca's face, the way she looks at me when I come back into the apartment—I recognize it from years ago. From when we first came to Red Hook, and she saw the less chic areas of our neighborhood. Equal parts curiosity and fear. She looks at me now and sees a stranger, and her mind accelerates to decide whether to approach or run away or simply freeze in place.

She grants me an hour; I'm positive she sets a timer on her phone before she starts walking. After an hour Rebecca comes back and says, "If you're staying I'm cooking . . ." and then fill in the blank with whatever she's making for herself. It's her way of trying to initiate a conversation.

"I should go," I say, putting my son back in his crib, or his vibrating chair, or on his back on the Technicolor play mat that Rebecca and I once dubbed his "Baby Acid Trip Funland."

"We should talk, Michael," she presses. "When do you think you'll be ready to talk?"

"Soon," I promise, vaguely. Then I leave. And once I'm away from the apartment, and where she cannot see me, I smile to myself because she still cares. She still wants me in spite of everything I'm doing to her. She's still an option—I'm monstrous for seeing it that way, fine, but it's warming to be loved and, even more, to be needed.

Insecurity gets the better of me sometimes. I don't know what Jenny does when I'm with Jackson, or when I'm in my shop, where I go almost every day. Strange to make the reverse trip, and to be so close to Rebecca and Jackson without seeing them. I ask Tony to photograph me at my lathe, ostensibly for a Web site. In reality, I'm texting the pictures to Jenny, to prove that I am where I say I am. She doesn't ask me to, but once a cheater . . . So with one eye on the lathe or the saw or any other sharp object, and one eye on my phone for Jenny's texts, I wonder what she's doing, whether she's in touch with Paul, whether he's at her apartment now having the conversation that I can't seem to bring myself to have with Rebecca.

I ask, in as nonconfrontational a tone as possible, "Do you still love Paul?" She drapes herself over me on the couch, filling in the *New York Times* crossword puzzle in ink. I'm listening to the Replacements over the speakers with my eyes closed. Jenny considers my question for a moment, completing a clue before answering.

"No, not anymore."

"You can turn it off, just like that?"

She snaps her fingers. "Just like that."

"I don't believe you."

"You asked me and I answered. If you wanted to give an opinion instead of asking me a question, you should have just said so."

I craft a response in my head. "If you love someone once, then a part of you always loves them. It never goes away completely."

"Don't speak for me. That's like saying 'people who believe in a Jewish God believe in the one true God.' If that's how you feel about Rebecca, fine. But declaring your beliefs with conviction doesn't make them any less idiotic."

Fair enough. "I think, and this is just my own opinion, that if a person, for example, like myself, loves a person, also for example, like you, then regardless of whether you are in my life or not, this person would, in part, continue to love you. And furthermore, again solely the opinion held by me and me alone, I believe that love, once felt, never truly vanishes."

Jenny turns her attention back to the vertical clues. "Better. You sound much less crazy. Thank you."

Later, in bed, when I'm cuddling her and not getting to sleep, and she can feel me squirming behind her and she's not getting to sleep, I say to her, "I love your hair. I love the rest of you, all of you, really, but I love love your hair."

"I'm going to lose it," she replies simply. "Not soon, I hope. But the women in my family go bald. My mother is in her mid-sixties and she's had a wig for a decade."

Was that an opening? Let's find out. "You never talk about your mother."

Jenny exhales, languid in my arms. "She once told me, 'Some people don't care what they got so long as you got less.' I guess that applies to our situation if we want it to, but I bring it up because it's one of the few expressions of hers that I remember. She and I don't talk very much." And we're done with this topic. We lie in silence for a bit until Jenny wiggles her ass into me to snuggle closer. "I just gave you more than I've given Fenn in the entirety of knowing him. Do with that what you will."

I run my palm over her breast and feel her heartbeat in between my fingertips. "When you start to lose your hair, I'll shave my head, and we'll be bald together. We'll move somewhere nobody knows us, and people will think we survived chemo together, but the reality will be that I'm just hopelessly, helplessly, completely, and unconditionally in love with you."

I hold her close until she drifts off. A few hours later, I finally roll over, slow as dismantling a bomb, and join her in sleep.

The next day, Rebecca comes back early from her walk. I'm feeding Jackson his first blueberries. Rebecca bought them this morning at the farmer's market, fat and purple and puckered at the top. Jackson can't decide whether he likes them or not, but he keeps shaking his hands for more. "If you'd like to stay for dinner, I'm making a stir-fry," she says. I stand up and hand her the cup of blueberries. Behind me, Jackson squeals in protest. "Are we going to have a birthday party for him?"

"Sure."

"Just family, I thought," she adds. "You, and me, and your parents. We don't need to tell them about all of this. I don't want to tell them."

"That's kind of you."

"I'm very kind."

"You genuinely are, Rebecca."

She rubs her eyes. "Michael, I need you to make a decision on how you think this goes forward. Not sometime soon, but immediately."

I go to her and hold her close, and she doesn't resist. She doesn't push me away. She doesn't even cry, standing like playing dead, a soft mannequin in my grasp. "Let's talk after the party. We'll get drunk and figure everything out. Okay?"

She shrugs because, really, what else is there to say?

Michael Gould

Two Days Ago: July 17, 2010

Jenny and I finally have our talk. It occurs in between discussions of which bread to buy and whether her sniffles are from allergies or if she's coming down with a cold. The most important decisions of our lives slipped into the liner notes of lesser conversations.

I say, "I could start over with you." I'm holding a loaf of white bread at the time, a generic store brand. Jenny thinks we should go to a bakery and get fancier bread, but if we're just using it to make bread crumbs, it doesn't matter. Now that I've released that bomb, though, she's looking at me wide-eyed; perhaps I've embarrassed her by starting this conversation in the middle of a grocery store. That doesn't mean we won't have it, though, standing before a neat bounty of loaves. "It wouldn't really be starting over. And it would be messy—I can't imagine it not being messy, especially for me, because of Jackson. But if you would be patient with me, and understand that I don't mean for it to get messy, then I think I'd like to knock my current world off its axis and give us a more legitimate try."

I hadn't unpacked my suitcase yet. Jenny hadn't cleared a drawer for me. We kept waiting for the large-scale event, like buying bread to make crumbs. Jenny takes that bread from my hand and puts our basket on the floor. Then she walks me out to the street.

"Do you mean that?" The issue has been forced, not that it hasn't in similar terms before. We've spoken at length about all the things that we could do, that we want to do, that we could make possible. It occurs to me that this is how couplehood works. It's not about making the leap, it's about acknowledging that you've already made it. Rebecca and I had been living together, sharing finances, sharing responsibilities, planning our family by the time we signed a piece of paper that said we were married. Jenny and I sleep together, wake up together, plan our days around one another. We are in a relationship, full-fledged, seemingly on the monogamous end of the scale. Now that we're standing up to our waist in that quicksand, it's merely a matter of agreeing that we're half-sunk.

"Absolutely. If you leave Paul, I'll leave Rebecca. Officially. Legally."

We walk the rest of the way to her place without speaking, Jenny deep in her own mind. She starts to say something a few times, turning to me and opening her mouth, as if she had a promise to make or a warning to give but stifled it. Once we get back upstairs she puts the chain on the door, right in front of me, then flusters. Pauses. Collects herself. Then she slowly slides it back off.

"I love you," she says.

"I love you."

"We can start from that." Her hand goes to my chest; she undoes my shirt buttons, one at a time, businesslike, with speed but not passion. I grip her wrist.

"Don't ever cheat on me."

For an instant she looks angry. Then it dissolves so quickly I think she may have misheard me.

"I won't." My belt follows, then my pants, like she's undressing a doll. When she's done with me, and I'm in her kitchen with my boxers around my ankles and not a stitch on me otherwise, she removes her own clothes, just as mechanically. When we're both finally naked, her look is so intense I wonder if she did all of this to check me for a wire, and to show me she wasn't wearing one either, that we could trust each other.

She drags me back into her bedroom and straddles me on the edge of her mattress. "Stay with Rebecca tomorrow night." She grips my face in her hands. "After the party, stay with Rebecca."

"Why?"

"I'm going to tell Fenn to come over." She reaches down and guides me inside of her. "Tonight you talk to Rebecca and I'll talk to Fenn. I'm going to ask for a divorce. You're going to do the same."

"All right." I move my hands from her hips to her face, but she grabs them, pins them back against her thighs.

"I'm not ready to marry you," she hisses.

"You're not divorced yet. Neither am I."

"Even after that. I'm not sure I'll ever want to get married again." She arches her back, leans into my shoulders. I grunt to accede. So we won't be married. I don't know why I thought we would be in the first place. "But I want to do something. Something for us. For this."

"Okay." I pant a little. "What?"

"We'll go to the Cloisters." She pauses, pushes me back down on the bed and shifts me up until my head is on a pillow. Then Jenny laughs, laughs with me inside of her. "We've never been to the Cloisters, so that's where we'll go. And we can go there once a year or something and it'll be our spot and that's where you and I will start because I love you and you are mine."

I come a few seconds after she does. The Cloisters. New territory for both of us, a place to plant our flag.

Michael Gould

One Day Ago: July 18, 2010

Dear Jackson,

Happy birthday, birthday boy! Before you were born, your mother and I sat down over ramen and spitballed ideas for traditions. We wanted our own, separate from the ones we grew up with. We had, in you, a tabula rasa of ritual. Your mom wanted to take a picture of you every day with her camera, one for each day of your life, from birth to when you turned eighteen. I don't remember why we nixed that. In fact, none of the traditions we brainstormed that night have come to fruition, but I've decided to start one of my own. I'm going to write you a letter each year on your birthday, and when you turn thirty I'm going to give them to you. If I'm not around, someone else will, I promise you that.

Why thirty? Well, that's the main point of this first letter. You're going to be told that you're an adult multiple times throughout your life. If we raise you Jewish, you'll be told that you're an adult at thirteen. This is bullshit. You won't know which hand to jerk off with when you're thirteen. Most everywhere else you'll become an adult when you hit eighteen, as if one day you are a young lad and then, poof, you've crossed over and have metamorphosed into a grown man. Again, this is bullshit. At eighteen your best-case scenario is to go off to college. There, you'll realize how young you are, a realization that renews itself every time you move on to the next point in your life. You'll graduate from college at twenty-two and then it's off to the real world, right? I mean, at twenty-two, you're an adult, right? Maybe. Twenty-two is a maybe.

I hope you are one of those extraordinary kids who goes straight from undergrad to the working world with a high-paying job in some fledgling industry that will pay you obscene amounts of money. If you aren't, and given your pedigree I don't hold this in high hopes, here's where you walk in on the ground floor. The lobby. Where the receptionist and the security guard work. It sucks to be starting out. But still, you're starting out, so opportunity is around every turn, and you can afford to dick around in jobs that intrigue you, even if you don't think they'll make for good careers. You can flirt and date and fuck and fall in love and get your heart broken and rebound and repeat the whole process over and over again, even blog about it. At *some point, you'll probably notice that you've started a ca-reer because you're finally working a job that doesn't in-volve a time card. I hope you love that career. I hope you love the day in, day out of it, because that is so fucking important I will say it loudly into your one-year-old face today and hope your mind absorbs it, stores it away for when you need it.*

Then you're thirty. It's not funny anymore. That's the theme of your thirties. It's not funny anymore. That end-less string of ill-conceived relationships? Some of your friends are getting married, some even starting to have kids. It's not funny anymore. That job you don't take seri-ously, so much so that you can come in hungover every so often and no one notices? Some of your peers are on a course that will carry them through the rest of their work-ing life. It's not funny anymore. Strangers as roommates isn't funny anymore. Not knowing how to manage credit card debt isn't funny anymore. Being uninsured isn't funny anymore.

When you read this, you'll be thirty, and I hope that you are in a place where you feel settled and secure, where you look around yourself with satisfaction at the work you do, and especially the people you share your life with. Still struggling to define yourself, still grasping and hoping and waiting for your life to begin at thirty is a terrible feeling. When you've made those choices, and you think you've made the right ones, you'll know it in your gut, and that's when your life is truly ready to be lived. That's when you're an adult.

I'm not there yet. I'm passing you this advice because I am your cautionary tale.

Your first birthday was a wild success. It's been a hot day, even hotter as the day progressed, but we still cooked outside and fed you a Popsicle. Orange. You devoured it.

Your grandmother hiked up your shirt and blew on your belly and you loved every minute of that. Your grandfather cradled you in his withered arms with a look of such deep and profound contentment on his face, as if to confirm his life's work had paid off. "What a beautiful specimen of a grandson," he said today.

I haven't told my parents, your grandparents, about my plans to leave your mother yet. I'd love to pretend that I'm sparing them pain or embarrassment, but the reality is closer to a sense of shame about how they will look at me. If you get past thirty and you still think it's better to ask for forgiveness than permission, you've made some wrong turns in life. Instead, everyone got to eat cake and sing to you and laugh at your giggles, as if you were telling the best jokes they'd ever heard. My mother finished it up by helping to give you your bath, wading into the tub with you, the water up to her shins, splashing around and beaming the whole time. Today was a terrific day for them; I helped to give my parents a terrific day.

After they'd left, your mother and I put you to bed. You were dangling limp in my arms before you even hit the crib. The attention wore you out.

Then your mother slept in her room, and I slept on the couch. And early in the morning, I snuck into your room and kissed you on your forehead and apologized for everything I was about to do. "I'm so sorry," I said into your sleeping ears. I hope I didn't change a dream into a nightmare at that point.

Then I walked out the door.

I never thought I was capable of loving someone as much as I love you, Jackson, and I never thought that love would get any bigger, or even could be bigger than the all-encompassing love I felt for you on the day you were born. But it has; it's accumulated. Today I love the one-year-old

Jackson Gould, who is smart and inquisitive and good-natured. He's not a finicky eater, loves to cuddle, smells good for a child who craps himself twice a day, and makes a surprisingly small mess eating pureed foods. You're a tidy child, Jackson, and it's just one of the countless qualities that make you extraordinary.

I need to go now. I told a fib before, four paragraphs ago, describing what happened after you went to sleep. I projected into the future. I'm going to put this letter down now, then I'm going to kiss you and apologize. If someday you don't understand, I hope you forgive.

All my love. Always.

Your father,
Michael Gould

I press the letter into a book, one of mine that I know Rebecca likes as well. She's not likely to put this out on the stoop, so I can come back and get it later. There's plenty I left out because it doesn't concern him; it's background detail to his story and personal to his parents' marriage. I left out that after we put him to bed, Rebecca and I sat down with a bottle of wine and dissolved our marriage. I left out that she cried like the dams had burst, like I hadn't seen her cry since Jolie died, not out of anger toward me, or a sense of betrayal. That will come later. Today she cried for the sheer tonnage of sadness that accompanies a wound you know will only open wider with each step. She did everything right, and still I'm leaving her for someone else.

"What does she do that I don't?" she asks me, so woefully. In so much pain.

"It's nothing like that. It's not one thing. It's something indescribable."

"You don't think you owe it to me to at least try to describe it?"

"It's that . . ." I seek out a possible answer.

"Do you love her more?"

"Not more. Not less. Just in a different way."

Rebecca pours herself another glass of wine. "The right answer was that you love her less than the woman you married and who gave you a child."

Gradually we wind ourselves down. Surprisingly little acrimony has passed between us. Rebecca makes no threats, instead asks me procedural questions. Would I be moving out? Yes. When would I come back for my stuff? When I can get the truck. A week or two. Does this mean we're getting a divorce? Yes. Should I get an attorney? If you'd like. I'm getting an attorney.

That takes her aback. "Why are you getting an attorney?"

"Jackson," I reply, and hope that answer suffices. She tucks that into the folds of her mind.

"I'd take you back, Michael," she says, her voice thick.

"Why? Why on earth would you do that?" I ask her.

"This is what I know, and I'm frightened by what I don't." She buries her head in her arms and cries more.

When she's decently drunk, when we're both exhausted and we've shed our tears and mourned our loss and even reminisced about the highs we hit, Rebecca kisses me like she did on our wedding day, her mouth pressed against mine with conviction. I watch her go into her bedroom—the one that used to be *our* bedroom—and leave the door ajar. A last invitation. A proper send-off.

Rebecca wants to fuck. That's what that open door means. It's not that I'm a rock god in bed, it's that I'm here. She didn't know the last time we fused ourselves together was the last time. Looking at that open door, I think that she is pathetic. Desperate. But those aren't the right words. I'm a horrendous person for letting them come to mind.

But I can't go in. I don't know why this absurd feeling hit me, especially at this time, but I can't go into the bedroom and be with her. Doing so would be unfaithful. So I place my phone on the floor in front of the couch, setting my alarm for before Rebecca will be up. Then I sleep, jittery about tomorrow, like I've just finished taking the biggest test of my life, and now all I can do is wait for the results of the exam.

Paul Fenniger

One Day Ago: July 18, 2010

The key still turns in the lock. That's a good sign. I push the front door open to find Jenny sitting on the counter, eating a sandwich. She regards me coming in. "You should have knocked."

"I'm sorry."

"You don't live here anymore, Fenn."

"I'm sorry. Should I go?"

"You're here already," she says, so I close the door behind me.

It's been a rough few weeks on my back. I spent two nights sleeping on the couch in Jacob Weinstock's office, showering in flip-flops in the building's locker room, keeping my suitcase stowed away under my desk, obscured by two heavy file boxes. It became difficult to go past the front desk, to look Manuel in the eye, or, worse yet, to avert. So on my third day away I came to Amir, another paralegal, and I knocked on his cubicle wall. "My wife threw me out," I admitted, point-blank. "I need a place to crash."

He analyzed me, ran the equations of what kind of life I must have if I'm coming to him for refuge.

"You can take my floor for a few nights," he offered. And so I have, ever since, sharing the same stale fart air of his tiny, rent-controlled Alphabet City apartment heated by the processors of three large computers. The floor isn't Amir's stab at domestic alphamaledom; he doesn't own a couch, only a mismatched set of computer chairs scavenged from assorted offices of Manhattan.

Jenny puts her plate in the sink and stares at me. "The air mattress is in the office closet." I nod. That's her concession to kindness, letting me take the air mattress. She washes her dish, done with me, so I get out of her space and go down the hall.

This room. This extra room. This office turned nursery turned office. This good intention turned mistake turned catastrophe. I want to rip down these beautiful shelves. I want to paper these walls. I don't want to leave here. I don't want to leave her. "Jenny!" I shout, my voice catching in my throat. She appears in the doorway. "Please." I whisper.

"You should get what you need and go, Fenn."

"Stop being cruel."

"I'm not trying to be cruel, Fenn. Going online and telling strangers about our dead baby is cruel. Cheating on me and pretending you're not because it's just chat rooms is cruel, Fenn. It humiliates me."

"I never cheated on you," I plead.

She rolls her eyes. "Fidelity shouldn't be a question of semantics."

I open the closet, carefully setting aside the garbage bags of baby clothes and toys we never threw out, anticipating that it would only be a matter of time before we tried again. As I lay them gently on the floor next to me, Jenny doesn't leave, standing in the room as if to make sure I don't steal anything. On the floor, in the back, is the small box with our air mattress, like a raft covered in coarse felt. It's patched with duct tape. I smile sadly to see it, this running into an old friend who has fallen on hard times. "Do you remember when we bought this?" I ask. Jenny doesn't respond. Doesn't even begrudge me the memory. "We didn't have a bed yet. We were in that awful apartment that you liked."

"I didn't!" she protests. "I hated it."

"I hated it too," I concede. "I only liked it because you were there. I remember we got our bed piecemeal. We got the frame first and then we scoured Craigslist for a mattress. And people kept writing to us so we kept taking trips to see mattresses that had weird stains. That's how we got familiar with a lot of neighborhoods, walking around trying to find people trying to sell us a mattress. Where did we end up getting one?"

"Murray Hill."

"You liked that one because a girl sold it to us and she was really skinny, so you thought it would still be like new. The guy with the van ended up charging more to transport it to us than we'd paid for the mattress itself. But we finally had a bed, and we were sooooo proud of ourselves because we were sooooo grown up to have a bed."

We replaced it a few years later. That's another story. We replaced it with the bed that we conceived our son upon and then our son died and then our marriage died.

"We earned that bed piece by piece," Jenny acknowledges, ruefully. I'm looking at her. Midafternoon summer light spilling over her. The sum of my lifetime.

"I'm not leaving," I say out loud.

"We're done, Fenn."

"I'm going to stay here tonight, and I'll cook you dinner if you want, and I'll go to work tomorrow. That's when you can change the locks and cut me out of your life, but right now I'm not leaving."

Jenny glares at me, incredulous. "I'll call the police."

Okay. I dig into my pocket and take out my phone, slide it across the floor to her. It's not meant to be a petulant gesture, I'm not triple dog daring Jenny to have me arrested. I'll accept her decision— whatever she decides—but if she's going to actually sever ties, it's going to be an active choice on her part, not me acquiescing and shuffling out of her life, slump shouldered and devastated, trucking a busted air mattress back to the subway.

Jenny picks my phone up off the floor, holds it out to me so I can see that she's clicked the button for an emergency call, hovering her finger over send. She's magnificent and fierce, her eyes wide and challenging, her jaw set. I married the most astonishing woman, and I've never loved her more than in this moment when she's threatening to call the cops and have me forcibly ejected from her life.

Phone still in the air, she asks, "What would you cook?"

"Is there still lamb in the freezer?"

"I think so."

"I could make a lamb tagine."

Moroccan food. Jenny has always wanted to go to Morocco, for the dinners alone. She winces at hearing the magic password. That's right, your partner knows your joys from dawn to dusk. Right now you're hoping there's still a dusty bottle of sambuca in the liquor cabinet.

"I'd like that," she says quietly.

I knew you would.

Assembly. Quick defrost. Toe the line between obvious slowness and toughening the meat by cooking it too fast from the freezer. Placate her with some olives she has in the fridge. I keep her talking as I cook. Happy topics. "Did you write today?" I ask.

"I did write today," she replies sheepishly. Jenny hasn't ever shown me anything she's written. I hear her typing away at night sometimes, struck by some midnight inspiration. Someday, I have total faith, she is going to show something extraordinary to the world. Jennifer Sayles will enter the canon and be taught in classrooms and people will bookmark the moment in their lives they first read her. I can't share how much faith I have in her. I have to dilute it with watery indifference. Otherwise it's too much pressure, to disappoint me. But she knows how true a believer she has in me.

The lamb comes out perfect, one of my best efforts in the kitchen. We eat it that night sitting across from one another at the table, sharing a glass of wine, literally passing it back and forth. When we were grindingly poor, we did that with beer, then mixed drinks, then fancier cocktails, our price point on the menu going up as we gained traction, still nevertheless sitting next to one another at the bar, sliding a glass from her lips to mine.

"You can sleep on the couch." Jenny stares into the darkness outside and relents, gets me pillows and a blanket off of the bed. It's too hot for either, the bedroom is the only air-conditioned room in the apartment, but asking to sleep back there with her crosses a line she's drawn. Tonight I'm going to sleep on the couch, and tomorrow I'm going to go to work, and somewhere in the thinking hours, Jenny will make her decision on whether or not to end us. I have faith. I have unshakable faith that it will be okay.

She closes the bedroom door, and I lie awake for an hour, sweating in place, eyes on the ceiling, listening to the street sounds. I wonder what she would do if I didn't go to work tomorrow, if I planted my feet on the floor and refused to budge. Would she call the cops then? What if I chained myself to the radiator in protest, safe until the landlord turns it on in winter, lived off her mercy to feed me scraps and let me simply exist in the same space as her.

In the quiet hours, the bedroom door opens and Jenny walks down the hall, past the bathroom, toward me. I could pretend that I'm asleep, quickly close my eyes, but there's been enough duplicity. She should know that I'm lying awake and thinking about us. "You're not asleep?" she asks.

I shake my head. She's in a T-shirt and boxers, more than she usually sleeps in when it's hot out.

"You let me treat you like a dog." She doesn't sound hurtful, just perplexed.

"It's how I love, Jenny."

"I wish you didn't."

"I'm sorry."

She sways from side to side. "I don't like having to make decisions, Fenn. I might get one wrong and then spend the rest of my life regretting it."

"I get that."

"Do you?"

"I'm a paralegal and a failed actor and I sometimes get off on pretending to be other people online. Decisions are scary. Inertia is scary. Everything is scary."

"Everything is scary. There's all of it in a nutshell."

"You're the only good decision I've ever been positive about. Whatever happens, I'm not going to change my mind about that."

Jenny climbs onto the couch, on top of me, lays on me like a second blanket. She works her hands around my waist, burrowing into the cushions until she's clutching me in her arms. I wrap myself around her and hold on for dear life.

Her skin is cool.

Michael Gould

Present Day: July 19, 2010

3:59 PM

In the movies, Jenny walks out of her apartment and kisses me full on the lips. Paul glowers as Jenny and I take each other's hands and go back into our place. Roll credits. Or, Paul takes a swing at me, which I nimbly duck and then counter with a right cross I didn't know I had in me but that drops him to the ground, blood trickling from his nose, Jenny looking down on him with disdain before unveiling an expert quip like, "I'm done with boys, Paul." Kiss on the lips. Hand holding. Exit into the house. Roll credits.

In the movies, it's not this oppressively hot. Paul and I don't stand slowly, helping each other, gripping the playground fence to get upright, then stare alongside Jenny, mute and squinting at the plume of smoke over Manhattan that has finally started to billow. Finally it looks like a cloud has emerged from the sidewalks of midtown and strives sullenly to climb back up to the sky. In the movies I don't turn my head to see Jenny's hand resting on Paul's bare arm.

"I need a shower." Paul breaks the silence.

"My towel is clean."

"A cold shower."

"We've been having brownouts along with everything else. The air-conditioning is working now, but it wasn't for a couple hours."

Paul rubs the back of her neck in sympathy. A stream of black smoke cuts through the cloud like a skunk's tail. We watch it for a while, watch it blow south toward Chelsea, toward Union Square, toward the Village, toward Wall Street and Battery Park and out over the sea. We watch the helicopters pull back, one at a time, a few breaking away from the pack, a few more taking their places. With a nod, Paul starts his way across the street. He pauses. "Is Michael joining us for dinner?" His voice rings out with a new authority, answering his own question.

For the first time since she came out of the house, Jenny looks at me. "No," she says over her shoulder. "Michael should get home." He nods again and walks across the street. Through the front door. Closes it behind him.

"You got burned," Jenny says.

"Had a long walk. Turns out the Cloisters are pretty fucking far away."

"I've heard," she mumbles.

"What's going on here, Jenny?"

"Paul and I talked . . ." She trails off, doesn't elaborate.

"Talked about what?"

"About us."

"Which us is us?"

"Me and Paul."

I try to keep my temper level. "I thought that conversation had already happened. I thought that you had the same conversation with Paul that I had with Rebecca and now those conversations were done."

She glances back at her apartment. "I've made a lot of bad decisions over the past year. Since the hospital."

"Don't blame this on a dead baby," I snap. That punches the air out of her. "*We* made decisions. *We* did. And I've done things I can't go back on because of those decisions. Did you just change your mind?"

"So many bad decisions," she repeats. Then, poking her head up, proper as a waiter about to read me the specials, she intones, "There's been an inordinate amount of horrible behavior on both of our parts."

I laugh and sneer at the same time. "There's been a lot of love as well."

"Go home. Please. Go home and work things out with Rebecca. I won't bother you again. I won't call and I won't text and even if Paul drops dead tomorrow I won't see you ever again."

"What if that's not what I want? What if I want to stay with you instead? What if I made my choice and I chose you?"

This is the part she hadn't thought about. Oh God. Oh God, it hits me full freight. This is all I've been thinking about for months. And she may not have thought about it at all. Or, she may have given it just enough thought to realize she doesn't care. "I choose Paul," she says plainly.

Jesus Christ. Jenny's got her arms crossed over her chest, stands back from me. I'm an unwanted visitor at her door, proselytizing. I'm a lonely cashier not ringing her up fast enough. Oh God, I'm going to have to walk all the way back to Red Hook. "I destroyed my marriage for you," I say idly. I don't know why I said that, possibly just to make her feel bad, or to continue the conversation. My water bottle swishes around in my shaking hands, it's nearly empty and I wonder if she would actually take it inside and fill it for me, let me come in for a minute and throw on a fresh shirt. She has clothing of mine.

"You have my stuff," I stress. "You have my clothes and other stuff."

She gets close to me and takes the water bottle from my hands. "Wait here," she instructs. Like I'm a dog at a post, like I'm fucking shameful. It can't end this abruptly. I've earned the right to the ebbs and flows, to the sluggish, turgid grind of a relationship turning and spoiling, rotting, then dissolving. She comes back out a minute later with my suitcase and a full bottle. She'd already had it packed. "Go home," she whispers.

I mount a last appeal. In the movie she cries and listens and brings me inside and then Paul sees us together and realizes he is the spare and he's the one who has to keep walking. "We made plans," is all I can come up with. Vague notions of vacations to take, restaurants to try, the life we would build together. I boil it down to three more words, and Jenny brushes them aside like gnats. "I love you." Hot tears well in my eyes. I'm fucking crying and sweating at the same time. I'd dive in the river if I could.

Jenny recoils, finally disgusted by me. "I didn't ask this of you."

"That's exactly what you did!"

She shakes her head, dismisses the very premise of my argument. "I want to love my life right now. For that to happen, we need to end. I'm going to go back inside now. Please leave us alone."

That was how she parried? That was her strongest comeback? I obliterated my marriage for her and she can't do better than to brush me off with peevishness?

I'm immensely frustrated because the answer is yes and there's nothing I can do about it.

"I'll call you tomorrow," I say finally.

She turns her back to me, faces a place I'm no longer welcome. "I won't answer."

Still across the street, I watch the door shut behind Jenny and stare up at their windows, waiting for her face to appear, for her to look out at me, see me and reconsider, understand that I was the better choice.

All the things I was supposed to say. Now they come to me. Not even worth repeating to myself. Plenty of time and distance to walk for that.

I'm still standing there ten minutes later, with two Clif Bars eaten, with both bottles of purple sugar water chugged, with only my bottle of water and now a suitcase to lug. If I follow the river and cleave to the coast of Brooklyn, I'll get home eventually. So I begin.

Paul Fenniger

Present Day: July 19, 2010

4:12 PM

The subway tunnel runs off me in a gray slick, a stream that stains the bathtub and swirls around the drain. Dark circles like cement dust splatter the tile walls when I rub my scalp. I'll shampoo twice, scrub myself three times, until my skin is pink and raw. Even then I won't feel completely clean. There are people who work in the tunnels every day. Do they have to wash themselves so thoroughly at the end of every shift?

The cool water does purify. Makes me forget that the sun scorched me on the walk home, that I felt like I was being pressure-cooked. Ten minutes ago I was desperately thirsty; now I open my mouth and let shower water in to splash around my gums, gargle and spit.

When I'm done with this shower I plan to lie down on the bed with the air-conditioning turned to full blast and sleep until my body doesn't want to sleep anymore. If I wake up in the middle of the night, that's okay. I may wake up and take another shower— that's an option. We have enough soap. Landlord covers our water bill. My head still swims; I sit down in the shower, in the muddy gray water, and let it rain down.

In a few days, whenever I next go into work, assuming the trains are running again, I will venture down to the Bedford stop, and I will wait on the platform for an L train. When one arrives, I'll wait patiently for people to get off and then swim with the crowd into the belly of the train. The doors will close. We will slide into the tunnel, beneath the East River. I'll tell Henry I love him as I pass underneath, as I do every crossing. I'll hang on to the metal pole, headphones on, staring into space. And when it gets me to Union Square, three stops later, I'll clamor out with the hordes, alight onto Fourteenth Street, and walk to the office. I'll do this again and again and again, five days a week, until I get a different job and ride a different subway.

The first few times those doors close and we dive into the tunnel, I'll remember today. After that, I won't. I'll listen to a podcast instead, and get wrapped up in it, and won't realize that I've even stopped thinking about the day I had to walk through the tunnel, until the next time my memory gets jogged, when the train stops in the middle to let the trains ahead get some distance. Then I'll remember again, but it will quickly evaporate.

This is how the trauma of today will work. First the shower washes away the evidence. Then rest makes me whole. And then it's simply a matter of time and repetition. However bad today is, the memories will fade in time. It's the good ones that get embedded. It might work differently for others, but I like how it works for me.

There's a gentle knock on the bathroom door. I stand back up. "Jenny?" She comes in, I hear the lid on the toilet clang. She sits outside of the shower. For a shampoo and rinse we stay silent, on opposite sides of the curtain. Then she speaks.

"What do you want to do for dinner?"

I'm simultaneously starving and completely disinterested in food. "I'm fine with anything."

"I could go out and get us something. I could cook tonight."

"No. Don't go out if you don't have to. Is there leftover lamb?"

"Some."

"Enough for two?"

"Definitely."

"I'll have that later. I'm going to lie down for a bit."

"Will you drink some water first?" I hear the catch in her voice.

"I will."

"If you're up at six, there's a press conference scheduled. Supposedly we'll find out what happened."

It doesn't matter. Something terrible happened. All that's left is the getting past it now. "I can find out when I wake up."

"I will too then. We can find out together."

"Once it's news it's news," I say. "Can't unlearn something. Can't unsee it."

"No," she agrees. More silence. I run the bar of soap across my chest, bury it deep in each armpit. What a silly, small pleasure. "Fenn?"

"I'm here."

"Tell me what happened to you today."

I will. I'll recount it. From the moment the train stopped to when I gathered you close to me and we lay on fresh sheets in front of the chugging hum of our air conditioner. I'll give you every detail.

But not right now. Right now I don't want to relive it. I want to get clean, Jenny. Please understand. "I'm still a little out of it," I say. "Can you tell me about your day?"

Jenny stops crying, gets it together for me. I love her grace. I love her glory. She'd be the New York today that stands bold and unruly, defiant and stubborn as the merciless sun, and she would tell all comers that she is here and she will not be moved. She opens her mouth. She starts to talk about what she ate when I left for work this morning. I close my eyes, let the water strip the soot from every pore. And I listen. I hear her soft and ethereal, in three-quarter time.

Michael Gould

Present Day: July 19, 2010

5:46 PM

Once I get past the tinted windows of the riverfront condos on the outskirts of Williamsburg, my journey back to Red Hook is more or less solitary. For blocks I'm the only person on the street, the only person walking through the Navy Yard, hauling my suitcase, banging it into my knee. The temperature has finally started its descent, still in the triple digits but on the downswing at least. Since I haven't died from heatstroke yet, that fate starts to seem a little less likely with each passing minute. My water bottle is still half-full from Jenny's; some curious nostalgia follows each sip, skipping all the other stages straight to bargaining that if I parcel out this last thing she has given me, this water from her tap, I'll retain some part of her.

Every few blocks the buildings part and I see midtown clearly, the smoke now more black than white, the air starting to smell acrid on my side of the river. The helicopters have all moved on save for one, a last sentinel. I can't tell if it's a news chopper or police. Something tremendous has happened today. And I walked through it.

New York exists as a single-celled organism at war with itself. Brooklyn resents Manhattan. Manhattan begrudges Brooklyn. Both ignore Queens, pity Staten Island, and fear the Bronx. But the density of the city forces us together. There are simply fewer square inches another person doesn't occupy on any given block. We bump elbows on the subway, sit thigh pressed to thigh at undersize tables in claustrophobic dining nooks. The smoke casts an ashen haze over the five boroughs, over all of us equally. Jenny and I came together partly because our bodies were literally smooshed together in a tiny office in Greenpoint, like handfuls of Play-Doh pressed into one another by a child.

Partly because we chose to. I pointed at Jenny and said, "I want you." The silent response to that call a resounding, rafter-shaking "And No One Else!"

It hasn't turned out how I thought it would. I take my long zombie walk to craft words of reconciliation. It's simple enough—Rebecca didn't do anything to make this a proportional apology. I'm sorry, Rebecca. I've done the worst possible thing I could ever have done, it will never happen again, and I will do everything in my power to deserve your trust again. That's the long and short of it, with some flourishes for how profoundly sorry I am. It's not insincere. Leaving Rebecca never felt *good,* but until about two hours ago it felt *right.*

At long last I stand outside my own apartment. The first thing I'm going to do when I get upstairs is kiss my son. The second thing I'm going to do is stand before my wife and let her make the next decision. She may be so happy to see me alive that we'll hold each other for a few days. She may be repulsed by me in myriad ways. When Jackson goes to sleep, I'll start on both knees and put my hopes in Rebecca's mercy. I turn my key in the lock and step back into our home.

The apartment is empty. I peek in Jackson's room, and he's not there, nor is his carriage by the door. Rebecca isn't in our bedroom. Even the basic-level detective work—cold oven, dry shower, made bed—tells me Rebecca hasn't been home in a while. A deep breath and it hits me: I don't smell cookies. The scent of our apartment without sugar baking has a sterile hospital smell to it.

I take out my phone to see if it's finally working and discover that it's completely dead. When I plug it in, though, it starts its slow refill. The power is back on, or here it never went off. While it charges I take the quickest shower of my life, every drop of cold water stinging my ruined skin. The sun and heat carved canyons into my lips; the tops of my ears show dead and white, skin peeling down, a horror movie effect I worry will terrify Jackson.

While showering, I listen for the door, now thinking up an apology to Rebecca if she comes home and finds I've jumped straight into selfish needs. I resign myself to this being my life for a while, watching the sword dangle over my head with each choice I make.

Forgoing the hamper, I plunge my clothes into the trash. My phone has enough juice to turn on, and thank Christ, I'm showing bars. Everything is returning, piece by piece. I call Rebecca and it goes to voice mail after one ring. One ring is what you get when she's in the subway or has her phone turned off. Four rings would mean she's ignoring me. This is a good sign. Another thing to resign myself to, reading every scenario of my life like tarot to identify the possible signs and signifiers. The affair has made my life a perpetual semiotics class.

If Rebecca isn't here, she's gone to my parents. And of course that's where she'd be—they would have come to grab her and Jackson the instant something went wrong, spirit them away to Midwood. Red Hook is on the water. Midwood is inland. Until the smoke clears, my parents would view Midwood as a fortress and Red Hook as Brooklyn's front lines. It takes four tries to call my parents, but I finally get a ringtone.

"Hello?" my father answers.

"I'm okay." I lead with that.

There's a deep breath on the other line, then quiet tears. I hear him say *he's okay* over and over again to my mother, who wails. "Thank God, Michael. Where are you?"

"I'm home. Listen, Dad, I need to speak to Rebecca." He conveys this backward to my mother, like my translator. *He needs to speak to Rebecca.* Then silence. "Can you put her on please?"

His voice is hushed. "Michael, we thought she was with you."

Blood drains from my head and I bend over the sink in case I throw up. The only scenario in which Rebecca was out of the house but still safe, the only scenario in which Jackson is safe, just fell by the wayside. I mumble some promise to call my father later and hang up. He's still talking as I bring the phone away from my ear.

I call her number again, and again it goes to voice mail after one ring. Underground, or turned off.

I search the apartment for some note from her, some indication of where she went. She could have gone to the police, to report me missing, but she wouldn't have wanted to drag Jackson to the station. There's no earthly reason she would have left this apartment with its locked doors and familiarity to venture out into the hottest day of the year with a one-year-old in tow. There's nowhere safer than where I'm pacing right now.

The clouds of smoke in midtown Manhattan. Whatever occurred beneath. There's no reason for Rebecca and Jackson to be there. There's no reason for them to be there. There's no reason for them to be there.

I can only hope routine will provide the answer. Rebecca took Jackson to Fairway, or to the Laundromat, or even to a bar along Van Brunt, needing a drink today more than ever and not caring about chiding looks. This is Red Hook. A mother can bring a baby into a bar and drink in front of it. This isn't Park Slope. I giggle at that, promise myself to tell that to Rebecca when I see her. After I hold our son.

Then I go running from the apartment as fast as my ruined legs will carry me.

I head straight for the tail end of Van Brunt Street, checking in storefronts, head on a swivel for strollers. Fairway has closed for the day, a bored security guard turning me away. He sympathizes when I tell him I'm looking for my wife and son, but he hasn't seen anyone like that since they closed three hours ago. I give him my cell phone number in case they come by. I run back out of the Fairway parking lot, and turn to run to the pier, where the view of lower Manhattan has drawn a crowd. I have to push people aside, calling Rebecca's name, looking for her amid the crowd. People mostly ignore me, a few jostle back, a few hush me, bearing silent witness to the spreading smoke. When I reach the end, I turn around and double-check, pushing the same people through the same crowd, calling out her name.

She's not at any of the bars on Van Brunt. However much our intentions had been to get recognized at the local places, no one on staff at either Hope & Anchor or Fort Defiance knows who I'm talking about when I ask them if they've seen Rebecca. "She gives you cookies!" I shriek to stunned, guarded looks. Why are they even setting up? Who the fuck is eating here tonight? Where are my wife and son? By the time I get back outside, the scent has changed. There's smoke descending over Red Hook, an electric winter scent, a char to the air. I'm breathing ash. I swear to God I'm breathing ash. Where are my wife and son?

I run down the streets of the Interior, even as my legs burn and my feet blister and every step brings worse pain than I can imagine. Still I run, searching for a woman pushing a stroller. I run up and down, block by block, past empty soccer fields, past the locked swim center, past the projects, where only a few people sit outside, everyone else glued to their television. I run through Coffey Park, the Interior park, where Rebecca has never taken Jackson, even though it's just as bucolic as any other New York City park, because we are afraid, because we live in fear of where we live and I've forced her to live here and now I don't know where she is or where our son is and I abandoned them both. I ask any group of people congregated, without hesitation, without dignity. I beg them to let me know if they've seen my wife and son. I force my phone into their face, the battery almost drained again, show them pictures of the two of them. Heads shake, eyes cast sideways, shared looks, as if it's a conspiracy, as if they have my family and aren't telling me.

No, it's that I'm sweating profusely and ranting and today has already had enough drama.

I collapse onto my knees in the middle of Coffey Park. This is where an older black man with stoic eyes is supposed to put his hand under my arm and help me up, hand me water, tell me everything is going to be all right.

He doesn't exist. Or if he does, he has his own trouble to deal with on this batshit day. The scattered few who see my spectacle don't want anything to do with the crazy white man, and I can't blame them, so instead I stay on my knees and heave.

The truck. The thought hits me upside my head. If Rebecca decided to try to come and find me, she wouldn't have done so on foot. If she didn't want to get my parents' help, she would have needed a car, and the easiest option is the shared truck from the studio. That's where I sprint to last, leaning my shoulder into the door as I turn the key.

She's not here. The key for the truck sits in the drawer where it always sits. Tony wrote on the chart that he parked it at Imlay and Pioneer yesterday evening. No further entries. I go there next and find an empty truck.

The walk back home feels longer than the walk from the Cloisters. I'll call the police and report her missing, along with Jackson, and hope they'll give this more attention because of the baby element, the mother-and-child element, than they otherwise would, especially today. After that, I'll call her parents, start by finding their number—we buried it somewhere—I don't have it in my phone. There's always the slim possibility that she got the fuck out of the city somehow, that she swiped a Zipcar and decided to drive to Connecticut. That she would seek her parents as a safe haven strikes me as the most ridiculous explanation of all, but any port in a storm.

I unlock the front door and climb the stairs, my knees buckling with every step. I'll need to spend the next few days recovering if circumstances let me. I'll need to recruit my parents, which means I'll need to explain why I wasn't with my family today, why I was at the Cloisters. My fingers fumble with the keys, salted tears sting the fissures the sun has carved.

The front door catches and the scent of cookies hits me. "Rebecca?" I call.

Her head appears in the sliver of door. She's put the chain on. "Keep your voice down; Jackson is asleep." I shut the door, let her slide the chain off, but nothing happens. I'm still standing in the vestibule outside of our apartment. I open it again and there she stands, just out of reach, still barricading me out with this chain. She shakes her head. No, Michael. No.

"Where have you been?"

Her eyes go furiously wide. These are her eyes from when Jolie would relapse. Incredulous eyes. "Where have *you* been, Michael?"

"I came home!" I fume. "I came home and you weren't here! And Jackson wasn't here! Where the fuck were you?"

"We took a walk."

"You went out in this? Have you seen the smoke? Do you have any idea what's been going on today?"

She clenches her fists and wraps her arms around herself. "We've been inside all day and I've been crying. It's freaking Jackson out, so I took him on a walk. We didn't go far."

"I was running around for an hour trying to find you. I ran all over Red Hook."

"I don't know." She sounds exhausted. "You missed us."

Start apologizing, Michael. Open your mouth and say, "I'm sorry."

"I know you are."

"Please let me in."

Her face turns to stone. I recognize this look too. This was the look she gave Jolie when she no longer trusted her and now aimed only to never get hurt again. Carefully, as if she had been rehearsing all day, she says, "You made a choice."

"I made the wrong choice. I made the worst choice. I chose selfishness and irresponsibility and cruelty. I'm so sorry. Please let me in."

She gets closer to the door. I could reach through and touch her if she wanted to be touched. I could rub her hands like I do when she's nervous and uncertain and needs me. Rebecca lowers her volume. "If there's something you need I'll pass it through the door, but you're not staying here tonight, Michael."

My eyes flit over her shoulder and land on the table I made with my two hands, of wood I bought and planed and shaped and smoothed and polished. A table to last us our lifetime of meals, for homework frustration and stilted family meetings, to sneak late-night cookies with our son, to toss keys onto when our hands are full and for me to sit at and watch Rebecca in her kitchen, in her element, dazzling me with her Rebecca-ness.

It lists to the side, imperceptible to everyone but me. I cut one leg an eighth of an inch shorter than the others, a careless mistake compounded by laziness, because it was the fourth leg I had cut, and because who notices an eighth of an inch? Who looks at a painting and sees its flaws?

It lists to the side because I had other places to be than in my workshop, cutting an eighth of an inch off of three more legs for a table I didn't want in the first place.

"I walked through Manhattan today. Someone attacked our city, and I thought I was going to die, Rebecca. I promise I did. And I realized that the only people who matter to me in this world are you and Jackson. You're who I love. Please let me in."

It's the luckiest excuse I've ever stumbled upon. I was in it and it was terrible and that's what inspired my epiphany. Take me back because I bore witness to tragedy. If I can convince her then I can convince myself. Rebecca's hand goes to her mouth, but I can't tell what the emotion is behind it. "Why were you in Manhattan in the first place?"

"Stupid reasons. I'm a stupid man and I'll never be this stupid again. I promise."

Dammit if I don't think for a hot second that she's going to relent. The beeper goes off on the fridge. Another batch of cookies is done. They smell like home. Rebecca lets it beep, lets it beep even though Jackson is sleeping and the cookies are overbaking. Dammit if I don't think it's because she's going to let me back in.

But she shrugs. "No, I'll bet you'll never be this stupid again, either, Michael. And I don't care what you saw today. You put yourself in the middle of it. You should have been here, with your wife and child."

"Rebecca . . ."

"We don't recover from this," she hisses. "I don't care if you never see her again and if no one ever finds out. I'll know, Michael. Every time I look at you I'll know that I'm your consolation prize. I have more fucking dignity than that," she seethes. "Jackson has more dignity than that. He's not the old toy you pick back up because you broke your new one."

"That's not what this is. Please let me in."

"Do you need anything?" she asks, with a heavy pause between each word. "If not, you need to go now."

I marvel at her dry-eyed face, her unwavering voice. All this time, I thought I was the stronger one. I take a few steps, slowly backing away from the door. There's no moving her today. "I'll call you tomorrow." Tomorrow we'll start to fix this. Tomorrow I'll beg. I'll beg on both knees. For now, do I need anything? Charger, change of clothes, toiletries, cash if she has any on her—I scamper through a list of what I need. Do I tell her item by item and wait in the hall?

No, wait. Don't start later. This needs to happen now. I kneel, one leg at a time, like dissembling. Like a building crumbling onto itself. I get on both knees and beg. "Please, Rebecca. Please don't leave me. Please."

"I'm not the one who left," she says, and shuts the door in my face. This time the dead bolt turns.

Paul Fenniger

Three Months from Now: October 20, 2010

I run the brush over the corner, touching up one of many patchy areas one last time. The wall seems to absorb the paint, greedy and spongelike. Or I'm using the wrong paint. Always a possibility. I don't really know what I'm doing, but Jenny seems pleased. She comes into what used to be her office and supervises my work, brings me autumnal cocktails of her own invention, runs her hands over the smooth walls and smiles to herself.

This should have been finished a month ago, but it's been a busy time, and Jenny has been good about not pressuring me. I got another off-off-off-Broadway gig, this one actually paying up front, to perform some Molière.

She's the one who brought up the idea of converting the room to an entirely new, as yet undefined purpose, or at least stripping the shelving, taking out every slat of wood, unscrewing every screw, spackling over every hole, and repainting so that the space would look completely different from before. From all of the befores. In August, when Jenny and I had our feet under ourselves a little more steadily, she came to me with the suggestion, and I bought tools the very next day. Jenny didn't explain why she wanted this done, just that she did.

I didn't need an explanation. Every brushstroke brings me new heights of contentment.

Dismantling the shelves took a few weeks. They were put together with an electric screwdriver, whereas I'm relying on nothing more than wrists and dedication. Jenny heard me cursing under my breath and came in to see what the trouble was. "He really screwed deep," I muttered, and she went red, and I went red, and Jenny and I avoided each other for the rest of the day. We stumble like that, or I trip over my own feet and take her with me.

It's not worth trying to resell the wood. It didn't cost much regardless, I'm not sure I paid for a minute of labor—at least not financially—so each trash day I haul slats of pine to the curb. Each trash day a few more disappear.

I lost a week when Jenny and I took a vacation to San Diego. We went online and looked for cheap fares, found a fantastic deal and a cheap hotel, and got on a plane and out of New York for a week. We both needed it. We went to the zoo and pretended to meet each other for the first time. Jenny appeared to be going for kink, but I found this really sweet, pretending to fall in love with her again. I got to be myself, and still my mind would slide, releasing all those endorphins. From across a seal enclosure, her eyes meet mine—Erik Satie scores each fresh introduction. We had a lot of sex—frustrated, grippy, needy sex that segued back into our routines, back into the places we like to be with one another. The apartment seemed bigger the day we got back.

She's been kind about the Internet stuff. More than kind. I don't clear my browser history, and she has a list of my passwords, and from there she told me she'll just have to trust. We'll just have to trust. She amended that pronoun. After enough time reading over my shoulder, she decided to create her own accounts. The anonymity of the Web appeals to her in a way she never expected. She loves the instant reinvention.

Sometimes she narrates to me what she loves about me. As if I'm a character. "Years later she'd take for granted the grace with which he cooked, his movements efficient, his steps minimal. He could navigate a stove and an oven and a pot and a pan without any extraneous movement, only pursed lips to show a focus greater than he gave to the usual tasks. And it was his secret, this strange talent in the kitchen, this yen for haute cuisine, this agility." If Jenny were to make me a character in her book, I hope she would be kind. I'd love it either way. It's the sum value of my life, her words. It's everything I live for.

I catch her staring sometimes, off into the middle distance for minutes on end, a completely new habit for Jenny, one I've never seen in our time together. She never used to go unfocused, and I know she's thinking about him, and she's wondering if she made the right decision, or if she'll ever know if she made the right decision, if she'll receive some confirmation one way or another.

And, to be honest, I don't know why she chose me, either. I don't know whether he did something wrong or I did something right.

Ultimately, I don't care.

Jenny comes in and ruffles my hair, charmed by the unintentional texture of the now yellow walls. She bends down and scratches a fleck of paint from my cheek with her nail, then kisses me where she scratched, then on my forehead, then on my lips, then on my lips, then on my lips.

And it's okay.

Michael Gould

Six Months from Now: January 18, 2011

This took a wrong turn somewhere.

My baby boy is eighteen months old today. I've promised myself that I'll stop counting in months once he hits two. He laughs at everything—big, full-belly laughs, guttural, dirty-old-man laughs that shake him like jelly and get everyone in the room laughing with him. Jackson Gould, the life of the party.

Rebecca takes him to Coffey Park, bundled up in the latest jacket that he'll outgrow in another week. We buy disposable clothing for our son. I sit on a bench and wait until she rolls him up to me. Rebecca and I catch up cordially while Jackson walks around the playground on fat legs. The playground part of this park frustrates him—everything is built for kids much older—but it's the closest to where he lives. Where he lives with his mom. It's taken me a while to make that mental correction.

She paid my parents back, every cent of the Becky's Bites loan. She made the executive decision to cut the mass of her cookies by 30 percent and the price per dozen by 25 percent, and somehow this math turned into an explosion of orders. When the economy is shit, a cookie for three dollars seems an affordable luxury. She's in coffee shops and restaurants across Brooklyn now. She's even hired two people for delivery, employees two and three of her empire.

Rebecca built something. I was looking elsewhere while she built something.

She thanked my parents with a glamour shot session for the two of them with Jackson. I came home to find a framed portrait of my parents holding Jackson, chin glistening and midsqueal. It's on the mantel where the picture of me and Rebecca used to be. I didn't ask my mother where she put the one it replaced.

When Rebecca and I have discussed all the latest business, most of it pertaining to Jackson, she takes out a cupcake and a candle, because candles won't stay in cookies, though I'm sure Rebecca will find a way soon enough. I carry a lighter now, and up to twenty things to light at a time, so I light it for him and we sing. The ceremony is a little lost on him—he just wants the cupcake and can't quite figure out why it's glowing with a danger stick, why Mommy would stick something he can't touch into something he's supposed to eat—but we blow it out for him and a minute later his face is smeared with icing and Rebecca bemoans the bath she'll have to give him and how hyper he'll be right up to the crash.

I had to stop eating her cookies. Rebecca still brings me a couple every time I see her, and I accept them, but give them to a homeless person when I can find one, or I throw them out. I couldn't go on any more Proustian journeys—those rabbit holes make for a dark dive.

We make plans for me to see him next weekend at my parents'. She'll bring him over. Then Rebecca and Jackson leave. I can't stay on this bench for long without a kid, but I don't want to go. I walk through the Interior back to the subway.

Today is also the first day the D train is running on its own line again. Six months and they've finally cleaned up the debris, set right the tracks, gotten the signals working again. It no longer shifts lines at Herald Square, picking up the thread again at Columbus Circle. The detour cost everyone three extra minutes of hassle every trip, and as of today we can find something else to complain about. I take the D up to Morningside Heights, to meet with a Columbia student who wants a goddamn apothecary table. I sit and fume and picture the check in my calloused hands for station after station after station. I don't even notice when the train stops again where it's supposed to.

The man sitting across from me on the train holds today's *Post,* which shouts the headline BEATS WALKING, with a picture of the mayor outside of Herald Square. The mayor grins, as does the guy holding the paper, staring right at me. "Beats walking," he jokes a catchphrase, long past frayed. I muster a nod in response. We're not going to high-five because the trains are doing what they're supposed to be doing, buddy. There are too many stops left on this trip, and I'd rather spend them with the inevitable subway mariachi band than connect with a stranger.

In the basement of a building on Forty-seventh Street, an antiquated boiler finally broke. It broke by exploding, sending the metal casing shooting through two floors before it lodged in the ceiling of the second floor, an out-of-business Judaica shop. Shrapnel also tore a gas line, and the flooding caused the circuits to spark, setting off another, larger explosion. Both explosions caused debris and flooding on the subway tracks below the building.

The building itself is empty. Every single floor is unrented office space, the landlord waiting out the swoon to hike up rents again.

Meanwhile, every day, the mayor's office receives assorted threats, both handwritten and typed, and it forwards these to Homeland Security. The mayor, on the morning of July 19, 2010, gets an early briefing not on the building explosion and fire, but on the subway damage, and the Department of Homeland Security can't say for certain that this isn't an attack on the transit system. The mayor yells, "Shut it down," bringing all public transit to an immediate halt.

Because it's the hottest day of the year, the electrical grid up and down the Eastern Seaboard takes on a catastrophic strain. Brownouts and blackouts cause some cell towers to shut down, generators kick on, but a few million New Yorkers all trying to call at once meant that no one got through. Crews couldn't get where they needed to go to make repairs because everyone with a car clogged the roads.

All of this gets explained to the mayor before noon, but he keeps the terrorism narrative going all the way through his press conference at six, when he insists that they continue to investigate the cause of the fire and that the MTA, New Jersey Transit, Metro-North, and LIRR service will be restored under heightened security. When the reports start to come out, the *Post* finds a picture of the mayor making the stupidest face possible and pastes it under the headline CHICKEN LITTLE.

My mother has kept me updated on every development in this saga. As soon as I learned I was wrong as to the cause, I tuned out. I'm rubbing my own nose in my own mess enough these days.

An appliance broke and I walked a marathon. The whole time I wanted it to be bigger than it was, but I wasn't the only one. It's the dirtiest of shared secrets. Every death that day was preventable, people who should have stayed put instead kept walking, and seven people died of complications related to heatstroke. But we wanted the four-figure body count, the benefit concert, the flags at half-mast. We wanted to be able to tell the world where we were on July 19. We wanted it to all mean something, because otherwise why did we go to all that damn trouble?

Things took a wrong turn somewhere. I'm well into my thirties and living in my parents' basement. My mother is mostly angry with me because I've made it harder for her to see Jackson now. But she cooks and fusses over me and gets upset when I stay in my studio too late, which I do with increasing frequency. I always shoot a text to Rebecca that I'll be there in case she needs anything, or in case she wants to bring Jackson by, and then I get my work done quickly and sit for a while, or go up onto the roof and stare out in any direction, though most often with my back to Manhattan, facing where I used to live, hoping to live there again.

My father looks at me with scorn now. He slapped me, actually slapped me, when I told him what I had done. My father has never hit me in my life and he put his palm across my face with intent. Take family out of the equation, take fidelity out, integrity and honesty as well. My father was raised to believe that you never cede what you have. Someone may take it from you, but if you love something, you never give it away. Same goes for people you love. He spends a lot of time in rooms other than where I am, and eagerly awaits the day I move back out.

I'd like to. I want to move out and back in with Rebecca and Jackson. She's not asking for a divorce yet, so that's good. The only time we've really spoken about it was a month ago, a slight thaw after five months. She said that sometimes she misses me, which reminds her of how angry she is with me. So every positive thought is counterbalanced by a negative one—not the best starting point for reconciliation.

I asked her if she hates me. She thought for a moment and said that no, she doesn't hate me, but seeing me reminds her of how passionately she is capable of hating herself. She didn't know that about herself before I taught it to her. That and our son are the two lasting gifts I gave my wife.

I still think about Jenny constantly. It's like I read nine-tenths of a mystery and then the only copy of the book was stolen from me. How the fuck does it end? The wondering consumes me.

If I'm supposed to hate her, I don't. I'm not angry at Jenny for having sharp teeth; she's an animal. I'm angry at myself for spending so much time in her jaws.

She's gone apeshit online, which isn't the Jenny I remember. She has a Facebook account where she posts her opinions on the stories of the day. The Jenny I knew was as political as an ear of corn, but now she's reading *The Nation* and listening to *Democracy Now!* and sharing her thoughts on every damn thing.

She posted the other day that she's pregnant again. I don't know who she's sharing this news with. I don't know any of the people she has listed as friends. Jenny never spoke of them in all of our time together.

But when I'm spinning wood on the lathe, or planing a tabletop, or doing anything where my mind can drift, it's Paul who occupies my thoughts. It's Paul Fenniger, who so happily and readily gamboled back into that relationship. Who still calls her his partner after she treated him like a prop. How does he live with himself? He posts pictures of the two of them grinning like children on the Staten Island Ferry. Like nothing happened. Like the whole year was just lost to a long blink. He's what keeps me tense, short of breath, awake at night. It's Paul I fucking hate.

Why does Rebecca not have that capacity to forgive?

They pose, smiling, his hand on her bump. Who took that fucking picture? Who else have they invited into their orbit? What does that person know about me?

Nothing. She's told that person nothing. And she won't. I will become another secret, as good as a lie. Until the next one hears a story about how I too was disposable, how everyone but him she could take or leave. Another lie she'll dress up as a secret.

But I remember. I remember every minute leading up to that day, and every minute leading away, and that day at its center, the rotted core of a faithless heart. I remember in wood, and I remember in steel, and in stone, in those tangible materials with which we rebuild once the smoke has cleared and the debris has been carted away, once everything razed is ready to rise up once more, slithering from the ashes, step by seething step.

Acknowledgments

Thank you, Kate Miciak, mentor and friend.

Thank you, early readers Emily Winslow and Martha Witt. The first drafts of this book were workshopped at the Sackett Street Writers' Workshop, and Erinn Kindig and Julie Sarkissian's contributions were invaluable.

Thank you, Ellen Levine, Scott Miller, and Alex Glass, as well as Susanna Porter, Caitlin Alexander, and the team at Lot 2. Your support got this book finished.

Thank you, Allison Hunter and Chris Russell. May every author be so unreasonably lucky.

Thank you to the teams at Stuart Krichevsky Literary Agency and Janklow & Nesbit Associates. Thank you to Brian Tart, Andrea Schulz, Kate Stark, Lindsay Prevette, and everyone else at Viking. Thanks also to Shelly Perron for her excellent copy editor's eye. If the designer on this book added a signature worth of pages, it wouldn't be enough to name everyone deserving of recognition.

Thank you to Kaori Miller, Ben Feldman, Stephen Luber, Victoria Horn, and to Kaori Miller a second time. Thank you to Ithacans.

Thank you to Melissa Ford and Wendy Isaac. Thank you to

Olivia, Sadie, Gabriel, Penelope, Jonathan, and Josh. Thank you, Cynthia and Todd.

Thank you to Robert Klein and Joan Klein.

Thank you, Morgan Geisert-Klein. That hyphen is what I'm most grateful for in this world.